W9-ABR-523

My Dear Cousin

Also by Peggy Hoffmann

A FOREST OF FEATHERS

MY DEAR COUSIN

by

PEGGY HOFFMANN

Harcourt, Brace & World, Inc., New York

First edition
Library of Congress Catalog Card Number: 74-78878
Printed in the United States of America

For the youngest Hoffmanns,

TESS SUZANNE

and

TWEED RICHARD

Contents

My Dear Cousin

Chapter One

A Goodly Heritage

When Thomas and Ann Hollingsworth's second daughter, Lydia Eliza, was born in their handsome three-story house in Baltimore, the young nation was almost as new as the dark-eyed baby girl at 15 South Street.

The United States of America was stumbling along under a loose confederation in 1786, trying to find its identity, to pay off its heavy burden of war debts and to hold up its head in the ranks of older nations. By the time the union had a firm constitution and a strong President—who would be called, significantly, the Father of his Country—Lydia Eliza was three years old and showing signs of the beauty that would one day make her a Baltimore belle.

Even at that age she strongly resembled her mother. She had wide-set brown eyes, dark hair with curly tendrils at the forehead and a gentle, introspective temperament in contrast to that of her lively sister, Ann Maria. Lydia could content herself with simple toys, or with trotting after her mother in their garden or climbing on her father's knee when he came in from his office at Hollingsworth Brothers, Merchants. She did not cry easily, but when she did, the tears came as from a deep well, and she was inconsolable.

Since Lydia was a miniature of her mother, her parents

watched fearfully for some sign of Ann's headaches, which could devastate the household, but Lydia was spared. Even the skill and attention of the good Dr. Donaldson could not lessen Ann's pain when the attacks came on; her husband, in his helpless sympathy, suffered almost as much as she did.

As Lydia Eliza grew, Thomas noted that she was like himself in at least one way, if not in many others: she had his sense of business and commerce, a liking for figures, for accurate records. It was an odd trait in a little girl. He took pleasure in giving her sums to add and then watching her quick response, even when she was quite young.

When Lydia was a clinging-vine four-year-old and Ann Maria a gangly six and a half, a baby brother was added to the family and named Thomas, Junior. Two other boys had been stillborn, and Thomas, Senior, had given up hope of having a son to bear his name. He admitted that there was more than a little tribal pride in his dream, although not all of his eight brothers and two sisters had been fortunate in their offspring either.

Samuel, who was also Thomas's business partner, had his own Samuel, Junior, as well as Jacob, named for another brother, and three daughters, but he and Sarah had had many sorrows too. Child after child was stillborn or had died at birth. Every lost baby, as in so many other households, took joy and vitality from the mothers and sent the fathers to work with heavy hearts. The ways of the Lord were inscrutable, Thomas tried to believe; a man must accept what he could not change.

After his first long, incredulous look at his son on a shining May morning in 1790, Thomas went out to walk the streets, his hands in his pockets, his eyes staring into the sky. He was not needed at home; in fact, he was in the way, as his eagerness sent him on tiptoe to the edge of Ann's bed, to grasp her fingers convulsively, to blink at the mewling little creature cuddled beside her. A boy? And alive?

He had to force himself outside, wishing he hadn't sent his little girls to Sam's. Perhaps he should stop in to see how they were. It wasn't far, just up at Number 9 Charles Street. No, they were probably taking naps. Sarah, who was Ann's sister, was a great believer in naps.

The Hollingsworths were a strong network of eleven brothers and sisters, children of Zebulon Hollingsworth of Elkton, Maryland, where Henry Hollingsworth, son of one of William Penn's colonists, Valentine, had established the family in 1711. Zebulon's first wife, Ann Mauldin, gave him one daughter and five sons, one of whom died at the age of ten, four days before her own death. Zebulon then married his second cousin, Mary Jacobs, who gave him six more boys and another girl. Their son David died at the age of twenty-one.

The remaining nine brothers and half brothers were known from Philadelphia to Baltimore as astute, farsighted, energetic businessmen and upright public servants. Three of them married Adams sisters from Christiana, Delaware, near Elkton: Jacob and Ruth, Samuel and Sarah, Thomas and Ann. The Adamses were from a family of eight sisters and one brother, George. One sister, Elizabeth, had married Thomas Tobin of Sassafras, later dying in childbirth and leaving four motherless little girls: Sarah, Rachel, Elizabeth and Ruth. The youngest Adams sister, Deborah, eventually married William Cochran and lived in Baltimore.

Two other Hollingsworth brothers married sisters: Henry married Jane Evans and Zebulon, Junior, chose Mary Evans, usually called Polly. Both stayed in Elkton, Zebulon at Elk Landing, their old family home nearby, and Henry in the center of town. Their half brothers Jacob and Stephen lived together on Queen's Way, west of town.

The huge clan, with its double cousins and other complicated relationships, was close-knit in spite of geographical distances. Levi was farthest from the others, having settled in

Philadelphia when he was eighteen, already captain of his own sloop and on his way to a fortune in the flour business.

Like Henry, Levi was an important officer in the Revolution. He was a founder of the elite Light Horse Cavalry (later called the First Troop) that always escorts the President of the United States when he visits the City of Brotherly Love. Their grandfather, the first Henry Hollingsworth, had helped to lay out that city, when he was eighteen.

Samuel and Thomas were in business together in Baltimore. Their oldest half brother, Jesse, also lived there and was active in many phases of business and civic life in that bustling port. The ninth, John, lived on the eastern shore.

Elizabeth, the older sister, married a Veasey from Bohemia Manor, and Lydia, the younger (named for Valentine's wife, Lydia Atkinson), became the bride of Samuel Wallis and went to live at the edge of the wilderness in Northumberland, Pennsylvania.

When their father, Zebulon, Senior, died in 1763 he had grandchildren older than several of his own children, making the tangled relationships even more confusing. Because of the family custom of naming their offspring for sisters, brothers, aunts, uncles and grandparents, there was a bewildering number of Elizabeths, Lydias, Anns (often called Nancy), Johns, Thomases, Stephens and Jacobs, but no one would consider changing the long-established pattern. So it was that on this wondrous spring morning, Thomas knew that he was giving his baby son an honorable heritage and a worthy name by calling him Thomas Jacob Hollingsworth, Junior.

He wandered toward the river, wanting to shout or to get down on his knees in thanksgiving. He finally climbed the steep road to St. Paul's Church and went inside to sit, unbelieving, in its stillness.

The new baby was several months old before his parents realized that Lydia Eliza did not share the family's affection for him. Several times she had given him a surreptitious slap or a hard pinch when she thought no one was watching. His howls would attract his mother or the nurse, but by the time someone arrived, Lydia Eliza would be playing innocently on the back steps.

On a hot August day her father caught her as she was about to hit the boy with one of her shoes, her pretty little face contorted and her teeth clenched. Thomas spanked her hard, for the first time he could remember, furious at her and furious at himself for getting so angry.

"Why did you do that?" he asked her over and over. "Now you can just sit here on this chair until I say you can get up. I've never seen you act like that! *Why did you do it?"*

Between racking sobs the child whimpered, "I hate him!"

"Hate a baby? A little helpless baby?"

"Why don't you give him away?" she cried. "Why don't you give *me* away? Somebody might want me. You've got *him* now!"

"Lydia! What are you saying?" Thomas tried to pick her up, but she pulled away, her tears stopped but her body quivering with dry, pitiful sobs.

"If you want a girl you've got Sister, and if you want a boy you've got *him,* and you don't need me any more anyway."

"Lydia! Lydia Eliza Hollingsworth!" In spite of her resistance, her father caught her and sat down with her, holding her on his lap by force. She was all arms and legs, lashing out like a trapped animal. He wanted to call Ann so that she could extricate him from this situation that was nearly too much for him; then he thought better of it.

"Daughter," he said quietly, "I shall hold you here until you stop thrashing around and come to your senses. Then I want to tell you something." He sat waiting, still holding her tightly.

"Is it a secret?" she asked in a strangled whisper.

"It must have been, but it should not be," he told her. "Did you know that we love you?"

"Who?"

"Your mother and I. And your sister. And even your little brother, because he is too young to realize that you think you hate him because you're jealous of him."

"What's that?"

"Just a big word. Now I'm wondering if I've been spending too much time with him, when I used to spend time with you. Can you forgive me?"

"What's that?" Cautiously she put her head against his shoulder, watching as if she feared he might push it away.

"Another big word. Will you be my friend again? I've been needing you, you know. A man with so much business to take care of must have someone help him with his numbers now and then. Babies aren't much good at that."

"He can't even walk, can he?" She twisted his watch chain with her fingers.

"Not yet. Or talk. Or help your mother with her flowers."

"He really isn't much good at all, is he, Papa?"

She fell asleep in his arms, and he carried her to her room to put her on her bed and drop a kiss on her damp forehead. He hoped that Ann had not heard the outburst, which had both sobered and shamed him. He might suggest some ideas to her—perhaps she too was unconsciously neglecting the quiet little girl who could keep her sorrows bottled up just so long. How could he have been so blind? She looked so vulnerable, her chubby legs getting long and slender, her hair tumbling around her shoulders. He wiped his eyes roughly and went back down the stairs.

When it became evident that there would be no more children, Thomas encouraged Sam's boys to come over as substitute brothers for his son, resolving that his daughters should never again accuse him of partiality. His pride in young Thomas steadily increased, but he was careful to speak of it only to Ann.

"There was a word that came to me at church," he told her

awkwardly, "a word that could describe our lad. Now what was it?"

"He's what I always dreamed of, Thomas." She reached to kiss his cheek. "Thank you for him."

"It is I who should thank you. Oh, I remember. The word was *radiance*. Am I too prideful if I say that Thomas has radiance?"

"It's a lovely word, Thomas. And he does have that." She kissed him again and went off to supervise Delia's work in the kitchen.

As soon as the girls were old enough, Ann took her husband's suggestion and began to draw them into her work with the Benevolent Society, a home and school for orphaned boys that she and Sarah had helped to establish through their church. One of Lydia Eliza's earliest memories was of going with her mother and sister in the carriage, first to the new rectory, high on a hill overlooking the town, to pick up parcels of food and clothing donated by church members, then to the big house out in the country to deliver them. Robert, the Negro groom, handled the team. Polodore, not long from Africa and showing traces of his proud royal ancestry, rode beside him.

There was always a swarm of little boys waiting to greet them, with a harried matron trying to enforce some kind of order. Often their exuberance frightened Lydia so much that she clung to her mother and tried to hide behind her or remained huddled in a corner of the carriage. When Ann remembered to give her an assignment, such as delivering a box of slate pencils to the teacher—a bearded old gentleman who looked the way Lydia thought God should look—she lost her fears.

By the time Lydia was ten years old, the Benevolent Society was as much a part of her life as was her school down the street from her home. She and Ann Maria, along with Betsy

Patterson, who lived across from them and was between them in age, were among the school's first pupils when it was set up by the Abbé Louis du Bourg, a friend of Bishop John Carroll. The teachers were French noblewomen who had escaped the guillotine with little but their aristocratic upbringing from which to create a life in the New World. The Abbé, known for his liberalism, was a crusader for education, especially for those who might miss out on its larger opportunities. Little girls of many local well-to-do families, who would otherwise have been privately tutored, were sent to his South Street school, regardless of their religious affiliation. On Saturday mornings the Abbé held special classes for Negroes.

In 1798 the routine of existence at 15 South Street was broken for the first time of any consequence when Thomas decided to take his wife and children for a week's visit to his old home at Elkton, fifty miles up Chesapeake Bay. It could be a belated half-century birthday present for himself, and it could combine business and pleasure, because he was involved in several ventures with his four brothers who lived there. He'd have a chance to show off his little brood and to get acquainted with an assortment of nieces and nephews he scarcely knew. They would go up by packet, if the weather allowed, and return by stagecoach. The trip would take most of a day each way; by going up by water and back by land, Ann could see which she preferred if they went again.

The youngsters were excited but apprehensive. What would all those Hollingsworth cousins be like? They knew the ones in Baltimore—Jesse's five, grown up and married and with children of their own, and Sam's five—but the ones in Elkton were a blank. Their uncle Zebulon had five children still living, there in the old home at Elk Landing at the confluence of the Big Elk and Little Elk rivers. He had inherited the property from his father, for whom he was named. Uncle Henry, a hero of the Revolution and named for his grandfather, had six—or was it seven?—there at Partridge

Hill in the center of Elkton. Thomas's children had heard that a little Adams cousin, motherless Ruth Tobin, lived with their childless Aunt Ruth and Uncle Jacob Hollingsworth on Queen's Way, west of town. Little Ruth's three sisters had stayed with their father.

How many more relatives were there? Would they descend on the out-of-town visitors like a flock of grasshoppers? Were any of them the right age to be good company?

Zebulon, Polly and their children and grandchildren met Thomas and his family at the wharf, a stone's throw from their house. From that moment until their departure six days later, the Baltimoreans were surrounded by relatives, young and old, and hardly saw each other at all, being parceled out all over town.

The three children stayed with Jacob and Ruth, who had suggested it so that the younger Ruth could have some companionship. There was a great deal going on at the big farm, so young Thomas could keep himself occupied if he got bored with female company, which he did at once. He rode every horse on the place. He went exploring with his bachelor uncle Stephen, who lived there with Jacob, and he gained seven pounds in weight, amazing even himself by his capacity for food after so much exercise.

When the visit ended, the five of them settled into the stagecoach for the long trip home, tired and hardly speaking, after so many days of doing little else. The driver climbed up on top and slapped the horses with the reins. A violent jerk and a complaining screech of wheels told them they were off.

Thomas, Junior, broke the silence. "Ruth Tobin," he announced, "looks like a tadpole."

"Now, son—" his father protested.

"That isn't nice!" Lydia glared at him. "And it isn't true either. Ruth Tobin is pretty!"

"Who said tadpoles were ugly?" He shrugged.

"I thought she looked like a fawn," Ann Maria argued.

"Sort of sweet and frightened. Big eyes, small bones. I was afraid she'd bound off into the woods any minute, just the way a deer does when—"

"How would you feel if you were the only young person around, except for servants?" Lydia brushed back her hair and took up an impassioned defense of her new friend. "And everyone was old enough to be your grandparents, and they watched every move you made, for fear you'd hurt yourself, and they worried if you sniffled, and wouldn't allow you off the porch unless someone was with you, and made you sit on a chair and do needlework and learn Bible verses?" She jumped involuntarily as the coach wheel struck a boulder at the side of the road. "Aunt Ruth won't let Uncle Stephen put up a swing for her in that oak tree. She might fall out of it and break her arm. She has a pet banty hen, but Uncle Jacob has to feed it so it doesn't peck at her. It's like living in a tomb! Or a prison!"

"Sister!" Ann Maria whispered.

"That house is so big and everything in it is so perfect, but it's dead, that's what it is. And full of old people. And the only one who comes to visit, except for Dr. Mitchell, is Grandmother Hollingsworth, and she's even older. Yes, I do too love her—a whole lot. But Ruth needs—"

"Uncle Jacob's house will be famous someday." Ann Maria tried to change the subject. "President Washington himself stayed there, in the room that Uncle Stephen has now. And two nights later his enemy General Howe slept in the same room. And that big giant servant—Richard Mills, that's his name—took care of both of them. He said they both snored."

Young Thomas pulled from his pocket a handful of pebbles he had picked up along Elk Creek. "Well," he said, trying to sound like a grownup, "when a man lives on the edge of a wilderness, he has to take in anyone who comes, doesn't he? Someone going from Baltimore to Philadelphia, or back, could get caught with no place to stay when night came. There are still wolves in these forests. Maybe even tigers and lions! A wolf carried off two of Uncle Stephen's sheep only last week. And there could be robbers—and all kinds of villains—"

"Thomas!" His mother gave the first sign that she was listening. She had been sitting with her head back and a handkerchief over her eyes. "You mustn't say such things."

"Ruth Tobin asked me what double cousins were." Ann Maria giggled.

"Twins!" Thomas began tossing and catching the pebbles like a juggler.

Ann Maria ignored him. "I explained that if your fathers were brothers and your mothers were sisters, you were cousins twice. Like Uncle Samuel's children and us. But Ruth's a single cousin instead of a double cousin."

"How was that again?" Her brother frowned. "I got lost way back there. Maybe Ruth's only half a cousin, she's so skinny. And I don't feel like a double anything. I'm just me."

"And Aunt Debby is an Adams sister who hasn't married anyone. Now if she'd just take Uncle Stephen—"

"I like Ruth Tobin," Lydia interrupted. "We're going to write letters to each other. She never gets any mail, and her tutor says she needs practice in penmanship."

"Write letters?" Thomas braced himself against the coach's swaying. "I'd rather do anything else! Why not be out riding horses or sailing boats or helping build something, like the fort over at Whetstone Point?"

"Mama said that Betsy Patterson was way out there with all those boys!" Lydia said. "Throwing rocks and climbing around like a regular tomboy!"

"Didn't you hear her screaming when old Xenophon came to get her?" Thomas laughed. "Her mother was waiting on the front steps, and they got her inside in a hurry. No thirteen-year-old girl of hers was going to act like that, she said. And Mama came and got me inside real fast too, just when it was getting interesting. How old is Ruth Tobin?"

"Almost eleven," Lydia told him, trying to curb the nausea

brought on by the roughness of the ride. "Halfway between you and me. Why?"

"I just wondered. I'd like to be eleven. Or twelve, like you. Or even fourteen, like Sister. I want to hurry up and be a *man,* like Papa."

Their father roused from trying to doze on the opposite seat. "The day will come, son, too soon," he grumbled. "And if you three jabberers would quiet down for a while, maybe your sweet mother could rest. And I could forget some of the names I've been calling this driver. A pox on all of them, drunken no-goods!"

"Hush!" Ann murmured.

"Isn't this blasted road anything but chuckholes?" He pounded angrily on the ceiling. *"Why don't you watch your driving up there? You're knocking our teeth loose!"*

"We should have gone by water," Ann said wearily.

"I got seasick," Thomas muttered. "Next time, mind you, they can come to Baltimore to see us. A man should never be dragged off from his own fireside. When they talk about homebodies"—he gave the ceiling another infuriated punch—"they're talking about me!" He rolled up his coat to use as a cushion for his back. "Yes, I know it was my own idea. Remind me never to try it again."

"I had a good time." Lydia began to pout. "I hope I can go again. Cousin Ruth wants me to, and I know they'll never let her come clear to Baltimore to see me."

"Your bones are young," her father conceded. "Mine are set in their ways."

The next summer Robert Hollingsworth, Zebulon's son, a lawyer who transacted the family's business in Europe, stopped in Baltimore on his way up the bay to visit his parents. Gratefully, Thomas accepted his offer of accompanying Lydia on the promised journey. "Don't let her out of your sight until Stephen or Jacob comes for her," he ordered, more than half-seriously.

"I understand, Uncle Thomas." Robert gave him a parting handshake. "Proper young ladies must be chaperoned at all times. Being at least twice her age should fit me admirably for the job. Now don't worry about her. And I'll use the opportunity to see how well she's learning her French."

It was hard for Lydia to analyze the exact ways in which Ruth Tobin had changed in that year. Possibly it was her clothes, somber in color and cut like those of a middle-aged woman. Ruth was scarcely out of her childhood, yet she was dressed in funereal garments, her hair severely done, her feet in sensible black shoes, her white collar unrelieved by lace or embroidery.

The two greeted each other as formally as strangers but with an undertone of excitement and anticipation. In her letters Ruth had declared that she was counting the days. Lydia had been doing the same. Her parents had wondered, with some exasperation, whether any of them would survive the long waiting.

"Mama sent this shawl for Aunt Ruth," Lydia said politely as she unpacked. "And this satin reticule for you—it's the very latest fashion from France—oh, here's a crystal vase for flowers, from my sister. We wrapped it in my new petticoat, so it wouldn't get broken."

"You're taller. A whole lot taller," Ruth said abruptly, hardly taking her eyes off her visitor. "Last summer we were the same size."

"I'm older than you are." Lydia smiled. "My brother says we're both too skinny. Mama thinks I should start wearing a corset so my back stays straight, but I tell her they're going out of style. Ann Maria wears one."

"My aunt stuffs me with milk and butter and cakes and light bread so I'll get fatter, but I never do," Ruth told her. "She doesn't want anyone to think she doesn't take good care of me. She's always having Dr. Mitchell weigh me and give me some nasty old tonic that tastes bad."

"Did you get my last letter?" Lydia went to put her undergarments in a drawer. "With the nasturtium pressed in it?"

"Yes. But the flower was all dried up. It smelled terrible. I wasn't going to mention it."

"But you can tell me anything, Cousin Ruth! Didn't we decide that last summer?"

"I guess we did, but I was afraid you—"

"Let's always have it that way, shall we?" Lydia suggested eagerly. "And we'll keep secrets from everyone else. But we'll tell each other everything—what we think about, what's going on in town, what clothes we're wearing and maybe even about our sweethearts—"

Ruth's face turned crimson. "I'm too young for that!"

"So am I, Mama says." Lydia was spreading some of her clothes across the big bed. "But that doesn't keep me from thinking about it, even if I don't tell her. Sister has two beaux already, but then, all the boys like her. She flirts, but Mama doesn't know it."

"These are so pretty!" Ruth caressed a taffeta petticoat. "And all this lace, even on—"

"Try on these shoes," Lydia suggested. "I think they're beautiful, with that French embroidery on the toes and those small heels. If they fit, we can dress up and we can pretend—"

"That would be fun!" Ruth's thin face brightened. "I have no one to pretend with, except for the black children, and I'm not allowed to play with them. Only, when you're here, it's more fun to have everything be real!"

On the afternoon before Lydia was to return to Baltimore—this time with Zeb's daughter Peggy Cooch, who was taking her little crippled son down for medical treatment—the two cousins wandered forlornly through their aunt Ruth's well-tended flower garden, not seeing the blossoms. A spatter of rain sent them inside, where their uncles were balancing their accounts. The men ignored them. The girls sat down, not talking, on the upholstered Georgian sofa that had supported such distinguished posteriors as those of President Washington, the Marquis de Lafayette, General Howe, several Signers of the Declaration of Independence and other notable citizens.

Jacob closed a record book and took a fresh one from the slant-top desk that their grandfather had brought with him in 1711 when he came from New Castle, Delaware, to the head of the Elk River and established the Maryland branch of the family. In a precise, careful hand, with florid capitals, Jacob wrote at the top of the first page:

6th Septr 1799 Elkton, Maryland

He sanded the ink, then looked twice at what he had written. "Is 1799 nearly gone already? Funny I hadn't thought of it. End of the century. H'm." He pushed back his everyday wig, which always made him perspire. "Be 1800 shortly."

"Eighteen hundred what?" His brother had been having trouble reading the figures he had set down by candlelight after busy days of supervising the field hands and freemen who worked for them. "Eighteen hundred short, did you say? Flour or grain? Was it a mistake I made?"

Jacob appeared not to hear him, looking out the window across their wide fields to the forests and the splinters of sunshine that were trying to break through the showers. Lydia and Ruth watched the two men without interest.

"You mean dollars, Jacob? Short eighteen hundred dollars?"

"H'm?"

"I wish to Heaven that Zeb wouldn't be so old-fashioned in his bookkeeping," Stephen said. "Levi and Henry both complain about it. Every single item that we ship through Elk Landing has to be translated from pounds to dollars and shillings to cents. Why doesn't he keep up with the times? We don't belong to the King any more! Doesn't he know that we won?"

"The *year* 1800," Jacob said crossly, as a fresh burst of rain smashed against the house. "The new century. I suppose we'll start hearing about some damned fool prophesying the end of the world. Papa used to tell Grandfather's story about a crowd of folks dressed in white and sitting on some high place outside Philadelphia all night, in freezing weather, waiting for Judgment Day, when the new century came in in 1700. Grandfather claimed that he didn't like the idea of starting out to *look* for Judgment Day. If they wanted him, they could come and get him. He was too busy to be bothered."

"He probably was, from all I hear of the old gentleman," Stephen agreed, pushing aside his papers and leaning back in his chair. "New century already, eh? Seems to me we ought to do something to let old Father Time know that the Hollingsworths are on to him." He reached for a dish of sweetmeats and handed it silently to the girls, hoping to lighten the gloom of their impending separation.

In spite of the fact that they were so scattered, all of the Hollingsworths—except for Thomas, who gave in grudgingly—were enthusiastic about welcoming the new century together in Elkton. The eldest sister, Elizabeth Veasey, was dead, and the other one, Lydia Wallis, sent word that it would be folly for her to attempt the long journey down from Northumberland, Pennsylvania, in December weather, but the nine brothers agreed to try it, egged on by their children and grandchildren, who saw only the chance for an unprecedented winter holiday.

The Celebration, as they called it, continued for nearly a week, since the trip from any direction was so exhausting that no one could bear to turn around and go right back. Elk Landing was headquarters for eating and gossiping. Guests slept there and at Jacob's and Henry's, with a few bedded down across from Jacob's, at the Manshon House on Queen's Way, which the first Henry had built in 1712. Food and drink were prepared and consumed in quantity. Zebulon had another "necessary" built out by the grape arbor.

When the incidents and accidents of the Celebration were totted up, there were only two broken bones and a sprained ankle, with an assortment of bruises and minor cuts. Ninety per cent of the injuries came from sliding down the polished mahogany banister that ran gracefully from the third floor to the broad front hallway at Elk Landing. For most of the hilarious reunion, there was a steady line-up of sliders of all ages climbing to the third floor and streaking down, some rolling over and over until they landed rump first against the front door, others braking themselves for a safer stop.

Lydia Eliza, overwhelmed by the noise and confusion, would remember the Celebration not only for the joy of being with her cousin but also for a sharpened appreciation of something she had been seeing and taking for granted all her life: the Hollingsworth coat of arms. A copy of it in a simple frame hung in their back parlor, but a much larger one looked down on the feasting from above the dining-room fireplace at Elk Landing. The crest had come down from the earliest-known days of the family in Cheshire, England, in the eleventh century, when the name was spelled many ways, often without the "s." It bore the words *"Disce Ferenda Pati,"* or, "Bear Patiently What Must Be Borne."

The field of azure blue was for loyalty and for the blue of the sky, silver for innocence and for the sparkling streams in the Land of Hol, and green for love and for the foliage of the holly trees that abounded there. A Saxon stag, for courage, surmounted the shield. For more than seven hundred years the emblem had been passed on in the family, through migration to Ireland in the seventeenth century and to the New World in the seventeenth and eighteenth centuries. It symbolized an ancient and honorable heritage. Lydia Eliza was singularly blessed. Her Adams ancestors, who had come to America at about the same time, were no less worthy.

Looking up at the crest through the haze of cigar smoke that fogged the house after the festive, long-drawn-out New Year's—the new century's—dinner, she had a powerful sense of belonging to a Family, in the noblest, sturdiest sense of the word. The rootless orphans at the Benevolent Society might have been from another planet; some had no real names, many knew only beatings and bestiality, never love. How could she have been so fortunate?

She wanted to share some of her thoughts with Ruth as they lay awake in the darkness after that first great day of the new century, but she could not find the words. Any mention of orphans was apt to upset Ruth anyway, sensitive as she was to her own loss of her mother and her separation from her father and sisters, who lived twenty-five miles away, across the Sassafras River.

Several first and second male cousins, who were attending the College of New Jersey up in Princeton, had allowed the two speechless girls to listen in as they shared tales of campus pranks, drinking bouts and challenges to duels, accompanying their stories with broad winks and knowing glances. Ruth, shocked but unable to pull herself away, began blushing at the first paragraphs and never stopped for the rest of the evening. Lydia got more and more self-conscious in the midst of so much maleness. She was all elbows and knees. Were the buttons on her new plum-colored worsted fastened into their proper loops? Was she as red in the face as Ruth? Did these men think she and her cousin were pretty, or were they secretly laughing? One had chucked her under the chin. She didn't know whether or not she should have enjoyed the impertinence. Her sister would have understood exactly how to handle it, but Lydia had never thought to prepare herself for such possibilities.

Later, in their room, still twittering about the wicked conversations of the college men, Ruth fell asleep in the middle of a sentence. Lydia tried not to move around and awaken her, but at last, unable to force herself into slumber, she slipped out of bed, found a warm wrapper and went to the window.

The world outside was frozen and silent. Lydia was not familiar with the Elkton countryside in winter. The stark beauty of the trees was surprising. Each limb and branch and twig had its own grace, uncluttered by leaves. The forest looked less secretive and menacing than in the summer; surely there couldn't be wolves out there? Maryland was too civilized. Her brother had been making up those yarns just to scare her. Was she afraid of the forest? Or of what? Of unknown and unexplored dangers? Of people? Of what was expected of her in the future? That might be it. Could she measure up?

In some ways her role was cut out for her: there would be dances, dinner parties, concerts, weddings, assemblies. She was getting small introductions to that life already, as Baltimore's social arbiters saw to it that she and her sister were on important guest lists for daytime functions. Then, in time, she would be expected to find the one man who was waiting out there—somewhere beyond the forest and the river. She would bear his children. What was it like to bear a child? Her sister had confided to her that it could hurt terribly, so terribly that you might not live. Ruth Tobin's mother had not lived. If you loved a man, and he was the right man—Ruth thought you'd know when that one came along. It would be something like a revelation from the Lord; there might be a great burst of thunder, or the sound of trumpets. When Lydia had tried to discuss the matter with Betsy Patterson, Betsy's bright laughter had closed the conversation. "If he has money and he's handsome and a good dancer, that's the one! And if that doesn't work out, I'll find myself a better one!" Ruth had been horrified when Lydia quoted this impudence.

At the Celebration she had noticed that the men's conversations had centered on business and politics. General Washington, whom several of them had served under, had just died, even though his physicians had bled him and had given him the finest medical care. There was sorrowful agreement that the nation desperately needed his leadership.

"He'd have made short order of those ruckuses we've been having with the French at sea," one of them had said darkly. "We were lucky not to lose a ship or two, or at least some cargoes."

"Well, Mr. Adams hasn't sold us back to Britain yet, in spite of all those gloomy predictions," another had countered, laughing. "I wonder if the old King will know that we intend putting Hollingsworth copper on the dome of the new capitol building down in the Federal City?"

"I hope we don't have to start making our plowshares into swords again," Henry had said in his croaking voice, which had been permanently damaged by a musket shot in the throat during the Revolution. "We ought to be able to figure out some way to get along in the world without slicing each other to ribbons every few years."

"Isn't that why Great-grandfather Valentine came over here with William Penn?" Jacob had asked. "And how many wars have we been tangled up in since then, even if we are Quakers?"

Lydia had noted that the women talked of babies and fashions and servants and illnesses. Probably she should try to have a greater interest in those domestic topics, but, except for the clothes, she found them dull. She was drawn to spots where she could eavesdrop on the men as they argued tariffs, shortages, markets, investments, politics and current events. There was meat and meaning in those conversations.

Suddenly aware that she was half-frozen, she slid back into bed, her toes poking around to find the copper warming pan someplace under the flannel sheets. Perhaps she could tell Ruth some of her ideas in her letters, which allowed more time for cogitation. Ruth was still terribly young for such serious matters.

Pulling the heavy comforters up around her ears, Lydia

Eliza could go to sleep in that house, that town, that state and that nation which had been so important in the rich history of her family. Suspended between childhood and womanhood and between two centuries, she looked only forward, to a new era and a new phase of her life.

Up in Philadelphia and at many other places, white-robed fatalists crept home in the icy dawn, disappointed. Judgment Day had not yet arrived. In spite of their careful preparations to meet it, the end of the world was not immediately in evidence.

Chapter Two

Put Not Your Trust in Princes

Lydia Eliza's summer visits to Elkton became a part of her life, as did the exchange of letters. The problem with their correspondence was that Ruth answered immediately. There was usually a reply by the next packet, leaving Lydia again her debtor, with her letters always repeating key phrases from Lydia's: "So sorry that Aunt Sarah has a cold," or "I know that your new bonnet must be pretty and that you like the velvet ribbon that matches your dress."

It took her a half page to get to the body of her message, but in that she was no different from Lydia, who penned: "I have been indulging in one of our old habits, my Dear Cousin, of napping after dinner, tho' my slumbers were not so peaceful as when we had the pleasure of being bedfellows, and have arisen to parley with you, at the same time to remind you that a fortnight has nearly elapsed since we parted, and we have not received any intelligence from you except through Uncle Stephen from whom we are sorry to learn that Aunt had been more indisposed, but I hope ere this she has recovered from the indisposition and that her ringworm is benefited by her regimen, and that it is no longer necessary to refrain from partaking of the nice bacon and smoked herrings."

Ending the message was equally slow. "Give my affectionate love to Aunt Ann and Uncle Thomas," Ruth would write, "and Ann Maria and young Thomas, and keep a large measure of it for yourself. I must now conclude with uniting Aunt Ruth's and Uncle Jacob's love to mine, and Uncle Stephen's also, and with much affection to you always I remain ever your attached Cousin, Ruth. P.S. Send my good wishes to Aunt Sarah too, and tell her that I hope she is soon well."

Before one of Lydia's projected visits after Jacob's death in 1803, Ruth wrote to request her to do some shopping, enclosing money and listing what she needed.

"I've been wanting her to do this!" Lydia exclaimed. "And now it's Aunt Ruth's idea! When they get out of mourning for Uncle Jacob, she wants Ruth to have prettier clothes, with more color and trimming. I can hardly believe it. Ruth is so excited that she's forgotten to be sad about losing Uncle Jacob last spring."

"I guess Aunt wants her to start looking for a husband," Thomas, Junior, suggested, with some of his father's practicality. "There's only Uncle Stephen to take care of her now, and when he's gone—"

"She's only fifteen!" Lydia retorted. "And girls shouldn't look for husbands. The husbands should look for them."

"I've heard that," Thomas said sagely. "I think that's what Papa calls a *theory*."

While Lydia was away late that summer of 1803, there was a widening ripple of excitement on South Street, giving her ample material for letters when she got home again.

There had always been flocks of young men coming to court her friend Betsy Patterson over at Number 18; the appearance of one more, even from out of town, was never particularly newsworthy. Privately, Lydia would not have objected if some of the gentlemen had joined the smaller coterie that arrived periodically at Number 15. She had grown to be a shy, willowy young woman, taller than her sister, her dark eyes dominating her delicately boned face, but she would have liked to be the opposite: small, sparkling, fascinating, irresistible. Like Betsy. Many other girls felt the same way. Betsy knew it and enjoyed it and never held it against any of them.

The beginning of the flurry could probably be pinpointed at the moment in August when the most flamboyant equipage in Baltimore came down South Street and the dashing Jerome Bonaparte, youngest brother of the First Consul of France, alighted. He bounded up the steps at Number 18, and, before he could lift the knocker, the door opened to admit him. He was expected, that was certain.

On that first visit he stayed only the proper twenty minutes. Before long, however, it was said that his horses could find their way there on the darkest night even without a driver.

Betsy—daughter of a Scotch-Irish merchant who had worked his way up from poverty to being considered the second wealthiest man in America, next to his friend Charles Carroll, one of the Signers—was inclined to pout. She was bored with Baltimore, bored with all her brothers and sisters, bored with the numerous but never quite suitable proposals that poured in on her, bored with the thought of spending eternity in what she considered the dullest spot in the whole world: Baltimore, the third largest port in America.

"Of course, I haven't seen the whole world," she would say sweetly, "yet." In darker moments she admitted to the thought of suicide as a way out of her discontent; Lydia, well acquainted with her moodiness, and fond of her because they had always known each other, knew that her threats were serious, partly because they were never public.

The spells of depression and boredom ended the instant the romantic young European came on the scene. Also disappearing were her local swains, outclassed and outmaneuvered. Betsy did not miss them.

Finding an eager audience, she kept Lydia and Ann Maria informed of the expected times of her suitor's arrival, saving them a great deal of bother. Young Thomas listened in on the girl talk just to have a chance to scoff later.

"That man!" he'd say with boyish contempt. "You'd never catch me dolled up the way he is. Velvet breeches. Bright green ones. And silk stockings—silk! He wants to show off his pretty little ankles. And one time he came in a sky-blue jacket and a red weskit. Our dear Miss Elizabeth Patterson said that it was a hussar's uniform, but I told her he was trying to look like a robin. She didn't like that."

"You're jealous!" Ann Maria teased him.

"Jealous? Of that snob? Anyway, Betsy's five years older'n me."

"She likes you, Thomas. She told me so. Lots of times." His sister knew how to get under his skin. He stuck out his tongue at her.

"You'd like to have high-stepping horses like his and you know it," Lydia chimed in. "And you wish you didn't have to learn to keep books for Papa when you aren't in school too."

" 'Hollingsworths always work!' " Thomas quoted. "I wonder why Great-grandfather didn't get someone to make that old motto into a sampler?" He glowered at Ann Maria, who despised needlework. "And I've got a horse, don't forget. All my own. So there!" He picked up a lump of sugar from the tea table and headed toward the stables to try to find Robert to help him give his horse, Starfire, a rubdown.

Ann Maria went to ask how long it would be before they were to eat, and Lydia was left alone. She dropped her embroidery in her lap. The needlepoint was only an excuse to be sitting by the window anyway, with a chance to view the activities of the street without being seen herself behind the heavy draperies.

What would it be like to have a handsome prince—for she thought of Mr. Bonaparte as a prince—come to see her, perhaps to woo her madly? She liked the phrase "woo her madly" and began spinning it around in her mind like a silver thread on a loom. "Woo her madly . . ." How would it sound if she could say "woo *me* madly"? She sat up guiltily and pretended to hunt for her needle. She must not think such thoughts.

Maybe no one would ever come calling on her, except for the boys in the neighborhood, who were really calling on Thomas. There were many maiden ladies around Baltimore withering on the vine, waiting for suitors who never came, filling cedar chests with linens, laces, embroideries and blankets, finally having to settle for a dry, sterile, unfulfilled life with relatives. They took young nephews for walks along the river or around the City Spring. They bought little pretties for their nieces in a secondhand stab at motherhood. They were at church services every time the doors were opened. Some were known to attend funerals of the remotest strangers, just to have something going on. To Lydia, these lonely spinsters personified tragedy.

Maybe her own life would end up that way. No one to bring her flowers or write those silly little notes she and Ruth Tobin used to long for. No one to sit by her at St. Paul's, close but not touching, just so she would know he was there, always there, beside her. No one to walk with through Howard's Park in the autumn, when the colors made her heart sing and the busyness of scampering squirrels was a warning to all to prepare for the winter that was sure to come. No one to hurry home with breathless news from the big outside world of men, eager to share it with her. No one.

Within a few days of Betsy's first meeting with the foreigner, she was calling him by his first name! Two of Lydia's aunts still called their husbands Mister after twenty years of marriage. It would be like Betsy to use first names just because it wasn't done. Especially for a man whose brother was the most powerful and ambitious man in Europe —a Bonaparte, no less. To Betsy, he was Jerome.

"You know how elegant the house and gardens are at the Marquis de Poléon's," Betsy always began. "Roses. And a little balcony. Lots of wisteria. Trumpet vine. Honeysuckle. That night they had lights all around the garden and along the drive. It was lovely."

"Like fireflies," Ann Maria could fill in from previous tellings.

"So their daughter—you know Henrietta Pascault—"

"Yes," Lydia would respond, not wanting to slow up the story.

"Henrietta and I were looking out over the drive. I must admit that I was prepared to be bored that night. Always the same: too much rich food, too much dancing, too much noise, never anything really interesting to do. Baltimore men are so *gauche*. And my gown—"

Lydia wondered why Betsy's dresses, stunning as they undoubtedly were, had to be called gowns, while those of everyone else were classed as dresses. "My gown was one I'd worn before, at a summer party the Ridgelys gave, out at Hampton—"

"Ann Maria and I were both there," Lydia reminded her.

"It's that pale soft green that brings out the color of my eyes. A very simple gown really, but with excellent lines, and I think quite becoming to my figure."

Lydia's mother had been heard to remark that Betsy's gowns were so skimpy and so revealing that the color didn't matter, so little was required. Lydia shot a quick glance at Ann Maria, fearing she might begin quoting.

"Another carriage arrived," Betsy continued. "We could hear two young men laughing. You know, even if a person is making small talk that you can't hear, you can still tell if the speech has an accent. So we got a little closer, where we could see better. Actually, Joshua Barney had already mentioned Jerome to Papa. Mr. Pichon at the French Embassy in Washington thought that Jerome ought to be in more, well, more sophisticated and elegant company. A nobleman from the First Family of France should never have second best, you know."

"Who was with him?" Ann Maria interrupted.

"With Mr. Barney? Oh, you mean Jerome. That was Mr. Reubell, son of one of the Directors of the French Republic. They were superbly dressed, in full uniform. And you could see by the way they treated their coachman and the De Poléon's footman that they were accustomed to the finest of society."

"And Henrietta said—" Lydia prompted.

"Henrietta said, 'I think I'll marry the tall one!' " Betsy giggled. "So I said, 'Fine! I'll marry the other one.' You know, Jerome is quite tall too. And then I said to Henrietta, 'I wonder who they are?' "

"Didn't you sort of suspect, from the accent and all?" Ann Maria smiled. "Are you really going to marry him?" she went on after one of the recitations.

"Of course! Why not?" Betsy's pretty little face was radiant.

"He's Catholic," Lydia whispered. "And you're Presbyterian. Does your father know he's a *Catholic?*"

"Does he know it?" Betsy's laugh pealed through the room. "Does he talk about anything else? Can't you hear him clear across the street?"

"You wouldn't turn, would you? You wouldn't!"

"Why bother? You can always manage things if you use your head."

In midautumn, Lydia saw Mr. Patterson rush off, angry and preoccupied, while his daughter stood in the doorway, red with fury, her delicate face distorted, her small body shaking. Lydia's father reported that night that William Patterson and the Bishop of Baltimore, the highest-ranking prelate in the country, had been conferring. There was a great deal of loose talk around town as to what might happen if an American girl, specifically a rich beauty from an important Protestant, Federalist family, were to marry the brother of the Catholic First Consul of France. There would be explosions on both sides of the Atlantic. Could Patterson and the Bishop head it off?

There were other whisperings in the market place, but never in the sacred confines of the homes, about the shadowy creature named Alexander le Camus, who was young Bonaparte's aide and constant companion. There was a sinister, unsavory quality about the man, in contrast to the undeniable Latin charm and regal bearing of his superior. Le Camus was reliably reported to have helped extricate Jerome from earlier feminine entanglements. More earthy commentators likened Le Camus to something found under a rock. Le Camus wore earrings.

The morning social calls of Baltimore ladies soon took on more life, after the required greetings and inquiries about each other's health and the weather. By late fall, their twitterings had become a magpie chorus of gossip. Too much of it was true.

The religious differences of the pair were only a fraction of the problem. Mr. Patterson was wise enough to have taken the measure of the self-seeking Bonapartes and the fierce old matriarch who was head of the family, called Madame Mère. Jerome had been born three months before her husband's death and was an uncommonly beautiful child, so she had spoiled him unmercifully, with his brother Napoleon, fifteen years older, contributing more than a little to the pampering. The marital adventures of the brothers and sisters were already scandalizing Europe. Patterson felt that, on the personal level, a marriage to any Bonaparte could lead to nothing but disaster.

On the international level, he suspected that Napoleon had plans for this colorful youngest Bonaparte. He was setting up kingships for all the others, regardless of their fitness for the thrones. Surely a prize of some kind was envisioned for

Jerome. Having him marry a foreigner, and a Protestant, would strike at the heart of the projected Empire. That she was rich and beautiful only compounded the problem—Napoleon knew that money meant power, but Mr. Patterson shuddered at the thought of Patterson money being channeled through the greedy fingers of the Little Corporal.

Betsy was a good Presbyterian, he kept repeating to himself. She could not, would not, must not marry out of her faith. He felt so strongly about it that he decided to disinherit her if she turned Catholic. The chilling thought struck him that she was so headstrong and reckless that she wouldn't care. And Jerome seemed to have unlimited funds, from somewhere. Patterson could only come out of his gloom by remembering that his daughter, next to herself, loved nothing more than money. Nothing on earth. She would never risk being cut off from the bountiful supply he furnished her. He hoped.

Young Jerome had a fabulous wardrobe and lived like a foreign potentate. Patterson didn't know the fellow's exact age, but he was surely little more than a boy. Jerome was one of the few Bonapartes who knew instinctively how to look and act like a king. Patterson, whose own wealth had come from sweat, hard work, canny wisdom and sheer stubbornness, decided to investigate the young man's finances as well as his private life; he owed that much to Betsy and to himself. What he found appalled him.

Confronting his daughter with the facts, documented and proven, made another humiliating scene. She laughed in his face, making him ill to think that any child could be so insolent to a parent. He detested himself for putting up with it. Why had all the rest of his big brood given him and Dorcas so little trouble, while this one, weighing one hundred and five pounds and scarcely reaching his shoulder, was systematically breaking his heart? He cursed himself for his spinelessness in not having tied her up long ago to take her completely out of circulation until she came to her senses. Ah, if Presbyterians only had convents!

Betsy was quick in learning anything, whether it was a foreign language or the intricacies of finance or outwitting her father. Lydia could testify to her easy absorption of the lady teachers' language at the Abbé du Bourg's school.

"Speaking good French may help me to escape from Baltimore some day!" Betsy told her and Ann Maria blithely. "You should work harder at it." She gave them a conspiratorial wink. "French opens doors!"

Until the arrival of Bonaparte, Betsy had often preferred her father's company to any other. She could discuss the affairs of the Bank of Maryland with the objectivity and shrewdness of a man. She was frequently of more sensible help to him than some of the directors. Times had changed. The more he tried to reason with her, the more obstinate she became. The hated Frenchman haunted their doorstep, charming the servants as well as the womenfolk. Patterson was horrified to find that even his wife, Dorcas, had been taken in. He felt like turning the huge key in the brass lock and forbidding the persevering suitor to enter.

"Betsy would like that!" he acknowledged. "She'd have material for all kinds of dramatic scenes, faithfully observed and peddled everywhere by the neighbors. And while my back was turned, the upstart would crawl in a window. With that slimy Le Camus giving him a leg up, and waiting outside to take him home. Ugh."

Patterson was getting accustomed to nausea, and there were no nostrums to relieve him. His business was suffering too. He turned for help to his attorney, and again to the Bishop. The Most Reverend John Carroll was one of the few people who understood his dilemma and who felt exactly the same way, for a different reason: a marriage between those two mad young ones would be a catastrophe. The lawyer suggested some legal moves. The Bishop turned to prayer.

Carroll felt that the matter was beyond religious bounds. Seeing Patterson's distress was like watching a great ship heading for the shoals when the lighthouse was dark.

Was it not his duty to aid the endangered mariner? Where else did his true responsibility lie? To God and the church, yes. To the Pope, yes. And to a fellow human being, tormented almost beyond endurance. The Bishop studied the Scriptures. He prayed. He waited for the voice of God.

"Does Napoleon know what's going on?" Patterson's lawyer asked him.

"I'm not sure. You know how long it takes to get messages across the Atlantic."

"He could cut off the young man's finances," the lawyer suggested. "That should bring him to heel in an instant."

"Should it?" Patterson asked cynically. "The fellow has diabolical skill in getting hold of money. I think there is nothing that would bring him to heel. I know exactly the size of some of his liquor and clothing bills in this town. The merchants think it's an honor to have a visiting nobleman on their books! And so far he has not paid anyone a red cent for anything."

"How does that affect the affairs of your bank?"

For answer, Patterson could only shudder.

His next move was to get Betsy out of Baltimore. She might have her head cleared of its nonsense if she spent some time down in Virginia. She did not. She and Jerome were in constant contact for the whole time of her exile. When she got home, unrepentant, Jerome was on the doorstep. The youthful lovers fell rapturously into each other's arms.

"You might as well accept it, Papa," she told him defiantly. "Jerome and I are going to be married. Nothing on earth can stop us! *Nothing.*"

"I cannot, and will not, under any circumstances, give my consent."

"We'll elope."

Patterson caught his breath. "You will not be able to find anyone to perform the ceremony," he said coldly. "This—this affair has not been any secret, I am sorry to say, and there is not a person in the country who hasn't heard of it. No minister would conduct the marriage service." He looked down at her with a kind of triumph, but she played a trump card with one word.

"So?"

The day before Christmas, South Street was choked with traffic from the first light of morning. Carriages brought callers, vans came with parcels of all sizes, elegantly wrapped and beribboned, errand boys shot in and out with messages and gifts. Servants polished and dusted and cooked and answered the door and never stopped grinning from the excitement. Florists arrived with armloads of such greenery and blossoms as they could muster in the depth of winter with so little time for preparing.

The curious paced the length of the street or lingered idly at the corners of the Philadelphia Road or Pratt or Water streets. None seemed to mind the cold or the drizzle of rain mixed with snow that was shrouding the town.

Lydia and Ann Maria were both up early getting themselves and their clothes ready for the wedding. Lydia decided on her rose velvet, which set off her skin. There were satin shoes to match. She watched the weather and the condition of the roadway for most of the day, wondering how she could manage to cross the street without ruining her shoes, feeling it would be undignified to arrive at so important a function with any detail of her costume less than perfect. Wearing a protective cover on the shoes would save them but not her pride. "Ah, fashion!" Her father laughed at her.

Ann Maria chose her best brown bombazine and her amber necklace, and wondered whether the head cold she had been fighting for days was going to keep her from going. She decided that it would not. What if she did have to spend a week or two in bed to pay for her recklessness? Would there ever be another wedding like this one? She would go.

As the appointed hour approached, every window in South Street had its collection of heads carefully screened by curtains. The whole affair was unbelievably romantic. Two beautiful young people—more than one person had called Jerome beautiful—madly, deeply, devotedly in love, finally marrying, in spite of the most determined opposition of family and church and government, probably to live in the glittering courts of France and to spend an enchanted life together. More than one matron in Baltimore, and elsewhere, found herself dissolved in envious tears, as squalling youngsters tugged at her skirts. Many a husband, sick to death of the frippery and the fussing and the gossiping, went out to find a fellow sufferer and get quietly drunk.

The calmest, gayest and most confident people in town on that fateful Christmas Eve were Miss Elizabeth Patterson and Mr. Jerome Bonaparte. He had stated on his marriage license that he was twenty-two years of age. He was actually nineteen and had been ever since November 14. In France, no person was allowed to marry without the consent of parent or guardian until the age of twenty-five. No person, high or low. But Jerome wasn't in France. His prospective father-in-law surely ought to feel better about giving his daughter to a mature twenty-two-year-old husband than to a nineteen-year-old boy, only three months her senior. So, he was twenty-two.

Early in the day, the young couple, sedate and proper, signed a remarkable document drawn up by Mr. Patterson and his lawyer. The other persons whose names were affixed were almost as remarkable as the paper. In accordance with Maryland laws, the French Vice-Consul at Baltimore, Pierre Jean Marie Sotin, and the Mayor of the City, James Calhoun, were required to be present. They were. The events of the day gave them conversational material for years.

Also signing were Lydia's good friend James Carroll; Jerome's secretary, Alexander le Camus; Jean Comegys, member of an important Dutch family of Baltimore merchants; and the colorful one-man navy and sometime privateer, Joshua Barney.

The first article in the agreement reflected Mr. Patterson's deep apprehensions. If there were ever any difficulty either in Maryland or in the French Republic, Jerome Bonaparte was to promise to "execute any deed necessary to remove the difficulty, and to confer on the said union all the character of a valid and perfect marriage."

The final article was to be dragged through the courts for the next half century: ". . . if the marriage should be annulled, either on demand of the said Jerome Bonaparte or that of any member of his family, the said Elisabeth Patterson shall have a right in any case to one-third of the real, personal and mixed property of her future husband."

At the bottom of the French version, the Vice-Consul set his signature under the phrase that translated as "Done at Baltimore the 3rd Nivôse, Year XII of the French Republic. The Vice-Consul [*signed*] Sotin." The word "Nivôse" was one of the flowery names of the new months selected for the French calendar, another of Napoleon Bonaparte's efforts to remake the world, even the universe, Patterson thought, in his own image. Feeling that his daughter's marriage represented one of the few great failures of his life, the banker could see her disappearing under the tidal wave of that new French Republic, destined to be an Empire. *3rd Nivôse.* It made him want to spit.

By afternoon, South Street was at fever pitch. The bridegroom arrived in purple satin, with diamond buckles on his shoes, and carrying in his hand a spray of flowers. Lydia's mother could not believe her eyes. That day was one of the few times when she allowed her curiosity to overcome her natural dignity and restraint. She had rushed around all morning getting gifts for the servants' Christmas, ordering extra food and making the house ready. Now she was permitting herself some time to watch from behind the draperies, along with her son and some of the kitchen help. Thomas, Senior, wouldn't dream of snooping like a silly woman, but moving nonchalantly along the street was different. He was almost an hour late getting home from work.

The girls were fluttering in and out for approval of their appearance, hunting for gloves and lace kerchiefs, choosing perfume. Ann wondered what their own weddings would be like if they were this hysterical about Betsy's. Well, Lydia would have enough to write to Ruth about; she wouldn't be coming around to ask for "anything, just anything" to fill up her letters.

Thomas, Junior, howled when he saw the purple satin. He went prancing along the hallway to show his disdain, his fingers crooked around an imaginary bouquet, but his mother shushed him. She did not want any undue racket to call attention to the huddled watchers at Number 15. Lydia Eliza leaned across her mother to get a quick look at the goings on, trying not to disturb the heavy draperies.

Jerome turned to speak to his driver, and Lydia caught a glimpse of his profile, dark, with flashing eyes, a fine strong nose, an aristocratic lift to his head with its straight brown hair; his romantically slender waist was partly obscured by the flowing cape he had flung over his shoulders. Forgetting the rest of the family, black and white, crowded behind her, she buried her face in her hands, wanting to keep that picture forever in her mind and heart. A prince, truly a prince!

Suddenly realizing how strange her behavior was, she fled from the room and caught up her wrap, her cheeks flaming. "Come on, Sister, it's time for us to leave," she said unnecessarily, since Ann Maria was at her elbow guiding her to the door. "Thomas marked out a dry path for us to take across the street. Wasn't that nice?"

"We both helped him, yesterday," Ann Maria reminded her. "We looked for rocks and high places. It was like crossing a stream up in Elkton, you said."

"Oh, yes, I guess that's right. Yes, of course. Where are my gloves?"

"On your hands, my dear. And I believe your head is still

in its usual place." Ann Maria reached to kiss her. "There are other princes, you know," she whispered. "Lots of them."

There were not many guests, because there was not too much space available after the immediate members of the family were placed. The Catons, looking like a bouquet of Christmas flowers in their bright velvets and satins, Henrietta Pascault, radiant and possessive on the arm of Jerome's friend General Reubell, whom she had vowed to marry and would very shortly. Sterrets, Ridgelys, Carrolls—just the younger ones with whom Betsy had grown up—Joshua Barney, his wife and sons. Every level place in the drawing room bore some kind of blossom or greenery. Large potted palms marked off the area between the front windows that was to be used as an altar. An ornamental velvet-cushioned kneeling bench mutely waited. William Patterson had resolved that the ceremony would have all the dignity, the solemnity, the Christian emphasis that he could possibly provide.

The Bishop, who had reluctantly consented to perform the ceremony, arrived in full ecclesiastical regalia, determined to be correct and solemn and the visual embodiment of his church. His eyes did not betray his sorrow or his concern. His handclasp in greeting Betsy's parents was warm and strong and reassuring, his smile benign, although their daughter had not changed her faith. She would always be a Presbyterian.

Lydia and Ann Maria stood near the fireplace, where they could see Betsy as she entered and would be able to view the ceremony clearly. Lydia suspected that Dorcas Patterson had planned the arrangement of the guests. Her daughter was known not to give a continental for the formalities of the occasion. With Jerome, the Bishop and herself all there, everything that mattered had been taken care of. She hadn't even had time to purchase a new gown and would wear an "old" one—one that had been worn once before to a dancing party.

"Sh-h-h-h!" The warning went around the buzzing room. "Sh! It's time!"

The Bishop took his place between the windows. The

splendiferous groom followed, accompanied by Alexander le Camus, uncommonly subdued. The two men turned to face the doorway. Mr. Patterson's usually florid face was drained of color, but his step was resolute as he escorted his daughter into the room, ignoring the sounds of quickly drawn breaths around him.

Betsy was dressed in a lace gown over muslin, exquisitely embroidered, her tiny feet twinkling in silver slippers, her dark hair under a shimmering veil. The neckline of her dress was low, front and back, and her arms were bare. One male guest reported with some pleasure that he could have put her gown in his pocket.

She stood close to her groom, her eyes brimming with happiness and more than a touch of triumph. Her father did not look in the direction of her mother, knowing he would see a similar expression there. She was on Betsy's side and always had been.

After waiting for the room to become completely still, the Bishop finally looked up and began to intone the ancient, beautiful words: "Dearly beloved, we are gathered here together in the presence of God and of this company. . . ."

Later, as the pair knelt before him, he read the traditional nuptial benediction of the Catholic Church and hoped in his heart that he had done what was best in that most difficult circumstance. More soberly than he remembered ever doing anything—and he was accustomed to weighty responsibilities—he wrote on the license:

Baltimore, December 24, 1803. By my authority I have today united in the holy bonds of matrimony, according to the rite of the Catholic Church, Jerome Bonaparte, brother of the First Consul of France, and Elisabeth Patterson, daughter of William Patterson, Esq., and of Dorcas (Spear) his wife.

JOHN, *Bishop of Baltimore*

The deed was done. All he wished now was to get away from the stifling chitter-chatter and lock himself in his study, where he could fall on his knees. Mr. Patterson came to steer him through the crowd around Betsy and Jerome and find a way for him to escape. The prelate suspected that his host would have liked to go with him. The two men exchanged a handclasp and a look of profound understanding. Patterson thanked him gravely and motioned for his driver.

Lydia Eliza's rose satin slippers took more punishment from the evening's dancing than from the muddy street. Jerome, gallant and graceful, managed to give every lady guest a few steps with him before he hurried back to crush his bride in his arms again and whirl her off her feet to the pulsing music. The two lovers moved in an almost visible mist of rapture. They slipped out of the room and up the stairs while the others were still dancing and eating.

Very late on that magical Christmas Eve, Lydia and her sister threaded their way across the street through the waiting carriages, accompanied for safety's sake by young John Barney. Her head a little light from the champagne, her eyes sparkling, Lydia posed an unanswerable question to her sister as they put their gowns back into their protective sheet-wrappers:

"What would it be like to be carried off by a prince?"

Chapter Three

The Dominion of Arrogance

With a wealthy American girl marrying into the First Family of France, fears of deeper foreign alliances were brought sharply to the surface. Thomas Hollingsworth even discussed the matter at home, which was unusual for him.

"They're saying around town that France and the United States are going to team up against the British, and that's why Betsy married that Bonaparte fellow," he reported. "A foot in the door, you might say."

"Papa!" Lydia said indignantly. "Betsy and Jerome married for love, and you know it! The government didn't have anything to do with it!"

"H'm." He cocked an eyebrow at her. "The government certainly didn't want to have anything to do with it—you probably didn't know all that was going on to try to head off that madcap match. It's just as well. You would have been upset. All I've got to say is that His Majesty had better wake up and send a full-fledged minister over here or he'll be mighty sorry. He and his tin soldiers can't get it through their heads that we're no longer a *colony*. One thing I'll say for that crafty Napoleon: he knows we're here!"

"Uncle Samuel thinks Mr. Jefferson was pretty nervy to buy that big territory of Louisiana," Thomas told his father.

"Of course, he said it was a good thing. That's a lot of land."

"It gets the Frenchies out of our West, son. But he should have had an act of Congress to back him up. Jefferson likes the French. He was there in the eighties as the American minister. Explains a lot of things," he said morosely. "And now Britain and France are in a shooting war again. I thought maybe that treaty at Amiens would cool them off. Well, we can't do much about it. And they'd better get a man over here, fast."

When the fighting had stopped at Yorktown in 1781, getting a treaty worked out and signed with the British had taken two years. It was ten years after the end of hostilities before any British minister was sent to the new nation. In September of 1791, a twenty-eight-year-old bachelor, George Hammond, was dispatched with orders not to present his credentials until the Yankees had chosen a suitable man to send to England. After weeks of delay, Thomas Pinckney was chosen, and Hammond could pay a formal call to President Washington, having sketched out some strategy while he cooled his heels.

He surmised that young Alexander Hamilton, Secretary of the Treasury, a man with an uncanny knowledge of finance, might be more receptive to British overtures than the Secretary of State, Thomas Jefferson, who was too close to the French and was in sympathy with their revolution.

Hamilton was friendly enough. He was also frank.

"What we need," he told Hammond, punching out his words with a pencil, "is to be economically self-sufficient. Commerce! Factories! Industry! That's where our wealth must come from. We must be able to stand on our own two feet, a free nation in the company of other free nations!"

Hammond had come with an attitude of benign condescension. He left the meeting a wiser man. If the Americans could scrape up enough capital to build manufacturing plants and perhaps pay transport for key workmen, the exodus from the British Isles and the resultant competition for markets would be calamitous. Too many Englishmen wanted to come to the New World anyway, especially men of the laboring classes. If ways were found to make it possible— Hammond stopped short. Did the men in Parliament have any true idea of what was afoot? If so, why hadn't someone briefed him? He began to comprehend the enormity of his assignment, and in self-defense retreated into the arrogance that was to bring his downfall.

In 1793 he was ordered to prevent the Americans from sending food, munitions and military supplies to the French, with whom Britain was at war again. Imperiously, Hammond announced that all American ships sailing for France were to be seized. The Hollingsworth brothers, who were just beginning to build up their shipping lines, were outraged, as was every merchant and businessman on the coast.

The uproar was so great that Hammond, who had married a Philadelphia girl, began to fear for his life. He moved her and their baby to New York City, where he could keep in closer touch with the British fleet, which might have to rescue him.

Hammond's petulance and total lack of judgment drove many fence-sitting neutrals toward the French. When he sailed for home in 1795, in a mental state dangerous to himself and others, and glad to escape with his skin, he was hardly mourned, even by his American relatives. Some of them became publicly pro-French.

Hammond did pass on one astute observation about the scene: the United States was so torn by internal conflicts that it would some day destroy itself by civil war. The report was filed with his others, probably with a reservation that the remark was a means of covering up his own deficiencies.

Having learned a small lesson, Great Britain began to look for an older man, more skilled in the delicate maneuvering that was obviously needed. Robert Liston, a fifty-four-year-old Scotsman, reluctantly consented to the appointment.

"I'd rather go almost anywhere else," he confided to a friend. The weather, the work—and especially the Yankees—would undoubtedly finish him off. His assignment to Philadelphia might be a one-way trip. With a sinking heart, he commenced choosing what to take and what to part with.

The capital was seething with intrigue. Liston was immediately in hot water with the French, which was to be expected, and also with the Spanish, who were under the thumb of France. He became a party to a plan to wrest the rich port of New Orleans from Spain through conspiracy with the Americans. When news of the British Minister's knowledge of the plot leaked out, there was fierce criticism of this flagrant breach of neutrality.

A senator was impeached before it was over, but Liston managed to skid safely through the crisis, a figure of ridicule and distrust. Pinckney, serving also as minister to Spain, obtained legal permission to use the port, through the Treaty of Madrid, without the need for connivance.

At the turn of the new century, when the scattered Hollingsworths were planning their own Celebration, Liston was caught in the midst of a more cumbersome and far-reaching migration. The capital of the United States was to be moved to the new Federal City on the banks of the Potomac, carrying out an act of Congress signed by George Washington on July 16, 1790. Hammond and his American bride had visited the site on their honeymoon and were not impressed. In 1792 Washington had fired its designer, feeling that "$5 a day was too much pay." By 1800, the city was still raw, unfinished, rutted with mud and infested with mosquitoes.

Several of the succeeding architects had doubts that the city would ever be a city or anything but a rough construction site of unfinished walls, unroofed buildings and impassable, weed-choked streets.

"If it weren't for those two terrible yellow-fever epidemics in the past seven years," Liston told his wife, "I don't think they'd ever leave Philadelphia, law or no law. It's a beautiful city, well situated, convenient to New York, Boston and Baltimore. Why move to that—that jungle?"

"Can't we get a leave of absence," she begged, "before all this upheaval begins? We could keep on going down the bay and to the Caribbean to visit my family and relatives there."

"You must remember, my dear," he told her patiently, "that Mr. Adams won the presidency in spite of his enemies' insistence that he was pro-British and wanted to take this colony back into the British fold. His Highness the Crown Prince, they called him. The least I can do is to stay with him awhile; the enemies might just have been right. Ah, what a feather I should have in my cap if I should bring *that* about! Perhaps a knighthood . . ."

By July of 1800, the public offices had all been transferred to Washington, and the Adamses were making do in a section of the partly completed presidential palace. The Listons never actually took up residence there; in late fall they sailed for the West Indies, their lives spared, their American adventure ended.

Liston could see the internal dissension that Hammond had reported and also beyond that, to the danger that the sleeping giant might be awakened and become a potent international force. Be on the alert, he advised, and don't stir up anything.

On the deck of their ship, Liston wrapped a blanket over his knees against the November cold and said without bitterness, "There was not a day when I wasn't attacked from one side or the other, usually about impressment first, then all kinds of other accusations. They claim we're stealing their sailors! *Their* sailors! Those traitors are our men, sneaking off to work on their ships! The way they talked to me you'd think I was going out as a privateer myself—"

"To kidnap sailors?" his wife asked.

"You don't think I'm a pirate and a liar and a thief, do you, my dear?"

"Not usually." She patted his hand. "But perhaps you'd better learn. You're going to miss all those insults."

Liston felt that he was leaving his post in good hands, those of Edward Thornton, who had come originally with Hammond. Thornton expected to stay only a few months, but he continued as chargé d'affaires for three years, his superiors assuming that all was well because his levelheaded diplomacy kept him from any explosive set-tos in the "raw and comfortless" capital city.

He was a fascinated eyewitness to the struggle for the presidency between Aaron Burr and Thomas Jefferson, two brilliant and capable men but different in every way. New York Federalists felt that if Burr were defeated it would be better to have no man at all in the presidency than to have Thomas Jefferson. Jefferson's backers returned the compliment. Partisan tempers were at white heat.

Thornton, accustomed to European politics, where the moves and countermoves were as stylized as the mating dance of the whooping crane, was flabbergasted at the outcome. Burr and Jefferson received seventy-three votes each. Neither would concede. The election was thrown into the House of Representatives, as demanded by the Constitution; the voting was by states. Ballot after ballot continued the tie. Finally, on the thirty-sixth time around, Delaware and South Carolina did not vote, and Jefferson was in.

Many Baltimore Federalists who had planned to attend the gala inauguration of Burr, coming up only three weeks after the tense election battle, were plunged into the deepest gloom. Young Thomas, in spite of his family's irritated protests, read out loud the newspaper's description of the day. The new President had gone to his inaugural on foot, dressed in ordinary clothes and surrounded by his ministers and other government officials. They were accompanied by a body of uniformed artillerymen.

"He may need all those guns," Thomas, Senior, chewed out his words, "for self-defense. I tell you, this nation is going to the dogs! Fast!"

"But, Papa, I've heard you describe how Mr. Jefferson himself planned those splendid celebrations for General Washington when he went into office." Lydia frowned. "I don't understand how he could change so much, and want everything so simple and plain."

"This is just the beginning," her father fumed. "The beginning of the end. You'll see, soon enough, where his *democracy* gets us!"

Unperturbed by the narrow margin of his election and by the howls of protest against him in the Federalist press, the new President attacked the problems and challenges of his office with great vigor. Within two years, the sounds of a quill scratching the signatures on the Louisiana Purchase were echoing and re-echoing into a roar of national triumph. Neither France nor Britain could comfort itself any longer with the thought of being indispensable to that awkward fledgling flapping around at the edge of the wilderness, trying to find its wings.

The news of the Louisiana Purchase startled the British, especially since Napoleon Bonaparte now had fifteen million American dollars in his pocket. What else that was dangerous to them might happen out there across the Atlantic? Wasn't there anyone in Washington to protect their interests but a chargé d'affaires?

In the scramble to find a suitable man for a full-fledged ministry, long overdue, they chose the Honorable Anthony Merry, taking him instead of Francis James Jackson, who was reputed to be "positive, vain and intolerant." They dared not send that kind of man.

What somehow escaped their notice was that Merry had the

same deep-seated contempt for Americans as did ninety-nine per cent of his countrymen; perhaps no one capable of handling such an important job was without it. Merry expected to be affronted at every turn. As it worked out, he was.

"I suppose they could have sent us someplace worse," he tried to console his weeping wife as boxes of clothing, furniture, bedding, crystal, china, silver and medicines choked their rooms.

"Where?"

"You must give me time to prepare a proper answer, my lady."

Finally landing after more than a month at sea, the Merrys were confronted with finding a way to get to the Federal City from Norfolk with their mountains of luggage. There were no through roads, so the trek had to be accomplished by water. After six days on the Chesapeake, they docked in Alexandria and completed the nightmare of their journey by "coachie" a type of vehicle that Merry had never seen before and that he found abominable.

It was late November when their entourage of people, parcels, bundles, burdens and boxes arrived in the muddy wilderness on the Potomac; they resembled aristocrats on a slumming trip. They had already made two serious mistakes before they even touched foot to the ground.

The local merchants began gossiping that the new man had imported quantities of British goods to sell in competition to the Americans. How else to explain the unbelievable tons of his baggage? In the kitchens and the bedchambers there were other whispers. The Merrys had brought along their own servants, like some kind of feudal lords. Did they think they would not receive decent care otherwise? Didn't American housemaids know how to tuck in a sheet? Couldn't American hands prepare and serve an edible slice of toast?

Ignoring the muttering, although he was aware of it, Merry put shells of two houses together, on K Street between

Twenty-sixth and Twenty-seventh streets, in order to get a habitable dwelling even partially suited to the ambassador from the first country of the world. In spite of promises, there was as yet no embassy. He and Mistress Merry set up their makeshift household and, as he attacked the problems of his office, each of them wondered exactly how much of their lifeblood they owed to the Empire.

There was still a furor over impressment. The Admiralty had given him figures showing that their men were deserting in droves—to the Yankees, of course—but the Americans were complaining that the British had no right to board their ships and take the men off—men who were British subjects. Albert Gallatin, Secretary of the Treasury, argued that it was perfectly legal to hire any man who applied for a job. American commerce was growing so rapidly that there was always a demand for seamen; if a man came into a shipping office asking for work, he should be taken on.

"These fellows are deserters from the British navy!" Merry contended. "Any deserter must expect to be apprehended and punished. That law is older than time! Your papers are full of notices about runaway slaves. You go after them, don't you? No matter where they hide?"

"Maybe our young men know how many are being killed in our war with France," his wife suggested once. "Nobody likes to get killed, does he?"

"The worst of it is that the Americans feed them better and pay them better than we do. They'll make our men *soft!* Are we raising a foot-loose generation of cowards?" he asked her angrily.

The Admiralty had ordered him not to accept any flimsy lies about deserters. Those fabrications about their being American citizens were being used only to save traitorous necks, and some of those necks must be summarily stretched, as an object lesson. The truth was that some of them did belong to bona fide natives, just as their owners claimed. The thumping of a hundred muffled drums could not have drowned out their tortured protests, as they were dragged, screaming, to a gallows or spun from a yardarm.

Several thousand sailors were hauled away; a horrifying number of them were hanged. Merry was assaulted by complaints and accusations from dawn to dusk.

Thomas and Samuel Hollingsworth were men whose names he soon knew, because Baltimore had been hard hit by naval losses and blockades imposed by the warring British and French. The brothers knew some of the kidnaped sailors, several of them being their own employees. Many of these had families in seacoast towns, some of them still living in the houses where they had been born. One was a Negro born in New England.

Anthony Merry might have been able to keep affairs on a more even keel if he had gotten on good terms with President Jefferson. The rawboned, public-spirited and many-faceted Virginian could live in elegance if he chose, could display great tact and courtesy, could handle tricky situations with skill and aplomb. He did not always choose to do so.

Even some of his admirers grumbled about his "democracy." He could look like the roughest farmer: hair uncombed, his corduroy overalls faded and dirty, a ragged red waistcoat sticking out under a country jacket, the tops of his boots turned down like some yokel's. He could look and act like the aristocrat that he was too, but there was no novelty in that, so his detractors ignored it. Only the judgment of history would emphasize his more sophisticated qualities.

Merry was doing his duty as he saw it by calling at the presidential palace in proper morning clothes, and by expecting courtesies befitting his rank at social functions, but there was something about the pompous and humorless British Minister that struck a nerve in the Jeffersonian anatomy. Merry was the kind of man that little boys like to trip up—Jefferson could scarcely resist sticking out his foot.

The cruelest stab at Merry's thin skin was to see the President acting most graciously toward a visiting beauty who was the sister-in-law of Britain's archenemy, Napoleon Bonaparte. Her companions were also her relatives, high in government circles, but Merry did not know that.

Betsy Bonaparte and her young bridegroom were certainly taking Washington by storm. The little bride's extremely daring clothes and witty tongue were the talk of the town; the Frenchman's irresistible charm was bowling over everyone he met.

"And he meets *everyone,*" the Englishman admitted grimly. "I hope his brother is paying him well for his services. He has earned it."

Before long, Mr. Merry began to wish that the Bonapartes were his only worry. The northern industrial states, known to be pro-British, approached him secretly with confidential information about a possible Northern Confederacy, as Hammond had foreseen. Merry's co-operation, they let it be known, could be of value to him as well as to themselves.

Drawing him into any such conspiracy amounted to near treason, but Merry was in for a more awesome confrontation from the highest of high places. The two propositions were not unrelated.

In one of the most shocking events in history, the Vice-President of the United States, Aaron Burr, killed Alexander Hamilton, his long-time rival and a former Secretary of the Treasury, in a duel on July 11, 1804. The tragedy occurred at the same spot where, exactly three years earlier, Hamilton's beloved eldest son had died, also in a duel. Somehow Burr escaped to safety, although he was indicted in New York for the challenge to the duel and in New Jersey for murder.

Burr still retained his high office until the last meeting of the Senate in 1805 before the new administration took over, and also presided at the impeachment trial of Justice Samuel Chase, which lasted from January 2 to March 1, 1805.

Earlier, Burr had sent a message to Merry offering his services and his talents, which were considerable, to the project of creating and developing a separate nation west of the Mississippi River. The stunned British diplomat could not forget that the man had been within a heartbeat of the presidency and was now ready, even eager, to destroy his country. When Merry had gathered his wits, he sent the information to London, as was proper, adding the thought that Burr would approach the French if England refused to help him.

Burr started out on a fact-finding trip down the Mississippi, scouting the territory for the support he might receive in his drive to set up the new Empire of Mexico, with himself as Emperor Aaron the First. The response surprised and elated him. He rushed back to consult with Merry.

"I have had no message at all from my superiors," Merry temporized. "I did send the information, by private courier. I thought that the wisest and safest method. It may not have been delivered. In any case, I have had no instructions."

"But look," Burr pressed the point, "once we get this western nation organized, the northern and eastern sections of the country will follow suit. I know you are aware of that. True?"

Merry did not answer.

"The Federalists have been having meetings. They are waiting for the support I can give them from the west. To do that I need help from you."

The Englishman watched him as he might have watched a cobra, transfixed. Burr opened up his hands. "In these ten fingers I hold the future of your nation on this continent, perhaps a brilliant opportunity for you as well. I am sure that you comprehend the value of the bargain I am offering." His face was within inches of Merry's, his eyes piercing into the Minister's brain.

"I have not received any instructions," Merry said in a low voice. "I cannot possibly commit my government to a course of action."

"Are you refusing?" It was Burr's turn to be stunned.

"I have no authority."

Burr pounded his fist on the desk and strode away. His hand on the doorknob, he said through his teeth, "The French should be quite happy to see me. They may kiss me on both cheeks."

Instead of slamming the door, he left it slightly ajar so that Merry was forced to go and close it himself.

By the fall of 1804, Merry's complaints about the burdens of his office became so insistent that his superiors gave him some help, appointing as secretary of the Legation an able and cultured young man, Augustus John Foster.

The new secretary was the son of an Irish M.P. for Ennis, and on his mother's side was the grandson of the colorful and eccentric Earl of Bristol, who was also an Anglican bishop. The Fosters had separated when Augustus was less than a year old, and he and his brother Frederick had lived with their father at Drogheda, Ireland, until the elder Foster's death, when Augustus was sixteen. His childhood home was about sixty to eighty miles south of the area from which the Hollingsworths had come to America in the 1600's.

His mother, talented in art and in politics, and with more than a little of her father's individuality, gave up her sons in 1781 and went to Italy for some years, before returning to London as the governess for the natural child of the Duke of Devonshire. In time, she became that gentleman's mistress as well as his wife's closest friend. Her two younger children, Clifford and Caroline, were sired by the Duke and brought up with his other offspring. Devonshire House was widely known as a rather unconventional *ménage à trois* and a gathering place for those in the innermost circles of British politics. Augustus John knew little, personally, of that irregular household until he was grown, but as his education and his career moved forward, his mother took an increasingly proprietary interest in his affairs.

Having heard nothing good of America in any of the four

languages he could speak and the several more he could understand, the new appointee was bristling and wary as he began the long, dangerous journey west.

From the pitching deck of his ship he watched the soft green shores of England fade into the fog and mist of a November day, in his arms a Scottish terrier his brother Frederick had given him. He was sailing into a watery abyss and leaving behind everything he held sacred. He pulled the collar of his greatcoat up around his ears and stayed by the rail until he could no longer see the land, straining his eyes to follow the last bird wheeling back toward home.

The coming of darkness brought a rising wind and the threat of a storm. Sailors scurried around, taking in sail and battening down the ship, as the waves became thrashing mountains of water. Trying to throw off the feeling that the storm was spelling his doom, he went below. After a time he gave up hope of sleeping and climbed back on deck. Within an hour they had outrun the worst of the weather, so he could stride awkwardly up and down, getting his sea legs, liking the salty punishment of the wind on his face, breathing in great draughts of the invigorating air. The puppy nuzzled close to his chest for comfort, whimpering in the cold.

On December 1, 1804, Foster turned twenty-four; it was the day before his onetime acquaintance Napoleon Bonaparte crowned himself Emperor of France in the presence of His Holiness Pope Pius VII. The flamboyant ceremony at the venerable Cathedral of Notre Dame in Paris sent a tremor of fear throughout the world. Foster was still on the high seas, but he was soon apprised of the details.

At Norfolk he saw British ships lying in wait to catch the French cruiser that was said to be bringing the new emperor's youngest brother, Jerome, down the bay on his way to France.

The boy's scintillating display of charm in American circles had not in any way pleased His Majesty, who had ordered him home. Since Jerome had married without consent and to one not of his faith, was underage, and was, or was supposed to be, subject to strict military discipline in time of war, his return to France could mean death for treason.

If the French didn't get hold of him, his capture by the British would give them a very large fish in their net. Any ordinary young man would have considered himself a hunted animal. Jerome Bonaparte had never been ordinary.

When Foster met him later, he thought Jerome a "well-mannered young man." Jerome was still circulating magically in Washington, Baltimore, Philadelphia and New York, his beautiful little bride on his arm. Neither the French nor the British had laid a finger on him. He and Betsy took a house in Baltimore at 36 South Street, a few doors from the Pattersons, with George Binner as their "botler." No mention was made as to who might be paying the rent, but it was common knowledge that Mr. Patterson felt that the pair must stay in the United States. It was nearly a matter of life or death; he knew it better than anyone else.

The Bonapartes' small dinner parties often included a childhood friend of Madame's, Miss Lydia Hollingsworth, who lived across the street and whose serene dignity offered a tantalizing challenge to Monsieur. He delighted in showing her home, if she had no other escort. She thanked him pleasantly for his courtesy, bade him good night and left him standing on the doorstep.

The Merrys welcomed their new secretary with great relief. Not only would his work as an amanuensis be appreciated, but his youth and his educational background might add some prestige to the sagging British image. Privately, they were glad to have a kindred spirit to share their exile. They prepared a room for him at their home, with a window view of the Potomac River and the low hills of Virginia.

This glimpse of natural beauty, especially at sunset, became one of the few bright spots of his life, along with the pleasant company of his little pet, who was supplied with a house near the service entrance.

Within a few months Foster, already overburdened by the immense paper work of their office, which had to be done entirely by hand—his hand, he soon learned—was absorbing the pessimism and bitterness of his chief, to whom he referred in his letters as Toujours Gai, calling their home Toujours Gai's Hotel. Every word that he had heard of America was true, even more so of the Federal City and its denizens.

On a particularly black evening he wrote to his mother, who had so blithely left him when he was a baby but who now eyed his every move with concern: "I shall forget how to be cheerful in this Sink of the Imagination."

He could laugh without amusement when he recalled the many notes she had sent him to warn against his bringing home an American wife. "Why doesn't she worry about my marrying a Hottentot?" he scoffed. "That might make more sense."

Chapter Four

A Man Mine Equal

Because Thomas Hollingsworth made it a policy never to mix business with domestic affairs, he was embarrassed when he had no choice but to break the rule. His work in partnership with Sam, and in less formalized co-operation with his other brothers, was his public world, his means of livelihood, his challenge, his cross at times, his satisfaction and reward at others.

His home was a completely private, sheltered, secluded haven reserved for his family and the large interrelated circle of Adamses and Hollingsworths. His wife had never set foot in any room or building where he transacted his extensive business affairs. In turn, he did not expect her to welcome any of those dealings to her hearthside. Home and business were two mutually exclusive areas of his life.

He had been in high dudgeon for longer than he could remember about the whole filthy blockade-and-impressment problem. Ships sat idly at the dock, cargoes rotting, men roistering in the grogshops, all because of the blockades. Once the ships were at sea, impressment was robbing the merchants of their seamen. If they escaped that piracy, the French were sinking their ships. The previous year, in 1805, they had destroyed a Hollingsworth merchant ship, *The Two Brothers,* with a frightful loss of life and property. The British were somewhat less dramatic than the French in their attacks on American shipping, but their steady erosion of the fleet by impressment and nuisance raids was keeping businessmen in a ferment.

Finally, in company with several other harassed Baltimore merchants, Thomas and Samuel shot off a protest to the government. They had heard talk of an embargo act, although Thomas didn't know what good it could do. The British and French were keeping ships from going out. An embargo act would keep them from coming in. Trade to him meant ships going out and ships coming in. Trade was the backbone of wealth. Wealth was the backbone of government. At least their signed protest might arouse a few of the powers-that-be down at the Federal City and get some action.

"What we need is a *navy!*" he was forever saying. "A navy with teeth!"

Long after they had given up hope of relief, a message came from the British Ambassador, the Honorable Anthony Merry, asking that his aide, Mr. Augustus John Foster, be permitted to call at their offices. Mr. Foster would be in Baltimore for the next fortnight, and Mr. Merry hoped that the Hollingsworth brothers would be so gracious as to arrange an interview with him at their convenience. He ended the letter "Cordially Yours."

They began gathering up notes of dates and places where their ships had been illegally boarded and their sailors dragged away. Three of the men had disappeared; one had been hanged. Their dollar losses from this mischief were staggering when all the separate columns were added up. They would have ample, documented ammunition for Mr. Foster.

Shortly after midnight of the day before their scheduled meeting, Thomas was awakened by an excruciating pain in his great toe. It struck him so suddenly that he leaped up as if he had been stabbed, frightening his wife and striking his left hand against the heavy walnut headboard with such force that he feared he had broken a bone. He sat up, holding his suffering foot with both hands, the right hand covering the other one to give it warmth and comfort. For several moments he rocked back and forth on the edge of the bed, nauseated with pain, while his wife fumbled for her robe and began trying to strike the flint for the candle.

"Forget the light!" he growled. "I don't need it. I've got the gout. Just go back to sleep. There's nothing you can do."

"Back to sleep?" she mumbled drowsily. "Can't I help you?" She crawled over beside him, patting him affectionately on the shoulder, trying to quiet him so that the whole household would not be wakened. He probably was right in saying there was nothing she could do. Gout was gout. She thought of the bottle of laudanum—perhaps a few drops would calm him enough so that he could doze until morning. She started out of bed again.

"Laudanum, Thomas? Shall I get it? Won't that help a little?"

"No!" he exploded, trying to put his weight on the throbbing foot. "If I can just manage to walk around a bit—*ouch!* Now go back to sleep." He could feel the joint at the base of his finger swelling as if in sympathy with the bursting toe on his foot. He felt like a spavined horse, hurting in every place at once, cross at losing his rest. He said a few fierce curses under his breath.

He spent the rest of the night in a chair by the window, staring out at the dark night with its occasional twinkle of light as watchmen came and went, his teeth clenched against giving way to his suffering, his mind in turmoil. He simply could not take the time to be sick.

The hope of getting any kind of settlement, concession, even a listening ear from the British was so tantalizingly close that he could think of nothing else. It would be rude to send word to ask for a postponement. He couldn't advise the gentleman, who was known everywhere for his extremely correct manners and his stiff-necked observance of the diplomatic niceties, that he had the gout—the word was as horrid as the disease—and must ask his indulgence. Out of the question! Impossible!

His wife was jolted from her sleep again as he snorted out loud in his annoyance. He muttered a halfhearted apology and slid farther down in the chair, his chin on his chest, his spirits low.

In the growing light he began inspecting the foot. A hideous sight. His ankle and leg were numb and cold, but the toe felt as if he might be holding it in a fire. The skin over it glistened redly in the slanting rays of the first sun, the veins around it like purple ridges, the nail disappearing under its puffiness. He could almost see the waves of pain leaping up and down and through it. And it would probably get worse.

To take his mind off his foot, he massaged his bruised hand and finally sat on it, so that the warmth of his body would give it some relief. The bone was not broken, he assured himself, although he had no idea what a broken bone felt like. It wasn't bleeding.

He felt the fingers on his right hand, then found that the corresponding sections of his left one were still functioning in the same way, although painfully. He probably had had only a bad knock. And if the bones were smashed, what could be done? Nothing, as far as he had ever heard from other people with broken toes or fingers. The doctor might strap them up to hold them steady, that was all. A kind Providence would eventually get the parts knitted together somehow. The thought of Providence, in Whom he had deep faith, both from heredity and inclination, made him bow his head for a short, wordless prayer. At least the prayer wouldn't hurt him, and any other treatment he might think up probably would. Thomas Hollingsworth was always impatient with pain.

He pulled open the neck of his nightshirt, suddenly smothered with heat and feeling weak. Getting up shakily from the chair, he slid back under the covers and fell asleep.

The day dragged miserably as he sat in the back parlor, his foot propped up in front of him like the prow of a ship, his diet restricted to barley soup, which he hated, and his temper at hair-trigger tension. Servants tiptoed; the girls looked in, brought him something to read and escaped. Young Thomas spent his spare time horseback riding in the fine spring weather so that he could be away from the house. Mrs. Hollingsworth seemed to be busy at an unaccustomed number of errands involved with the Benevolent Society and the summer clothing she was collecting for the children out there. Her husband wondered why Lydia wasn't doing it—Ann usually assigned her all those tasks.

In the evening he sent for Sam, who came over from Charles Street to commiserate and to agree with him that something had to be done about the upcoming visit of the British representative.

"I guess I could handle it by myself, Thomas, if I have to," Sam offered. "You know, we ought to be realistic about this. As I've said all along, if the British government wants to stop impressment and raids, it can. The point is, they don't want to. It isn't just a group of hotheads pulling these stunts; it's a government policy! Truth is, this young fellow can't do anything one way or the other. He isn't the government, you know. He isn't the Admiralty. He isn't the Foreign Office. He's just their messenger boy. They're sending him around to soothe our feelings a little, hoping we'll soften up enough to stop squawking about what they're doing."

"Maybe we ought to cancel the appointment—"

"No! Oh, no," Sam said. "It's taken us this long to get any rise at all out of them, and I want to see what happens. I was merely saying that we shouldn't fool ourselves with false hope. Don't you think you'll be well enough to get there by tomorrow? It isn't until three-thirty."

"You ever have the gout?" Thomas snapped.

"Couple of times," Sam admitted. "Worst pain in my whole life. I keep my fingers crossed all the time, afraid I'll get it again."

"Was it over in one day?"

"One day? Lucky if it was gone in a week."

"Then why ask me about tomorrow?" Thomas tried to shift his uncomfortable position, wincing from the effort, annoyed with his brother's obtuseness. Sam ought to have more sense.

If they did get anything out of the Secretary of the British Legation, their combined efforts would hardly be enough to make even a dent in the British armor plate of righteousness. In his rising anxiety, Thomas began to loathe Augustus John Foster before he ever saw him. Impudent young upstart! Soft-soaping pettifogger! Arrogant fop!

"Well?" Sam asked a little impatiently, putting the burden of decision on him. Since Thomas was ten years older, he was the senior partner, but he didn't always enjoy the honor.

"We have two choices, I guess," he said heavily. "Cancel—and I can't quite bring myself to doing that. Too much is at stake. And I don't have the gumption to ask for a postponement. I'm sure every minute of Foster's time in Baltimore is filled with appointments."

Sam lighted a cigar, blowing the pungent smoke toward the ceiling as he disciplined himself to appear relaxed while Thomas cogitated. His second choice would probably end up by being the only choice.

"I guess what we'll have to do," Thomas said with a sigh of resignation, "is to have him come here."

"Here? At your *home?*" Sam turned to his brother with a half-smile, thinking he was joking. "Here?"

"We might even ask him to stay for tea," Thomas responded, with a slight smile of his own, now that the decision was made. "It's here or nowhere, as I see it. And tea wouldn't be out of place, would it? You don't invite a gentleman, especially an important one, to your home—your castle, you might say—and then not offer him any kind of hospitability, do you? Well, do you?"

"No, of course not. But this will be a business conference—a quite irregular conference. I can't picture it at home like this—"

"No? Then can you picture those figures of your losses, down there on your desk? Dollars, cents, men, ships, goods, trade? That's what I'm talking about! Losses! Just the drop in our shipping tonnage in the past six months scares me. Have you noticed the lines of ships tied up at the docks? How many of them are ours? Another year like this one—"

"All right! All right!" Sam had never seen him so ruffled. "Shall I bring over a tot of my best brandy? We don't want their little messenger boy to report home that we're barbarians, do we?"

Thomas grinned for the first time. "Make sure it isn't French. And another thing, don't let me touch a drop of it. One swallow and I'd probably lose both my hands and both my feet—or wish I had. Damn! Damn all gout! You know what those fool women are feeding me? *Barley!* Like a sick horse. Barley—" He made a motion of disgust. "No meat. No alcohol. No wine. No *nothing!*"

"Pox take it!" Sam sympathized.

Lydia came in with a Sèvres cup and saucer on a round silver tray, and pulled up a mahogany piecrust table to her father's chair. "Hot lemon juice, Papa. Mama says you have to drink it. And if Uncle would like to have some too—?"

"See?" Thomas gestured angrily. "Lemon juice! *Hot!* Why don't you try some, Sam? It's *delicious.*"

"Thanks just the same. I'm doing fine." Sam's heavy front joggled up and down with his struggle to keep from laughing.

"Shh-h-h, Papa." Lydia handed him a Madeira linen napkin and fussed with the cushion propping his feet. "This will help you get better. Drink it all now. No cheating." She slipped from the room with a wave of her fingers for her uncle.

"When are you going to get those girls married off?" Sam asked bluntly.

"Married off? You've got some at your house, you know," Thomas reminded him, playing the game in which they often indulged but which was annoying him now. "Ann Maria's only twenty-two and Lydia's twenty. They aren't so damn old."

"Molly's been married to James Cheston for three years," Sam reminded him. "And Betsy's snaring young Sterret Ridgely, and Sally's just a girl. We're not doing so poorly. Got grandchildren too. I'm warning you"—he chuckled—"you'd better get busy or you're going to wind up with a houseful of old maids!"

"Two unmarried young ladies do not make a houseful of old maids," Thomas retorted sharply, unable to enjoy the banter. "I'll expect you at three-thirty tomorrow, or shortly after, with young Foster. You might as well plan to stay for tea too. Tell Sarah you won't be home until later. Business conference. And don't tell her we're having it here. Might not set well. I'll have to figure out how I'm going to handle Ann so she won't get excited and bring on one of her headaches." He waved in a gesture of dismissal and picked up the steaming cup of lemon juice, knowing he'd have to drink it sooner or later. Polodore was waiting to help him up to bed, an attention that would ordinarily have embarrassed him but that he now found touching and suddenly welcome.

Thomas dressed with care for the meeting. The linen at his neck was crisp and spotless, his trousers carefully brushed, and his sore foot wrapped in a dark flannel bandage to diminish the attention it was sure to draw as he sat with it stretched out on a stool, his back to the window in the handsomely furnished front parlor. The visitor would have to face him, thus giving Thomas a better opportunity to study the man's expressions while his own face was in shadow. Ann had been bustling around all morning, getting ready, asking his advice on the menu, arranging flowers from her garden on the mantel and a bowl of fruit on the tea table, instructing the servants, finding invisible specks of dust.

He noticed that she had put out the Waterford glasses for the brandy, which Sam's black boy had brought over in the morning. Thomas was going to be hard put to resist it. For one thing, his courage needed bolstering, but he knew from previous agonies that any alcohol would increase the conflagration in his foot tenfold. Sam was reputed to have one of the finest cellars in Baltimore, almost on par with young Bonaparte's. That one was already becoming legendary.

"I guess this will show me exactly how much strength of character I have," Thomas sighed. "Ah, the high cost of self-denial . . ."

Within five minutes of the scheduled conference, Sam brought their visitor up the steps. Polodore—head high, dignity unassailable, face impassive—went to the door and let them in. He took their hats and sticks, ushered them into the parlor and bowed himself out.

"Quality," he summed up the new arrival for the other black folks in the kitchen wing. "Quality!" He went over the tea dishes with a critical eye, disappointed that he didn't find any greasy spots or tiny chips in the rims to fuss about.

The bell rang, and he hurried back to the parlor. Mr. Thomas must want him to serve the brandy, a task he performed with polished skill. He pulled down the tabs of his best jacket, nodded to his master and began the ritual, wishing he could hum.

Apologizing for not rising to greet him, Thomas stared at his guest. The fellow was only a boy! He felt a moment's annoyance that the British would have such disrespect for

America that they would send out this stripling and expect him to know how to handle important international business, especially in such explosive times. They had shown astonishingly poor judgment in the first men they sent over, and there hadn't been an ambassador of any kind for almost four years, just a chargé d'affaires. Then they had dug up that arrogant and thin-skinned Merry who was always getting his feelings hurt and who was rumored to be tangled up with the traitor Aaron Burr. And now this—this child! *They take us for fools!*

The youngster's face was round, almost cherubic, his eyes a bright dark-blue, with the air of wonder of a child trying out a new pony. His hair had the same red-gold coloring as Deborah Adams's; she had recently married William Cochran. On a woman the color was beautiful, but on a man it looked somehow unfinished. His hair was fine and silky in texture, and it gleamed with cleanliness. Even more amazing, the fellow blushed!

Sam couldn't resist a sudden startled raising of his eyebrows when he first noticed the red flush rising above Foster's utterly English, utterly correct neckpiece. Nobody blushed any more! It was a lost art! Sam's and Thomas's glances crossed briefly. Both of them felt at once disarmed, fatherly, generous, protective. The boy was afraid of them!

Foster's back was ruler-straight as he sat on the proffered chair, accepted the brandy from Polodore, passed it delicately under his nostrils and allowed himself a wintry smile of approval, even of pleasure. Sam's eyebrows did another small jump; the youngster knew fine liquor! Or was he acting?

"I hope you will forgive my asking you to come here. We know you are very busy, sir," Thomas was saying politely. "As you can see I am, shall we say, discommoded?"

Foster nodded gravely. "We sometimes suffer the same ailment in my country, Mr. Hollingsworth." His speech was British in all its consonants, but the vowels had a certain soft quality that was baffling.

Sam, who had more contact with the shipping captains and was more often at dockside than his brother, wanted to keep him talking so he could identify the sounds. In a lull in the conversation he asked suddenly, "Do I note a slight Italian accent in your speech, Mr. Foster?"

It was the Englishman's turn to be startled. There was never any telling what Americans might do next; they were so unpredictable as to be predictable. "I lived in Italy for a short time," he answered, the blush rising again.

"Going to school?" Sam pressed for more information, having been so accurate in his first guess. The British always sent their young ones off to be educated at such frightfully early ages. He never knew how the parents stood it, to say nothing of the poor little tads.

"I went to school in Ireland as a child, then Christ Church College at Oxford, and in Germany later," Foster said frigidly. "In Italy I was on the Grand Tour, which you may have heard of." He cleared his throat discreetly and took the initiative, to forestall any more impudent probing. "As you know, gentlemen, Mr. Merry has asked me to call on you to ascertain in more detail the exact complaints which your firm has against His Majesty's government—more specifically, of course, the Admiralty, if I understand it correctly?"

He took from his pocket a small leatherbound book, opened it to a fresh page and waited for them to speak. Sam fumbled for the lists and figures he was sure he had brought with him.

"You sent them over at noon, Sam, remember?" Thomas reached for the portfolio on a table near him. "Shall we start with, perhaps, 1801, five years ago, sir?"

It was dark when the Secretary of the British Legation, Augustus John Foster, who was always embarrassed because he looked so young, left the house of Thomas Hollingsworth, merchant, escorted with great courtesy and geniality by his brother, Samuel Hollingsworth, also a merchant.

Sam knew for a certainty that the gentleman was no adolescent, inept, frightened, disconcerted boy. Sam was wondering privately what had hit him.

Equally stunned, Thomas sat rubbing his injured finger—which he'd forgotten until that moment—waiting for Sam to return. "I surely never thought," he greeted his brother ruefully, "that the day would come when I'd find myself feeling sorry for the British Admiralty!"

"Sorry for them!" Sam whistled. "For a while there, I was ready to sign over every ship and every man we have to keep their country from going to the dogs. I thought I had to get out there bodily to protect those poor devils from the French. I'd like to hire that young man myself. Maybe he could do something to persuade Mr. Jefferson—"

"Mistuh Jefferson!" Forgetting his foot, Thomas swung himself around and pounded on the arm of his chair with his good hand. A streak of pain through his toe made him gasp as he said again, *"Mistuh Jefferson!"* spitting out the consonants as if he were spitting out the man himself, eliding the r's so softly that they disappeared. His slurred speech sounded like that of one of his slaves. "That country mule is selling himself and the whole nation to that—that Bonaparte and those Frenchies. What does he want to do? Put all the mongrels in the saddle? Get himself named a prince, or even a king of something, for groveling at their feet? Does he want to break our *backs?"*

Hearing his angry shouts, his wife hurried in, their three young people at her heels.

"Never mind, sister," Sam laughed. "Thomas and I were just letting off a little steam about what goes on in Washington. Levi calls it an indoor sport. That was a very nice tea you served us and the young man. The gingerbread was excellent."

"Young Thomas's favorite food." Ann Hollingsworth smiled her thanks. She had the best cook in the neighborhood, and everyone knew it. All of Delia's pastries were superlative.

"He knows Betsy!" Lydia said. "He's known her for a couple of years, ever since she and the Prince used to be in the Federal City so much. He even said he had been at the Pattersons to call on her, so he knows our street well!"

"Betsy is a married woman with a baby!" her mother reproved her. "Perhaps Mr. Foster was calling on her father."

"That Jerome! Another Bonaparte, the worst of the whole lot!" Thomas pounded the chair arm again. "Where is he now? Left her on the ship in Lisbon and no country in Europe would let her land. And that baby due to get born, and so Great Britain had to take her in. Shameful! And does he support his wife now that she's back here with the child? Has he ever even seen his son?"

"Some prince she got herself," Ann Maria said lightly. "But he was what she wanted. She told Lydia and me she'd rather have Jerome for even a year of her life and be unhappy forever after than to—"

"He was a wonderful dancer," Lydia whispered loyally.

"And where is he now?" Thomas roared.

"Hush! Idle gossip does no one any good!" Mrs. Hollingsworth went around drawing the curtains and lighting more candles. "You just hush, all of you!"

"That Mr. Foster surely knew a lot about a lot of things," young Thomas said admiringly. "I sat beside him at tea. Ships! He must know as much about ships as the McKims. He's been on all kinds of them, big and little. And he's got a pet terrier named Tartar—"

"You hardly let him eat, asking so many questions," Ann Maria chided.

". . . and horses. And rigs. He sent clear to England to have a curricle shipped over for him to drive around in, and he's going to have it all painted and polished up, and he's buying a spanking team of bays to pull it. He tried to pretend that he didn't know much about handling the horses because he hadn't had any driving lessons, but he wasn't fooling me."

"He seems awfully young," their mother mused, "to have done so much."

"I didn't dare ask him if he'd heard about that woman down in Norfolk who's helping Britishers pose as Americans when they want to jump ship." Sam grinned. "Seems she has a big cradle, man-size, and when some young rascal wants to come over to our side she rocks him in it for a few minutes; then she can swear that she's known him from the cradle!"

"Do you think there are many Englishers really coming to work on our ships?" Thomas broke into the laughter. "I never figured the British had a leg to stand on when they insisted we have their men. It sounded like a big lie to give them an excuse to kidnap our fellows so they can keep their navy afloat."

"A big lie, Thomas?" His wife's eyes and mouth were three round O's.

Thomas ignored her. "And if young Foster ever finds out about that cradle-rocker down in Norfolk, she'd be in for it, you can bet!"

"Oh, *I'd* never tell him," Sam protested. "But it's a true story. And you ought to know, if anyone does, how many British we have in our crews. Not a tenth of what they think we have, but you can't deny we've got *some*."

"They like American wages. And not getting shot at by the French," his brother conceded. "Of course, that can't excuse the British piracy—"

"Thomas!"

"Whose side are you really on, Papa?" his son asked.

"On *my* side!" Thomas retorted, his face twisting in another surge of pain. "All I want to do is to go on about our affairs, sell our merchandise, sail our ships where we damn well please with *nobody* sticking his nose in where it doesn't belong! French, British, American! I'm fed up, by damn!"

"Thomas! The children!"

"Children? They're old enough to hear a few of the facts of life." He turned to Sam. "I knew we shouldn't have that fellow come here. A man should never mix business and family. Women ought to stay out of it, every bit of it. Say, I got the idea from the way he asked you about the Society of the Cincinnati that he figured it should be something like an order of nobility for America. Or maybe knighthood?"

Sam stood up to leave. "Is that right? Guess I'll have to get Henry to get me voted in." He tried to make a courtly bow from the waist but gave it up.

"Well, don't let it go to your head. Thanks for sending the brandy. The smell of it nearly finished me off, I can tell you that," Thomas said glumly. "Give our regards to Sarah and the family. Now, for some more hot lemon juice to finish off a gala evening—ah, glorious hot lemon juice! A brew fit only for a dead man!"

Long after Ann Maria was asleep, Lydia Eliza stared into the night. She had never met anyone quite like him—he had subtly handled every person there in the way to make that person well disposed toward him. With her brother he was a contemporary, interested in animals and ships; with the women he was chivalrous without overdoing it; with the men he was direct and unflurried, although his unwilling blushes seemed to vex him. Without bragging, he had hinted at his wide acquaintance with important people abroad. He even knew Napoleon himself, and the capricious Jerome, now truly a prince and possibly soon to be a king!

There was a good scent about the man—Lydia had not for an instant thought of him as a boy. He smelled of fine shaving soap, the best of leather in his gloves and shoes, British wool in his clothes, the faint aroma of expensive tobacco, although he had not smoked in their house.

Had she and Ruth Tobin thought there would be a revealing burst of thunder or a blare of trumpets . . . ? Guiltily she decided not to mention the evening or the visitor to Ruth, not for a while anyway. Maybe never.

The linen cuff at his wrist had brushed along the fine reddish hairs on the back of his hand as he wrote in the little notebook—sometime in the night, Lydia Eliza woke with a start, dreaming she had touched him.

Chapter Five

As a Piece of a Pomegranate

South Street, burgeoning in spring beauty with early roses, lilacs, flowering crab, jonquils and tulips, had a mystical glow as Lydia Eliza slipped to her window early the next morning. An unfamiliar kind of secret joy made the corners of her mouth turn up and gave her eyes an amber luster as she studied herself in a cloisonné hand mirror and tried ways of piling her hair high on her head. Could this reflection be true? She pulled back the sheer undercurtain to give herself more light. Her skin was so pale. Even this new inner excitement did not give her any more color.

She tried pinching her cheeks, a technique she had experimented with before. There was a quick redness, but the improvement lasted only moments, leaving ugly blotches the shape of her fingers. She licked her lips, hoping a gentle biting would create more rosiness, but it did not.

Once, when they were younger, she and Ann Maria had moistened their fingers and rubbed them across the deep red of the large cabbage roses in the wallpaper, smearing their cheeks and achieving a most mischievous appearance, which delighted them both. They were giggling and admiring each other and indulging in elaborate posing when a boyish snicker betrayed the presence of their brother.

"Thomas! You get away! Be gone!" they squealed.

"Right!" he shouted as he raced down the steps. "I'm going to tell Mama!"

They were at his heels, ready to defend themselves, forgetting that their appearance was a complete giveaway.

"See!" he told their mother triumphantly. "Didn't I say they had themselves all painted up like Indians? Isn't that what I said? And the wallpaper is all streaked too. That's where they got all that red stuff. Right off the wallpaper!"

He watched with unrestrained glee while they were forced to wash their faces until all vestiges of the paint were gone. Their cheeks burned for days, both from the humiliation of getting caught and from something that caused a skin irritation that would not go away. Neither girl ever put cabbage roses on her face again. Ann Maria, although her hair and eyes were lighter than Lydia's, did not need them.

Andrew Aitken, an enterprising apothecary at the corner, was mixing and marketing a new rouge-pomade, but ladies of quality were not patronizing him. Or at least Lydia wasn't. She tried to avert her eyes whenever she went past his shop, to avoid temptation. When she had to enter, to make purchases of laudanum, flaxseed, sweet oil or camphor, she prepared a written list and bought only the exact items, hurrying along, saying that her mother needed her purchases right away. In her haste she found it hard to wait for him to count out her change.

Mr. Aitken, who had known her from the day she was born, was puzzled by her attitude, never dreaming that its true cause was the display on his shelves of the little jars of rouge.

On this spring morning after the Secretary's visit, she wished again for the courage to buy and use the cosmetic, but she knew she never would. For one thing, Thomas's sharp eyes would notice, and for another, her mother would scold and make her scrub it off, just as she had done eight or ten years before.

Now if I were Betsy, she thought. But Betsy, with her vivid coloring, would not have had the problem in the first place. Even if she had, it would not have been a problem, not for Betsy.

She reached for a new *flacon* of perfume she had purchased for herself after first choosing it for Ruth Tobin. She found the scent so pleasing that she had bought the second bottle, carefully subtracting the purchase price on the bill that she would send up the bay with the parcels for her cousin. She thought fleetingly of confiding in Ruth about *him,* but then . . .

She touched the stopper lightly behind her ears and spent several minutes turning her head swiftly to the side to catch a whiff of the scent. It was gay and subtle, with the freshness of a daffodil. Would he like it?

She spun around, thinking that her sister had caught her, but Ann Maria was still soundly asleep. Glancing again in her mirror, she saw that her cheeks were flushed. It was most becoming, she had to admit.

A blush was the mark of a lady, her grandmother used to tell her. Lydia suspected that it might also be the mark of some secret guilt, an indication that one's thoughts had pushed into some forbidden garden and were wandering around among all the tempting blossoms that were not to be touched.

She dared not wonder why their visitor had blushed so easily. Even to wonder would be sinful.

The vivid picture of Mr. Foster's hand came back again and nearly smothered her. She tiptoed off to wash her face in some cool water and to get into some clothes so she could go outside, where it was easier to breathe. Her mother's garden was always beautiful in the early hours, sparkling with droplets of dew on the complicated webs the spiders had built from flower to flower. A walk there would steady her nerves.

Mr. Foster's carriage appeared in their street two days later, drawn up in front of the Pattersons. But of course he was calling on Betsy's father, who kept his countinghouse on the lower floor at Number 20. Lydia watched from behind the curtains, at the same spot from which she had observed the visits of the French prince. It was some time before the young man came out—three rows of needlepoint, to be exact—from the door at Number 18, raising his hand to Mr. Patterson, who was standing on the top step. Did Lydia only imagine that he glanced across the street to Number 15? She was sure she wasn't dreaming it. He had looked for as long as she could hold her breath, fearing she would betray herself by movement of the drapery in front of her. She knew he had looked.

Foster actually had been calling on Mr. Patterson, with a list of topics given him by Toujours Gai, on an errand similar to his visit at the Hollingsworths, with an emphasis on banking matters. As the two men were beginning their conference, Betsy came into the room to ask her father a question. Foster jumped to his feet, reddening because he knew that he had hoped she would appear.

"Madame Bonaparte!" he said, bowing in his formal way. "I'm so happy to see you again!"

She gave him her hand. "Mr. Foster! I didn't know you were here. I'm sorry to interrupt—"

"You might like to join us, Betsy, if Mr. Foster doesn't object," her father said gruffly. "You have a sharper mind than I when it comes to international finance. All three of us know that, I suspect."

Startled, but pleased to include her, Foster held her chair and moved his own so that he might have a better view of both the Pattersons. He inquired about her son, saying nothing of her absent husband, then waited for her father to explain briefly the points they had already discussed. She appeared to give Patterson her complete attention.

When Foster left, he knew that he must get to his room at once to write down the details of what Patterson had agreed to and the suggestions he had offered; if he didn't, all his recollections of the meeting would be so blurred that it would be as if the older man had not been there. He was disconcerted to realize that Betsy, whom he had known for so long but had never seen except with Jerome, could affect him so much. He did not pity her, as some did. She did not need pity. If anyone could manage her own life, she could. She had some of the spunkiness of Foster's mother.

That young lady could knock a man right off his feet! he thought distractedly. But not this man. I plan to keep my head . . . but it wouldn't take much—now let's see, what was it he said about interest rates after June first? Or was it July? Where are my notes?

Going out their door, he had glanced across the street. Mr. Thomas Hollingsworth was one of the directors of the bank next to his house. Had Merry told him to stop there too? He looked at his list. No, not this time.

Lydia saw him again that weekend at the Strickers', where an afternoon garden party given in his honor was suddenly driven indoors by a torrential rain. The house was a mass of confusion, of damp, wilted dresses and hats, of gentlemen trying to be charming though their shoes were squishing-wet and their carefully powdered hair was becoming pasty and streaked.

Mr. Foster stood by himself in a corner of the downstairs parlor, brushing his clothes as tactfully as he could, to avoid the appearance of a shaggy dog coming in from a swim. His eyes were twinkling with amusement, his round face glistening with drops of rain and his unpowdered hair showing an attractive curliness as it dried. Lydia's first reaction was of irritation with him. She had heard that in Ireland and England it rained all the time. What was so terribly amusing about this dreadful situation and the misery of their distraught hostess? It was a stroke of bad luck that could have happened to anyone. How dare he think anything was funny?

Mrs. Stricker went up to him then, and Lydia saw the quick mask that dropped over his face. He straightened his shoulders, got his dripping pocket kerchief out of sight and acted as if nothing untoward had happened. He spoke a few words to his hostess, and she went on to her other drenched visitors, somehow revived. Her day was not ruined after all.

In that brief moment, Lydia Eliza knew more about Augustus John Foster than did anyone in Baltimore. It was a precious secret.

When Mrs. Stricker was out of his sight, he stood by a window and allowed himself to survey the noisy, steaming room, not showing any alarm when violent cracks of thunder threatened to smash the house.

If I hear trumpets too, I'll die. . . .

His eye caught Lydia's. She saw the flush begin to rise above his collar, just as it had at her home. He started toward her, smiling a greeting. She was almost choking. She put her hands over her flaming cheeks and made her escape.

He was to be in Baltimore a few more days, she knew. Her father brought in occasional reports of Foster's dealings with other businessmen like himself, saying gloomily that all the young man did was listen.

"I thought that was what you'd been waiting for, Papa," young Thomas said quizzically. "I heard you and Uncle Samuel say you were glad he would."

"Yes, I guess so. Even that was more than we had hoped." His father dropped into a chair and pulled out a stool to give his foot some rest. He should have known better than to try to walk all over the whole flour mill up there on Jones Falls Road, he told himself. After all, he wasn't young any more. He could have had his son do it for him. The lad had turned sixteen the previous week, time for him to get into at least a part of the business. Good training for him.

Lydia's shopping expeditions began to take on an extra dimension as she tried to plan her itinerary so that she wouldn't seem to be in the neighborhood of the Indian Queen Tavern on the Philadelphia Road at Hanover Street, where he was staying, four blocks from her home. Busy as he was, of course, he could be almost anywhere.

She wondered if he had discovered the beauty of Howard's Park, high on the hills back of town. (Her brother had been quoting him endlessly about birds and small forest animals and the trees that were native to America but new to him.) He must surely have met John Eager Howard and been invited to his estate at Belvidere; if so, she hoped they had suggested that he roam along the rough paths in the woods.

When she shopped for Ruth she usually went on foot, for it meant going from one place to another for small items, with little Pansy tagging at her heels to carry the parcels and often as not getting lost because she was not tall enough to see over the counters. Her frightened shrieks brought clerks running. Laughing at her terror, Lydia sometimes threatened to tie the child to her wrist, like a pet kitten, and Pansy would begin smiling through her tears. Next time, she'd be lost again.

If her purchases would be bulky or heavy, or there was a great deal of used clothing, toys and furniture for the Benevolent Society, Polodore and Robert took her in the carriage. Pansy would struggle toward the door of the school tugging some large parcel—a carton of underdrawers or a donated straight chair—and the schoolboys would laugh at her, making her drop her burden and try to hide behind Lydia's skirts. She wondered if the skittish urchin would ever become a useful servant.

Polodore usually completed Pansy's tasks, his dignity a little ruffled by her behavior. Robert sat stolidly on his high seat, talking to himself and the horses, inclined to drop off to sleep. Boys swarmed everywhere, climbing on the back of the team, making up games of hide-and-seek and teasing Pansy. Unless the animals snapped at them or started to move, Robert never noticed the goings on. His job was to drive.

A few days after the garden party, her brother went with her to gather up the gifts for the school. The two of them stood on the steps of the rectory looking out toward the water, with the growing, bustling city at their feet.

"Someday I'm going to get on one of Papa's ships and go right down the river and out into the bay and on into the ocean and see the whole world," he told her confidently. "I'll go everywhere! And I'll bring magnificent presents for you and Mama and Sister."

"What if some privateer sinks your ship?" Lydia asked, laughing at his boasting. "There were three wrecks in the papers this week, you know. And they don't know how many others that we haven't found out about."

"Mr. Foster said—"

Lydia jumped, unconsciously. "Did—did you see him?"

"No, why?" Thomas turned to her, puzzled. "I saw him at our house last week, same as you. Say!" He hurried down the steps, trying to catch up with her. "Say! You must like him! I know you do! Say!"

"Hurry up. We're late," she scolded. "I have so many more things to do today. Get in. Robert, you can take me to the school. Papa wants Thomas to come to the office to help him for a while, so we can let him out at that corner."

"He does?" Thomas asked. "It's the first I'd heard about it."

"I forgot to tell you," Lydia lied, wondering how she could get out of it later. "Come on, get in! Mama expects me to be home for dinner at one. Hurry!"

Lydia always came home from her tasks refreshed, although she felt a tinge of sadness as she thought about other deprived children who hadn't been found by Dr. Bends or by those women like her mother at St. Paul's. And what of the girls who were growing up without any father to support them or any school like the Benevolent Society to protect and educate them for some kind of useful trade? No one ever talked about orphaned *girls*. And a school like the one she had attended there on South Street, run by the Abbé du Bourg and taught by French gentlewomen, could not accommodate such waifs. And what about those filthy scamps who infested the waterfront, begging, stealing, lying, staying precariously alive? Lydia Eliza knew that she wasn't supposed to be conscious of such people. Ignoring them somehow was supposed to make them disappear. Polite ladies should not make themselves sad by meditating on the plight of the poor, who would always be with us. Something was being done about the poor, she knew, but what about the dirty, the dishonest, the thieving, the starving, the desperate?

"Let them eat cake!" Marie Antoinette's infamous phrase popped into her head as she rode along on her way home. Lydia shuddered at the memory of the gory descriptions that had been bandied around of the brutal, horrifying death of the French queen. In spite of her parents' efforts to keep their children's ears sealed to the atrocities that were reported anew every time another ship arrived from Europe, all three of them had heard too much to be able ever to forget it. She wondered if the children in England could have been kept in ignorance of the goings on so close to their own shores. Was Mr. Foster a child then too, or was he older, perhaps already at the University? She could only guess at his age.

"Mr. Foster!" She was startled to hear herself say his name aloud as Robert guided the horses into their street. If he heard her, he gave no sign. She gathered up her gloves and reticule and rushed into the house, knowing she would probably have to face Thomas and admit to her fibbing. Lydia never found it easy to dissemble.

"Liars must have good memories!" Uncle Samuel teased when he was trying to find out whether she and Ann Maria had found sweethearts. "Or tell more lies to cover their tracks."

She was saved this time by a letter from Ruth Tobin, which was lying by her plate. She broke the seal and unfolded the page, relieved that it had arrived so providentially. She scanned its contents quickly and passed it around to the others.

"Everyone is fine," she said cheerfully. "Ruth wants me to buy some dress goods and some lace trim for her. And possibly a new bonnet. You know she likes yellow—you should see how pretty she looks in yellow. I may try to find something at Bedford's for her. And she'll want gloves to go with it, I'm sure. And possibly a light shawl. And I saw a beautiful mosaic brooch at the jeweler's shop yesterday."

"Chatterbox!" Ann Maria chided her. "Why don't you stop for breath? I never heard you talk so much and so fast."

"Me?" Lydia feigned surprise, her face getting hot. "I'm always excited when I get a letter from Cousin Ruth. And I might be able to get some of her shopping done this afternoon. It's such a fine day. I have to go out anyway."

"In the afternoon?" Her father frowned. "I didn't know you ever shopped in the afternoon. You attend the fashion parade over on Charles Street pretty faithfully, of course, but do any of you ladies ever do any useful work then, such as shopping? I don't think so." He began slicing the joint of beef in front of him so that he could serve the plates. "We need a spoon for the gravy, Pansy. By the way, girls, the young man who was here last week stopped by our office a moment this morning. Just happened to be passing, he said. Oh . . . what was his name? It's terrible to get so old that you can't remember names!"

"Which young man, Papa?" Ann Maria asked. "You know there are several young men who come here off and on. Quite a few, to be honest."

"Lydia knows, doesn't she?" young Thomas put in. "It was that new Britisher, wasn't it, Papa? Mr. Foster. Lydia's sweet on Mr. Foster."

"I am not!" Lydia said furiously.

"Son, be quiet!" their mother silenced him. "What did the

young man have to say, Thomas?" she asked her husband, steering the conversation away from Lydia, who sent her a quick look of gratitude.

"He was making sure he had all the facts we wanted him to know about," he answered, finishing his serving. "He's going back to the Federal City in a day or two, depending on the weather and the road. He sends all of you his best regards. He says he remembers you most pleasantly."

Lydia studied the food on her plate, not seeing it. She must try to think of something else except that he would soon be gone and that he had not come a second time. He sent best regards. That was nice. Best regards.

Deliberately she turned her thoughts to her cousin, glad that she had decided not to mention her interest in the Englishman, blinking her eyes in an effort at control. She stabbed at a spiced peach, and it slid crazily onto the tablecloth.

Where was it that she had seen that nice sprigged muslin? Ruth had asked for something that could be worn in late summer and early fall. Possibly a high-crowned poke bonnet could have feathers in one of the colors in the fabric.

Ruth's tastes, although having more life than when she was younger, were still simple. In any case, too much ostentation was out of place up there in the country. Elkton did not yet have a church, usually the most effective place for displaying one's wardrobe.

Four of the Hollingsworth brothers had helped set up a fund to establish a church in Elkton as long ago as 1785, but the choice of a minister—as well as of a denomination to join—threw the village into such controversy that the building was never anything but a dream. The Episcopalian clergymen who were available had made themselves so unpopular that no one would vote for any of them, although the once-Quaker Hollingsworths leaned strongly toward that faith. Methodism was just beginning its rise to prominence, having been formally organized in Baltimore for the United States in December, 1784, but good Episcopalians, Presbyterians and Quakers were not about to become Methodists. The impasse left Elkton with no church at all.

"I won't be going up there for at least another month or so," Lydia said thoughtfully. "Perhaps I could find the things that Ruth wants right away and send them to her by Captain Biddle's packet on Saturday. Then if they don't suit, she can get word back to me by the packet early next week and I can exchange them."

"That sounds reasonable," her mother said amiably. "Why don't you get right at it, dear?"

Was there a glint of amusement in her mother's eyes? Lydia dared not look at her directly. The two of them were so much alike, not only in appearance, that she knew her mother could read her mind. Her mother was heavy and Lydia was thin, but their eyes, hair, face, even their walking pace were the same. Both of them could say a great deal without making a sound.

Had her mother once been young enough and eager enough that she too might have made excuses to be out, and very busy of course, just in case a special young man came along? Had she found all the others dull and disappointing until the right one appeared? The right one? She glanced at her father, who looked like, well, like a father. Rather square-set face, a twinkle in his eyes when he felt good, his hair graying in little twigs over his ears, his body thickening and settling as he moved into his late fifties. He must have been young then too!

She could hardly resist smiling as she tried to picture him as a dashing suitor. Had he been a gay and light-footed dancer, always her choice in a young man? Had he thought of amusing little gifts and surprises? She couldn't imagine it. Had he been romantic and irresistible in the moonlight, so that his touch could set a girl on fire? Her *father?* Had he made that long-ago-young Ann Adams, who must surely have been pursued by other swains, feel that life without him would be only dust and ashes, but with him would be roses and stars and diamonds? He must have! Incredible.

She realized that her mother was watching her, half-smiling. As quickly as she could, Lydia excused herself from the table, gave her mother a quick kiss and left the room.

"Well, what was that for?" Ann Maria asked. "Is there anything going on around here that I don't know about?"

"Why?" Ann asked innocently. "I think it's still quite proper for a young lady to kiss her mother."

"Yes, of course," Ann Maria apologized. "But Lydia—"

"She's busy, dear. She has a great deal to do. She's going shopping for Ruth, you know. You heard her say so. She's quite busy."

"Yes, I heard her."

When Lydia returned to South Street late in the afternoon, little Pansy was carrying a number of small packages. The larger ones would be delivered in the morning. Lydia admitted that her feet hurt. She had been to a great many places. Too many of the streets were uphill.

On the tea table there was a small bowl of white-petaled flowers with golden centers, like captured stars.

"What are those?" she asked, staring. "I never saw anything like them. Where did they come from? Aunt Sarah?"

"Plain old daisies," Thomas said. "From *him*."

"They are not daisies, Thomas," Ann Maria said severely. "They are called marguerites. Aunt Debby was here when they came from the greenhouse and she said she had a book about flowers, so she could find out about them. One of her black boys came over just now and said that marguerites are for tranquillity. Peace and all that sort of thing. You should have seen how excited Aunt Debby was when the messenger came!"

"Tranquillity?" Lydia bent her head over the engraved card that lay just under the bouquet. The letters of his name leaped out at her. Above it he had written: "With best wishes to the Family of Thos. Hollingsworth, Esq."

Ann Maria was still talking. "When Aunt Debby saw that it was from a man, she asked a thousand questions. You know how romantic Aunt Debby is. A born matchmaker."

Lydia was not listening. She looked again at the engraved name: "Augustus John Foster." There was no mistake.

If Lydia Eliza Hollingsworth could have seen her face in the cloisonné looking glass at that moment, she would have liked well what she saw.

Chapter Six

The Horn of the Unicorn

When Great Britain's young and personable Secretary of the Legation returned to his room overlooking the Potomac River, he unpacked his luggage and sat down to reorganize his notes. He could not afford a valet, and the man who served the Merrys considered that the extent of his duties, so Foster had to make his own arrangements for having his clothes brushed and freshened. Well, that could wait. He stretched his legs to the needlepoint stool that Mrs. Merry had put there for his comfort. For the first time in more than two weeks he could let himself unwind.

Looking back over his mission to Baltimore, he was forced to admit to a mixture of feelings. It was one of the first where he was entirely on his own. He had tried to represent his government honorably and to the best of his ability, to listen with an attentive inner ear, and in speaking to marshal his facts and his thoughts before opening his mouth, so that his listeners would react in the way he wanted them to. Doing so was both a talent and an art, perhaps even a craft, although he disliked the word as being too close to the truth.

He was aroused by the sound of his pet terrier scratching at his door. The dog nearly knocked him over in his joy at their reunion.

"Hello, hello, hello, my good fellow!" He tried to get the animal to settle at his feet. "Come in and make yourself comfortable. Yes, I know you're glad to see me. Yes! Yes! I know! Now tell me, Tartar, my friend, how many beautiful little wives have you found for yourself while I've been away? A lucky thing for these American mongrels that I have brought you here to improve the breed, eh? It may be our only contribution to the great muckland of American culture!"

The greetings finally over, Tartar curled up on Foster's bed, ready to have his ears rubbed. "One thing I learned," Foster confided, "is that there is a damned sight more to diplomacy than having a good tailor. Matter of fact, a good tailor would either starve to death or lose his mind over here. Or both. Remind me, I must order what I need for next winter. It will take that long. Broadcloth, I'd think, for one . . . I'll probably be here the rest of my life. Maybe buried here. Should plan to be properly turned out."

The questions had been hurled at him from every turn in Baltimore, although more than once he thought he detected a note of sympathy for his country. "What about this new war, Mr. Secretary? Do you think England and France can ever stop fighting? I thought the peace of Amiens had settled their squabbles." Any answer he might venture to such queries was usually drowned out by more questions that were closer to American hearts and pocketbooks.

"Are there going to be any more blockades? Is the Admiralty able to understand that the United States is a *neutral, independent country?*" He had heard "neutral, independent country" so many times that it was like a drumbeat. And the "Yew-nited States." He winced whenever the syllables came to his ear, which was at least every other sentence. The more he saw of the "Yew-nited States" the less united they seemed. The South was agricultural, all of its economy hanging on the skeletal bones of tobacco and cotton, but even those states could not be said to have any kind of mutual rapport. The

North was industrial and commercial, but the only unity in those states was in their opposition to the federal government, which had driven them into a possible separate confederation. Merry had been told about it; it would surely bear watching.

Foster wondered how many were aware that both Britain and France were dependent on neutral shipping, since neither one would allow the other to pass its blockades. He had to be neutral and independent himself, but he felt drawn to the North because of its British sympathies. On the other hand, he could see that its growing manufacturing was going to tear the heart out of British industry.

His inborn love of the land in turn sent his sentiments to the Southerners, who by temperament, heritage and geography were landowners, land users and land preservers. Baltimore, close to the Mason-Dixon Line that separated slave and free states, represented in one city the best—or the worst—of both the North and the South. And then there was the West, that vast untapped empire that Aaron Burr wanted to set up, with himself as the emperor of Mexico, an idea that had also appealed to the lamented Alexander Hamilton, many said.

Burr, whom Foster considered "a little man . . . mysterious and unquiet," had taken many pointers from Bonaparte, except that he would fail and be disgraced before he tasted imperial fruit.

"A close squeak for old Toujours Gai, eh, Tartar?" he asked his pet. "Lucky for him, and for us, that they didn't have anything on him when the Yanks tracked down their traitor, eh what?"

He wondered how anyone could consider a nation "yewnited" when it was ripe for a split, each state cloaking itself in isolation and selfishness, each wanting to be a kingdom. Seventeen sovereign states pulling in seventeen stubborn directions did not sound like a nation to Foster.

"I hear rumors," one Baltimore merchant confided, "that there might be another Order in Council that will blockade the coast of France from Brest to the River Elbe. Then where could we trade? France is already trying to destroy all our British commerce, as you well know. Britain makes us stop and pay tribute before we can go on any place else, like a medieval robber baron. We're barricaded from every side. We're a neutral, independent country, sir, and we depend on the freedom of the seas for our living!"

"I have heard no such rumors," Foster could say truthfully. "I'm sure that my government will advise—"

"This impressment is nothing short of piracy, sir, if I may say so!" That complaint was clothed in so many different phrases, from courtesy to the grossest rudeness, that Foster could have shut his ears if he dared. He was relieved that his assignment required him only to listen, not to give answers. Listening was difficult enough to scare off a lesser man.

Would he have been better off in military service? He had enjoyed his months in the Royal Horse Guards Blue just before the turn of the new century, but, being honest, he had to admit that the life was better in retrospect than in reality.

"Otherwise I would have stayed, wouldn't I?" he asked Tartar.

Did his miserable trait of blushing ever betray his true thoughts? The problem had no remedy. He could not discuss it either, certainly not with Anthony Merry.

He was getting used to the Merrys, being thrown in their company a great deal, and was privately amused that he was often invited to social functions when they were left out. When Congress was not in session he traveled widely, being entertained by many of the nation's most prominent citizens of all ranks and parties. His open, persevering mind, his limitless curiosity and his wry sense of humor were assets totally lacking in his chief. Before A. J. Foster had been long in the New World, he was personally acquainted with more of its geography, its politics and its people than almost anyone else, native or foreign. What he learned did not always soften his prejudices.

Mr. Foster liked the Ambassador's wife, who could be witty

and stimulating, having some of the brighter traits of the well-known Madame Bonaparte, without some of her more daring fashion innovations. Madame B., as many called her, was said to wear nothing at all under her fashionable French gowns, some quite sheer. Her arms and throat were always bare, her wrists twinkling with bracelets, her specially blended perfume slyly seductive.

American women, whom Foster deplored in a letter home as "a spying, exuberant Race, and yet as ceremonious as Ambassadresses," could have learned a great deal from the circumspect behavior of Mistress Merry, whose life was anything but easy. There was a goodly supply of feminine beauty in nearby Georgetown, which many of the Federal City's bachelors had discovered with delight, but Foster was experiencing no difficulty in escaping any American traps.

"It's not my manly resistance," he confided to Tartar. "It's the bait they use."

Occasionally some of the woe that had nearly overtaken him in Italy in 1802 returned to darken his days. He had written to his mother about Tivoli and the Grotto there. "Whoever is extremely melancholy—if his Melancholy is not chased away by that magnificent Scene before his Eyes—he may have the finest Suicide in the World by jumping in to where the River hides itself in that most gloomy of all gloomy Caverns, and make his Exit from this Life through the most beautiful Gate that Death ever opened."

He had managed to resist the lure, if indeed he had meant the comment seriously.

By 1805, in America less than a year, he was already lamenting the intellectual vacuum in which he found himself. "If the Congress met at Philadelphia," he wrote home, "one might employ one's time but here there is absolutely nothing, not even Books to be had."

A week later he amused himself, and, he hoped, his family, by describing the second inauguration of President Thomas

Jefferson the previous March, three months after Foster's arrival.

"I don't know whether I have yet transmitted to you an account of the Installation of the successor to Montezuma in last March," he scrawled in his interminable sentences and capitalized nouns. "On the 4th he proceeded on horseback from his Palace, which is of white Stone and the largest building here and attended by his Secretary and Groom rode up the long Avenue of Pennsylvania to the Capitol, which is an unfinished Rival in Stone of the Roman building of that Name, and dressed in black silk stockings delivered a speech of some length which you have, to a mixed assemblage of Senators, populace, Representatives and Ladies—it was too low spoken to be heard well. He then kissed the Book and swore before the Chief Justice to be faithful to the Constitution then bowed and retired as before when he received Levee at which all who chose attended and even towards the close Blacks and dirty Boys who drank his Wine and lolled upon his Couches before us all—the jingling of a few Fifes and Drums finished the Day. There was nothing dignified in the whole Affair—he is about 65 years old and affects great Plainness of Dress and Manners. *Au Reste.* He is a Philosopher of the Political Speculative kind, unbounded Freedom reigns in this unbounded Land and the shameless abuse of Britain in their Papers is not at all creditable to the Country, particularly where there is no Wit to soften the Asperity."

In his 1805 inaugural address the "successor to Montezuma" had pointed with pride to American successes in putting down the Barbary pirates, although he did not believe in a navy or in appropriating money for one. His policy of "no entangling alliances" had kept the United States out of the renewal of British-French hostilities, he declared. Foster sat shaking his head in wonder, almost in pity. How could a sprawling infant nation with no navy and with scarcely an army become entangled in a battle fought three thousand miles away, unless the battle came to it? Which it surely could. There were men in important positions already screeching for it.

By the spring of 1806, before he was sent to Baltimore on his own, Foster was tense and restless. Mr. Merry had gotten himself so crossed up in every direction, especially by the mounting rumors of his involvement with Aaron Burr, that his recall seemed almost certain. Foster considered Merry the ideal man for the post, however. He was "slow, indefatigable, clear-sighted and vigilant . . . does his business like Clock-works, has a tenacious Memory of everything said to him, and a quick Observation—but as to Imagination I never saw a Man with so little concern for it."

Yes, old Toujours Gai was the man for America. Dull, plodding and with an unfurnished mind.

Only Foster's trips away from Washington and from Toujours Gai's petulance served to revive him. Increasingly, he was trusted with assignments where his personable manner, his facility with languages—he spoke French, German and Italian with ease, and sometimes missed interesting dinner partners because he had to stay beside a visiting notable who spoke no English—his retentive memory and his sense in keeping his mouth shut made him a good listening post and a safe spokesman.

John Randolph, whose swings at both political parties delighted Foster and sometimes startled him, became his intimate friend, opening doors for him that might ordinarily have been closed, giving him behind-the-scenes glimpses of government that no other outsider could have had. He found Randolph's sallies in that high-pitched, insolent nasal twang a joy, and more often than not a reflection of his own opinions, which he dared not express.

"I'd never have thought that you were a cousin of the President!" he told Randolph. "You sound like a very *distant* cousin."

"I'm luckier than he is," Randolph parried drolly. "One of my ancestors was an Indian princess. Royal blood always improves a man."

On a stifling night in early summer soon after his return from Baltimore, Foster was reminiscing about the happenings of recent weeks. One evening there had been especially pleasant. He snapped his fingers as he remembered something.

Did I send those flowers? I must have. And there were some for the Strickers—that dear lady was so flustered because of the rain—and the Ridgelys. Yes, the Pattersons. Some others too. I must have taken care of it. But of course, now I remember the old gaffer there in the office at the greenhouse. Talky, very talky. Pleased with the size of my order.

He smiled as he recalled the embarrassment of two wealthy merchants whose toes had been stepped on by the British. They had entertained him graciously, if a little irregularly, in the home of one of them because that poor fellow was confined with an attack of the gout.

"Well, Tartar, no one can blame the British for giving him the gout! That's some satisfaction." His pet flipped one ear and went back to his snoozing.

There was an eager young boy at that house. What was his name? Thomas. Thomas, Junior, to distinguish him from his father. The lad had pelted him with questions, but not the irritatingly controversial kind that everyone else was flinging at him in Baltimore. The young fellow's fine mind was so similar to his own that he would have enjoyed spending more time with him. He was a seeker, a dreamer, a boy who in England would be given the best possible education and trained for important public service. Like himself, he thought immodestly.

He had not been blind to the fact that two young ladies had joined them for tea. One had a slender face with an aquiline nose and merry blue eyes, with a scarcely restrained sauciness.

The other, paler and quieter—Americans were always pale, he thought—had large brown eyes like her mother's, a graceful long neck and a willowy figure. She barely said two words all evening, but he was conscious that she watched him and that her changing facial expressions whenever her father mentioned business matters showed that she knew a great deal about it. And could keep silent! He knew how to do a few things himself without seeming to; it was an essential asset to his work. That reserved young lady had learned the art well. He did not find her awareness of him in the least unpleasant either.

As a matter of fact, her subtle attention had combined with some excellent brandy they had served him to make him feel warm, comfortable, his best self. He had been reluctant to leave. In his year and a half in America he had never felt so well.

"I hope to Heaven I didn't stay too long," he said aloud. "One thing my father taught me was that a gentleman knows when to leave as well as when to arrive. I *surely* hope I didn't stay too long. It was so—so pleasant there." He and the dog set off for a ramble under the trees along the Potomac. "What was her name?" he asked, as if he expected an answer. "The quiet one, the one with the eyes. I'll bet those eyes could look at a man with—no! Mustn't let myself speculate in that direction, eh, Tartar? Here I am, talking to myself again. Sure sign of approaching dementia."

There were so many beautiful women in Baltimore. A visit there was like walking through a garden of roses. And such roses! The finest homes in town had opened their doors to welcome him. There was a great deal of color, inside and out. Some houses were painted blue and white, making a pleasing contrast to the dull red of the newer brick ones. He was sorry to see brick replacing the wooden structures. Wood was so scarce in Europe that its use meant the greatest luxury.

One businessman he had met, Mr. William Cochran of the

home begging that some way be found for him to leave. He was planning to spend some time with the Merrys up in Lancaster, the capital of Pennsylvania, but he hoped that his time in North America would be short.

"Must I remain in this Sinkhole all my life?" he complained. "If I do, I must look out for an American wife, which will be the worst thing in the World, for the American women are miserable anywhere but in their own Country."

Had he considered the equal, if not greater, discomfort of his own countrywomen as they struggled to transplant themselves in alien soil? Had he overlooked Mrs. Merry? He followed up his sweeping generalization with another bitterly introspective question in his letter to his mother: "Who in England will have me if I stay till I have passed the Line and go home with my dried-up Brains from this parched Country?"

He was twenty-five years old.

"You know what my friend Talleyrand said about this place?" he asked Tartar as they climbed the steps to his room at the Merrys. "He said it was a place where anyone would sell his pet dog. Sometimes I think he was right." The terrier looked up at him as if to question him. "Not you, my good friend," Foster said indulgently. "And I'm not an American, thank God. And I never will be. I can have that much to be grateful for."

He went to a window, flinging it wide, admitting another influx of flies and mosquitoes along with a surge of withering heat that took his breath away. There must be a spot for him somewhere else in the world. Britain? Never that much luck. Anywhere in Europe? The first nation of the world had embassies and consulates over most of the earth. South America? Perhaps if he served this terrible apprenticeship well . . .

He reread his letter: ". . . indeed this is a painful and disagreeable Country for any Man of refinement or of any feelings to have a Situation in. . . ."

He dared not confide, even to his mother, that he was hoping he might be assigned to replace Anthony Merry. He knew in his bones that his chief's days in the United States were numbered. He felt also that there was no person more qualified to take over the post than himself. He had done so much of Toujours Gai's dirty work—successfully, he hoped—and was well acquainted with many of the nation's leaders. He knew everything that was in their confidential and state papers because he had often been up half the night writing them himself, in duplicate.

There was some ambivalence in his feelings about the matter, he had to admit. He hated the country and almost every feature of it, and yet here he was, dreaming that he could be named ambassador! Facing himself honestly, he decided that he could learn to adjust himself if he were in the top place instead of having to move always in Merry's long, unhappy shadow. There was something about power that could change many other elements of a situation. He hadn't had to study books to learn that.

There was always talk in Washington of moving back to Philadelphia, which would certainly make for vast improvement. If he lived to be a hundred he would never be able to understand why the enigmatic Americans—who seemed so simple-minded and charming at one moment, crafty and scheming and utterly corrupt the next, and whose official representatives were often little better than country bumpkins, to his way of thinking—should have decided to locate their Federal City there in the marshes of the Potomac River.

Why not in that beautiful city of Baltimore on the inverted cup of hills overlooking the Patapsco River and the Chesapeake Bay? Why had they ever left Philadelphia anyway? It was George Washington's idea, some said, for a more central location away from the maelstroms of trade. The yellow fever of the 1790's, others told him. Yes, he knew of the yellow fever: forty-four hundred deaths in one short season, and another siege two years later. Mr. Samuel Hollingsworth, whose

Philadelphia brother, Levi, had been on the Committee of Forty-five that had battled the scourge up there, had helped to work out plans to protect his own city. Baltimore had escaped, because, it was thought, one of the solutions had been to cut off all commerce with Philadelphia. Many people, including Foster, believed that the fever was carried by ships.

Washington had been spared the deadly fever. It had no people then either, an excellent reason.

Foster had walked over many square miles of the Columbia District, his pet at his heels, recalling the long rambles of his childhood in Ireland. He looked at trees, birds, fish, making notes on snakes, insects, wildflowers and the abundant small animals dwelling in the area. Whenever his mind rebelled, as it frequently did, at the goings on in the frontier village being fronted with marble, the open country would refresh him. There was much natural beauty, but the low swamps must alert the residents to the danger of ague, that terrible shaking and debilitating ailment that always struck those living where the miasma could waft the sickness to them. Georgetown was higher, and had people and homes of both good taste and charm, a delightful village. Why not choose Georgetown?

Unfortunately, when Congress was making its plans some years earlier, no one had asked Augustus John Foster for his opinion. Nor were they likely to do so now. A pity.

Bringing himself back to the realities of the moment, he looked over his letter and signed it, "Your affectionate Son, Augustus John Foster," folded it, dropped a blob of sealing wax on it, pressed his heavy ring into the wax and went off to mail his thoughts to England.

In Baltimore, the brown-eyed young lady who had shown him that she could keep her thoughts to herself was packing for her summer trek to Elkton. She checked her list for Ruth Tobin and the accounting of Ruth's money, marking off each item as she put it with the others. Ribbons, lace, bonnet, hooks and eyes, a fashionable new spencer in pale-blue velvet—Ann Maria, advising her that if it did not fit Ruth or if her aunt would not permit her to wear the smart jacket, she would be happy to oblige and take it off her cousin's hands.

While she folded and wrapped, Lydia Eliza made a mental list of topics that she might discuss with Ruth, all of them avoiding the slightest hint of a heart flutter. Ruth liked to hear of the social doings in Baltimore, so Lydia could spend a great deal of time in descriptions of the Spring Cotillion, the food that was served at this and that dinner party, the attention being paid a talented new actor in the theater. There had been enough young men calling on her so that she could recount incidents yet honestly deny any true excitement over them.

In the days preceding her departure she reminded Polodore, Ann Maria, Thomas, Junior, her mother, her father and Delia, each separately, and forgetting that she had mentioned the matter to any of the others, that if a letter came for her it was to be forwarded. Captain Biddle would bring it up on the packet. They could write on the outside, underneath the previous address: "At Mrs. Ruth Hollingsworth's, Elkton." Or they could put: "At Mr. Stephen Hollingsworth's, Elkton." Biddle would understand.

At the same time, Ruth Tobin was begging their uncle Stephen to find some suitable young men who would be available for social affairs during Lydia's visit. "Not just our cousins, Uncle! We can always see our cousins. They aren't any fun. We're old enough for real beaux now."

"How about a preacher fellow?" Stephen asked slyly. Since Jacob's death he had become more like a father to Ruth, and they were good friends. "There might be three or four preacher fellows running around, looking for female souls to save."

"Uncle! How you talk!"

"Then there's *me*. Handsome. Spry. Wonderful dancer.

Reliable. Good team and a good-enough rig with fresh paint just this spring. Got enough money some Saturday nights that I could buy you young ladies a bag of licorice if you don't ask too often."

"Uncle!"

"Let me work on it," he asked solemnly. "I suppose you're so highfalutin that you'll want someone under eighty-five years old. Well, they're getting scarce. Mighty scarce." He walked away, shaking his head, his shoulders sagging. "You may even have to settle for a Methodist."

Chapter Seven

Her Candle Goeth Not Out

There had been some headshaking when Deborah Adams married William Cochran. Not for any personal objection to the gentleman, but because he was several years younger than she, and he had two children. A ready-made family was never easy for any woman to take on, especially for Debby, who was considered flighty and sometimes irresponsible. Of the eight Adams sisters and one brother, she was the one the others loved the most. The youngest, and naturally coddled by the older ones, she had a special quality that set her apart, a sparkle, a giddy fluffiness that masked a sturdy heart and a solidity of character that outsiders never got to know.

Two of her three sisters who had married Hollingsworth brothers—Ann and Sarah—encouraged her to accept Mr. Cochran because they lived in Baltimore, where Mr. Cochran had his office in the Baltimore Insurance Company at the corner of Water and South streets, close to both families. Marrying him would assure Debby's residence in Baltimore and bring some of her bubbling warmth into their lives.

The third, Ruth, now widowed, took the opposite tack. Wasn't it possible for Debby to find someone in Elkton or in their home town of Christiana, Delaware, which was just up the pike? And there was still Stephen, a most eligible bachelor. Why not make the Hollingsworth-Adams mergers a foursome? And bring Debby to live in Elkton, close to Ruth?

In any case, all her relatives thought it was high time she married someone. Even with Deborah's attractive qualifications, her chances of finding a husband got steadily slimmer. All of them admitted to being selfish, and all of them finally said that she should follow her heart, which was what she had been intending to do all along.

Deborah Adams and Mr. Cochran, whom she never called anything but Mr. Cochran, were married at St. Paul's Church in Baltimore on December 20, 1804, in a ceremony so simple and so beautiful that she could never think of it without tears. If she mentioned the day or any tiny fragment of memory about it, Mr. Cochran would swallow awkwardly, the backs of his ears turning red, and sit in his chair very quietly as he shuffled the papers he had brought home from the office. Later he might look up at her and say in a half-whisper, his eyes brimming, "I love you, you know."

"And I you. Forever."

Debby was old enough to know her own mind. She was thirty-three when she changed her name to Cochran, and had turned down as many proposals as the gayest Baltimore belle. After four or five of these refusals, her brother, George, advised her that she'd never find the ideal man she seemed to be waiting for.

"When they made me," he told her, "that was it. No more perfect ones. Too hard for other people to live up to." But when his ten-year-old son was taken from him by a Providence he could no longer consider all-wise, he stopped teasing Debby. He had a fear that the Devil had been listening.

He was openly relieved when she accepted Mr. Cochran, but looking at that worthy gentleman from a man's point of view, he found her decision hard to comprehend. Mr. Cochran was so underdone. Not handsome either, to speak of, but then, that was no drawback. Cochran was as serious and steady

—he almost said stodgy—as Deborah was fluttery. His sober mien made him seem six or eight years older than he was. George would have guffawed if he had known how it was between the two.

One October afternoon Mr. Cochran had called for Debby when she came from Christiana to visit Thomas and Ann. His rig was polished and spotless, his graceful roan mare prancing in new harness. He was shaved to the quick, his hair and chop whiskers carefully trimmed.

After escorting her down the four steps, he lifted her into the gig, settled himself beside her, picked up the reins and headed toward Whetstone Point, where the view in several directions was of opalescent water, fringed with trees. The wide river was bobbing with sails, and a light breeze kicked up small ripply waves. Orange, russet, yellow, red violet and olive gold in the leaves, blues, grays and greens in the water and the sky made a whole spectrum of color and beauty enveloping them.

They sat near the water's edge, the horse nodding lazily, and watched the panorama. Deborah felt a strange kind of peace in the company of this silent man. After a long time, he said diffidently, not looking at her, "Your hair is like honey with the sun shining on it."

Just in time she stopped herself from saying, "What?" He was giving her a compliment, she was sure, but she had heard others more flattering and more original. Many, many others. She could not know how much courage it had taken for him to say the words, or how many days he had spent in shaping them in the first place.

After an interval she said, "Thank you. You are very kind to say so."

He jumped. "I am?"

"Of course!" A mischievous dimple appeared in her cheek. "You are most kind," she told him.

"Do you like me?" he asked bluntly.

"Why—why, yes, I suppose I do." She began pushing back

the fingers of her gloves so that her nails made sharp little ridges at the ends of the fingers. Always fastidious, she noticed a tiny thread breaking loose and tried to decide whether to ignore it or to break it off, which might loosen the seam. She allowed her gaze to stray to that other pair of hands, idly holding the reins but shaking visibly.

Quickly he clucked to the mare, and they moved on. Debby tried to look at the graceful elms and the thick growth of alder bushes that would probably have to be cleared off if they ever finished enlarging the fort they had built there during the Revolution.

The goldenrod was nearly spent. The oaks wore blankets of discarded leaves and acorns over their feet. There were several large V's of Canada geese in the sky, arriving for their winter's stay and looking over the accommodations. A great blue heron posed majestically in the shallow water, ready to have his portrait made. The air was hazy and cool.

Mr. Cochran guided the horse out toward Mount Clare, letting the animal trot at its own speed, his hands still shaking, his face averted.

"The children like you," he volunteered a mile or two later. Again she caught herself and refrained from asking, "What children?" Of course he must mean his own. She had barely met them, both girls.

She continued to study the broken thread in her glove, not consciously trying to fathom his mind, but knowing very well what she might find. The quavering fingers suddenly tightened on the reins; the sensitive mare jumped slightly in response and then began a brisker trot. Deborah stole a glance at the man sitting so tensely beside her, very much aware of the direction her life was taking.

He drove her, finally, back to Thomas's home. As he reached up to help her to the ground he said swiftly, as if he might completely lose his nerve if he tried it any other way, "Then it's settled?"

For the first time they looked squarely into each other's

eyes. Deborah saw there a depth of love and strength that would carry her and sustain her forever, no matter what. Mr. Cochran saw adoration. He was to see the same look from those hazel eyes under the curling auburn lashes every day for the rest of his life.

In that other brief marriage, ending so soon in death and leaving him two small children, he had never hoped to know that kind of rapture. He had known only peace, which he had thought was enough. He caught both her hands tightly in his, and she could feel the trembling in his fingers.

"It is settled," she whispered, as Lydia and her brother came flying down the steps to invite him to stay for tea. He made a hasty excuse, and the two escorted their aunt back into the house as his carriage rolled away, his deportment giving no hint of the hurricane that was sweeping through his heart.

Debby Cochran took to her new domestic responsibilities like a tiny bright bird building a nest. The household on Calvert Street soon added a small sweet daughter, looking like her mother and named Elizabeth for Debby's lost sister, the young Elizabeth Adams Tobin. Somehow, along with the children to love, the servants to supervise, the busy social life of Baltimore and her relatives to keep up with, Deborah had a talent for knowing when there was illness or other deep need for comfort. Not only for being aware, but for arriving at the precise moment when despair had set in and her cheery presence was like an answer to prayer. Perhaps the doctor was being let out the door, frowning and discouraged as he reflected on his inability to forestall the hand of fate. Mrs. Cochran's handsome equipage would pull up out front. The lady would alight, nod briefly to the physician and speed daintily to the door, followed by a black man bearing a bowl of fresh custard.

If the doctor knew her, and most of them did, he could square his shoulders and lift his head. Deborah Cochran's sunny positiveness was the best possible medication; the gloom in the sickroom was sure to lift. He could comfort himself with the thought that the custard, of which he had had many verbal reports, would probably not kill his patient.

Debby's domestic talents never did include cooking. Custard was her only specialty. The results were generally edible, occasionally delectable, sometimes impossible. Mercifully, no one ever told her of the batches that were thrown away after a one-bite sampling.

She made the concoction with enormous energy and enthusiasm and carried it to the sick in bountiful generosity. When her footsteps skimmed across the floor overhead, Miranda's rheumy old eyes would roll back knowingly. "Somebody sick," she'd mutter. "Miz Cocken flyin' down them steps."

"I don' hear no flyin', Gram." But before the sentence was finished, Miz Cocken would swoop into the kitchen, tie on her big ruffled apron, send to the springhouse for milk and eggs, all the time making a great clatter of pots, giving orders about the fire, pulling down serving dishes to choose one that was suitable in size and color for the lucky recipient. Custard required a bright dish, Debby always thought. She shopped for cheerful bowls the year round. In summer her basket always had a sprig of flowers from her garden, and in winter a bright ribbon on its handle.

Any other cooking going on at the time would have to be delayed or abandoned. When she departed in triumph, her face rosy, her hair disarrayed, every pot, mixing bowl and cooking utensil would be dirty, every fresh towel used, and her kitchen slaves left with the feeling of trying to breathe in a sudden vacuum.

"Lak I say," Miranda would say fondly, "somebody sick."

From the moment he had met her, through her brothers-in-law, Mr. Cochran realized that her cameo fragility was only on the surface. Her ladylike empty-headedness and her pretense of helplessness were what was expected of well-brought-up young women, but they were really only a façade for a character as strong as the tides in the bay. She was impulsive, moody, imaginative, artistic, eager and tender. Her shimmering red-gold beauty did not diminish as she grew older. For her husband, his sober world took on an aura of enchantment from the moment he carried her over his threshold in an uncommon gesture of gallantry. The exertion, even though she weighed only a hundred pounds, set him to coughing, but she did not tease him about it, then or ever. In her bridal happiness, she resolved to put his welfare first in everything, to make sure he was fed nourishing meals, kept from anxiety, and coddled night and day, so that the coughing, which always left him weak and shaking, could be overcome.

On the first Sunday in September of 1806 they were invited to have dinner with Thomas and Ann. Their girls were to have come in from Elkton on Saturday after a month's visit. There would be a great deal to talk about, or rather to listen to, Mr. Cochran said to himself. Well, Debby needed some brightness. When she was happy, he was happy.

Mr. Cochran enjoyed his meal. The cooking at that household was of the best, and Delia had prepared special dishes to please Lydia and Ann Maria. There was a plate of steaming hot gingerbread, which sent young Thomas into exaggerated sighs of pleasure. The house was full of autumn bouquets in every hue.

Thomas, Senior, was in an expansive mood, having all his brood home again and with Debby, always a favorite, sitting next to him, more beautiful than he ever remembered her, although she was thin and pale. He looked at her again out of the corner of his eye. He fervently hoped that she was not already expecting a second child. His own first two had been too close together and they had lost the stillborn boy. Then a second son was stillborn after Lydia's birth. No wonder young Thomas was so precious to him that he dared not face the depth of his feeling. If Debby was to have another baby, there must be some way to make sure that it would live.

His daughters were trying to cover all the events of a month in the few minutes. Ann Maria had had no plans of accompanying her sister, then had packed her clothes and gone running to catch the boat, impulsive as ever. The two of them had so much to tell—when Ann Maria was around, twice as many things were bound to happen, somehow. And Ruth Tobin had been in a glow of enchantment to have both of them there. She had *loved* the pale-blue spencer, and everything else that Lydia brought. Yes, she was still thin as a toothpick; no, Aunt Ruth was no better and spent a great deal of time lying on a sofa. Young Ruth seemed to them to be tied down in taking care of her, but she did not complain.

Thomas had a sudden, aching wish to keep his family always close to him, never to let them go, somehow to be a magician, so that he could have his children always young, himself no older, his wife across the table looking at him with pride and fulfillment just the way she was, her dainty sheer cap crowning her expressive face. Three days of headache the past week had wilted her, but she said nothing of it to her daughters.

Thomas liked making a ritual of his serving chores, slicing the meat like an artist painting on canvas, reaching for the spoons to apportion the mounds of fluffy Irish potatoes, the dried corn, the butter beans from their own garden. He noticed that Ann was using their hand-woven Irish linen cloth, one of her most treasured pieces, with the lace-edged napkins to match. The day meant much to her too. She had missed church for the first time in months to complete plans for the meal.

"Uncle Stephen said he'd be our beau!" Ann Maria was laughing. "All three of us were to be his sweethearts. I think he really enjoyed it."

"He should have been an actor," her brother scoffed. "If he made you think it was fun squiring three girls around, he should be in a theater, getting paid for it, that's all I have to say. Three girls! Giggling. Chirping. Losing things. Trying on clothes. Eek!"

"We saw our cousin Peggy Cooch—you know her little boy

died. And Cousin Hannah Partridge." Lydia was deliberately ignoring him. "I learned to row the skiff. And we got to watch them unloading hay in the big barns. And Aunt Jane slipped on her front steps and sprained her ankle but she's all right now. Cousin Ruth wants new curtains for her room. You should see how pretty she is, Thomas. You'd like her. She asked all about you."

"Cousin Robert Hollingsworth was there for a few days," Ann Maria recalled. "He said to tell you he was still hard at work on your lawsuit against the French government for the loss of our ship, Papa."

Her father's benign expression darkened. "I suppose he is. They sank *The Two Brothers* in 1805. I'm willing to lay a sound wager that it will be *1905* before we get any satisfaction out of them, no matter how hard Robert works. When's he going back to Marseilles?"

"Thomas! You're not betting on Sunday!" Ann spoke for the first time.

"It is not a bet, my dear, when you know you're going to win," he said easily. "That's the only kind of wager I ever make. As safe on the Lord's day as on any other. Maybe more so." He turned to Debby. "How was church, sister? I'm afraid we were a household of heathens this morning. Too much excitement in getting our young ladies home again."

Mr. Cochran nodded sympathetically. He would have infinitely preferred staying home. He and Debby had sat dutifully in their pew, trying to listen to the sermon, trying to make some sense of the words the choir was battling through and trying to stay awake. He hoped he hadn't embarrassed them both by snoring. He was afraid to ask. Debby was hoping that her physical misery meant she was having another child and, if so, that she could carry it to full term. The first one had been nip and tuck for them both.

Little Elizabeth was on the verge of cutting teeth and was so fretful that her mother was up with her almost every night.

Deborah trusted her woman to care for the baby during the day, but any whimpering in the night brought her out of bed in an instant, her feet shoved into warm slippers, a wrapper around her shoulders, her eyes trying to see in the dark. She was impatient of the amount of time it took to get a light and had not much skill with the flint anyway, so she inched along to her daughter's cradle, guided by the wails, and caught her up, hugging and soothing her and pacing up and down. In her anxiety she usually stumbled into the blanket chest or the bedpost or the rocker or the ornamental iron doorstop shaped like a fanciful cat. The noise eventually wakened her husband, hard as she tried not to disturb him. He would stagger from bed, trying to stifle a cough, and would soon have a candle lighted. He would poke around on the medicine shelf under the washstand until he had found the paregoric.

"Sometimes, Mrs. Cochran," he told her once, "I feel that I should give the painkiller to you instead of to the wee one. She goes back to sleep long before you do. And after all, your husband does have to get up and go to work in the morning. When you don't sleep, he doesn't sleep."

"I know, I know," she said fretfully. "I shouldn't let myself get so upset. But little Elizabeth is so—oh, Mr. Cochran, if anything should happen to her . . . Oh, Mr. Cochran, I could not bear it. . . . She is so . . . so . . . precious. . . . Oh, Mr. Cochran . . . I do love her so."

He had folded her silently in his arms then, and comforted her as she had comforted the baby, until all three were asleep. Days and weeks of these wakeful nights were taking their toll. The baby could sleep during the day, but he worried about Debby; her skin was too pale.

Responding to some deep but unspoken need in his wife, he had resolved to go to church with her each Sunday; perhaps in that way he could find strength for himself too. He had less and less of it.

Mr. Cochran liked the rector. A good man, although inclined to be a little unworldly for a businessman's taste. The official board, noting Mr. Cochran's faithful attendance, approached him for advice on fire safety for their new building, and he was astounded—but pleased—to see the extent of their ignorance about such a basic need.

"Dr. Bends preached an excellent sermon this morning," Debby was saying loyally, startling her husband from his reverie. "Excellent. Although I fear I might have been dozing for part of it. Wasn't it something about the sowing and the reaping and the harvest and all, Mr. Cochran?"

"I'm sure it must have been," he answered dryly. "This is the ideal time of year for the subject, wouldn't you say? I could eat one of those apples, Miss Lydia."

"Oh, of course." Lydia picked up the bowl. "These apples are from the orchard at Elk Landing. Uncle Zeb had them ready for us when we got to the wharf, so it was no problem to bring them with us. Early Winesaps, I think they are."

"I certainly should be able to remember his name," Debby said, her fine brows drawn into a frown, her fingers drumming on the table.

Mr. Cochran darted a quick look at his wife. There were times when her conversation was completely irrelevant to anything that had gone before. It was not that she intended to be devious, but her mind could wander to far pastures with little effort, not realizing that other minds were not following the trail. The dear sweet thing wasn't well, he thought compassionately. He wanted to reach out to touch her to see if she had a fever.

"I surely have heard enough about him," she went on, putting her hands to her temples with a nervous little laugh. "Oh, dear, oh, dear, whatever *is* his name?"

"Man? Boy? Child? Here in Baltimore? Help us with some hints, my dear."

"Oh, *you* know, Mr. Cochran. We saw him in church this morning. I nudged you and I said, 'There he is,' and you said,

'Who?' and I said, 'Him!' and you didn't want to look right then because it was time for the long prayer and you thought that wouldn't be proper and that people would notice you, and I said, 'You could look real quick so you don't forget to later,' because sometimes, Mr. Cochran, you do forget later, and you said, 'Oh, all right, but don't whisper any more.' Remember now?"

"Oh, of course!" He smiled with relief. He had caught up with her ramblings. "All she's trying to say is that we saw that young Mr. Foster in church this morning. The British fellow."

"Mr. Foster?" Lydia's fork fell on her plate with a clatter, and she choked for breath. Polodore came to fill her water glass.

"He's in town?" her father asked. "What for? Is he here on business?"

"I wouldn't know, Thomas," Mr. Cochran said simply.

"He has sort of reddish hair, and he's real young. And his clothes look British, and he's got a real straight back." Debby was relieved too that her puzzlement was over.

"He's no child." Thomas laughed. "He may be young in years and young in looks, but he's got the wisdom of Methuselah."

Lydia sat trying to compose herself, sipping at the glass of water. He was in town, in Baltimore. It could not have been more than an hour or so since the Cochrans had seen him.

That must mean that he was on his way back to Washington from his summer trip to Pennsylvania. There had been an item in a Philadelphia paper she had seen in Elkton that said that Ambassador and Mrs. Anthony Merry were spending some time in the "delightful environs of our capital city of Lancaster." Her cousins Levi and William, Uncle Zebulon's sons, who were both in the state senate, had a more than passing interest in national politics. Both of them said that the Ambassador was bound to be relieved of his post, and there was widespread speculation as to who would replace him. They had heard from Washington that Merry's Secretary of the Legation had accompanied him north, perhaps for extra briefing in taking over the job.

Lydia hoped they did not suspect her interest. Levi had come to Elkton from Baltimore to ask his father's advice about a business proposition that had come from his uncle Levi in Philadelphia. He and his brother had sat out under the big oaks at Elk Landing, catching up on the news. Ruth Tobin and Ann Maria were spending the day visiting their cousins at Uncle Henry's house. Lydia had chosen to walk to the Landing with an invitation to all of them for dinner with Aunt Ruth and Uncle Stephen the next Sunday. She was in no hurry to leave. The distance was not great, but the day was warm, so she had stayed to enjoy a cool glass of lemonade with her aunt Polly and listen to the man talk at a polite distance, not appearing to be eavesdropping.

"Too young, I'd think," William had said, forgetting how young both of them were when they began their public service.

"Has too many of Merry's sore spots." Levi had laughed. "All those Englishers are touchy. But the ladies like the fellow."

"They'd like him even more if he got to be the ambassador." William had countered. "There'd be a rush like at the ticket window at the races."

The ambassador! He could handle it, Lydia was sure. Even her father thought so, although she had never asked him a direct question about it. And that would mean that he would stay in America. Her heart suddenly felt too large for her body.

He was in town. If he planned to go to Washington by stage, he could not do so until the next day. One left every morning but Sunday, at six o'clock, getting to Washington in time for dinner.

Chapter Eight

My Heart Is Not Haughty

Mr. Foster's second visit to the capital of Pennsylvania had been a pleasant one. He had had enough travel in America to be able to appreciate the little city, enough of Washington's muggy heat to appreciate Lancaster's summer coolness and refreshing breezes, enough of the company of Toujours Gai to be looking forward eagerly to that gentleman's imminent departure for home.

One of the things that Foster had observed in his study of America was that the various state capitals were either in sleepy, unimportant country towns or in brand new ones carved out of empty spaces miles and miles from nowhere, as savage and unpromising as Washington. He decided that the reason for this peculiar folkway was that those bumptious bumpkins who were being sent to govern their peers would be outclassed in an academic or intellectual community, such as Princeton or New Haven, or outfoxed by the sharper businessmen in a big city.

It was safer for all concerned to build a new town, or to select a remote and undistinguished one where nothing of any consequence ever happened and where the weighty business of government could be conducted without other distractions.

Less danger to the rough diamonds, he thought wryly.

Actually, more of the nation's business was transacted in Baltimore than in Washington. Important social functions would draw the President himself, along with other dignitaries, who would make the uncomfortable journey north for the occasion. The capital city's finest ladies shopped in Baltimore and were well known to dressmakers, milliners, jewelers and merchants of luxury goods and imported specialties.

Foster could only speculate on the blindness of the nation's planners, writing his thoughts in his notebook and specifying on the last page that none of it was to be published or used in any way until everyone concerned was long dead and out of harm's way. Talking to himself by way of writing in a personal diary allowed him to say the things he dared not voice.

He had made plans to take the curricle back with him before he decided to spend a few days in Baltimore en route. The groom could take the rig for him if the weather was bad and he could go by stage, but if the rain or sun didn't beat down too unmercifully he might ride along, perhaps pick up a few more driving tips; he'd been doing quite well on the pretty country roads around Lancaster. His riding horse could be hitched on behind.

The Pennsylvania folk had thought the curricle very sporting indeed. The thills and the spokes of its two wheels had been painted bright red, the remainder a shining black; the harness was decorated with red and silver. His team pranced when they pulled the carriage.

Foster always preferred to travel on his own terms rather than be a victim of stage schedules, besotted coachmen and passengers whose odors made him ill. He liked to stop to eat where he pleased; there were adequate, if not elegant, facilities on the main roads. He liked to take a chance on a country inn. For one thing, he could move on if the place was impossible; for another, it gave him an opportunity of meeting some rare "originals," who always fascinated him. On occasion, he had been forced to ask for food or lodging from some farmer and had not been invariably well received. He learned, however, that the farther he was from civilization, the more gracious were his unexpected hosts. In some of the more "civilized" hostelries, his driver might well be seated at the same table with him, with no consideration of rank or propriety. Shocking.

As it turned out, the weather was unco-operative, and he was forced to go from Lancaster to Baltimore by public stage while the groom took the horses and curricle himself. The man beat him to the Indian Queen by hours; he had had time to wash and polish the curricle, so that it looked new again and was attracting extravagant attention.

Promptly at four on Sunday afternoon, Foster drove it around the corner of the Philadelphia Road into South Street, proud of his increasing skill in handling the team. Riding a horse was one thing, when your knees did as much of the guiding as your hands; driving a carriage with a fractious team was another, not much like the pony carts of his Irish childhood. He had taken on the job with the same resolve with which he tackled everything: he had to succeed.

In the summer he had written home from Lancaster: "It is the best settled and the most cheerful quaint Country I have yet seen in North America. I drive out every morning at seven o'clock and every evening in the Duke's Curricle which I have it lined will be the most perfect Carriage that the Yankees have ever seen. I have two good bay Horses that would not disgrace Hyde Park and the best saddle Horse in the Land. He belonged to John Randolph. . . . I mean to sell my Horses in October to keep the Curricle for another pair next Year unless His Majesty's Ministers are good enough to order me home. The young Ladies here are not so *squeamish* as your English Fair and I am honoured by being allowed to drive some of them about."

He hoped that Miss Lydia Hollingsworth—he had learned her name by the simple expedient of asking the rector after the morning service—would also not be squeamish and would show him some parts of the city he had not visited. His pride would receive an extra boost by his being seen with such a beautiful young lady by his side, a pleasure not to be discounted.

He walked briskly up the few steps to her door, studying the iron fire mark with the crossed hands (which signified that the house was under the protection of a company that Sam and his brother Jesse had helped to found, the Baltimore Equitable Society), waiting for his knock to be answered. He had seen the same symbol in England. The hands were of painted wrought iron, mounted on a wooden plaque. He smiled to himself, like a proud uncle who finds a nephew trying to walk in his own big footprints. The Yankees were even dependent on their British cousins for their symbols. The Hand-in-Hand Company in London had almost the identical fire mark.

The door opened, startling him. He could so quickly dream that he was home. The proud colored man that he remembered from his spring visit bowed him into the entrance hall. The young lady soon appeared, looking fresh and lovely in a soft pink gown, modestly cut, with a large cameo at her throat. She was not as pale as before. He found her added color attractive and wondered what had caused it. The country girls around Lancaster had much the same look. She was carrying a small parasol that matched her dress. A wise move. The afternoon sun could be blazing hot. He would have appreciated some such protection for his own fair skin.

Lydia settled into the seat beside him, hardly having said more than to reply to his greeting, although she had shown pleasure in seeing the curricle and in noticing his pride in it. Lydia was very much aware of the hidden audience that was watching their every move. Apparently he was not; he must believe that the street was as deserted as it looked.

"I should like to see more of this fair city, Miss Hollingsworth," he said as he picked up the reins. "Perhaps you will be so kind as to suggest . . . ?"

"Oh," she said, surprised. "Oh. Well, have you seen Fells Point? Or any of our lakes? Or the Jones Falls? Of course, that flows right through the city. My brother tells me—" She caught herself. Was she getting too talkative? She could hear Ann Maria laughing at her. *Chatterbox!*

"Yes?"

"Perhaps we could go east, Mr. Foster."

Obligingly he clucked to the team, and the bays set out, their necks arched, their hoofs making a smart tattoo on the pavement. Lydia sat with her head bowed under the parasol, trying to keep her thoughts from his hands as he guided the horses. Perhaps she should comment about the rig, but what should she say?

There was silence between them as they rolled along Pratt Street, with its view of the river and of the ships at anchor beyond the wharves, quiet on this early autumn Sunday. A few other carriages were out. A gig sped past with a physician hurrying to a patient; some children in a pony cart almost forced them off the road; a dreaming couple on horseback held hands across the space between their mounts. A closed carriage, its curtains drawn, its driver impassive, made both of them wonder about its occupant, but neither spoke. The shouts of two boys rolling hoops were the only noticeable noise outside the crunching of their wheels and the snorts of the team.

"But what shall I talk to him about, Mama? He's so important, and he's been everywhere and he knows so much!"

"He's a man, dear. Just let him talk about himself."

"But how do I get him started?"

"You'll know, dear."

"Ask him about the Indians, Sister. He knows a lot about the Indians," put in young Thomas, eavesdropping again.

"You might turn here, to the right, Mr. Foster."

He gave the reins a tug, and the silence began again.

I might ask him if he likes America, she thought anxiously. But what if he doesn't?

He cleared his throat. "How long is it before the leaves begin to get their autumn colors here?" he asked. She looked up in relief. Perhaps he was trying to help her get him started talking about himself, although it did seem the long way round.

"In a few weeks," she said eagerly. "You'll notice some of the young maples already getting orange, and the sumac bushes there by the river—"

"Is that the shrub that looks rather purple?" He seemed relieved too that they could speak with each other.

"Yes, rather purple." She felt that the subject was closed and could not think of another word. Swallowing hard, she finally squeaked out, "How do you like America, Mr. Foster?"

A flush of scarlet rose instantly above his collar, and she knew she had said the wrong thing. Hastily she tried to correct herself. "I mean—what do you—well, is there anything—what do you—well, consider especially interesting in our big country?"

"Many things," he said with an effort.

"My—my brother said—"

"I remember him. A fine boy."

"I guess he is. Anyway, he said—he suggested—he thought you might tell me something about the Indians."

"The Indians?" Astonished, he turned to face her. "Oh, yes. He must mean the ones your President Jefferson has been entertaining in the Federal City. Come to think of it, I should probably have answered your earlier question by saying that I find the Indians—well, interesting."

Lydia began to relax, hoping that the conversation was launched. "If you turn right here you'll be at the waterfront. How did you—I mean, aren't all the Indians—what I mean is, I thought they were wild and a bit—a bit dangerous."

"You've never seen one?"

"Oh, my, no."

"Well, they aren't like anything or anyone I've ever seen." He smiled.

"But why—why were they in Washington? Did you see them there?"

"Your President—you mean you don't know that your President is trying very hard to, shall we say, *charm* the aborigines who are now a part of your country through the purchase of Louisiana?"

"No. Why?"

"Because . . ." He hesitated, trying to organize his thoughts. Were all women as ignorant of what was going on? But then, why shouldn't they be? Did any man, British or American, expect his wife to be involved in public affairs? He realized again that his mother's intuition and information on political and national issues were most singular. He should not judge every woman, or any woman, by her. Perhaps her very brilliance was one of the reasons she and his father had separated when he was a baby. Women weren't supposed to know so much. It wasn't healthy.

He began again. "President Jefferson told me that he surmises the Indians—he was actually speaking of the Cherokees, just one of the many tribes—might soon even have a representative in Congress. Chief Doublehead, who was there last year, thought it was a very fine idea."

"In Congress?" Lydia murmured, having visions of feathered headdresses and tomahawks mingling with frock coats and polished boots.

"Last December, Mr. Meriwether Lewis—have you heard of Captain Lewis?"

She shook her head, playing safe by being honest.

"He was one of the men who explored your vast western territory," Foster told her. "He and his men went up the Missouri River and down the Columbia, clear to the Pacific Ocean! A fantastic journey, believe me! A modern Marco

Polo, in a way. He sent many reports of the Indians in the West."

Lydia sat up straighter, not wanting to miss a word but wondering if he might be making up the whole thing. She must watch the tone of his phrases to hear any hint that he was teasing her.

"Last December," he told her, "Captain Lewis and his partner Lieutenant Clark persuaded some Osages and other tribesmen to come to the Federal City as guests of President Jefferson. There were Sauks, Pawnees, Sioux and Missouris, some from twelve hundred miles away, requiring sixty days of travel. They were housed across the street from their enemies, the Cherokees, who were also visiting Washington."

"Was there any trouble?" Lydia looked alarmed.

"Not that I heard of. It was strange to see all the tribal markings and the shaved topknots. The young Sauk braves pierce their ears in two places as a sign of manhood. . . ."

He cleared his throat and went on resolutely. "Some of them put on a show at a rope-dancing theater. A chief got up and roared a question about his bravery and how many men he had scalped. Then the others leaped and shouted like crazy men, making a great spectacle of themselves to show they honored him as a great warrior."

He stopped talking. Perhaps one did not describe such affairs to proper young ladies. But there had been young ladies in attendance. And this one was such a rapt listener. Her eyes were wide open as she waited for him to continue. Neither was noticing the scenery along the riverbank, of willow trees dipping to the water's edge, ducks bobbing around on its surface, people walking along or sitting on the grass. The water was a roughened mirror of the sky.

"Yes?" she prompted.

"Then there were some fireworks. There was so much applause for the Indians that they performed again. Pretty soon they were all hacking the air, making the most unearthly yells."

"Were you scared?"

"No!" He laughed, startled at her naïveté. "It was a great show. The yelling was the same kind they did when they first passed by the President's house. It must be a whoop of triumph."

"How were they dressed?" Lydia asked innocently.

"They weren't," he said, half under his breath. "Only a—well—a simple girdle." He signaled the team, which broke into a brisk trot. "Did you say there were lakes somewhere near your city?" He was astounded at the turn the conversation had taken and at his own lack of judgment in letting it get out of hand. There was something about the girl that made him act like a schoolboy and that sent his pulse leaping. She could be so still.

It might not be wise to tell her of the marriage customs of the Western tribes, although he found the subject intriguing. A man who wished to marry a girl would tie four horses to the wall of her father's tent. If the father took away the horses, the girl was his wife. Not only that girl, but all her sisters, in a sort of Old Testament arrangement. No, it would not be wise to mention that. He had already said too much.

"How is your father?" he asked as the team began to pull them up a slight rise in the road.

"Papa? He's fine."

"And your uncle?"

"He's fine too. You must mean my uncle Samuel. I have several."

"Yes, of course. Your uncle Samuel."

"He's fine."

There was another long silence as they spun along past scattered houses and toward the open country. Lydia wished the day could go on forever, finding the steady trit-trot of the horses' hoofs soothing, not conscious of the passing of time.

Foster wished he could stop thinking about the Indians. What had gotten into him to make him so obsessed by those children of nature who were rapidly taking precedence over all the other visitors to the Capitol? If it came to a choice between the Indians and even such an august caller as an ambassador, Mr. Jefferson would put the ambassador second. Their bizarre headgear, their garishly painted bodies with great slashes of red, green or white, their nauseating odor, their long slender pipes shaped like tomahawks at the end, their near-nakedness in any kind of weather—none of these features of the red men was proper conversational material for a Baltimore belle. Or for any lady.

He had been told that the Indian girls were easily approached by presents to their papas, but that even in the "most interior parts of the continent, the Roses are not always to be counted on as being without Thorns."

He could picture his friend Caroline Ponsonby, the Duchess's niece, if he told her such tales. Or his mother! He could be more graphic in describing the savages to his brothers—who might not believe him—but he'd never mention them to the two women. And he *shouldn't* have talked about them to this gentle girl.

When he brought Lydia to her door, she thanked him, and he thanked her, and he got into his carriage and drove off, his back too straight as he tried to appear to be handling his team like a professional.

All of Lydia's family, black and white, waited just inside the door, ready to scramble into hiding if the gentleman happened to come in. "Where did you go?" "What did you do?" "What did you talk about?" "What's he like?" "Is he coming again?"

She tossed her parasol into a corner and flew up the stairs to her room. *"He told me about the Indians!"*

In Washington the Honorable Anthony Merry was rereading a note that had come to his hand. "Ill-health?" he asked his wife. "I thought I was in excellent condition. Do I have ill-health?"

"His Majesty," she told him acidly, "is giving you a leave of absence because His Majesty has undergone a change of government. Ill-health is their idea of a good excuse. I surely have no objection to going home."

"Neither do I."

"I do wonder"—she smiled—"what civilized people have been doing these past three years."

"They may have forgotten us, Mistress Merry," he reminded her. "And anyway, Mr. Fox is known to be such a friend of America that I should find it extremely difficult to work under him. He simply doesn't know the facts."

If Toujours Gai was surprised at his recall, no one else was. Foster found it hard to accept the rebuff of not being chosen to replace his chief, or at least left in charge until a new man was sent. It was a humiliating slap in the face. He knew that many persons around Washington felt that he was the right man for the job too.

All of his disenchantment spilled out in a letter to his mother in late September, 1806. "You don't mention when Erskine leaves England," he told her. "As soon as I know of his appointment officially, unless I am left Chargé d'Affaires, which now I do not expect as I was not appointed to it at first, I have made up my Mind to ask for a Leave of Absence."

"My stay here will not lead to anything," he continued, "my Pay is no Object as the Country is expensive and both Health and Mind suffer in a land of Swamps and Pawnbrokers. Nothing can make me amends for another Summer spent here if I am once strongly seized by the Climate and ten Months a Year spent at such a Botany Bay place as Washington is enough to kill one's Imagination and every Germ of good Amour or Temper. I am resolved to take my chance on returning. To be on the Spot is a great advantage when Appointments are making. . . ."

So a promising young envoy was being consumed by the yawning wilderness of North American geography, climate, food, manners and diplomacy. A. J. Foster's self-esteem was at an extremely low ebb. He did not get to go home, even though he pleaded that he must be in Ireland to take care of his father's property. The man appointed for the job he wanted was David Montagu Erskine, son of Britain's Lord High Chancellor, sent by Charles James Fox, America's friend.

The colonists had never forgotten Fox's tribute: "The resistance of the Americans to the oppression of the mother country has undoubtedly preserved the liberties of mankind, and the freedom of the seas will be one of the blessings of Revolution." Many British had not forgotten it either, but the incorrigible and outspoken gambler had somehow survived his political foes and arrived at the post of Secretary of State for Foreign Affairs in 1806. One of his supporters had been the charming Duchess of Devonshire, Georgiana, who bought at least one vote for him by kissing a shoemaker as a bribe.

While Erskine was on the ocean, Fox passed away at Chiswick, one of the homes of the Duke of Devonshire and of Foster's mother, Elizabeth. It was an irreparable loss. For one thing, Fox's antipathy to Napoleon could have changed the course of the war. Foster wrote to his mother as soon as the news reached him. "The hope of Peace I suppose is buried with William [*sic*] Fox. To have been present at his last Hours, to have almost caught the breath of so great a Man . . . in the very House where you were must have been very affecting to you. It is melancholy to see our greatest Men cut off in such Numbers just when we have most Occasion for them."

His letter sounded so somber that he added: "However the Spirit of the Nation is still high and I am convinced we have more Men of Integrity and Talents in prominent situations to boast of than there are in all the World besides."

When Toujours Gai finally left—after having stayed on for

an embarrassing length of time following Erskine's arrival, and having persuaded the new minister to take his house—Foster loaded him down with mail. On December 6, as the Merrys were ready to depart, Foster wrote his mother: "It is impossible for me Love to remain here unless I was in the Nature of a puppet showman and inclined to lick the Shoes of the dirty democratic Tribe here."

It could be truthfully said that the autumn of 1806 brought the greatest disappointment and feeling of failure in all of Augustus John Foster's life up to that time—as it did also to a blossoming, pensive Maryland girl, Lydia Eliza Hollingsworth.

Lydia saw him again at a Christmas frolic in Baltimore, where she had gone with James Carroll. The couples swung out onto the floor, first in pairs, then in fours, then in eights for the Grand March. As the dancers made a large circle, Lydia reached back to catch a masculine hand and turned to look at its owner. In her surprise she nearly let go. She had not known that Foster was to be invited or that he would come.

"Hello, Miss Hollingsworth," he said shyly as the circle gained speed.

"H-hello," she answered, feeling her palm get too warm as she clung to his fingers to keep from breaking loose. He gave her hand a quick squeeze as the call came to "Swing your partners!" and Carroll whirled her away. She tried to see through the dancers to find out with whom Foster was dancing. A flash of cherry velvet and the curls of a dark head that came just to his shoulder told her that the lady was the former Miss Elizabeth Patterson. He was chatting with her as they danced, his face showing his pleasure.

Later he found a way to get to Lydia to ask to see her program. "May I have—let me see—a waltz? Do you like to waltz, Miss Hollingsworth?"

"Yes. Yes, very much."

"A. J. Foster," he wrote in the line. "There is also a quadrille later in the evening," he said gravely. "I believe you are not yet engaged for that one. Perhaps . . . ?"

"Perhaps," she answered as she saw Betsy being guided toward the punch bowl by two gentlemen, one on either side.

Lydia could never remember the exact moment when it happened, but sometime during that magic evening, which had started out as just another of the gay affairs that filled the festive season, she fell in love, for the only time in her life. He had not encouraged it, he had not asked for it, she knew, but it was there, inevitably and undeniably. She had not really thought that love would come that way, like a sudden stifling radiance in the heart, or that it could make one blind to everything and everyone else on earth.

In the moments of conversation that were possible, he had found that she, like himself, had both Irish and English ancestry. She could feel herself blushing when he said with a low chuckle, "Perhaps we are cousins, Miss Hollingsworth!" Had he blushed too?

After the quadrille he had escorted her to her chair and, with a deep bow, had said, smiling, "Thank you for dancing with me, my lovely cousin!" And he had disappeared among the other merrymakers.

The next morning she saw him get into his carriage at the hotel as Robert was driving her out to finish her Christmas shopping. He was probably setting out for the Federal City, for he had said he was not going to stay in Baltimore long. He also caught a glimpse of her; he touched his hand to his hat in salute and appeared for a moment to be dismounting again, but when she did not stop, he went on too. She dared not look around. The swirling snowstorm soon swallowed them both.

When he did not get in touch with her afterward, she was cross and resentful, although she could not have given a sensible reason for her feelings. Surely he was not expected to send notes to every lady he danced with; what other excuse could there be for writing her? He had not remained in Baltimore long enough to do much calling. At the ball he had been charming, but he was charming to everyone. He was quite the lion of the evening. Endless feminine chatter about him filled every social function for days. His attention to Betsy Bonaparte had not gone unnoticed, but neither had his attention to Lydia Eliza Hollingsworth.

"I saw how he looked at you," one of the Catons told her.

"He knows my father," Lydia answered simply.

If others had noticed it, could she have been imagining that warm expression in his eyes, the tightening of his fingers on her hand? She wished she could confide in someone, but then they'd be watching her, asking sly questions—she must get busy. There was no sense in moping. Over nothing, really. The orphans? The church? Shopping? Shut-ins? Her relatives —ah, Aunt Debby!

It was early on a crisp, cold morning when she stopped in at the Cochrans' to deliver a jar of blackberry jelly from the ample supply in their cellar. She found her aunt in her ruffled, lace-trimmed blue peignoir, her tawny hair tumbling down her back, her expression agitated and perplexed. Her pregnancy made her movements graceless and unbalanced.

"Do come in, my dear," she called as she heard Lydia's voice in the front hall. "I just can't seem to find—let me see, now where could I have put it? Did the maid take your wraps? I'll ring for some tea. I'd lose my head if I didn't have it—here's a chair. You always look pretty in a green chair." Her nervous laugh chimed through the room.

"What's the trouble, Aunt Debby?"

"Nothing for you to worry about, my dear. I had bought a new brooch—oh, I was going to ring for tea. Why don't you do it, Lydia? The bell pull is by that door, but of course you know that, don't you? I'm so confused this morning." She tried to smile, but her eyes betrayed her.

"Did you lose it, Aunt Debby?" Lydia knew that the brooch would be valuable. Deborah never had any other kind.

"Well, I hope it isn't really *lost*—" She sat down abruptly. "Oh, my goodness, I'm not even dressed. Well, you see, my birthday is this week, so I bought a gift for my husband to surprise me with. It's small, like a bowknot, with rubies and diamonds sprinkled through it. So pretty! Oh, my dear Mr. Cochran will feel *terrible*—"

"Does he know you've lost it?"

"He doesn't even know I've bought it! It was to be a surprise for him too! What will he say after I've spent all that money? And nothing to show for it!" She began to walk around the room, running her fingers under the edge of doilies and ornaments, sliding her toes cautiously around the legs of chairs and sofas. The maid came with tea, but her mistress never noticed her. Lydia motioned for the tray to be set near her so she could serve their cups.

"But, Aunt, if he doesn't know you have it—"

"Oh, but I intended to tell him. Today. And I can't bear to have anything upset my dear Mr. Cochran. He's so good to me."

"Are you sure you had it in here? Was it still in its box?"

"This morning, after he went to his office, I got it out and pinned it on my robe to see how it would look, and then little Elizabeth began to cry so pitifully and I—" Her hand flew to her throat. "Why, here it is, under this double ruffle! I've had it on all the time. Oh, my!" She accepted the cup of tea that Lydia brought her and sat fanning herself weakly with her free hand. "And I kept thinking of all I had to do today. Old Mrs. Ireland is ill, you know. And she's so fond of my custards. I always send twice as much because her husband likes them too. He told me he had never eaten anything like them, particularly my butterscotch custard. I made up that receipt myself. Oh, Lydia dear, how glad I am that you came, to help me find my lost brooch! I don't know what I would have *done* without you. Can you stay for dinner?"

"Thank you, no," Lydia said, sliding forward on her chair.

"There are a number of errands I must do. And Robert is waiting out in the carriage."

"And what of your young men? Isn't there a certain special one?"

"Now, Aunt Debby! Don't try matching me up with someone this early in the morning!" Lydia hoped her laugh didn't sound as hollow as it felt.

"You would be a fine catch for some man!" she said fondly. "Even my dear Mr. Cochran thinks so, and you know he never gives out compliments lightly."

"You want me to be choosy, don't you?" Lydia asked, rising. "I really stopped in for a selfish reason, Aunt Debby. Would you allow me to take little Elizabeth as my special charge for a while? You need some rest, and I need to get better acquainted with her, and I do have free time, now that the Lenten season is coming and social affairs are slowing down."

"How sweet you are!" Debby accepted. "And it will give you some important practice for your own little ones someday. You know, Mr. Cochran's partner, Mr. Comegys, is a fine man. And he's not married."

"I'll look him over," Lydia said, as she did every time Deborah mentioned another eligible bachelor. "If you think I should. I brought some jelly from Mama. Clorinda took it to the kitchen. Don't bother to come to the door with me. You've had a difficult morning."

Once he accepted the fact that he had been passed over for promotion, A. J. Foster, never one for wallowing in self-pity, took himself in hand. Growing up without a mother and with only the indifferent mercies of his father to sustain him, he had made up his mind that there were two areas of his life in which he would not fail: his career and his marriage. They were strongly interrelated. Even if there had been a great fortune to fall back on, he would have been forced by his pride and the gift of his high intelligence to use his talents in some worth-while way, probably in public service.

Marriage for love and a home and children was important to him too. He had not the slightest interest in being "just another Diplomatic old Bachelor." His parents' marriage had been a disaster, and his grandparents' nearly so. He was too close to both failures to try to fix blame, but he suspected that the husbands were more than halfway at fault, and that both breakups might have been foreseen even before the rites were performed. Indicating a measure of the regard that his maternal grandmother, Lady Bristol, had for her son-in-law was the fact that in writing of him she referred to him simply as "f."

It behooved Augustus to be objective in his choice of a wife. His problem would be to combine that calculating coolness with the warmth of love, which was basic and outweighed all other considerations. A diplomat's lady had more than the ordinary burdens of life thrust upon her, so she must have enough spine to survive. She must leave her home, likely forever, so she must have a rugged heart. If she had the advantage of inbred culture, such as upper-class Englishwomen enjoyed, his own work would be enriched.

When he first arrived at the Federal City, he had met and actively courted a girl who might have fitted his needs. She was half Irish and half Portuguese (he called her "particoloured") and shared his dislike for the United States, but the poor dear died of consumption within six months.

Secretly he realized that he was eager to leave, so that he could avoid accidentally falling in love with an American girl, who would not make a suitable wife for a British public servant at all. And Americans were so reluctant to pull up stakes and go back to the Old World. It was odd too that they put no great premium on coming from an ancient family line of wealth or distinction, or both. A man was what he could become.

William Patterson, one of the country's wealthiest men, "came over here from Ireland . . . as a Redemptioner," Foster wrote to his half sister, and went on to explain that "that is a Person who sells his Services for a certain period to pay for his Passage from Europe, and he became an hostler. He is now universally respected as a Merchant and is one of their most honoured Dealers in Baltimore."

Mr. Patterson's daughter and another girl who lived across the street from her had both upset the rhythm of Foster's heartbeats, although the two were as different as mountain and ocean. The gossips had told him enough of the Patterson girl's marriage and the scandalous behavior of her husband, who had divorced her through the French Senate, to make him plan to watch his step. She did have many traits that would be useful to him though; he could see her moving confidently, surely, enchantingly in almost any circle. But the criticism and whispering that would go on if he were to marry her—could his career survive it? And would he eventually be only tagging along behind her, drowning in the wake of the ripples she always created? He'd better play safe.

And the other one, the dark-eyed, quiet Lydia—when he thought of her, his objectivity flew out the window. Best to stay in Washington and fill up his time with appointments, meetings, Shakespeare, Vergil and politics.

In the spring Merry sent him to Baltimore again for a conference with several bankers, notably Mr. Patterson. He dashed up the steps at Number 20, and in a half hour ran back down, jumped into his carriage and drove away.

Miss Hollingsworth, getting ready to go over to spend some time with her little cousin at the Cochrans', would have been flattered to know that the gentleman was deliberately keeping himself from crossing the street and dashing up the steps at Number 15 instead of urging his groom to get him off to other pressing matters, which were not pressing at all.

He had inquired about Madame Bonaparte, conscientiously using her correct title, although she was already addressing him as Augustus. He hoped that his expression conveyed the same kindly interest as of one inquiring about an elderly aunt.

Patterson was not fooled. "My daughter," he said with a wintry smile, "is in good health. She and my grandson have gone to the country for a short holiday. I'll tell her you asked."

"Is the boy well?"

"Yes, he is well."

Chapter Nine

The Disquietness of My Heart

Spring was late and miserly, as if the cruel King of Winter was refusing to give up his death grip on the earth. A March snowstorm—which happened every March but invariably caught everyone off guard—froze tender sprouts, caused countless accidents and sent children flying out for a final snowball fight. Several elderly people fell and fractured hips or shoulders. Brittle branches snapped under the weight of ice.

On Liberty Street, a horse pulling a heavy drayload of liquor lost his footing, and the dray smashed into an iron hitching rail. The barrels split open, and the driver landed head first on the road. In no time, an enormous crowd of people, black and white, was finding a way to get under the golden cascades of liquid, mouths open, gullets ecstatic. The drayman, stunned and bruised, finally got his bearings and joined them. A number of dogs and cats, attracted by the racket, behaved very strangely for the rest of the day. By the time the police arrived, there was little for them to do or to drink. The dray was righted, its owner sent a message of the mishap and the driver carted off to a doctor for patching up.

Deborah Cochran, doing errands before the birth of her second child, got her feet and head wet and was soon very ill.

Lydia, who had been spending afternoons with little Elizabeth, found her services very much needed. She took over almost the total care of the frail, china-doll charmer, who liked to be cuddled. It would be hard to give her up when Debby was well again. When the child was asleep, Lydia would stand by her crib marveling at the fine hair on the pillow, the nearly invisible lashes on the soft baby cheeks, and wondering. She had always thought that any child of her own would be dark because she was, but Mr. Cochran was dark, and here was his little flaxen child with coloring like her mother's and hardly any resemblance to him. Somehow, blond babies seemed more precious and fragile than brunette ones . . . and if the father had fair skin . . . and reddish hair . . .

Debby's son was born three weeks prematurely, bright-eyed and dark-haired, named William for his father. They had to hire a wet nurse for the boy, and he was soon thriving. Mr. Cochran became so alarmed at the slowness of his wife's recovery that he set his foot down in a way most unusual for him. Early in the summer, when Deborah was still shadow-thin and more absent-minded than ever, he hired an extra nurse to stay full-time with his family while he packed Debby off for a change of scene. Lydia found herself superseded by the capable, no-nonsense Mrs. Lavinia Lanfear, who took over like a martinet. No outside assistance of any kind was needed, she let it be known, and the less interference she had to put up with, the more smoothly and peacefully the household would run.

Lydia watched the departure of the Cochrans through a film of tears. "Oh, Mr. Cochran!" Debby kept saying as they waited for their luggage to be put aboard the chaise. "How good you are! How very good you are! Oh, my *dear* Mr. Cochran!"

Later, when Ann Hollingsworth suggested that she, Lydia and young Thomas go on a trip into Maryland and Pennsylvania, Lydia accepted eagerly. "We might find some mountains!" she exclaimed. "I've never seen a mountain."

miral Berkeley, demanded the right to search the ship for British deserters. Outraged, the Americans refused.

The *Leopard* commenced firing. In no time the decks of the *Chesapeake* were awash with blood. Three men lay dead in the slime. Twenty others dragged themselves out of the line of fire, wounded and screaming vengeance. The unarmed *Chesapeake* was forced to strike her colors. A boat put out from the *Leopard* and men scrambled up the ladder to haul off four sailors, under a steady torrent of abuse. Within hours, one of the men was hanged from a yardarm of the *Leopard,* his body an ensign of insolence swinging heavily in the wind.

As soon as the news reached land, the nation was up in arms. If there had been an organized military force, well-equipped for battle, war would have ensued in a matter of hours. Foster said a few personal, heartfelt prayers of gratitude that his earlier prayers for promotion had not been heard. His chief was in the direct line of fire of American fury. There was no hiding place.

President Jefferson immediately refused permission for any British warship to enter any American port. None was to leave either. The kidnaped men must be returned and the British government must make restitution to their families and to the United States government for the damage that had been done. He insisted again that impressment must stop.

The British were adamant: the *Leopard* was completely within its rights.

Unable to affect the course of history but only able to record it in his post as secretary, Foster was amazed to find, as the days passed with one angry exchange after another, that he was still in the United States instead of being shipped home, because of the possibility of a declaration of war. The threat of immediate hostilities was paralyzing everyone with dread; escape to Lancaster was a gift from Heaven.

On a summer morning he went into the town and was walking along the street toward a tobacconist's shop. From the corner of his eye he caught a glimpse of a girl who looked like the one he had been trying to shove out of his heart for nearly a year. For a moment he was again concerned with his sanity. He'd been working too hard. He was seeing things.

Hadn't he heard that the Hollingsworths had relatives someplace in Pennsylvania? Perhaps this young lady was one of them. He understood it was a large family. He didn't know what town they lived in; it could be Lancaster.

The resemblance was remarkable. The set of her head, the firm but delicate line of her chin, the proud ladylike way of walking, almost like an English gentlewoman. The young fellow strolling with her, looking into shopwindows, was so much like that younger brother, the one who asked so many questions and was such a handsome, cheerful lad.

Foster quickened his pace. It wouldn't hurt to investigate, and after all, a chap should be polite. And supposing that it really was the Baltimore girl, and she had seen *him* out of the corner of *her* eye—the pair had disappeared from view.

"There are such things as mirages," he told Tartar. "Remember that time when we were coming over to this God-forsaken wasteland and we thought we saw a castle rising out of the ocean, with turrets and flagpoles and everything? You were pretty young then, but it was a frightening sight. So, they have mirages in Mr. Penn's Woods too. Fellow rests his mind by letting it go off on a tangent and dreaming about a beautiful girl, and there she is! I may just try it again, it's that pleasant."

He wandered into a small tavern to sit drinking ale and reflecting on the state of the world. He did not like the results.

"Here's the tollgate Ann Maria described," Thomas told his mother as he paid the seventeen-and-a-half-cent fee. "Let's watch for Conestoga Creek. She said there was an elegant bridge supported by large pillars."

"What I remember, son, was her remark about the State

House. She thought they were going to run into it, because it was fixed in the center of the street."

"Let's drive through it!" Thomas suggested. "Do you think the horses would do it? Shall we try?"

"Thomas!" His mother never knew when to take him seriously.

"Ann Maria went on to Lititz," Lydia was reading from a letter she had brought. "It's a little Moravian town, and the people are mostly Dutch."

"I wonder if they wear those fat pants," Thomas said. "All the pictures I ever saw of Dutchmen showed them wearing those big fat pants that make them look like sausages."

"Hush! I think they're really German, son."

"She went to church there at night," Lydia continued reading. "She said all the prayers were in Dutch."

Thomas was suddenly serious. "Do you suppose God speaks Dutch, Mama? I think He'd have to. Or at least be able to understand it. What good would their prayers do otherwise?"

"Son! I'm glad your father isn't here! I never heard such talk in all my born days!"

"I didn't mean anything wrong, Mama. It's just that I wondered. Somehow at St. Paul's a fellow gets the idea that—well, never mind. And I really am sorry. I shouldn't have said it out loud."

The streets were busy and full of people, even though it was summer and the Pennsylvania legislature was not in session. Lydia looked covertly in as many directions as her parasol would permit. Window shopping with Thomas gave her the added dimension of looking for passers-by mirrored in the glass, but she saw only strangers, absorbed in their own worlds and with the characteristic gait and garb of Americans.

She was reluctant to leave Lancaster, but finally there was no more time. The pull of Elkton was always strong, and she had much to tell Ruth Tobin, except for the one thing she could not tell because there was nothing to say.

☆

Foster resolved to avoid the girl when he stopped in Baltimore on his way back to Washington. After all, his situation was so shaky that he might be recalled at once—Merry's orders had been waiting for him when they got home the previous year. If he were to undertake a serious courtship—which would not be any strain, he admitted—and then were to be transferred, just as he was getting the girl convinced that leaving her home and family and going off with him would not be the total disruption she probably feared—but how did he know *what* she thought? Had he ever tried to find out? She might turn him down flat, refuse to see him. A girl as attractive as that one was probably spoken for anyway.

The long ride south had left him stiff and uncomfortable, so he set out for a brisk walk. Pacing along Baltimore's hilly streets, he found himself unaccountably at 15 South Street, lifting the knocker and staring up at the crossed-hands fire mark. The sound echoed through the house. No one home, not even a servant. He started to knock again, thought better of it and left.

An hour later the travelers returned, exhausted and happy from their adventure, a round trip of nearly three hundred miles. They were warmed with thoughts of family doings at Elkton but saddened by the death of their grandmother, Mary Jacobs Hollingsworth, who had outlived her husband by forty-four years.

Lydia leafed quickly through the few pieces of mail that had come, but there was no letter with the magic of his scrawl on the address. Why had she expected one? For the thousandth time she told herself that she must put him out of her mind. There were many other men in the world. Several not-impossible ones lived right in Baltimore, and Aunt Debby was always finding more. Some of them would soon learn that she was home. One or two of Uncle Stephen's "preacher fellows" had been surprisingly attractive. A tall, sober one had made a tentative conquest of Ruth Tobin's heart. She and Lydia had had several serious talks about him.

Giving in to her weariness, Lydia climbed the steps to her room, to unpack some of her clothes and to set herself once more to the need for forgetting the Englishman. What real cause was he giving her for remembering him? She looked out at the sun-blackened remnants of her mother's garden. Neglect had done it, yes. . . . Ann Maria had probably never once thought of tending it. But a little watering, a little pruning and weeding, a little care . . .

Forget him? As soon forget the moon, or the stars, or the eternal sea.

Britain's Secretary of the Legation, who had watched Anthony Merry's persecution by the Americans at close range, was forced to watch again as the squirming David Montagu Erskine was blasted from both sides of the ocean over the *Leopard-Chesapeake* affair. Erskine was deeply affronted when his government sent over a special envoy, George Henry Rose, to try to soothe the Americans, the scrabbling, clamorous Brother Jonathan. Rose was told to keep the *Chesapeake* negotiations completely separate from any other Yankee complaints, and to hint strongly that if the Americans were to withdraw their proclamation against British ships their conversations might be more productive.

Meanwhile Erskine continued his extraordinary efforts to effect some kind of accommodation, sending word home that he was certain the Yankees would go to war against the French and on the side of the British if only the hated Orders in Council were withdrawn. For this bit of wisdom, he was called a deserter who had gone over to the Americans, the enemy.

Foster, his hands tied by his subordinate position, could see only disaster ahead, in spite of Britain's greatest sea victory of all time, the defeat of the French at Trafalgar in 1805. Knowing that he could never win a naval war after that, Napoleon then announced his bold and brilliant Continental System, closing off the entire European continent from the British

"Nation of Shopkeepers," who were dependent on that trade for their survival.

Norway had come into the fray, against England. Holland was a kingdom with a Bonaparte on the throne. Austria, Spain, Italy, Germany—nations of Europe were being knocked over like pins in a game of bowls, or subverted by the use of some of Napoleon's fifteen million American dollars.

There were enough Bonaparte brothers to supply kings for several thrones. The youngest, Jerome, had married a fat and wealthy Prussian princess, for which the Emperor rewarded him by canceling three million francs of his debts. His splendiferous coronation as the King of Westphalia—a kingdom created by the Treaty of Tilsit after the defeat of the Russians and Prussians at Friedland—was set for December, 1807. His friend Le Camus was to be named Count Fürstenstein, but he could not pronounce it. The best he could manage was "Furchetintin," at which he and Jerome laughed the loudest of all. Jerome was said to have offered his cast-off Betsy a castle at Schmalkalden, thirty leagues from his own royal residence; she retorted that Westphalia was not large enough for two queens.

There were many kings but only one emperor. He was proving to be a formidable one. When Foster first met him, around the turn of the century, he was impressed by the fellow's good manners and good sense, traits he admired. It was beginning to appear that the Corsican's sense was most uncommon and his manners, at best, superficial. The Trafalgar defeat was a serious blow, but Bonaparte had not yet used up his bag of tricks.

And now Britain had stirred up this hornet's nest in the New World! "This variegated Nation—composed of British of all descriptions, of French, Dutch, Swiss, Africans, etc."—as Foster had described it in a letter home soon after his arrival in America—had inherited stubbornness and scrappiness and self-sufficiency from all its forebears. "Such a gang to have the Affairs of an Empire wanting little of the size of Russia entrusted to them makes one shudder," he had told his mother. Lately he wondered if he'd been shuddering for the wrong reason.

Now and then Foster told himself loyally that *he* might have been able to avoid some of the worst blunders that others were making, but he had long ago given up the idea of volunteering his advice. In view of his unusually wide acquaintance with the Americans, he might have been helpful in contributing some light instead of heat to the raging controversy. He seemed to be the only person who knew it.

These times of frustration and self-doubt brought to the surface again his need for a wife, as support to his pride, as distraction from the maddening pressures of his job, and, quite simply, for love. He had tried several times to spell out for himself what he truly wanted. A business partner? God forbid. A political adviser? He laughed grimly. He was already overburdened with advice from his mother. A decorative chatelaine? Yes, he thought. Yes! But that's not enough. A healthy cowlike creature who would give him a houseful of healthy calflike children? The thought was revolting.

If he was to stay in America, he must forget his resistance to the idea of taking an American bride. The prejudice was a little ridiculous when he faced the facts. Many Americans had truly admirable traits, from sturdy inheritance and the buffeting of a pioneer culture. If he found the right one, possibly he could train her. Again he was shocked and ashamed. Would she be like a pet puppy, for Heaven's sake? Tartar tugged at his shoelace, wanting to romp.

"Well," he said aloud, "the way things look now, we'll all be booted out. If they decide to ship me to Samarkand, they'll do it. Perhaps I should look up Samarkand on the map. Don't believe I *quite* know where it is."

Alerted in the early summer of 1807 by an urgent notice, the Maryland militia was ready for a display in October. The Governor came to Baltimore to witness the spectacle, a brilliant troop of hussars commanded by Joshua Barney having made the trip to Annapolis to escort His Excellency safely and with honor.

Samuel Hollingsworth, who had volunteered in the Revolution when he was eighteen and was now a captain, was singled out for a special presentation. He stood as straight as he could, trying to tuck in his waistline so that his military jacket would cover the gap at the top of his trousers. Sarah had been after him to get a new uniform; she could not move the buttons over any farther. His pride held him back. He was hardly a pound heavier than when he had had the last one made. The wool must have shrunk.

A week after the big day, Lydia sent Ruth a first hand report, remembering to inquire first about their aunt's health and about all the other Elkton relatives. "Aunt will have to be more careful of her rheumatism now," Lydia noted sympathetically. "When you wrote, the cough from her attack of influenza was somewhat troublesome. I hope it is quite removed—sore lips are quite fashionable here, since the 19th, that blustering day when we all flocked to the doors and windows to view the gay and splendid appearance of our Companies. It was very unpleasant on the ground where the Governor reviewed them. Miss Cheston presented Uncle's troops with a set of colours. The ground yellow, festooned with blue velvet marked with gold, Valor and Mercy being represented in painting by two bare arms, one with a drawn sword, the other in the act of sheathing with the motto: 'By Valor drawn, by Mercy sheathed.' On the band beneath, 'For our Country we serve.' The Captain gave an extemporary address."

Ruth Tobin was about to make her first trip to Baltimore, or to any place other than Sassafras, some twenty-odd miles from Elkton. Lydia thought of little else. She urged Ruth: "Do not forget South Street is nearest the Philadelphia Road and I hope you will make our house your first home; all join me in the request. Mama says the driver will let you out." She ended with the reminder: "Cousin, be sure to come here first, you promised me so to do. Mama and Ann with Papa unite their best affection with mine for Aunt, Uncle and you, with the expectation of soon seeing you, your ever affectionate Cousin, Lydia E. Hollingsworth."

She folded and sealed the letter, tossed on a coat and went to the dock to hand it to Biddle herself. She would have been nonplused if anyone had asked her what was going on in the larger world or why the militia was suddenly so active. She knew that her father was cross and preoccupied and that there was constant talk of wrecks and disasters at sea, but that was the way of fathers and of the sea, wasn't it?

If A. J. Foster had seen that "gay and splendid appearance," he might have revised some of his observations about America's readiness for combat. "The Army of the United States," he wrote in his notebook, "according to a Report from the Secretary of War, Dec. 3, 1807, consisted of 1 Brigadier General, 1 Regt. of Artillerists consisting altogether of 1,629 Persons of which 20 were [*illegible*] and 1120 were Privates—2 Regts. of Infantry, consisting altogether of 1614 persons of the Number of Americans 200 being wanting to complete the Establishment, and a Corps of Engineers consisting of a Lieut. Colonel and 30 others."

The Baltimore *American* reported that the Fifth, Sixth, Twenty-seventh and Thirty-ninth regiments had gathered up two thousand men that summer, uniformed at their own expense, many carrying their own weapons, and the men were "in a very respectable state of military discipline." They had also organized "several Corps of Artillery, and one of Cavalry." And Maryland was only one of the seventeen states. Others were mobilizing just as rapidly.

While he was at it, Foster added details of other military matters. "In the British Army at Halifax," he wrote, "a common Soldier receives 13 pence per day, 6 pence being deducted for his Rations and the Remainder is paid to the Captain, who accounts for the Amount monthly to the Private. Shirts, Shoes and Washing are to be paid out of it."

He was amazed that the British had any men in their army at all. The figures spoke for themselves. Conditions in the hellholes of the British navy were even worse, with the floggings, the unspeakable food, the miserable pay and the sadistic brutality of the officers. Mutiny was not unheard of. The story of what had happened on the H.M.S. *Bounty* when Augustus was eight years old was known to every schoolboy. The whole British fleet had been lined up in the Channel and required to watch the hanging of three of the mutineers from the yardarms of the *Brunswick,* a treatment of the symptom instead of the disease. Those habitual cruelties were too deeply ingrained for any change in that direction. It wasn't hard to see that impressment was the only way the British had of getting their men back, in order to keep their ships from rotting at the docks and their nation from ruin.

"The Russian soldiers," Foster added, "wear about their feet a Towel smeared with Tallow instead of a Stocking to guard them against the Cold. They have besides large Pantaloons and Boots." His inquiring mind had discovered another use for tallow: "The smell of Tallow drives away Insects from Fur," he noted elsewhere. "The Empress of Russia's Sables are placed on a Table in Service with Tallow put about the Room in various Places."

The horses' hoofs pounding briskly on the road, the driver's long-drawn-out "Whoa-oa-oa!" and the grinding of heavy brakes were sufficient announcement of Ruth Tobin's arrival. The metal rims of the wheels clanging on cement added to the clatter. When the team and carriage stopped moving, the air was almost still. Thomas, Junior, who had been waiting at the corner, stepped forward to open the door while the driver jumped down to get Ruth's luggage from the boot of the coach.

"Hello, Cousin Ruth!" Thomas saluted her. "Welcome to the Port City! Mama sent me to watch for you. Is this all you brought? Two big cases? Now, when my sisters go away—yes, driver, I think I can manage them. Muscle, you know. Yes, I'll take care of her now."

Ruth was talking at the same time. "This is such a big place! And all those buildings! And so many people everywhere, and so much noise! Is this the paving that Uncle Jesse got for the city? We saw so many exciting things on the way down here. The iron works at Principio—"

"Aunt Debby calls it Prince Scipio." Thomas laughed. "Mind your step. It's right this way, only a few houses."

". . . and the race track at Havre de Grace. We crossed by the ferry there. Thomas, I believe you've grown two inches taller since August!"

The family rushed out to smother Ruth with greetings while Thomas got Polodore to help him with her luggage. Ann Hollingsworth came to inquire about her ailing sister and other Elktonians.

"One at a time, my dear," her husband said gently. "If we bother our dear Miss Ruth with so many questions, we'll run out of things to talk about!"

"Oh, Papa!" Lydia hugged him. "You don't give us credit!"

"I've never been so happy in my whole life, Uncle Thomas! There isn't anything more wonderful in the wide world than to come to Baltimore!"

"H'm. My girls say the same thing about getting out of Baltimore. There's something about going almost anywhere that brightens a woman's heart. I'll never quite understand it."

"What would you like to do while you're here?" Lydia asked at tea. "Aunt Debby will want to carry you off every minute—wait till you see those two beautiful children!—and Uncle Samuel and Uncle Jesse and their families will be after you, and Uncle George Adams and Aunt Eliza—they'll keep you so busy—"

Ruth looked up shyly. "I'd really like to learn the new dance steps. Is that silly?"

"No, not at all," Lydia said, trying not to look surprised. "Does your preacher man like dancing?"

"Never! He thinks it's the work of the Devil!"

"And so you want to look into it, eh?" Her uncle grinned. "Well, we've got some pretty good dancers right here, and as far as I know Old Beelzebub hasn't come around to claim tribute."

"I'll teach her," Thomas, Junior, offered. "George Howard and Cousin Jacob keep up on the newfangled ideas, and they show me."

"Really, Cousin Thomas?"

"Of course. Anyway, Papa said I had to be a gentleman while you were here and volunteer for nice things to entertain you."

"Now, son, don't give me away!"

"I don't want to be a burden, Thomas."

"My services as escort are figured by the hour," he said smoothly. "My excellent and witty conversation costs extra."

Lydia was surprised that Ruth was well-informed on several things of which she knew nothing, but then she recalled that their uncle Stephen talked with her a great deal. Neither of them had anyone else to chat with, Ruth Hollingsworth being absorbed in her illnesses.

They were sitting by the fire sipping mulled wine, after a festive oyster supper at Sam's and a brisk walk home through the autumn night. Ruth looked from one to the other, as if memorizing their faces.

"I can't bear to leave," she said sadly. "It's like another world, to be here. But maybe I can come again. Uncle Stephen says that we'll soon be going up and down the bay by steam, and that we can go like the wind!"

"He must have heard of that fellow named Fulton!" young

Ice still holds, I hope you will do me the Honour of accompanying me on either Wednesday or Thursday of that Week. The Favour of a Reply is requested.

Respectfully Yours,
Augustus John Foster
Secretary of the Legation
of His Britannic Majesty
Washington, D. C.

When he saw how pompous his title looked written out that way, he tore up the note and wrote another one. "Don't want the dear lady to think I'm an insufferable ass," he told Tartar.

The second note was a little shorter. He signed it, "Yours, Augustus John Foster." It was a dangerous slip of the pen. Perhaps he was hers, in spite of himself. But he must never say so. He made the paper into a tight ball and threw it into the fire, watching until it was consumed. He wrote a third, being careful of his penmanship, so that his meaning would be perfectly clear, and signed it, "Respectfully, A. J. Foster." No use adding his title. Surely she would know who he was.

He sanded and sealed it, and turned in, praying for cold weather.

Why had he thought of skating? Why not the theater? Or a concert? Baltimore had many cultural offerings. He smiled to himself in the flickering darkness. He knew exactly why: it meant that he could touch her. And perhaps she'd stumble . . . or slip . . . and he could catch her. . . . He knew why he had suggested skating.

She neither stumbled nor slipped, but he did. Catching his swan-shaped skate on a slight lump in the ice, he went sprawling. It was the most humiliating and undignified thing that had ever happened in his whole life. He couldn't imagine that anything could be worse, unless it be one of those nightmare dreams of addressing Parliament in the buff.

Somehow he got his feet back under him, and she helped

him to a fallen log on the bank of the frozen inlet, where twenty or thirty young people were also skating. He collapsed by her side, puffing and embarrassed, glad of the dim light and that she had offered him neither pity nor ridicule.

Finally getting his breath, he could manage to see himself as a figure of fun. "Came a cropper, didn't I?" he said with a shaky laugh.

"Are you hurt?" she asked with quick sympathy as he bent to rub his throbbing ankle and brush off the worst of the snow from his clothing.

"My pride," he admitted.

"That will heal," she said serenely. "Ankles take longer."

They sat for some moments, out of sight of the other skaters, Foster trying to gather up the remnants of his shattered composure, Lydia resting quietly at his elbow.

There was a bright full moon. They could look out across the gleaming ice to the dark trees and shrubs on the opposite shore. A few tongues of red flickered from small bonfires the skaters had built for warmth. Now and then a couple would glide by, hands crossed, bodies moving in graceful rhythm, but none of them noticed the two on the log.

Lydia was wearing a burgundy velvet skating outfit with sable at the neck and wrists and a snug hat to match. Even the coldness of the crisp winter night could not cool off the flush in her face as she sat close beside him, wanting to comfort him but not knowing how.

"It was most thoughtful of your mother to send that flask of hot coffee for us tonight," he said at last. "A fine person, your mother."

"Yes, she is."

He turned to look at her. "You're beautiful!" he blurted out. "Simply beautiful. I wish—" He caught himself just in time and bent over again to assess the situation with his ankle.

After a silence, Lydia asked, "Did I remember to tell you that my brother asked me to say hello to you? He remembers you."

describe a traveler's last-minute reluctance to leave. "I'm journey-proud, that's all it is." He steamed his face with a hot towel. "It's one of those American diseases for which there is no cure but a change of scene. Thank God, they won't be able to put some of their hideous leeches on my veins to cure me of this one."

In his years in the New World he had met one or two great men, dozens of mean men, crude men with cruder manners, scheming women clawing their way upward for a social position they had not attained by inheritance or marriage. He had seen many varieties of geography, of architecture, of nature, had subjected himself to the horrors of public transport and his digestive tract to countless indignities, but he had survived. Surprising, but he had.

He dreaded the job of sorting and packing, and found chances to stop and look out the window or relax in front of the fire. The bleak landscape outside was gray and brown and empty. He pulled the curtains shut, lighted extra candles to dispel some of the gloom and forced himself to select the books that he would put in the boxes lined up outside his door.

From the pages of one of them a paper fluttered to the floor. He picked it up, recognizing a letter that his mother had written him on his eighteenth birthday. He had not looked at it in a long time.

"You are eighteen this day, my dearest Augustus. . . ." He could almost hear the tones of her voice, even after three years' absence. He stretched out on his bed, deciding to read it through, another delay in the thankless job of packing. Tartar curled up against him for a snooze. "Many, many happy years may you see, and may those encreasing years ripen every virtue in your breast and bring them to their full maturity. Let not this anniversary of your birth, my dearest boy, pass without forming new resolutions for the year to come. Examine your own character; see what you think you can find there to alter and amend. You are young enough to counteract any tendency yet old enough to be soon in danger from the influence of habits and custom; indulge in a fault today, it will be harder to resist it tomorrow; the fault which you acknowledged to me, that of too easily giving way, would insensibly make you act not according to the errors of your own judgment but those of others: be on guard against this, dearest Augustus, yet the contrary extreme, an unyielding disposition, is still less amiable."

Irritated, he got up to poke the fire. What did she expect of him anyway? Don't be this, don't be that. "Act not according to the errors of judgment of others. Good Lord!" he exploded. "That's the way I make my living! Errors in judgment! Even Toujours Gai didn't make as many as Erskine does. And Mr. Rose is giving up and going home. And the Americans! Errors in judgment! That's what they're trying to build a nation on!"

He almost pitched the letter into the flames, but something stopped him, perhaps a subconscious thought that it, and letters of his own that his mother was keeping, might be of interest someday to his children and grandchildren. This idea drew forth another bitter laugh.

"I do know, almost as well as you do, Tartar my busy friend, how a chap *gets* children and grandchildren, or at least I think I do, but I don't seem to be doing very damned much about it." He kicked angrily at a heavy trunk, yawning open by the wardrobe.

He scanned the last few lines of the letter. "Be firm, therefore, only when the pure dictates of your heart tell you you are right, and if ever wrong, fear not to acknowledge it; above all, fear it not to me. Some means of reparation a friend may generally point out, but where can you find a friend so true and so affectionate as your mother?"

"Shall I tell her?" he asked the terrier. "Shall I really tell her? And where was she when I was growing up and needed just such a true and affectionate friend?"

"All the great fundamental qualities of your character, I trust, are right. I have never know you fail in them; strict inviolable truth, a religious observance of one's promise, a sacred observance of another's secret, and prudence for one's own; as your situation and connections in life enlarge duties increase also, and amongst the foremost I hope you will ever feel the purest [regard] for women, and never risk their happiness to gratify your vanity or even passions."

He refolded the letter and stuck it among some others in a portfolio. All these preachments, from a woman who was openly the mistress of her best friend's husband? Even if she was his own mother, he wanted to snap at her: *Are these your own values?*

Well, Stockholm was a long way off. Six, eight, maybe ten weeks from this wilderness. As nearly as he could figure from the map, Sweden was a third of the way around the world from Washington, and from Maryland. In a frenzy of tossing his books in a heap on his bed, pulling out his underclothing and deciding what to keep, what to burn, trying on jackets and weskits that no longer fitted him well, one word spun around in his fevered mind: *Lydia.*

Thrilled to see his handwriting again, on the note that came to her several days after the skating party, Lydia Eliza nevertheless had a feeling of foreboding as she found a place by the fire in her bedroom and sat down to read it. It looked like the others, except for the stiffness of the writing.

The few previous messages she had had from him had excited her so much that her fingers shook trying to open them. This one she held in her hands, turning it over and over, as if it might speak to her, as if the act of breaking the seal and unfolding the page might release something frightening. She folded her palms over the letter in a gesture of sheltering it, perhaps from her own eyes or from the light of day. Finally, realizing that she was being melodramatic over something that was probably only a courteous thank-you note for her company, or an assurance that he had recovered from his spill, she reached for the brass letter opener on her writing table and slid it under the wax seal bearing his initial.

"Dear Miss Hollingsworth," he had written, in such careful script that it reminded her of some of her own early efforts when Miss Becky Love had made her follow a ruled line to keep the bottom of the letters straight. His other notes had been almost as scrawly as her own penmanship, but this one showed a great deal of exacting care.

"I am grateful to you for your Company on my recent Visit to Baltimore," he had written. "It was pleasant to meet some of your Friends and to enjoy the beauty of the fine Skating Place near your City." She wondered if he was going to mention his mishap. She hoped not.

"Upon my return to the Federal City"—she could almost feel the tension in his phrases, as if the words had been hard to put down—"I was advised that I am ordered by my government to . . ."

She could read no further. She put her head down in her hands and allowed herself a few moments of the agonized weeping she had been holding back for so long.

"I am ordered by my government to proceed to a new post . . ." The words smeared into a mishmash of ink through her tears. A new post . . . what did it matter where? He was going away. Even Washington was six hours distant. Any other capital might as well be on the nearest planet.

". . . a new post in Stockholm, Sweden." She managed to finish the line. The letter slipped from her fingers and fell to the floor. Another freshet of tears overcame her. "I am to proceed to that City at my earliest Convenience," he had added. "Your company has been one of the most pleasant Experiences of my stay in America. It has indeed been a pleasure to know you."

There are ways and ways of saying "This is the end," she thought bitterly. One of the worst is "It has indeed been a pleasure to know you."

"My warmest regards to your Family," he concluded. "I remain, Respectfully yours, A. J. Foster."

In a postscript, added hastily and with none of the precision of the first handwriting, he had scribbled, "I trust you will enjoy having a little Book that has always been one of my special treasures. It is a prayerbook given me by my aunt, Lady Hawkesbury, on my twenty-first birthday. I have wanted somehow to leave a true part of myself in the New World. A.J.F."

As a gesture of trying to wipe out his memory, she tore the letter to bits and dropped them into the fire, regretting it instantly. When the book arrived several days later she put it away at the back of a dresser drawer, still in its mailing wrapper. There would be time later to look at it. Time? She was rich with time.

She threw herself again into helping her mother with the orphans, taking along little Gracie, hoping she would prove more useful than Pansy, who had been moved to one of the farms. She accepted every bid to assemblies, tea parties, balls and dinners; she attended services at St. Paul's with a devotion and fervor that did not escape her mother's notice. Sensitive and compassionate, Ann said nothing, but she was acutely aware of her daughter's struggle. Debby, realizing that something was amiss, called on Lydia frequently to spend time with Elizabeth and William, pleased to see the way she brightened up when the little girl rushed to her arms. Ann Maria arranged her own activities so that her sister was never left alone.

The fact that the Britisher had been transferred was no secret. He had many Baltimore friends. George Oakley, who took Foster's place and whose fame for his ways with women had preceded him, soon discovered the saucy charms of Madame Bonaparte, who was living with her father and emerging from the despondency of Jerome's betrayal of her. Soon Oakley's team could also find its way there in the dark without a driver.

Neighborhood gossip was intense, but Madame B., to whom the French Minister pointedly referred as Mademoiselle Patterson, had never been disturbed by gossip. Half-married, half-divorced—depending on which side of the ocean one used for a judgment seat—she was steadily taking on more imperial ways as she got farther from the need for them. There was snide talk of "brummagem royalty" as she sat in a box at the theater in Philadelphia, holding court, her son on her lap, like a queen with the Crown Prince on display.

Lydia rarely saw her, and then only for a passing word of greeting. She knew that Foster had been friendly to Betsy, and was afraid that his name might be mentioned and that Betsy's sharp intuition would ferret out her secret. Around town there was talk that Foster had been courting Betsy, but Lydia passed that off as mere idle speculation.

As John Carroll, now raised to the archbishopric, had feared, the Pope had been dragged into the distasteful negotiations with the Bonapartes but had reinforced Carroll's views that the marriage was valid and the child legitimate. For the boy's sake, the Archbishop was glad that he and Patterson had gone to such lengths to avoid legal and ecclesiastical loopholes. The one in need of guidance and protection was young Jerome Napoleon Bonaparte, nicknamed Bo. His mother was not so helpless.

After the French Senate voted Jerome his divorce, Betsy toyed with the idea of having Bo baptized as a Catholic, in order to pry some concessions from France. The boy was already two years old. She finally backed off; the risk of being cut off from her father's fortune was too great. She was lucky that she had not already been disinherited. For the same reason she had not herself become Catholic, although she said it was "the religion of kings."

Bishop Carroll, concerned for the child's immortal soul, was deeply grieved at her cynicism. Attractive and unbelievably willful, she was not above any kind of scheming for personal advantage, with her child as a pawn. Was the sacrament of baptism something to be bought and sold?

When the Britisher had been gone for seven or eight months, Lydia wrote to Ruth to report her safe arrival home after the summer visit to Elkton. The two had considered the merits, pro and con, of several young men who were courting Lydia, and had agreed that Ruth's decision against the tall and sober servant of the Lord was the right one. Lydia did not admit that she had no interest at all in any of her suitors.

It would probably narrow down to the choice between taking second best or sinking into that dry life of spinsterhood that spelled horror.

Her letter told Ruth that Aunt Debby was "thin and well, her children enjoy good health. They were all here an hour yesterday. Tell Aunt Betsey [Mrs. George Adams] William is a fine boy, it will be news for her. He looked very well in his dimity pantaloons. Elizabeth looked like a little doll, in her short clothes, sleeves and bonnet tied with pink ribands."

She was noncommittal about herself. "Morning calls I have made to all." Ah, that morning calling. What a time-filler it was. She was confronted at every third or fourth house with some comment, not always well put, about her and Ann Maria's continued lack of husbands. Deadly.

"I dined and spent an evening at Uncle's and took tea with Molly [Cheston] who made tea below stairs for us. She is perfectly well, little Samuel not as coarse an infant as his brothers were, and his eyes are blue at present, a good baby. Poor Uncle Jessy has had the ague though it is now conquered. He had three shakes. The rest of our friends are in good health. Mama has had her old headaches since her return."

That summer, King Jerome had dispatched the brother of his trusted aide, the Count of Fürstenstein (né Le Camus), to get his son, whom Jerome had never seen. The boy was three years old, with the good looks of both his parents. The young

King of Westphalia felt that his child should be brought up in a court in Europe as befitted his station in life. The demand that she give up the child impressed Betsy as being a royal decree. Furious, she refused.

She wanted an imperial title for herself as well as for her son, and would never be content with less. She often said that if she could get to Napoleon himself she could manage anything she wanted, but she never succeeded in meeting him. (The only other man she really wanted to know but never did was Lord Byron.)

"Well!" Sam stormed into Thomas's house with the evening paper. "This is the last straw! Mr. Bonaparte has added something he calls his Bayonne Decree to all his other decrees so he can rule the world by starvation!"

"What's it say?" Thomas was ready to settle down for a quiet smoke and didn't relish being upset all over again after ten hours in his office.

" 'Any neutral ship caught in European waters will be captured and confiscated.' " Sam slapped at the paper with the back of his hand.

"Oh, my God," Thomas said under his breath.

"And what do our great President and our noble Secretary of State think we should do about it?" Sam roared. "Nothing! Not one damned stinking thing!"

"Not even get us some kind of navy? Or arm our ships?"

"Nothing! Says either side can be brought to its knees by economic pressures. We just won't trade with 'em! We'll trade with ourselves and forget any business that has to go across the water. Like two charwomen scrubbing each other's floors! I guess they figure Baltimore can trade with Havre de Grace and Elkton can trade with Annapolis and we can anchor our fleets in the Chester River! That'll be just dandy!"

"Oh, my God."

Hearing all the noise, Lydia came in from the back of the

house. "What's the matter, Papa? Oh, hello, Uncle Sam. Bad news in the paper?"

"Nothing for women to worry their pretty heads about," Sam said sourly. "But you'd better learn to weave cloth for your clothes, the way your great-grandmother did. And eat only what you and your sweet mother can grow in your little garden plot. And live without sugar. And coffee. And tea. No silks from the Orient, no cottons or woolens from England; can't ship them in. Tobacco, hides, wheat—all our produce will pile up on the docks until it blots out the sun; can't ship it out. Frenchies'll get us. The good old U.S.A. is going to have to crawl into a hole and pull the hole in after us. The whole damned country might as well take the veil—"

"Now, Sam—" The presence of his daughter put some restraint on Thomas, although he agreed with every word and felt that he was being backed inexorably against the wall by powerful enemies at home and abroad.

"Sorry, Lydia. I hope your father won't want to send our ships and our men into that deathtrap. We're cornered. All the neutral shipping is done for. And I get riled up."

"So do I," Thomas said as his shoulders sagged. "It may cheer you up a little, Sam, to find out it's just as bad over there. Lydia, could you find that letter from my sister, Lydia Wallis, up in Pennsylvania? She sent a bunch of clippings from the *Republican Argus* in Northumberland, spelling out what our embargo is doing to Great Britain. I can't see any end!"

Impatiently, Sam took the papers and commenced to read.

. . . against whom does the Embargo operate? Is it not most severely felt by the British, whose government forced the measure on ours? It is much to be deplored that in any country, millions of innocent and industrious people should suffer famine, oppressions and misery to gratify the pride, cupidity, envy and vindictive rage of a few individuals, who compose a corrupt administration; but this is the case in England—and these unfortunate people have but the dernier result of uniting and rising *en masse* to hurl to destruction the authors of their woes.

Sam whistled and took out a handkerchief to mop his brow.

"That isn't all," Thomas told him. "They quote a letter that was brought in from Falmouth in forty-eight days, I think it was on the *Thalia.*"

"Oh, yes." Sam read it aloud. " 'The times are very bad here. The disaffection among the mechanics and manufacturers has arisen to an alarming height, particularly in MANCHESTER and BIRMINGHAM.' They put both those cities in capital letters. Let's see. . . . 'In these places the government has been obliged to call out the MILITARY to disperse the different, tumultuous assemblages. Numbers of the half-starved inhabitants have been killed but the tumult still continues—*and the people cry for vengeance.*' Sounds bad, doesn't it, Thomas?"

"In Manchester, there were 'serious rioting and commotion among our working weavers,' " Lydia read from another clipping, " '. . . hundreds out of employment . . . oatmeal and other provisions advanced in price.' And at Stockport and Bolton the rioting was severe, and when they called for the militia, nobody would come! They said, 'in all likelyhood we shall tomorrow or the next day have occasion for every man ourselves.' Papa, that's awful!"

"I guess you know what the *Argus* thinks the answer is," Thomas said grimly. "Revolution! If it worked here, it can work there. Here's another little piece they reprinted from the Hudson *Balance*: 'Every man in his senses would prefer drawing a tooth, however severe in its operation, to the continual torture of the toothache and its consequences. And no man is fit to live out of Bridewell or Bedlam who would abuse and destroy the operator for his agency in producing the pain inflicted by the operation. If thy tooth offend thee, pluck it out and cast it from thee; thou fool, is it not better thy tooth should be destroyed than that thy whole body perish?' H'm, paraphrasing St. Matthew to stir up a revolt!"

"Nothing funny about it," Sam said as he rose to leave. "I hadn't thought about those poor devils having so much torment just because *we* embargoed *them*. It's the little people that catch it, isn't it?"

"It's everybody, Sam. And when you come up with a nice neat solution, let me be the first to know. Revolution did it here. More or less." He saw Sam to the door and came back to his daughter. "Did you hear about the emperor's new clothes?" he asked with a scowl. "I mean our emperor, Mr. Jefferson. Turned himself out at the Fourth of July doings in a suit made of homespun. Everybody that's anybody these days is doing the same. Pretty soon we'll all look as if we're dressed in slave cloth. I feel like laying in a good stock of quality fabrics just for ourselves, but then, where can I get hold of any if it doesn't come in?"

"I'd better go right away and get the things Ruth wants me to bring her," Lydia said anxiously. "I had no idea it was so bad. There seemed to be ample supplies in the stores last week."

"Sam's a prophet of gloom," Thomas tried to soothe her. "We're not licked yet. And you and Ruth will still be nicely clothed for some time to come, my dear. It doesn't take much for her, does it? Anyway, you let Sam and me do the worrying. We're experts."

The *Leopard-Chesapeake* affair was eased a little when Britain agreed to pay indemnity for the men it had captured, but that was only part of what had been demanded. Jefferson had asked for three things: return of the captured men, indemnity to their families and the government and the immediate cessation of impressment. Releasing the men and paying compensation for them left the even more vital point still up in the air. If impressment didn't stop, all American shipping would stop, and Britain would strangle itself by its need for imports, if it hadn't already. And were the British going to mete out any punishment to Admiral Berkeley? After all, he was the man who had ordered the attack on the unarmed *Chesapeake*. Was it punishment to promote him?

An angry editorial shrieked out in the Baltimore *American and Commercial Advertiser* of July, 1808:

AS WE EXPECTED

We all remember the hypocritical disavowal of the attack on the *Chesapeake* by the British Ministry, and particularly by Mr. Rose and his correspondence with Mr. Madison, ADMIRAL BERKELEY was to be severely PUNISHED for his attack on our national sovereignty and violation of the laws of nations. Now, fellow citizens, mark the punishment. He is to be entrusted with the command of a secret expedition of the first importance which was to have sailed from England after the departure of the *Osage*, perhaps designed for America, to commit new enormities, to perpetrate new murders. *Huzza for our old friends!*

Mention of the *Osage* stirred up even the British sympathizers. The ship had been seized at Falmouth and all its cargo removed so that the British could look for contraband goods being sent through without payment of tribute. When nothing was found, the *Osage* was reloaded and allowed to go belatedly on its way. In taking inventory, the ship's master discovered that items listed on the original manifest were missing: a carton of this, a barrel of that, several cases of something else. The British were pirates! On both sea and land!

When James Madison—small, quiet and reserved, but with the priceless asset of a gay and clever wife—succeeded to the presidency in March of 1809, the Embargo Act was gone, but it was soon followed by more restrictions that brought even louder outcries from the common people in England for the repeal of the Orders in Council.

Mr. Erskine, hounded and harried by the Americans and called pro-American by his own people, made the worst mistake of an erratic career by taking matters into his own hands. Madison had told him quite frankly that the United States was going to arm its merchant fleet—one hundred and twenty thousand men—and give them letters of marque if their neutral shipping continued to be hampered. Brother Jonathan had come to the end of his patience.

Convinced and intimidated, but with absolutely no legal assurance to back him up, Erskine pledged His Majesty's government to suspend the Orders in Council forthwith. For this flagrant insubordination, Erskine was recalled, after the most blistering rebuke ever sent a minister.

He was replaced by Francis James Jackson, previously passed over because of his rudeness and intransigence. In 1802 he had been forced out of Berlin by Napoleon, and he was sent to Denmark. The Danes gave him the name of "Copenhagen" Jackson because of his callous mistreatment of them.

In Sweden, Augustus John Foster heard of the appointment with the greatest misgivings. He felt like holding his hands over his ears to shut out the blast from the inevitable explosion.

Jackson, his Prussian wife and their two children arrived in Washington with pyramids of luggage, a troupe of liveried servants and a splendid landau, the like of which the Yankees had never before seen and were quick to notice.

He took over the Erskines' house, making some acidulous remarks about its filthy condition. Mrs. Erskine had been American-born, which was sufficient reason to expect such neglect. The Jacksons would have to have the property painted, papered, whitewashed and scrubbed, an inconvenience that gave them limitless conversational fodder.

Jackson's fame had gone ahead of him. His initial impact on the Americans confirmed their worst fears. It wasn't long before some of the newspapers were goading their readers to band together and tar and feather Mr. Jackson before he had a chance to Copenhagenize Washington. Ignoring the insults, Jackson, armed with his arrogance, set out on the necessary rounds of diplomatic calling.

Military evidence of American anxiety began to appear. In

August the sloop of war *John Adams* anchored in the Baltimore harbor, her cannons visible, her uniformed sailors spilling into the streets. Lydia and her sister were among the guests invited aboard her. It was a "novel and pleasant entertainment," they later told Ruth. "Mr. D. Murray invited us with several Ladies and Gentlemen to visit. She was lying between the Point and the Fort, therefore we were conveyed to her in Barges from the Wharf—and had a pleasant *row*. We were then hoisted on board in a large armchair ornamented with red cloth and our feet well-secured. This ceremony was rather awkward and looked like the triumphal cars introduced on the stage, however our curiosity was fully gratified by seeing the Vessel in the most beautiful order, the Officers and crew were all on board which to us Girls was quite unexpected and you may suppose a little embarrassing when we perceived the deck lined with soldiers. We went into the Cabin which was very handsomely furnished and were regaled with Cake, Punch, etc. After having seen every part of the Vessel we returned to the barges and were rowed near the Fort, then proceeded home highly pleased with our excursion."

Jackson chose to ignore the saber-rattling, and went on his blustering way. By November, he had gotten himself in so badly that the President would give him only the most elemental courtesy. Secretary of State Robert Smith refused to deal with him at all except in writing. Ann Maria wrote to Ruth that "Mr. Jackson is very handsome. The news of the day is that he and the Secretary of State have had words and that they have refused to negotiate. I am not politician enough to venture the result."

"Have had words . . ." Indeed they had. Through Secretary of the British Legation Oakley, Jackson had requested a special passport for his family so that they might travel in safety when they were in the United States. The Secretary of State responded by announcing in the public press that "as

the same time we drew the dividend on your 12 shares at 12 Dolrs. each amounting to $144, placed to the credit of your Account. You have been informed of the long indisposition of Mr. Cochran's little Daughter and of Sister Deborah's removal to Govanstown about 5 miles for the trial of Country Air, the poor little Creature is yet being a most pitiable spectacle. Sally or Nancy [Ann Maria] visit it almost daily and say if it recovers it will be a miracle. Brother Thomas's family except himself are well, he now goes out a little . . . you can judge how he bears confinement. . . . Sarah sends her love to you and Ruthy as does our Boys and Your Affect. Brother, Sam Hollingsworth."

There was no miracle, except for the little girl's valiant, fruitless struggle to live. At her death she took with her a large part of her mother's heart, and of Lydia's. Little William, already greatly cherished, would never again be scolded or punished. His father, coughing oftener and harder and finding that he needed more and more rest, learned to make excuses so that he could do much of his office work at home, where he could lie down. Deborah found it easiest to sit near him, not speaking, her hazel eyes worshiping him but shadowed with grief, her fingers picking at her dress.

The parlor draperies in South Street were fluttering again as Mr. Oakley stepped up his courtship of Betsy Bonaparte. Lydia, preparing for her summer visit to Ruth and wanting to get away from the memory of the loss of the precious little girl, wrote early in August: "Mme. Bonaparte keeps our street quite gay. Oakley, Secretary to the Legation of His Britannic Majesty [*where had she seen that title before?*] is devoted to her. Every evening that he is here, and he is very little in Washington, he takes tea and is with her until ten at night. Betts are made whether he will offer, and if so whether she will accept or decline. He celebrated his name in Europe by eloping with the Queen of Prussia's sister, then a married woman. Betsy is dressed with care every visit he pays and will make a conquest if she can. How far beyond no one knows."

"It is not proper for her to entertain that man!" Lydia's mother said frequently. "She is married and has a child. And he's not a proper man anyway."

"I know, Mama." Lydia answered absently.

When she finally turned Oakley down, Betsy let him know that it had been an extremely difficult decision because her father had told her that he would disinherit her if she refused him. Or so the gossips said. At any rate, the French were quick to come up with twenty-five thousand dollars to soften the blow.

Lydia herself refused two proposals that winter. The first, from a long-time family friend confounded by the staggering task of raising five children after the death of their mother in childbirth, was painful for her only because she pitied him. That was the only emotion she felt.

With the second turndown, her parents expressed concern for her future. "Theophilus Barry has excellent prospects," her father argued, with his usual practicality. "Good bank account, sound future in the sand-and-gravel business."

"Yes, Papa."

"And he stammers only when he's real scared," her brother put in.

"Yes, Thomas." She pinched his cheek too hard. "So keep quiet!"

"Ouch! That hurt!"

"Oh, really?" She turned to her parents. "Mr. Barry is indeed a fine man. Sober, solid, dependable, good to his mother, money in the bank, keeps his nails clean, goes to church every single Sunday of his life, is a major in the militia and is about as exciting as a river scow. There, I've said it!"

"Lydia!" Her mother's eyes flew wide open.

"And what's more," she said with more fire than she ever remembered allowing to show, "I don't think I could *bear* to spend the rest of my life wondering *which eye to look at!* Now, leave me alone, all of you. Please!"

"Do you want to be an old maid?" Her father put bluntly the question that was just under all their conversations about Lydia's suitors.

"No, Papa, I do not. But I also don't want to marry just anything that comes along, hat in hand, and proves he has enough money to take care of me. Is that all that life amounts to?"

"Such talk!" Her mother gasped. "Honestly, the young people these days! You'd think that—"

"I'm sorry, Mama. I'm truly sorry. But that's just the way it is." She was close to tears. Couldn't they ever understand? Had her mother forgotten so soon?

The climax of the Christmas assemblies was the annual Twelfth Night ball, which was "celebrated by one Mrs. Smith Hollins," Lydia wrote to Ruth, "and transferred to Miss Stricker, as the succeeding Queen. Thomas was chosen her King."

She had never been prouder of her brother, now taller than she, and with a bubbling gaiety under his surprisingly good manners. He and Elizabeth Stricker, who had known each other from their childhood, made a stunning pair, she in ivory taffeta and diamonds, he in immaculate evening clothes, a ruffled jabot on his shirt, his dark hair in gleaming waves. If only Ruth could have seen him! She was so fond of Thomas.

"Madame Jerome was there," she continued, "as handsome as ever but a little more in the fashion of uncovering."

"How could she be?" Her mother sniffed.

"She is delighted with her late excursion," Lydia wrote. "Her coach has not yet been exhibited. She showed me her livery—drab-coloured cloth with scarlet trimmings. She tells me neither she nor her son, which surprised me, has a title yet, though Napoleon supports them now, and promises the other, at a time not specified. We have seen Madame Reubel [Henrietta Pascault], she has improved in her manners, they are softer and more affable. Those ladies have not met."

So Betsy was finally beginning to live in the grand manner that Jerome had prescribed for her but had never undergirded with money. Now Napoleon was paying for it. When she accepted the Emperor's offer, Jerome had laughed, but Betsy retorted that she'd rather be under the wing of an eagle than of a goose.

Sometime around her twenty-fourth birthday, on February 13, 1810, Lydia decided that she would try to consider seriously the next proposal that came her way.

There were probably worse things than not being in love with your husband. Not having one, for instance. And sometimes love came afterward, simply from propinquity. In Oriental countries marriages were never for love, she had heard. Some were said to be happy ones. The percentage was probably about the same as in the more enlightened nations.

At approximately the same time, Augustus John Foster received a curt note advising him that his services were no longer needed in Sweden. His old acquaintance, Napoleon Bonaparte, was taking over the country and the Honorable Mr. Foster was therefore an enemy alien.

Chapter Eleven

I Am Like a Green Olive Tree

The following winter Mr. Foster was forced to go to Ireland to look over the affairs of his father's estate. It was a long overdue journey and not too pleasant in the season of high winds, rain and cold. He had been courting a young lady named Annabella Milbanke, but he was not completely sure of his feelings about her. He was puzzled by her occasional withdrawal and moodiness. In many ways she would make a suitable and acceptable wife for him. She had a title, was intelligent, attractive, attentive, and both her mother and his mother approved of their romance. Being at a distance and across an expanse of water would give him time to put his thoughts in better perspective. I may not be in love with her, he brooded.

On a particularly chilly and depressing day he received a letter from his mother, who, after long years of their irregular relationship, had married the widowed Duke of Devonshire. When the first Duchess died in 1806, Lady Elizabeth Foster was inconsolable; they had been the most intimate of friends. Nearly three years passed before she married the Duke. Augustus was almost twenty-nine years old when he acquired a stepfather, and his illegitimate half brother and half sister, to whom he was devoted, were nearly grown.

He settled down by the fire to see what tidbits of gossip and information about people in high places she was sending him. Her close contacts in the top strata of British political and social life were his most valuable asset, and he knew it. He slit the seal eagerly. He was lonely there in Ireland.

A second letter on distinctive crested stationery fell into his lap. He picked it up with only moderate curiosity. It was not uncommon for his mother to pass along to him some of the communications that came to her or the Duke. He opened the folded page, then caught his breath as the full import of the words struck him.

"I have the pleasure to announce to you, my dearest Duchess," he read, "that I have this day assented to the nomination of Mr. Augustus Foster as Minister to the United States of America. I hope this will meet with your approbation as nothing can ever afford me more pleasure than whatever I know can convey satisfaction both to yourself as well as the dear Duke—I remain ever most truly and sincerely your affectionate Friend and humble Servant, George, P.R." The letter was dated "Carlton House, Feb. 14, 1811."

"I say! I say!" He held the paper close to his eyes to make sure he was seeing it correctly, and raced through it again. "I say! The Prince Regent! I say! *America!*" There could be no mistake.

He wanted to laugh, to shout, to skip, then just to sit still and pound the palm of his hand against his temple to knock loose any cobwebs that might be fogging his thinking. "America! Minister! Not just an underling. *Minister!*"

Finally getting control of himself he began reading his mother's letter. He laughed aloud as he read her disclaimer. "You will believe that I never said one word about you to him or anybody else." The statement was probably true, as far as it went. She could say all kinds of things without speaking.

The historian Edward Gibbon, whose marriage proposal she had refused, said of her that "If she chose to beckon the Lord Chancellor from his woolsack in full sight of the world, he could not resist obedience." Gibbon had read her a chapter of the manuscript for his new book *The History of the Decline and Fall of the Roman Empire,* and she had listened with such rapturous attention that he fell in love with her. In spite of her rejection of his offer, they remained friends for life.

"Well, let's see what else she gives me," her son murmured. "So, he sent her the message at the play. H'm! Mr. P. Regent didn't want the appointment to be kept secret anyway. A nice touch." He continued reading: "The Prince . . . makes me suppose that in the present situation in which we stand with America it is considered as an important and advantageous mission and it is one in which you are first and therefore all the credit will be yours and distinctions will probably follow . . . a period of great consequence to this country . . . if she [Annabella] has any liking for you the idea of going would make her decide in your favour."

He walked over to look out a window at the sleeting rain. "Come now, Mother, let me handle my own affairs of the heart," he muttered as he went on with her letter, ". . . perhaps get it exchanged for some other Country she would like . . ." He tossed the letter onto a table. "Some other country! Does she think I am a complete nincompoop? *America!*"

He astonished himself by leaping in the air and kicking his heels together, something he hadn't tried since he was fourteen. A quick look around assured him that no servants had seen his outburst, and he began rereading the note from the Prince Regent, savoring every word. He knew that the awesome weight of responsibility would descend upon him soon enough, but for that day, which suddenly seemed sunlit and shining, he could exult in this new milestone on the thorny path of diplomacy, which he had chosen as his way of life.

He would have some weeks to prepare himself and to be instructed in great detail by his government; it had taken them more than four years to become aware of his existence and of what he considered his great potential. There had not been a minister in Washington since Jackson's precipitate departure.

In Baltimore, Mr. Cochran's health had become so alarming that he resolved to seek some sunshine, and, he hoped, some strength, on the island of Barbados, where he had some business connections. Deborah was torn a dozen ways. They had never been apart since their marriage, and she had an absolute horror of the sea. Her husband often teased her that an inch of water in a birdbath upset her.

She even debated going to the wharf to see him off. The sight of the boats and of the icy, choppy waves was sure to be terrifying. But if she did not go she would be deprived of those last few moments of her adored husband's company, so she went, clinging miserably to his arm until the very last instant, admonishing him to take care of himself, wear warm clothes, write to her every day, come home safe and well and strong again, and not to ever, ever go near the rail of the ship.

She had a few private words with the captain, who tried to hide his annoyance at being advised of his duty. She lectured the dock hands, huge Negroes who were toting the shipments into the hold and would not, of course, leave with the ship. "Take care of my husband! Take care of my dear Mr. Cochran! Don't let anything happen to my darling Mr. Cochran!"

Ann and Thomas took her to their house for tea to help her get braced for the long lonely weeks ahead. Lydia had watched the parting of the pair with envy. The warmth of their love was the sort of thing she dreamed of, something nearly holy in its beauty. Did all marriages have such devotion and adoration at their core?

"At least there's a doctor with him," Debby said tearfully, for the twentieth time. "My dear husband trusts Dr. Donaldson, and I know he's in good hands. And the Lord will protect them, don't you think, brother?"

"Yes, my dear, I know He will," Thomas soothed her, embarrassed at the glimpse he was having of her innermost heart.

"And our dear Dr. Bends sent a message to some friends of his in Barbados, also ministers of the Gospel. I'm sure they will welcome him."

"Of course," said Ann. "And he'll come back so strong and so refreshed that you will hardly recognize him."

"I hope so," Debby said sadly. "I devoutly hope so. I greatly fear for his lungs."

Six weeks passed before she had any word from him, weeks that were as difficult for her relatives as for herself. Deborah was never one to disguise her feelings. On February 4, 1811, Lydia wrote to her Aunt Ruth the good news that "Mr. Cochran has arrived out safely, with a passage of 27 days. One of the owners who went with him has written from a different port. Aunt expects a letter by the *Hiram* daily. This news is most acceptable to her. She has perused the Marine lists with great interest every evening."

"If I know Deborah," Stephen commented when the letter arrived in Elkton, "she has not only perused the marine lists, she has nearly devoured them."

On the twelfth, Debby could gather up paper, pen and ink and send her own joyous message up the bay. "I can write you now, my dear Sister, and give you the information more greatful to my feelings than anything on this Earth except that of seeing Mr. Cochran. I yesterday received a large packett of letters from my dear Husband, two lengthy ones to me, one to his brother David, and one to Brothers [Thomas and Samuel Hollingsworth]. They contain everything that I could possibly wish and a great deal more than I could have expected for at this time. I hope I may be sufficiently thankful to the Almighty for His great goodness in protecting and restoring those whom I hold most dear on earth. . . . He was never an hour sick, relished every meal and arrived safe at Barbados the 28th Ulta after a passage of 3 weeks, which was spent as agreeably as the nature of the situation would admit of—since leaving home he says I have felt no symptom of any of my former complaints, and have enjoyed an excellent appetite nor has it failed me on shore, where the fare is better than I had expected, the Island being well supplied ever with Irish potatoe's, Butter, etc., by a Cork Fleet which had arrived only two days before then . . . to a person coming from a Northern climate and in the winter Season, the appearance of all nature in complete bloom and verdure is astonishing and delightful beyond my poor power of expressing."

Deborah had read that line to any and all she met. It was so poetic.

"The Town," she went on with her copying, "which is said to contain only 20,000 Souls, ⅕ Whites and ⅘ Blacks and Coloured, including about 3000 troops, is if possible more complicated in its plan than even New York. The streets are very narrow, but quite clean, being either paved with stones or covered with a kind of gravel, Marl and sand which absorbs rain and renders them always pleasant. The Gentlemen to whom I brought letters have been very polite in their offers, he observes, I spent last Evening at a pretty large party of both sexes and all ages where music and dancing constituted the principal amusements of the Younger part, while the more advanced and sedate among whom I ranked myself, entertained ourselves with conversation. Dr. Donaldson, Mr. Walker and himself retired about 11 o'clock but the rest of the Company did not break up until 3 o'clock in the morning.

"He has dined and suped with an intimate friend of Dr. Bends in Barbadoes, is under an engagement also Dr. D. to visit another friend of Dr. B. 14 miles distant also to spend a rural day with Mr. Cadogan at one of his Plantations where he is to shew him his sugar works."

She pushed away a stray lock of hair from her forehead, stopping for a moment to imagine herself sitting beside her loved one, looking at tropical plantations and reveling in the summery sun, but the vision was so painful that she went back to her paper. ". . . attended several of their places of worship. One Sunday morning they went to the Episcopal Church of St. Michaels where he heard a sermon of about 15 minutes preached, in a handsome House to a very thin and listless congregation of fashionable looking people. Also visited the Barracks. Saw the General, Sir Charles Shiplet, and heard with delight a Band of the 66th Regiment composed of about 40 musicians.

"Mr. Cochran says they are comfortable fixed in lodging . . . expects in a short time to find a sheet sufficient. He says their time as yet has been chiefly occupied in making and receiving visits and walking through the Town and its environs; the latter of which towards the North and East have delightful outlets, the one leading by the Governor's or King's House and the other by the Castle or Barracks, about a mile out of Town . . . mornings passed in reading and eating oranges until breakfast is ready which is after nine o'clock, dine at 4 o'clock . . . the Citizens he is exceedingly pleased with. . . . I wish you could hear all. He says you may therefore conclude that I will pass a few months as agreeably as it will be possible separated from you and our dear Son . . . indeed this is the only want I feel; but this want recurs every day, and every hour of the day."

She had read and reread that paragraph to Lydia and Ann Maria so many times that Lydia had to shut her ears. Every day, and every hour of every day was something she understood quite well. And the Cochrans had hope to sustain them.

Mr. Cochran was not expected home until mid-May, but early in April Deborah received a brief message saying that he was so much better and so lonesome for her that he was taking an earlier ship. Immediately she started watching the winds, the marine lists, the sky—wearing herself out with her eagerness and her worry. Within three days of his message he arrived in person, ringing the bell late at night and calling out for her. She came flying down the steps in her wrapper, having just retired, and was in his arms, weeping and laughing and covering his face with kisses.

The next morning she brought him to be shown off to the relatives, and Lydia could report that "the voyage has been highly beneficial." She could not, and did not, add that the sight of their happiness in being reunited after his long and dangerous absence was almost more than she could bear.

That night she and Ann Maria lay awake, talking of the numerous balls they had attended that spring, since a group of Philadelphia belles had again been in town.

"Four dancing parties last week and two this week," Ann Maria counted up. "And now all these weddings. Everyone is getting married. Except us! The last leaves on the branch," she said lightly. "Not that I care. There was your old flame, J. Carroll, marrying Achsah Ridgely. And Cousin Levi's announcement at the New Year's Day dinner! He's already past forty! Ann Dorsey is lovely."

"What about old Mr. Ben Williams?" Lydia asked, glad to get away from their own affairs. "He must be eighty! Everyone says that Mrs. Crosby doesn't know how she's going to run her boardinghouse without him. He's lived there for most of his life. And he's marrying that French widow, Mrs. Moreton, young enough to be his granddaughter."

"I was guessing that Cousin Sally wouldn't accept young Dr. Gibson," Ann Maria said sleepily, "but Uncle Sam says she will, and he's delighted. A professor of surgery at the medical college, and with a fine private practice too—if he'd asked me, I'd have taken him right off, instead of making him wait the way Sally has."

"Me too." Lydia yawned and stretched.

"Really?" her sister's voice was soft and reflective. "I half thought there was someone a little extra special in your heart. . . ."

☆

The announcement of the appointment and imminent arrival of the new British minister was made early in the summer. Lydia had come in from a tiring day of shopping in preparation for her trip to Elkton, wanting to have all the things Ruth Tobin had requested ready and in good order so that she could take everything with her. She had slipped off her shoes and was sitting on the Chippendale sofa in the back parlor, checking off the items on her long list. "Corded gingham . . . I hope she'll like these colors—red, blue and buff. A purple shawl for Aunt Ruth. I thought the white ones with the flowered borders not quite suitable for her. I must return her change, twenty-five cents. A paper of pins, four yards of ribbons—"

With a gay whoop, her brother burst into the room and announced in a dramatically impressive voice, "It gives me great pleasure, my dear sister, to inform you—" he stopped to find his place in the newspaper he had in his hand, "to inform you that the Honorable Augustus John Foster, recently secretary of the British Legation in Naples, Italy, after a similar post in Stockholm, has been named minister plenipotentiary to the United States of America and will arrive in Washington sometime before the next Congress convenes in October."

His voice raised in intensity until he was almost shouting. "Mr. Foster was in America for three years . . ."

Lydia's long-built-up defenses crumbled without warning. She sat shivering and nearly ill as her brother boomed through the remainder of the news paragraph. "Mr. Foster is a bachelor, stepson of the Duke of Devonshire, nephew of Lord Liverpool, grandson of the late Earl of Bristol and Bishop of Derry. It is understood by the Department of—"

Lydia heard only the first phrase of the pedigree. He was still unmarried. Maybe he was the type who chose to remain single, being either too fussy, or too arrogant, or too insufferable, or too selfish—none of those adjectives fitted him. The truth must be that he had not yet found anyone. And he was coming back. An impossible dream was becoming a possible reality.

Almost with apprehensiveness she began to watch the mails. It was the only thing she could do, since it would be the height of impropriety to make any overt move to reach him. There was a chance, of course, that he did not remember her, or for some reason might not wish to see her. When no message came, she was convinced of it.

Numbly she went off to Elkton, laden with parcels for Ruth and messages from everyone. She looked forward to the fresh brightness of the country and the lift to her spirits that she always found there. Ruth and their uncle Stephen were waiting near the wharf, Stephen announcing that he had rented a section of Zeb's warehouses to have a place to store Lydia's burdens until he could make several round trips with his biggest wagon and get them all transported for Ruth. Each year he had some variation of the same joke to greet her with; if he had forgotten it, she would not have felt welcome.

Ruth fell on Lydia with delight. "How's Thomas? And Ann Maria? Are your parents well? Does Thomas enjoy his new boat? You wrote me that he had one. Could you find the dress linen?" The barrage of her questions set Lydia talking and laughing immediately, which was what she had been hoping for.

Aunt Ruth had just had another of her frequent brushes with death and was crotchety and demanding, hardly allowing her niece to leave her side. Lydia saw that the confinement was hard on Ruth, and resolved to find ways of getting her away from the house while a servant stayed with the old lady. Rain or shine, Ruth must escape at least once a day.

The two cousins took long walks, with the slave Rachel posted in the sickroom. Lydia felt the need of storing up memories of the breadth of open sky out in the fields, the beauty of the deep forests, the soft cheerful gurgling of creeks and rivers, as a kind of bulwark for the days ahead. That name which she had not spoken in all the long months since his departure would now be in the papers and on everyone's lips, as politics and business inevitably collided. So much depended on him; she had been saying silent, secret prayers for his wisdom and strength.

Young Thomas would keep an eye out for every mention of him, and would never fail to call it to her attention. Ann Maria and her mother would be watching her covertly. Her father would be inquiring as to why the young Englishman that he had liked so well hadn't come around, at least on business. Yes, she would need every ounce of inner strength that she could manage.

The day for her departure came all too soon. Ruth and Stephen went to the Landing with her, kissed her fondly and stood waving and trying to smile. Biddle, long familiar with this annual leave-taking, gave the boat whistle an extra toot as they passed some of the islands and slipped out of sight. Lydia pulled herself away from the railing with resignation and went to find a place inside for the boring hours ahead. There was a storm brewing. The trip down the bay would be rough. Some people could sleep on the packet, even in the worst weather, but she could not. She wished belatedly that she had brought along something to read, or perhaps some needlework, anything to occupy her time.

Aunt Polly and Uncle Zeb, both quite feeble, had come out to the dock and had given her a bountiful lunch to take along, as well as the bushel of apples they sent each fall. Polly prided herself on her picnic lunches, packed in one of the special straw baskets that the Hollingsworth ships brought in from Bermuda. Lydia had a rather amazing collection of them at home, colorful and useful, in several sizes. Occasionally Aunt Debby used one for carrying some of her custard to the sick. The baskets always brought the shut-ins much pleasure, whether the custard did or not.

She found a sheltered place under her seat for the lunch so that she could keep watch over it. There was often a rowdy crowd on the packet riding down from Havre de Grace, men returning from the races, either drunk because they had won or drunk because they had lost, carousing, unruly, loud, dirty and altogether unpleasant. She wanted her place to be secure before any of them boarded.

Sometimes there were other, more respectable travelers as well, businessmen who had come down the Turnpike from Lancaster—mothers and children visiting relatives, old gentlemen looking over property in Baltimore—but such passengers were in the minority. When she was younger her parents always made arrangements for some member of the family or some close friend to accompany her as a protection, but in recent years she went alone.

"Just stay by yourself," her mother warned her. "Don't talk to anyone."

"Yes, Mama. You've told me before."

"If anything happens, scream for Biddle," her father advised. "He'll watch out for you. Biddle's a good man, known you all your life."

"Yes, Papa."

"And always take good care of your money. Put it in a *safe place,*" her mother added meaningfully. "Thieves and robbers are everywhere."

"Yes, Mama. Thieves and robbers."

The storm, gathering momentum and beginning to spit angry fountains of water, almost obliterated the docks and the hurrying, pushing crowd of people who were waiting to get on board when they finally reached Havre de Grace.

She had chosen a seat well forward to starboard, so that she could watch for the spires of Baltimore and see more quickly who had come to the pier to meet her. Polodore of course, his ebony face shining. Her father, if at all possible, smiling from ear to ear. Possibly her brother, although he had not been well since he had taken a bad dousing in a sailing accident earlier in the summer. His hands had spells of painful aching and were beginning to twist out of shape, the skin over the joints puffed and shiny. Sometimes he would waken at night with such a stab of agony that his cries woke up the household. Those incidents embarrassed him greatly, and he would be quiet and apologetic the next day, staying off by himself and not wanting to talk of his pain.

Lydia worried about Thomas. Even Dr. Gibson, Sally's suitor, whom her family considered the finest medical man in Baltimore, could not find an effective way to relieve him. Hot compresses, plenty of rest, a good diet. They followed his instructions to the letter, but there were no visible results. Dr. Donaldson was equally baffled.

Young Thomas had been so happy that summer. He was spending every spare moment on the river, and when there was time, out on the bay, sailing the sleek little sloop his father had surprised him with for his twenty-first birthday. His conversation, which for most of his life had centered on horses and saddles and fox hunting, shifted abruptly to spinnakers, sheets, bowlines, masts, winds, tillers. Every Friday he watched the weather carefully, hoping that his time off from his father's office on Saturday could be spent in the sloop.

Getting braver and more confident of his skill, he had asked Elizabeth Stricker to go for a sail. It was a perfect day, a day designed for a sailor, he had announced at breakfast; his father, seeing his own youth reflected in his handsome son, agreed.

"Miss Stricker," he told her with a gallant bow, "you are to be skippered today by the safest and bravest and strongest sailor in the whole State of Maryland. I had to convince your father, and your mother, and my father, and my mother—everybody—before I even dared ask you."

"I believe you, Thomas," she had told him brightly. "I trust you."

But they had upset, far out in the bay. Miss Stricker had nearly drowned because she couldn't swim, and it was a very long time before men on a workboat from the docks saw Thomas's frantically waving white shirt and managed to haul them to safety. They were both badly chilled in spite of the warmth of the day.

"We were skimming along as nice as you please, Papa," he told his father through chattering teeth as he finally sat wrapped in a blanket at home. "You know how it is, you always go farther than you think you do. And the day was so perfect. Wasn't it a perfect day, Papa?"

"Yes, I guess it was, son. For a while anyway," his father said under his breath, wondering what great good fortune had spared the boy to him.

"We had a following breeze, the water was smooth . . . it felt like being a bird flying along. Miss Stricker was so pretty in her blue dress—just the color of the water. I guess that's why they didn't see her at first and thought I was out there alone. Did you see her, Papa?"

"I saw her," he said quietly. "I helped to lift her into the carriage. Hardly weighs more than a canary, even when she's soaking wet."

"Well, when I saw how far from home we were, I decided to tack to get us headed this way again—I don't see how it could have happened, Papa, I really don't. I'm a *very* careful sailor, and I told her exactly what to do, but she must have moved the wrong way at just the wrong moment. She knows better . . . she told me so . . . and the boom hit her . . . not hard, but it scared her. You know how skittish women are, don't you, Papa?" he asked anxiously.

"I guess."

". . . and she fell backwards and I tried to grab her and the sheet froze somehow. It was all so fast. The sail went down and under like—like someone throwing a flag into the water. And we—we capsized . . . and I told her . . . I told her . . . hang on to the boat, I told her . . . *hang on to the boat!* Is she all right, Papa? I've got to go see if she's all right!" He tried to squirm out of the blankets, his face flushed with fever. "I need some dry clothes."

"Stay where you are," his father said sternly. "Ann Maria

just came from the Strickers. The girl is doing fine, just scared, but she's all right. And her parents don't seem to be blaming you. Here, take some of this whiskey. Are you warm enough? Your mother is getting some soup."

"I'm burning up, Papa. And I must have cramped my fingers trying to get that sheet loosened out there in the sloop. I—I can't open my hand. Is she all right? Are you sure, Papa?"

"Miss Hollingsworth?" Lydia jumped as she thought she heard her name through the tumult of the new passengers who were scrambling for seats, stowing baggage, cursing the weather and each other and their luck, stumbling over feet.

"Thieves and robbers," she thought quickly, "thieves and robbers . . ." She had wrapped herself in such a cocoon of thought, worrying about her brother, that she found it hard to realize where she was.

"Miss Hollingsworth? May I sit down?" The words were unmistakable, the voice well-modulated and courteous, the accent undeniably, crisply, beautifully British.

In disbelief and confusion, she allowed her gaze to move slowly upward from his polished shoes to the hands that were her first memory of him and at last to the round face that she had given up hope of ever seeing again. She looked quickly away. Her mind, deeply troubled and concerned about that other young man so close to her heart, must be playing tricks.

"Perhaps you don't remember me?" The voice had an edge of laughter.

She could reply only by a sustained exhalation of breath. "I—" She covered her face with her hands; then, coming to her senses, she pulled her skirts tighter around her, her face flaming, her pulse thumping wildly. "Please do sit down. There's—there's plenty of room."

"How are you?" he asked conversationally when he had settled himself and made sure he was not crowding her. "I'm very happy to see you, Miss Hollingsworth."

"I—I'm fine," she gulped. "And you?"

"I'm doing very well now," he said with a slight smile, "but for a while there I was a little anxious, thinking that I had miscalculated and that you might not be on this boat. These other stalwart citizens taking up most of the space seem not to be quite your kind." She noticed that there was a dimple in the side of his cheek. He was a little heavier, but not much, and only subtly older, but vastly more self-assured.

"On this—on this boat? How—what made you think—I mean, how could you know? Were you hunting me?"

"I've been corresponding with your father," he said with a touch of smugness. "I wrote to him soon after I reached America, to find out—well, to ascertain . . . Well, I have very much wanted to see you again—" He was stammering just as she had been, and the well-remembered color was rising on his neck.

"You've been writing to *Papa?* Have you *really?* He didn't tell me!"

"I asked him not to," Foster confessed. "You had already gone to Elkton when he responded to my inquiry, and so I thought I could—well, I hope you like being surprised, Miss Hollingsworth?"

"I love it," she whispered too low to be heard.

"I've been up in Pennsylvania, getting away from Washington's heat, just as I used to do. I waited for this packet at Havre de Grace and sent my man and my luggage on to Baltimore. I understand that some person named Gadsby has bought the Indian Queen? It won't be quite the same with a new name. Say, I *am* glad to find you! A ride down the bay in this weather would be insanity otherwise. Are we in one of those hurricanes I've heard about?"

He went to catch her gloves, which had gone flying from her lap as the ship tossed like an eggshell in the violence of the storm. He leaned down to look her full in the face. "Yes, I was right," he announced happily.

"Right?" She thanked him for the gloves and returned his gaze for only a moment, fearful of betraying her feelings and worried that she was still dreaming.

"You are beautiful. I was right. Beautiful."

"O-h-h . . ."

Great sheets of rain were pelting the windows. Ordinarily Lydia would have been terrified and nearly as hysterical as Aunt Debby, but now she was so overwhelmed by the magic of Foster's presence that she scarcely noticed it. A fearful crack of thunder and lightning was followed by a sudden quiet in the crowded ship. Surely they would have to tie up somewhere, she thought, as dispassionately as if she were not at all involved.

"How is your family?" he asked, after a bad pitch had nearly sent both of them to the floor.

"Very well. At least they were when I left home. My brother has been ill."

"Thomas?"

"You know his name?"

"Of course. What has been wrong with him? Nothing serious, I hope."

"He was in a sailing accident. There is swelling in his hands and sometimes in his ankles. But you don't want to hear of our troubles. Please tell me what you've been doing. . . . I mean, where you've been since you left America. I—I thought you'd never—"

"Never be here again, eh?" He smiled. "Well, neither did I. But here I am, and with a great deal of hard work ahead of me."

"I know," she said anxiously. "All the talk is of war. Everywhere. Even among the farmers up in Elkton. And my two cousins who are state senators—and the people in Baltimore—everyone is worried! We mustn't have war! Is it really so bad? Is there anything that—?"

"That I can do?" he finished her sentence. "I hope so."

"So do I." She dared to smile at him for the first time.

"I shall do my best, my—my dear cousin," he said with a twinkle in his eye. "And now, perhaps I should go look around this magnificent frigate and see if there is some kind of buffet—"

"Buffet?"

"Some place where they can prepare some food for us to help us pass the turbulent hours of our journey, in case the skipper wins out over the storm."

"Food? Oh, I have a picnic basket with me. My aunt Polly sends one because she thinks the cooking on the packet doesn't amount to much. This time she brought a simply enormous lunch." Lydia reached under her seat and pulled out the gaily colored basket. "Why, she sent enough for—tell me, Mr. Foster, did my aunt Polly know that you would be on this boat?"

"Aunt Polly? I never heard of anyone named Aunt Polly. Is she another Hollingsworth?" he asked blandly.

"She sent enough food for six people!"

"How nice! I am a bit hungry. But there are only two of us. Unless perhaps some of these other creatures are in your circle of admirers?" He looked around curiously, frowning and shaking his head.

"There's even a little note for you! Uncle Zeb wants to welcome you back to America! Oh, Mr. Foster!"

"That was kind. I hope all your countrymen feel that way, Miss Hollingsworth."

"They knew!" Lydia gasped. "Everybody knew! Everybody but me!"

"Sly, that's what I am," Foster said contentedly. *"Sly!* Perhaps you should warn your government to watch out for me, my lovely and blushing cousin!"

Chapter Twelve

Vine and Fig Tree

Their turbulent ride down the bay gave them hours for conversation. No one on the packet knew either of them, and Biddle was desperately busy trying to save his ship and his passengers. In spite of their apologetic efforts, the pitching of the storm frequently threw Foster and Lydia against each other. After a while it seemed witless to resist.

When the first confusion of their meeting wore off and they could smile at each other and breathe in anything but short, excited gulps, Foster began talking of his hopes and dreams. Lydia's absorption in every word he said and her encouragement by the right kind of questions, combined with their isolation in the midst of the noisy crowd, had set him to talking in a way that stunned him when he looked back on it later. There was no one in America with whom he could speak freely, except his long-time friend John Randolph, and he had much on his mind. He had forgotten how raptly she could listen.

I must have rattled along like a runaway stage.

Lydia had guessed correctly on many of his tastes and attitudes. She never repeated any of that conversation, even to Ann Maria. She appreciated the privilege of being let in on some of the deeper thoughts of a man with far-reaching responsibilities on his shoulders. She had had no idea that such a person might have a serious worry as to how he was doing, a secret doubt of his abilities. Beneath his outward self-assurance, she could sense he was striving for answers, struggling to know that whatever path he chose was the right one.

He had such hopes! From listening to her father and uncles, she could see that his hopes were theirs, on a much larger scale. He had in his hands the power to achieve them, which they did not. He was careful not to mention names, but she was aware that there were men of power and influence in the government whom he hoped to be able to persuade to his point of view. By convincing a few he hoped to influence many.

She saw him again on Sunday morning at St. Paul's, his back as straight as ever, his deportment sober and dignified, almost withdrawn. He sat in the pew and listened with concentration as the rector admonished his parishioners to look to the Lord for guidance and assured them that their faith would see them through the Valley of the Shadow and bring them finally to the glories of Heaven. During prayers, a stolen glance showed her that he was on his knees in an attitude of the greatest supplication and humility. After the service, as she waited on the steps while her parents exchanged pleasantries with Dr. Bends, the Englishman came up to her, his face showing his delight in seeing her.

"Miss Hollingsworth! It's a fine morning, isn't it?"

Lydia was aware that several pairs of eyes were focused on her, and that most of the viewers were aware of the gentleman's identity. Never one for public display, she nevertheless felt a moment of pride at his attention. He stood near her, greeting others he recognized, until Thomas and Ann came out, then fell into step with them as they walked to their carriage. Handing Lydia in, he asked, "May I call on you, Miss Hollingsworth, perhaps sometime today?"

Not waiting for Lydia to reply, her father interjected, "Glad to have you, sir. Do come for tea."

"About five o'clock," her mother said, as the carriage door closed and Robert lifted the reins to drive them off.

"Papa! You *shouldn't!*"

"Shouldn't what, daughter?" he asked serenely. "I like that fellow. Know your mother wouldn't mind having him for tea. Knew we had to let him come when he wants to come. He's a very busy man."

"But—but he was asking *me!*" Lydia felt like a sullen child.

"I notice he didn't refuse," her father grunted. "Seemed pleased."

"What if *I* had refused? What if I didn't want him to come?"

"Never once thought of that. Never once. Maybe I'd better ask Robert to turn back and see if we can find him."

"No, Papa. It's all right."

In the evening, the two of them sat in the emerald brocade wing chairs at either side of the fireplace in the front parlor, chatting easily, like the good friends they were getting to be.

Polodore, sent by her mother, stepped in now and then to see if anything was wanted. Young Thomas came home from calling on Miss Stricker, wanting to greet Foster but apologizing for not shaking hands. Foster noted how wan and pale he looked. His gait was slow and awkward; he was not at all like his usual self.

"I'm not being rude, sir." He grinned. "It's just that my fingers are giving me a bit of trouble. Glad to see you again."

Ann Maria brought a tray of sweets and stayed for three or four minutes on the edge of a chair, leaving the door ajar as she went out. Lydia was aware of her family's none-too-subtle chaperoning, but the moments with the Englishman were so precious that she would not allow anything—not anything—to rob her of enjoying them.

She told him of the exciting and dangerous voyage that her cousin Jacob, with his friends George Howard and George Pinckney, had made that spring to Portugal, finding life in

Baltimore discouraging and unrewarding for a young man wanting to get started in business.

"With the blockades—" she began, then wanted to bite her tongue, wondering why she had to say just that. "Well, anyway, Jacob decided very suddenly to go, and Aunt Sarah called us to come and hem cravats for him. They had to get him ready for that enormous trip with only a few days' notice. What a flurry! Then it was more than three months before we had any word from them at all. Weeks and weeks and weeks. We didn't even know—"

The unfinished sentence hung in the air. Finally she went on, "Many of the ships that leave here don't get to—"

"My men sink them," he said bluntly.

"Oh, I didn't mean that!"

"Neither did I." He grinned. "But we get blamed for it, don't we? Tell me, what ship did they go on, and did they get back safely?"

"The *Rockingham*. Yes, they're back. It was a tremendous adventure. And the moment that Jacob got home he rode thirty-six miles to visit Anne Gooding, our little neighbor, who was staying at a summer place in the mountains. It looks like a wedding! And George Howard is to marry Prudence Ridgely shortly. My sister and I will be attendants. Those fellows nearly talked an arm off anyone who would listen when they got home. They had seen so many things."

They sat quietly, feeling no particular need for saying anything, both of them content. Her brother came in again, excusing himself for interrupting. "I wanted to ask Mr. Foster," he said eagerly, "if he saw that comet we had last month. We were supposed to have an eclipse of the sun on the same day! Imagine! I saw the comet from our third floor, but it didn't have any tail on it, just a circle of light around it. And my cousins and I smudged some old pieces of glass so we could look at the eclipse, but it didn't amount to much."

Intrigued, Foster leaned forward. "I did hear talk of it,

but I was in Pennsylvania then and saw nothing. An eclipse and a comet on the same day! Perhaps that's some kind of omen—or aren't you superstitious?"

"If I'm going to be superstitious, I want only good things to come of it," Thomas said lightly. "If there's to be an eclipse of something, I want it to be quick and soon over. None of this lingering-death stuff for me. And if there's a comet—"

"That should be something new and bright and wonderful, eh?"

"That says it! New and bright and wonderful. And it should do great things, like making everyone in the world happy. Say, how's that for wishing on a star?"

"Make everyone happy?" Foster mused aloud when Thomas had left. "I wonder what it would take?"

"Health, I'd guess," Lydia ventured. "That would make Thomas happy, I know. Friends. That's what I enjoy."

"Yes?"

"Peace. That's what everyone wants, isn't it, Mr. Foster?"

"I suppose. But only on his own terms, his own kind of peace," he said cryptically. "Wealth? Wasn't it your Ben Franklin who said something about being healthy, wealthy and wise? How do you feel about wealth, my dear cousin? Is it important?"

Lydia didn't answer immediately. Finally she said thoughtfully, "No, not really. I'd think that some of the world's goods would be needed, of course, so that one could live, but wealth just for—for spreading out on a table and counting—"

"I like that phrase!" Foster laughed. "Just for counting! Do you mind if I use it sometime in one of my memorable discourses for the great men of your country?"

Was he teasing her? Lydia could never determine. "Well, what I mean is—I'm not a great thinker, Mr. Foster. That's no secret. But I feel that wealth is . . . well, it's a responsibility, and it's to be used, isn't it?"

"And people who have wealth?"

"They are to use it, I guess," she finished lamely.

Some moments later he went on, "We didn't explore Mr. Franklin's ideas of wisdom. That sort of speaks for itself. But—"

Lydia swallowed hard, not replying.

"I suspect that you agree with me," he continued, trying to choose his words carefully, "that everyone, rich or poor, prince or peasant, everyone needs love?"

A candle in one of the wall sconces guttered into darkness and Lydia went to a drawer of the Pembroke table to replace it, lighting it from another. The heat from her face could have ignited it, she thought shakily.

Foster was glad of the interruption. He was treading on dangerous ground. He almost said thin ice—but of course it had not been thin ice that had tripped him up on that unforgettable evening so long ago. Not thin ice, but an unsuspected obstruction frozen into thick ice, quite a different matter.

He pulled from his waistcoat pocket the heavy engraved watch that had been his grandfather's. "I really should be going," he said, easing himself reluctantly toward the door. "I have much to do in your fair city, and I shall have to make several kinds of preparations so that I am not asked questions I cannot answer. My government—God rest its soul—seems to intrude on all the pleasant moments of my life as well as on the more ordinary and humdrum ones."

Lydia turned to face him, making him catch his breath as the soft candlelight fell across her hair and throat. He asked quickly, "May I call on you again soon? I have my curricle with me as I did before. If the weather is nice, perhaps, shall we say Tuesday afternoon?"

"If the weather is nice . . ." she whispered, praying silently that the sky would be cloudless.

He ended up by staying most of the week when he discovered the help that he could get from Lydia and her aunt, Mrs. Cochran, in furnishing his embassy. When he headed south from Baltimore he could hardly understand why he was in the United States at all, except to visit delightful people and to perform the ceremonial rites required by Great Britain's Foreign Office. He couldn't remember that there had ever been a quarrel between the two countries or that on several occasions they had been threatening to cut out each other's hearts and draw and quarter the remains. Even the Baltimore businessmen, who flocked around him like bees when they found that he was in town, had been amenable to all his suggestions, had treated him with great respect and kindness. For a brief interlude A. J. Foster, thirty years old, in excellent health and with an important and challenging career in his grasp, was a complacently cheerful man.

Two days in the Federal City brought him back to reality. He would not soon escape from it again.

Washington had grown to almost ten thousand persons during his absence, but it still had a crude, unsettled look, as if its residents had not yet decided to stay, which in truth they had not.

Seeing the area again had been almost a physical shock for him. He remembered how his brother Frederick had looked when they were little tads and Frederick had managed to cut all his front hair, clear to its roots, startling everyone who saw him. Washington looked the same way: cropped, exposed, vulnerable. There were slashed, wounded spaces everywhere. Houses had been slapped together indiscriminately, of brick or stone or wood; some were still hollow shells.

"I do not think this will ever be a great City," he wrote his mother. "The Demon of Speculation has already fixed himself here and instead of giving premiums for building, the Land is very dear. There is no Commerce whatever & all the Increase arises from the demand for Houses from the members of Congress & those whom they bring here; but I heard so bad an account of this wretched Settlement that the only thing I was disappointed in was the hope of finding great

Forests of fine Trees, instead of which the Land is mere waste in the City and all the trees have been cut for Fire."

The Federal City, now eleven years old, made him think of a sprawling army camp, where the tents could be quickly dismantled and moved someplace else. Even the marble-fronted government buildings looked temporary and not fastened down.

In wet weather, marshes and swamps were much in evidence. In dry weather, there was a Sahara of dust. In rain or snow the roads were nearly impassable, although the introduction of paving was some improvement.

In spite of these shortcomings and of his memories of the caliber of some of the men who came there to make the nation's laws, he was happy to return and was greatly challenged by the assignment. Washington had changed a little, but Foster had changed a great deal. With skill, wisdom, tact, hard work and imagination, he hoped to bind up some of the needless hurts made by his predecessors and to establish firm bonds of understanding and mutual respect between the two nations. He was bursting with ideas, his brain afire with ambition.

Arriving from England the day before Independence Day, he had found the capital nearly deserted except for shopkeepers and hostlers, but the quietude was welcome, because it would give him time to settle in. He took a house at the corner of Nineteenth Street and Pennsylvania Avenue—actually, three houses put together, with passageways cut between them. He had brought some furniture with him, planning to fill in the gaps with local purchases, another means of ingratiating himself with the Americans.

Because he felt that more could be accomplished in one evening over a good dinner, with fine liqueurs, unobtrusive but skillful service and an atmosphere of sophisticated relaxation, than in days of stodgier contacts in a business office, he took great pains to establish the setting for such meetings.

He planned to buy only the finest of American-manufactured articles, thus accomplishing two shrewd aims: to show the Americans his appreciation of their best work and to emphasize British taste and insistence on quality. Many Washingtonians had long memories of the staggering amounts of baggage that the Merrys and the Jacksons had brought with them, stirring up gossip that the Britishers were planning to set up their own shops in competition with their American hosts. Foster knew better than to make that kind of mistake.

On several occasions when he chose a piece that he liked, he was surprised to find that it had been made in his own country. At first he was pleased, knowing that the workmanship of British goods was undoubtedly the finest in the world, but he was puzzled. Why should Americans be sniping at the British and cutting off trade with them when there was such a demand for British products? Why should any country set up such self-defeating restrictions when it was prospering? The 1807 Embargo Act, designed to hurt his country, had been a disaster for the Americans, but when it was repealed, the Non-Intercourse Act had been almost as bad for them. Someone should talk some sense into their heads.

He knew of the increasing development of American textiles—Americans were now doing their own weaving on a commercial basis instead of just making threads and yarns. British technicians were itching to get across the ocean and into the infant industry. If they did, it would not be long before the crude homespuns being flaunted by political leaders as an encouragement to local manufacturing would no longer look crude, but would be purchased and used for their own merits. The democrats he had met on his previous stay were strongly in favor of national industrial growth, but the Federalists, especially in New England, were suspicious of such reckless independence. The Federalists there, who could trade with England through their next-door neighbor, Canada, were not eager to disturb the *status quo,* a condition he understood. Mr. Foster was courageous and inventive in many ways, but basically he was a conservative.

During his time in Baltimore he managed to have a number of conversations with business leaders there. The Hollingsworth brothers had talked quite freely with him.

"We don't want war, Mr. Foster. We don't want war with you, or with France, or with anybody! All we want," they told him several times, "is to be free to trade and to use the seas for that purpose. Your restrictions, which in effect make us pay tribute to Great Britain and support her war effort, are bankrupting us. And the waters are infested with pirates. Sorry, sir, but you did ask us to speak freely."

Foster said nothing, hoping his color did not betray him.

Once Thomas, the senior partner, asked him quietly, "Do you realize, sir, what it's like to have to meet a payroll? At least fifty families in this town depend on us for their livelihood."

"Seamen?"

"Many of them. When our ships lie at anchor, they starve. Many men work in our mills. Flour has to be sold after it's made, you know. We have a store, which depends on goods from the Caribbean, from Europe, from the North, all of them coming by ship."

"It would seem," Foster suggested thoughtfully, "that your interests may be more closely tied up with ours than you realize, since we have the greatest navy in the world, actually, the only one to speak of. You need us to protect you from the French—"

"That's the way I feel," Sam snorted. "We know that President Madison is as belligerent as they come, even if he does look so meek and mild. Seems hell-bent to fight someone. And I say, if he's so rarin' to fight, why not Napoleon? There's our real enemy!"

"We don't want the rest of the world to laugh at us, you know," Thomas told him, "and say we're afraid to fight."

"Laugh at you? Afraid? What do you mean?"

"It may look as if we are cowards if we try to get our just due by negotiation instead of by cannon and musket."

"Cowards? I can't believe that anyone would consider it cowardly to seek diplomatic answers to a problem." Foster frowned. "Negotiation is always desirable, it seems to me. More than saber-rattling and bloodletting."

There was an interval of silence and contemplation; then Thomas asked him, "I'm wondering if you saw that item about yourself in the Philadelphia paper, sir? They said you were sent here as an opiate. An opiate to lull us, I believe they had it."

"Is that so bad?" Foster countered. "I was rather flattered."

"Nothing wrong with an opiate if it cures what ails you." Sam chuckled. "Damn sight better than a blister—I'd almost rather die than to have one of those crushed-beetle plasters slapped onto me. Have some Madeira, Mr. Foster?"

Foster was to recall that conversation frequently. There was an almost incomprehensible belief, widespread, that America had to fight in order to prove its manhood, like an Indian brave bringing home a dripping scalp. The antagonist in the fight, so long as he was a bona fide enemy, was not half so important as the fight itself. Such childish thinking was hard to counteract.

His chief assignment in his new post sounded like a simple one: Settle the Chesapeake affair. In one way, the Yankees had played into his hands, because in May the American frigate had returned the fire of the British corvette *Little Belt,* thinking it was the battleship *Guerrière*. Some of the crew were killed. The American commander, John Rodgers, had acted without instructions; the incident was nearly an exact reversal of the British attack on the *Chesapeake* four years earlier, or so Foster chose to consider it. He planned to confront Secretary of State Monroe with the facts of the case. He had been advised to avoid any more disasters by handling both the shipping people and the government with great care, speaking softly and remaining calm.

His second instruction was to try to get the Americans to

use some sense about Napoleon's sinister double-dealing, not only because France was England's enemy, he tried to think, but because Great Britain still had an avuncular interest in the breakaway colony and hated to see its leaders taken in by the crafty Corsican. Explaining the truth to them would be in the nature of doing them a favor, an unselfish act of kindness.

In the so-called "Cadore Letter," the Emperor had told them that the Berlin and Milan decrees had been repealed and that, in consequence, the Americans were no longer under any restrictions from the French. No one bothered to ask for proof. However, everyone in Europe knew that no such repeal had occurred or was likely to, but communications were so poor and seizures of ships in French-held ports so widely separated geographically that the gullible Americans were easily sucked in. Correct information about anything, trivial or important, took months to arrive and be verified. In the interim, all kinds of mischief could go on. And did.

Napoleon was making sagacious use of one of the most fundamental quirks of human nature: Make the lie big enough, and everyone will believe it. With the same brashness he had used the Rambouillet decree to cheat the United States out of vast land holdings to the tune of four million dollars. When confronted with the factual evidence of this treachery, the simple-minded Yankees who had been victimized blamed the talebearers instead of the wrongdoers, a second facet of human foibles that Napoleon could exploit for his own purposes.

The new ambassador was nonplused. How could an honest man, which he considered himself, even begin to counteract such monstrous ignorance and credulity? The enormity of the problem staggered him. He had no idea of where to begin or how to proceed.

As in any other riddle, he must begin where he was. Washington. What he had to deal with was Congress. The make-up of that colorful body had changed radically in four years. The Republicans had swamped the Federalists in the election and had brought in a number of Western and Southern men, who were a new breed. Henry Clay, a fiery thirty-four-year-old Virginia native representing Kentucky, was speaker of the House, second in power only to the President. He saw to it that his side-kick, the twenty-nine-year-old John C. Calhoun from South Carolina, as bellicose as himself, was appointed to the Committee for Foreign Affairs. Peter Potter, a Yale-educated New Yorker, was chairman. Several men of similar outlook clustered around them. The group was soon known as the War Hawks; they were anything but peaceable.

They had plenty of ammunition to support their ferocity. Out in the Northwest two Indians, Tecumseh and his mystic-fanatic brother called the Prophet, had been goading their people to unite in self-protection against the encroachments of the white man. While Tecumseh was away, William Henry Harrison and his men destroyed the village of Tippecanoe in the Indiana Territory, known as the Prophet's Town. There were immediate and murderous reprisals. Most Westerners were convinced that the British were backing the Indians in their attacks on the white intruders, operating subversively beyond the border of Canada. The British reasoned that if they did not use the Indians against the Americans, the tables would be turned and the Indians would work against the British.

The way for the Americans to handle that threat once and for all was to attack and annex Canada. A simple matter, fortunately. March North. Take Canada. There was a hue and cry up and down the land: To Canada!

Foster was convulsed with laughter to hear his old friend John Randolph declaim in his high-pitched voice, "Canada! Canada! Canada!" sounding like the whippoorwill that he said the War Hawks really were. If Randolph's mockery was funny, nothing else about the whole thing was, except its absurdity. There was no army, no money to support one, there were no military planners or leaders. No one seemed to know how many men would be required for overwhelming Canada, or what points they should plan to attack first, or how they should even start to go about the job. . . .

Then, to the south, there was trouble in Spanish Florida, which made a perfect hiding place for escaped slaves, renegade Indians and spies. Spain was now England's ally and so welcomed any anti-American move.

Foster found that he could rest his mind from his troubles and confusion by working on plans for his house. The women in the Hollingsworth family had been most helpful on that score, but he had been hard put to keep his attention on the choice of a tea table, for instance, when it was so easy to visualize the lovely Lydia—the American Lydia—using it to serve his guests. A fireside chair had so much more grace when it was occupied by the same young lady, who had sat in it to test its comfort and design, thus making it somehow her own forever. A console table for his entrance hall cried out for a pair of her gloves to be lying on it.

"The ones she wore that day came from Italy, I noticed," he murmured to himself. "Good taste, even in gloves." He missed the company of little Tartar during his reflections. His pet had been killed by a runaway horse and sledge on a frozen day in Stockholm; he found the loss almost intolerable. He thought for a while of trying to obtain one of his terrier's numerous and varied descendants in the Washington area, but decided against it. No other animal, even a blood relative, could replace Tartar. "Have to talk to the wall now," Foster grumbled.

Deborah Cochran, startled and excited to be asked, had thrown herself wholeheartedly into the task of advising him with his furniture. Her suggestions were sought by every fashionable young man in Baltimore when he was setting up his household and wanting every detail to be in order before he carried his bride over the threshold for her first glimpse of her new domain. Fluttery and feminine and impractical as the lady might appear at first meeting, she had sense and vigor in decorating a home.

Debby never saw the three-part house on K Street in Washington, but her vivid imagination took her there as truly as if she had made the journey and had flitted through the rooms, studying the view out the windows, the available wall space, the exits and entries. She suggested drapery patterns and color schemes to set off the pieces he had brought from abroad. She advised the placing of serving tables, lamps, chairs, sofas, suggesting a footstool or a decorative screen at a spot she felt might be drafty on cold nights. She knew the value of a conversation grouping at one site and clear open spaces for traffic at others.

Lydia had watched her with fascination. Debby had the sure touch of a born expert. The Englishman realized it too, and was impressed that in spite of her personal liking for frilly trappings she had chosen handsomely simple, masculine furnishings for him, the kind of well-designed pieces that would never go out of style. Watching both of the women was a dividend of householding that had never previously occurred to Mr. Foster. He could have shopped for hours.

Braced by his stopover in Baltimore, he got back to Washington in time for the arrival of many government officials. Decisions on some of the troubling problems of arranging his embassy had been made for him, and correctly, by Mrs. Cochran—a great blessing—but now some questions were rising in his mind as to why he should keep wondering about Miss Annabella Milbanke's feelings toward him. Who was it, he asked himself as he swung out alone for one of his invigorating walks along the Potomac—who was it who had been the prime mover in that romance? Himself? Perhaps. She was attractive, and when he was with her he surely forgot his loneliness.

But her mother had taken more than a perfunctory interest in the affair. Lady Milbanke realized that he was quite a catch —so did he—and was forever easing the way for his courtship of her daughter. Lord Milbanke—Old Twaddle, as Foster's mother called him—was known to be under his wife's thumb, so her parents were presenting a solid front of approval, even encouragement, of his suit. Annabella blew hot and cold. He sensed that she wanted to marry great wealth, which he did not have, although he was far from being a pauper. His future was bright, even brilliant, if he played his cards right.

For some reason also, the Lady Annabella was uncommonly attracted to young George Gordon Lord Byron, whose poems were rocking the country.

He couldn't help but contrast the Milbanke parents with the Hollingsworth parents. The latter treated him kindly, with the innate good manners for which Marylanders were noted; they seemed to enjoy his company, but they kept themselves as something he considered essential: private persons. They allowed him to be a private person too, respecting him both for himself and for the responsibility and prestige of his office, but never—he tried to think of the right word—never *intruding*. He liked that. They neither smothered him nor froze him out, they never pressed for answers he was unable or unwilling to give and they never asked him questions which would force his hand.

And Lydia! He had not been mistaken in his memories of her. How he wished that his family could meet her; surely their blind prejudices would ease. What did any native-born English girl have that she didn't? A title, perhaps. How much did a title contribute to warming the heart, strengthening the character, bracing the arm? He knew of titles that were empty façades for decadence, immorality, poverty of the spirit. Being called milord or milady was no guarantee of sterling worth.

His mother had warned him so many times about entanglement with an "American beauty." Why? What was she afraid of? Did she know any? Did she believe that all American girls made such deplorable failures of marriage as the Patterson daughter?

The Duchess Elizabeth was sending him frequent reports of King Jerome's scandalous involvement with women of all social levels and of various nationalities. But the sinner there was Jerome, not Betsy! Foster had always liked Betsy, and he knew that she liked him. The word was that she would spend most of the winter social season with her Washington relatives, thus getting away from "dull" Baltimore and into the vortex of political and social excitement. He must call on her as soon as it was convenient. He wrote her name on the long list he was making. The protocol of calling and returning calls was going to keep him very busy for the first weeks of the autumn season.

One of his planned approaches to the enormous task of trying to build a bridge of understanding with the Yankees was to give a series of small dinners for ten or fifteen people, choosing his guests with care after one thoughtless pairing of Irish visitors had nearly resulted in a duel; if anyone should have been aware of the trigger-tension of Irish tempers, it was himself.

He instructed his maître d'hôtel that the food was to be superbly prepared and that the table service, linens, wines and liqueurs must be faultless. Proper chilling, proper heating, proper serving—every detail must be attended to.

Remembering the backwoods simplicity of some of his guests he tried to plan his menus with just enough sophistication to embody British culture but with enough lack of novelty to avoid any inadvertent embarrassment. International brouhahas could come from such unexpected and sometimes ridiculous incidents. An ambassador needed to be more of a tightrope artist than any circus performer.

He learned to his sorrow that serving foreign and unfamiliar delicacies could be, to say the least, unwise. There were large quantities of sturgeon in the Potomac River just above Georgetown, and he found that the roe could be cured into a very acceptable caviar. He taught his chef the method of preparing it, using a receipt from the famous *Chambers Universal Dictionary of Arts and Sciences,* a practical and indispensable book. He soon had a bountiful supply of native-grown caviar for his parties. Alas, the only guests who appreciated the treat were the Russians. The others, thinking that the serving dish contained blackberry jam, treated the caviar accordingly, spreading it lavishly on the crisp crackers placed near it. Watching the results nauseated him, so much so that he made a note of it in his diary, his only safe way of venting his irritation.

"In Britain the very word 'spit' is considered indecent," he exclaimed. "The very *word!*"

His table and his social doings lacked one element: a charming hostess. How could gentlemen withdraw for smokes and more masculine conversation when there was no one to withdraw from? He rarely invited wives with their husbands because of his own situation, but he would have liked to, and there were indications that many wives would like to come. He enjoyed the treat for his senses of having attractive, well-dressed women around, although he found their intellectual furniture inclined to be skimpy. The women of America were not like those of the Devonshire House set. But then, who was?

Whenever he could find a spare moment—often late at night, when his house was full of echoes—he wrote short notes to Lydia, wishing that there might be some way he could send himself instead. His days were choked with activity, his mind trying not to lose sight of the larger vision while he was encompassed with details. It piqued his interest that she never initiated any correspondence, never sent an impulsive note to inquire about this or that; she waited at least three days after the arrival of his letter, then wrote a friendly and circumspect response. She told him that they were well and busy. If he had asked a specific question, she answered it. Her brother was better, the Cochrans were pleased to know that he had sent them greetings, her uncle Samuel had been ill with a cold but was improved. Yes, they too had had inclement weather for some days. She hoped that his work was going well.

She gave him no hint that her letter was written and rewritten until it managed to create just that warm but impersonal tone. She had her own arts and her own self-discipline. His attention, sporadic as it was, was nevertheless transforming her. It was as if a hearth fire, long unused and cold, had been rekindled, and the warmth of its flame was gleaming on everything it touched.

Ruth Tobin, who had known all along of Foster's planned surprise of Lydia on the packet but had never tipped her hand, had asked her several times what was going on. In one of her letters she had advised Lydia to be cryptic in her answers in any personal message or else to send important letters only by hand. Their aunt Ruth was prying into everything, opening her mail, accusing her of secretiveness, getting more difficult as her illness increased and her mind grew more twisted.

Early in November Lydia wrote her: "I think the style of dress this winter very elegant and costly, white satin with lace overdresses are most worn, ornamented with flowers or french trimmings. You ask if I am to be invited to the Delaware frolic; no, my dear Cousin, I have not been invited, and if such an honour should be done me, I could not accept. (In confidence, I am pre-engaged, the thing I wrote you of by Samuel, has taken quite another form and we may have a Christmas frolic. It was communicated to me this week and the compliment of attendance asked of me.)"

She had been deliberately mysterious not only for Ruth's sake, but also in case her letter reached other prying eyes by accidentally going astray. The Ambassador had mentioned that every move he made was reported back to England, seldom accurately, so Lydia resolved that she would protect him in whatever way she could. She did not know, of course, of his remark to his secretary, Mr. Anthony St. John Baker, when the first such garbled gossip made a round trip to England and stung him with its distortion.

"Damned if I'm going to live like a cloistered monk, Mr. Baker! Why doesn't someone tell that to the old biddies?"

In due time he found his way to Madame Bonaparte's. She was more than pleased to see him. For a moment he feared she was going to give him a peck on the cheek. A maddening blush suffused his face, but she saved the moment by turning away to find a suitable chair to offer him and by ringing for tea.

"Or perhaps brandy, Mr. Foster? Cognac? Whiskey?"

"Tea is best," he said simply. "I must make a number of calls yet today. I can stay but a few moments, alas."

"It is such an honor to have the ambassador of the first nation of the world come visiting!" She smiled up at him. "I hope you are comfortably settled in your embassy. An imaginative idea, to put several houses together! My uncle says he has seen you now and then, but I didn't know whether or not you would find your way here."

"Had I followed my personal inclinations," he said graciously, "you need not have wondered."

As he watched her pouring tea, he saw that she was using her petite femininity as a banner in a strongly masculine world, where her frailty would naturally need protection. The Britisher was charmed and amused; in the course of his career he had met many such women. As a matter of fact, they were often marvelous company, and he never objected to what John Randolph referred to as their "velvet claws." A. J. Foster enjoyed playing games too.

Little Bo came in during the short visit and climbed disarmingly onto his lap. He was touched. How long had it been since he had held a child? He couldn't remember.

"Son, you mustn't!" his mother scolded. "He likes men," she explained, laughing. "It's hard for me to be both father and mother, so little Bo tries to attach himself to every male who comes along. Here, Bo, come and have some cookies."

Solemnly the boy crawled down and backed away. Foster tried to pat him on the head, but he was out of reach.

Would she ever take another husband? She had enough chances, he knew. The men in Washington swarmed around her. Watching her, anyone could see that she would have had little trouble taking on the role of queen, perhaps even empress.

There was much speculation as to why her aunt, Miss Nancy Spear, usually referred to as being "redoubtable," had never married. She was attractive enough and had an uncanny sense of business. It was said that she could put up a wet finger and ascertain the direction of the financial winds, a rare gift for a woman.

Foster knew why she remained single. She was too successful. She had to win, which meant that someone else had to lose. No husband wanted that kind of humiliation. With Foster's own need for a wife, which amounted to downright eagerness at times, he still had a peculiar sympathy for women. When his long-time friend Caroline Ponsonby, niece of the first Duchess of Devonshire, married William Lamb (Lord Melbourne), he was deeply distressed and wrote home: "I cannot fancy Lady Caroline married. How changed she must be—the delicate Ariel, the little fairy queen become a wife and soon perhaps a mother. . . . it is the first death of a woman—they must die twice, for I'm sure all their friends, their real ones at least, receive a pang when they change character so completely."

After his first formal call, Foster rarely saw Madame Bonaparte alone, but he found that her "salon" was an excellent window on the world, and a place where he could meet assorted Frenchmen who avoided him elsewhere.

The French minister, Louis Barbé Charles Sérurier, who

like his predecessors referred to her as Mademoiselle Patterson, subtly encouraged his underlings to drop in there. Not too obviously, of course, but they might pick up morsels of information that had value. He gambled also that she knew more than he did about what was going on in the splendid, if corrupt, courts of the expanding Empire. In return for M. Sérurier's snubs, the lady told one and all that she was educating her son in hatred of the tyrant, a direct-hit bon mot that enraged the Minister.

Foster watched the uneven battle from ringside, all the more partisan because he found the Frenchman so easy to despise.

Reports soon flew back to Britain—and to Baltimore—that His Excellency the British Minister was courting the former Miss Patterson, who was not yet divorced by American law, and who two years previously had finally asked the Archbishop to baptize her son as a Catholic, in a ceremony at St. Peter's in Baltimore. (She remained a Presbyterian.) Foster did nothing to counteract the talk. For one thing, he knew very well who had started the rumors. For another, that phase of his life was nobody's business. And it might serve a good cause to have the people at home think he had an inside track for confidential information about the doings of the Bonapartes. He guessed at how much Betsy knew of the goings on of her former in-laws: exactly nothing that wasn't common knowledge. His refusal to react to the gossip about him added an air of mystery to his dealings, precisely as he had hoped. Why admit that there was nothing going on?

He was willing to do anything humanly possible, explore every avenue, be alert to every opening that might help him extinguish the sputtering fuse that was creeping toward the point of igniting the dynamite of war.

When his small dinner parties proved to be moderately successful, he got the idea of giving a great ball for the Queen's birthday, coming up in January, a ball such as the

Americans had never seen. He did not have the limitless space and splendor of such a residence as Devonshire House for his soiree, of course, but he could manage. He threw himself into the plans with the utmost enthusiasm: music, flowers, food, liquor, extra servants. He would ask everyone he knew in Washington. When he got his first tentative list made up, there were almost three hundred names.

"My rooms will be crowded! Fine! Everyone will have to be friendly. Maybe some of those hard heads can be softened up a little."

The next day he added an out-of-town name and made partial arrangements for a place for her to stay. His first thought had been Madame Bonaparte's home, but a voice at the back of his mind warned him against it. The Carrolls—he would approach them, for he knew they would be in Washington most of the winter. He had nearly rented their house himself, and he knew they were friends of the Hollingsworths.

On November 12, he could write laconically in his diary: "Settled the Chesapeake Affair." After four years of argument and disappointment, he could take the credit for the end of the quarrel, because he could confront the Secretary of State with the facts about the *Little Belt*.

Monroe and the President took the blame for the action of their frigate and Commander Rodgers, and accepted Britain's apology and indemnity for the *Chesapeake*. Foster felt a little like snapping his fingers in a gesture of nonchalance. One down! And how many to go?

He had achieved the first step up the towering mountain, but his real work was just beginning. He went off for a new round of maneuvers with congressmen and statesmen, lighter in heart and warmed also by the thought of a Christmas frolic in Baltimore. By that time he would have earned a holiday.

Chapter Thirteen

My Friend or My Brother

Christmas on South Street was bittersweet. The Hollingsworth household was glowing with reflections of Lydia's joy but inwardly hushed with alarm about her brother. He had never completely recovered from the swelling and stiffness that had come on after his sailing accident in the summer. Now and then there had been a span of a few weeks when he was relatively free from pain, but the return of damp weather would bring on new spasms of torment. The fingers of his hands were distorted and tender. His knees and ankles were occasionally swollen and pained him frequently, forcing him to avoid any chill or sudden exposure. He hated the necessary coddling. He occupied himself with learning his father's business, rarely going sailing, horseback riding or hunting, activities requiring physical dexterity he no longer possessed.

Keeping books and writing letters for the firm were part of his work, but there were times when he could scarcely hold the pen. He made many errors, then had to copy and recopy until his temper wore thin. His father said nothing but set him at other tasks, his heart twisting.

"Important for you to get into the mill and learn some of the operations there," he'd say gruffly. "Maybe you should get down to the wharf and see about that shipment your uncle

Zeb claims he sent down from Elk Landing. The Pratt Street Brewery needs those barrel hoops, and they're already late. I'm getting tired of having them jump me about it." He had to be careful that his voice didn't sound like an old bear as he tried to keep from showing his feelings.

Early in the fall he sent his son on a long trip to Boston and the Falls of the Niagara, hoping that the change of scene would be good for him, and that he would profit from a first-hand look at some of the rest of the world. The duties of commerce would tie the lad down soon enough, Thomas knew; let him live a little, while he was still young and unencumbered.

The womenfolk in his family were the real gadabouts, going up to Elkton to visit relatives, kiting off for the day to visit Sam's daughter Betsy, now Mrs. Charles Sterret Ridgely, at her home, named Oaklands, out in Elkridge. Well, he didn't mind. If women could leave, he supposed they should. As for himself, he liked staying home.

Ann and his daughters could turn over the household to Polodore—who was as dependable as daylight—give instructions for the other servants, get Robert to hitch up the team or a driving horse, and off they'd go, with not a care in the world. Now a local riding academy was giving lessons; frightfully expensive, he felt. He'd learned to ride a horse simply by climbing on its back and hanging on, there on the farm at Elk Landing. But ladies had to be taught, and some fellow with nothing better to do had to be paid for teaching them. Which also meant all kinds of new clothes. Ah, women! He sighed, finding that thinking about them took his mind off his son, if it did nothing else for him.

Lydia's new happiness was bringing in a fresh flock of suitors and social invitations. She accepted some of the attentions pleasantly enough and brushed off the others. Any man who was a good dancer was most apt to be accepted. She was turning down every invitation for the busy Christmas season, not being sure how much time the Ambassador would be able to spare from his work, and not daring to have any spot on her calendar filled.

"First things first, eh, Sister?" young Thomas teased. "And what if your Englisher doesn't come at all? What if His Majesty the Crazy King sends word that the Honorable Minister is to stay in Washington?"

"He'll come."

"Are you really sure? If he doesn't, you are certainly fixing it so that you'll be sitting home bored to death and thinking how much fun everyone else is having. Don't come complaining to me!"

"He'll come."

Ann Maria was catching some of Lydia's admirers on the rebound, in addition to handling her own, and the house was humming with talk of ball gowns, party slippers, hairdressers, perfumes, supper favors, jewels. Messengers came and went. The dressmaker stitched for long hours. There was constant danger of sitting on a pin that had fallen from something while the girls were parading around in their partly finished gowns. There was so much to be done that Ann finally sent over to her sister Debby's to ask if she might borrow a servant to help them get caught up.

Debby, busy getting Christmas ready for little William and his half sisters, said she could dispense with her day woman for a while, if that would help. Fronya often worked for Ann in a pinch, as well as for Debby, so Ann was grateful for an extra day of her time.

Fronya ironed. She was fantastically slow—in movement, in thought, in perception, in response—so slow that she could give the impression of being completely motionless when she considered herself quite busy and working at top speed. Her only special possession was a small ruffling iron, invaluable for doing up fancy cuffs and neckpieces. The lower section cupped hot coals under its corrugated top. The upper part of the iron was a matching corrugated roller with a handle. The

Her husband was too upset to do more than shake hands, putting such pressure into his grip that both men withdrew their fingers as quickly as possible. They were ushered into Thomas's room.

It seemed to his parents that their examination took an eternity. Finally they came out, and Donaldson spoke for both of them. "We think you are doing exactly the right thing for him, Mrs. Hollingsworth, by keeping him in bed. He will need quite a bit of rest."

Keeping him in bed, his father echoed silently. But he can't get up!

"Dress him in warm flannel, see that he's covered, don't let the fires go out upstairs," Gibson advised. "We saw that he keeps tossing off the quilts, but he must be kept warm. You can bathe his face in cool water to reduce some of the fever. We may bleed him sometime later."

"Most important is bed rest," Donaldson reiterated, starting down the stairs.

"Bed rest?" Ann asked despairingly. "Is that *all?* Isn't there anything else we can do for him?"

"Watch his diet," Donaldson replied. "But I know you do anyway. Plenty of good meat and vegetables, nothing that will be hard to digest. Liquids. Fruits."

"How about . . . ? Well, could we . . . ?" Thomas, Senior, was searching for anything practical that he could do instead of distractedly pacing the floor, rattling coins in his pockets and staring out the windows.

"Rubbing would be good," Gibson suggested. "Use oil of wintergreen and massage him gently on any of the affected parts whenever he wants you to. Let us know how he is by the weekend."

"By the weekend? But that's five days away! Won't there be any change in him for *five days?*"

Donaldson said nothing further until they were at the front door. Pulling on his gloves and turning his coat collar up around his neck, he said soberly, "Thomas, I wouldn't be honest and I wouldn't be your good friend if I didn't tell you the truth. It may take a while, Thomas. It may."

"We'll do all we can," Gibson said quickly. "Try not to worry."

"Yes, try not to worry. And the best wishes of the season for all of you!" Donaldson added.

"I'll stop in when I can," Gibson promised. "Good day."

The Hollingsworths stood in the open doorway and watched after the retreating backs of the two men as if they had been a couple of pallbearers.

"It may take a while," Thomas said dully. "They were telling us more by what they didn't say than by what they did." He pulled his wife into his arms, and the two of them clung together like lost children, aching for reassurance. "They didn't say he was going to—"

"No, Thomas! *No!* They just said—"

"It may take a while," her husband repeated.

Lydia dressed with meticulous care for the gala evening with Mr. Foster, two nights before Christmas. She had chosen a rich satin the color of country cream and had her hair dressed modishly high. She spent the day fluttering the way her Aunt Debby did, a most unaccustomed thing for Lydia, rushing upstairs, downstairs, talking, laughing, looking in on Thomas, remembering small details for the evening. In midafternoon the Ambassador sent his man with a message saying that he had arrived in Baltimore and was established at Gadsby's as usual. With the note was a box containing a delicate corsage of roses and a coral velvet ribbon for tying it around her wrist. Lydia raced up to Thomas's bedside to display the flowers. She spun around in a pirouette and then held them in front of him.

"Smell! Aren't they beautiful? Aren't they wonderful?"

To her horror, her brother burst into tears. *"Thomas!"* She put the little nosegay on the chest of drawers and hurried to sit beside him. "Thomas! What is it? Why—why, you never cry!"

"Go away!" Painfully he pulled himself up so that he could turn over with his back to her. *"Go away!"*

"Thomas! You mustn't!" She flew to the other side of the bed and tried to force his hands away from his face. "What is it? What is it?" He was so fevered that she nearly let go. "I'll get Mama."

"No, don't. Please don't!"

"But what is it? Are you worse? We can call the doctor—"

"I'm all right." He was gradually getting control of himself. Lydia found a handkerchief and watched mutely as he wiped his face and his eyes. He slid farther down in bed, pulling up the covers so he could avoid her gaze.

A sudden insight came to Lydia. "You had planned to go to the ball too, hadn't you? You were going to be Elizabeth Stricker's escort, weren't you? Is that it? Oh, Thomas!"

He nodded. "She knows I can't go. I sent Polodore over with a note several days ago. I—I had planned to give her roses—she's the kind of girl who should have roses, don't you think?"

"Yes, Thomas. Yes, she is."

When he was calm again he asked, averting his eyes, "Will you do me a big favor, please?"

"Of course. Anything."

"Don't ever mention this to anyone."

"But—but—"

"It won't happen again, I can tell you that. Never." He drew a long shaking breath. "It's just that I—that I—well, I just can't seem to get used to it—"

The ball was all that she had dared to hope for, and more. Foster, in full-dress uniform, by far the handsomest and most distinguished man there, flattered her by engaging her for nearly every dance. He permitted John Comegys, Mr. Cochran's business partner, to have a cotillion with her, and her cousin Jacob to be her partner for the Sir Roger de Coverley later.

Madame Bonaparte came in late, surrounded by a small coterie and radiating charm with the air of conferring royal favors. Foster went to ask her for a dance, but her program was already filled. He was a little disappointed, because she was a superb dancer. Hardly an eye in the room missed seeing the quick kiss she blew him from her finger tips as he moved off.

I could have done without that, he thought, his face burning.

Returning to Lydia, he said with mock gloom, "Since I must share you with these other gentlemen for two dances, I have made very sure of their credentials. Mr. Comegys and Mr. Jacob Hollingsworth should pass all the tests. I notice that almost everyone in the room is looking at you with admiration, my dear cousin. Not that I blame them."

"They are looking at you, Mr. Foster," Lydia corrected him. "Almost everyone knows me. And they know who you are. Their real interest is in seeing me with you. It's quite simple."

"Then we should allow them to rest their eyes, Miss Hollingsworth. I shall bring you some punch, if you wish, then perhaps we can find a—a relatively quiet place where we can talk without being on display."

"Whatever you say," she answered breathlessly.

"There is something I want to discuss with you," he began when they had found a sofa in a secluded bay window. "I am planning to give a ball for the Queen's birthday, coming up in January—"

"In Washington?"

"Where else?" He grinned. "I live in Washington, you know."

"I'm sorry. . . ."

"I'm not. You are especially attractive when you blush, my dear cousin. Or did you mean you were sorry that I live in

Washington instead of, perhaps, Buenos Aires? Never mind. I have talked with the Carrolls—"

"The Carrolls? Why?"

"They are spending most of the winter there, and I have asked if they might accommodate you as their house guest when you come for my ball—"

"I? Come for . . . ?" Lydia gasped. "What do you mean?"

"But of course you understand that I want you to be there! It appears to me that your presence would add greatly to the—to the charm of the gathering." He was covertly watching her unconscious responses to his conversation. Ah, if only politicians were as transparent. "And, in case you are concerned about possible protection on the stage journey there, my friend Mr. John Randolph will be up here shortly before then and has kindly consented to accompany you—"

"You think of everything," she whispered.

"I try, my dear cousin. I try."

Lydia sipped her punch, hardly lifting her eyes from the rim of her glass. Foster waited. "You will come?" he asked finally, but still she did not reply. "It means a great deal to me, Miss Hollingsworth."

"And to me . . ."

John Comegys came hunting her, his program in hand, reminding her that the cotillion was about to begin. Foster took her glass as she moved away, glancing shyly back over her shoulder. Setting the glasses on a convenient table, he went to find Miss Caton, who was to be his next partner.

The precious corsage was beginning to wilt when he bade her good night very late in the evening, but Lydia was as fresh as morning. She had forgotten her nagging grief for her brother, living only in the spell of the moments she had spent with the man looking down at her.

"The ball will be at my embassy on the twentieth," he reminded her. She noticed the fleeting dimple in his cheek. "In the meantime I shall stay in Baltimore until you have made up your mind. We British are a stubborn lot. We Irish are even stubborner. To pass the weary hours until I can see you again, I may have to occupy myself with fragments of His Majesty's business, alas." He brushed his lips across her hair. "May I call tomorrow? Just to keep my invitation fresh in your mind?"

"Tomorrow." She could hardly hear herself. "Yes, tomorrow."

Christmas Day was quiet. The servants were up early to "cotch Massuh's Chrismus' gif'," and Ann had prepared generously for them, but they were as subdued as the rest of the family. Thomas, Junior's illness had shown no sign of abating. If anything, he was worse, and was much thinner. The ailment was a kind of rheumatism, which several family members knew well, but was more painful and more generally spread over his body.

The feast that was usually the most important part of the day had lost most of its savor as the other four sat at the table without him. No relatives had been invited, for the first time ever, and the meal was eaten without enjoyment.

When Lydia went up to see her brother, he lay stiffly in his bed, not turning his eyes toward her as she came in. His gifts lay unopened on the floor beside him, and his hands were white and useless against the hand-woven blue coverlet. The tray with his dinner sat untouched on a chair.

"What's the matter, Thomas? Can't you eat any of this fat goose that Delia cooked especially for you? Or the squash? Not even the fruitcake? It's the best we've ever had," she lied, not remembering one bite of the food she had choked down.

"Not hungry."

"You must eat! I'll send Polodore up to feed you."

"Never! I couldn't put up with that."

"But you have to eat, to get your strength built up. You know that. Isn't there something—anything—I can get for you?"

He shook his head. "One thing I would like, though . . ."

"Yes? What is it?"

"Is he still here?"

"Who do you mean? Papa? He's right downstairs."

"No, not Papa. The Englisher. That Mr. Foster."

"He's in town," Lydia said quickly, her face glowing. "Mayor Johnson insisted that he spend the day there, and of course he had to do so."

"I didn't get to see him," Thomas said. "Is he going to come again? Could he possibly come up to visit me for a few minutes?"

"Why, I'm sure he would. I know he would. He's always liked you."

"He has? Of course I used to be more of a man than I am now—"

"Thomas! I will not listen to such talk. And I'll ask Mr. Foster."

The Ambassador was surprised but pleased when Lydia relayed her brother's request the next afternoon. He looked at her mother with a question in his eyes as to the propriety of his entering the more private area of their home. She relieved his concern by telling him, "Thomas had us move some comfortable chairs into his room, and of course we keep the fires going all the time for him, so he has a sort of drawing room for himself, he says. Please do go see him. At the head of the stairs. My daughters will show you."

One glance at Thomas's distorted hands showed him that he should not extend his own in greeting, although he had picked up that Americanism some time ago. He accepted the proffered chair and noticed with admiration that there were several fine ship prints hanging on the walls. An inlaid mahogany chest, topped by a pair of silver-trimmed military brushes, was a handsome masculine piece.

The Englishman wondered uncomfortably what they should talk about. He had done very little calling on the sick, and when he had, the person was usually someone very old to whom death would come as a friend. He knew better than to ask how Thomas was or to mention his appearance, which shocked him beyond words. And he had had enough of politics, God knew, at the Mayor's. Thomas's interests probably didn't go in that direction anyway. Foster reflected ruefully that his host had stuffed him more thoroughly with politics than with roast duck and smoked ham.

A servant came with the tea things, so for some moments he was occupied with being served and saying thank-yous. On a window sill he noticed a crudely carved gull, its head thrust forward, its wings poised for flight.

"Is that something you made?" he asked.

"When I was maybe ten or eleven," Thomas answered. "I worked and worked on it, and that's as far as I got. I guess I couldn't make myself throw it away, but it doesn't look like much. I hope you can tell that it's supposed to be a bird."

"I like it," Foster said simply. "It has good lines and a feeling of—well, a feeling of being ready to fly off into the sky."

"Do you have gulls in England?" Ann Maria asked, doing her bit.

"Some species." Foster set his teacup on the tray. "That reminds me—when I was coming back here, back to the United States last summer—you know that I lived here before—"

Thomas and Lydia exchanged glances. Ann Maria put her teaspoon on her saucer, not looking up.

"When I came back, it happened that the day was very clear as we came nearer and nearer to the land. Really a beautifully sunny day. And I stood on the deck, straining my eyes, watching for my first glimpse of America."

"Something like our Christopher Columbus, eh, Mr. Foster?" Thomas was smiling broadly for the first time in weeks.

"Exactly!" He got up and struck a pose. "There I was, on the deck of my flagship, the *Santa Maria,* peering through my spyglass—"

Thomas shouted with laughter in appreciation of his quick wit. It was a sound that had not been heard at 15 South Street for much too long. "And a dove came out with a tree-branch in its beak . . ." he prompted.

"It was a gull instead of a dove." Foster smiled as he sat down, a little surprised himself at his antic. "And it probably had a fish in its beak, but I didn't see that. The first hint of land we had was the smell of pine trees—marvelous and tantalizing—then there was just one gull, long before I could see anything but water. Then there were a couple more, then maybe a dozen, then—oh, I don't know how many. It was exhilarating. They were like a welcoming committee. I half expected some of them to be bringing invisible lines that would tie up and pull the ship right to the shore. I couldn't see anything but peace and beauty and hope on the horizon that day, believe me."

Ann Maria passed him the dish of sweets and went to give one to Thomas. When he had nibbled at it, he asked, "Sir, do you remember when I asked you about the eclipse and the comet? Last fall?"

"I certainly do. A most interesting coincidence."

"Well, my old schoolteacher, Mr. Cyrus King, came to see me the other day, and he was telling me that he had read something about Tecumseh. Do you know about that Indian, Mr. Foster? He's some kind of big chief out in the Northwest."

"I've heard of him." He tried to keep from frowning, wondering what the fellow was getting at.

"Mr. King said that Tecumseh was a very smart man and that he knew about both the comet and the eclipse beforehand. I don't know how he could have, but he did. I guess Indians are all pretty smart."

"So they say."

"Well, Tecumseh was trying to get the tribes—many, many tribes—to let him be their leader. They had been ambushing and murdering white people all along the frontier—that was in the paper—anyway, he told them, 'I'll show you how powerful I am. Tonight there will be a new star in the sky because

I am going to put it there!' So that night, there was the comet. Right where he said it would be." Enthused by his story, Thomas was trying to sit up straighter. Lydia made herself ignore his efforts. They had been told to let him do what he could.

"Must have scared them from red to green." Foster laughed.

"Then, the next part of the story is that he knew about the eclipse too. He knew the exact time it was coming. So he said to them, 'All right, men. If some of you think I don't know Big Medicine—' that's what they call their magic, Big Medicine—'If you think I don't know Big Medicine,' he told the other Indians, 'just you watch. Just you watch! *I might even turn off the sun!*' "

"Oh, Thomas, such wild stories! Surely you can't believe all that!" his sisters scoffed.

"I heard the same thing in Washington," the Englishman admitted. "It must be true. At least our red-skinned brothers must have some kind of magic. That gives me an idea."

"You mean you know some Big Medicine too, sir?" Thomas's eyes were feverishly bright, and the visitor knew he must leave.

"I wish I did, my boy. I was thinking that perhaps I should move my embassy to a tepee, possibly paint my face with green and white stripes. And study the heavens for the arrival of the next comet." He stood up. "I'm so glad you invited me," he said warmly. "I really am. You have given my spirits a lift."

"I?" Thomas tried to shrug his shoulders.

"Is that so hard to believe?"

"Hard? Impossible." Thomas managed a slight grin to take the edge off his words.

"May I come again, my friend? I must be here for a few more days, for several reasons. There is some chance that the French consul, through the good offices of your Mayor Johnson, will at least give me the time of day. And I must use a little more persuasion to get your sister talked into attending my ball in January."

"Oh, she's coming!" Thomas blurted out. "She's having a new dress made. And she and Ann Maria lie awake half the night talking about it. They wake me up with their giggling. Didn't you know? She's more excited about it than with anything that ever happened to her! You mean you didn't tell him, Sister?"

By the time the Ambassador returned to Washington, with Lydia's acceptance verified, Ann Hollingsworth was close to exhaustion from caring for her son night and day. The servants helped, but she trusted no one to take the main responsibility at night.

The fire must be kept going, with care that it didn't smoke, since he had trouble breathing. He must be kept covered. If he couldn't sleep, he should be rubbed until he could relax and drop off into unconsciousness for a while. An occasional sip of wine seemed to comfort him. Thomas, Senior, had brought his choicest bottle and made a place for it in the room. He must have fresh night clothes if he perspired too heavily, but he could hardly manage to change them himself without help. Someone who could be trusted must be alert to his slightest needs.

He was beginning to improve, almost imperceptibly. He slept better. Some of the swelling left. His appetite picked up. As he got stronger, his mother got wearier, until her husband decided to take charge.

"My dear, we are going to get someone to stay with Thomas at night, so you can get your rest," he announced. "You won't let me do it. You don't trust anyone else. *But*—all he needs now is to have someone who can hear him if he calls for something, and someone who can keep watch over the fire."

"I won't ask any of the servants," Ann said stubbornly. "They have enough work during the day."

"It's not a hard job," Thomas argued. "Just a responsible one."

"Fronya," Ann said. "Maybe she could stay nights for a week or two."

All Fronya said when the idea was broached was "Yes'm." She moved in at once, her luggage consisting of the ruffling iron and of the clothes she was wearing, three layers deep to bring them all at once. Where she had come from, no one asked. She never left. Ann made her a pallet on the floor in the hallway, outside Thomas's room.

There was an extra space in the cellar that could be cleaned and whitewashed. When Thomas no longer needed night care, Fronya moved down there. Otherwise the pattern of her life did not change.

Basically, Fronya ironed.

Ann's long weeks of loving care of her son finally put her down in bed with a heavy cold. The only member of the family who caught it from her was Lydia. She tried prayers, tears, whiskey and every kind of human struggle to throw it off as the time for the great ball drew near. Nothing worked. She was flat on her back.

When John Randolph got off the stage in Washington, the only thing he had to deliver safely to his good friend the British Minister was a carefully worded note saying that a certain lady who was to have decorated the evening for him was ill and could not come. Lydia had written and rewritten the message several times, trying to hide her overwhelming disappointment, which was as great as his.

Seeing the expression on his friend's face, Randolph pressed Foster's shoulder in a gesture of sympathy and left him alone to face an evening that no longer seemed important.

Chapter Fourteen

Mischief Is in Their Hearts

When Augustus John recovered from his regret at Lydia's absence, he had to admit ruefully that he would not have had a moment to spend with her. His secretary, Anthony St. John Baker, would have had all that pleasure while Foster buttonholed one after another of his guests, using on each whatever tactic might prove effective in his larger strategy. At most he might have had glimpses of Lydia as she swirled past in some other man's arms, or was made acquainted with foreign dignitaries by Mr. Baker, not by Mr. Foster. She might possibly have felt that he was neglecting her. He finally discarded that thought as an unworthy and unkind one. Surely she would have had sympathy for his situation.

By the next stage he dispatched to her the flowers he had bought for her, violets and lilies of the valley. He had asked the florist to pack them with extra care so they would not freeze. If only he had nothing more world-shaking to worry about!

The previous week had been an alarming one. The War Hawks had goaded, cajoled, threatened and ridiculed the members of Congress until that body had been forced to vote an increase in the regular army to thirty-five thousand men. They had backstopped the vote by a million dollars for arms, equipment and supplies, with another four hundred thousand dollars for the navy.

"They don't have a navy!" Foster had protested to some English industrialists who were visiting in Washington. "They'll have to create one from whole cloth. Not one capital ship!" He could not mention to them his dismay that so many of his Federalist friends had voted for the increases. Even Josiah Quincy, a sharp-tongued New Englander, said publicly that to vote against the measure would be to betray his country.

Congressman Langdon Cheves of South Carolina wanted to put several million dollars, not just thousands, into building twenty-five ships of the line and forty frigates. This suggestion was scorned, and before long the whole program for building up the navy was abandoned. They would patch up their few rotting frigates as a token navy, then spend their energies and their money on preparing for land defense, which all the War Hawks were foreseeing as a necessity.

Defense in the west from the Indians, British and French, in the north from the British and in the south from the British and Spanish—those were their needs. Foster watched poker-faced as they discounted any program for defense from the east, which would be the sea. All of their enemies were based across the sea. How would they get to the New World and keep themselves supplied except by the sea? Well, the War Hawks' shortsightedness made part of his work easier.

He stepped up the tempo of his conferences and notes to legislators, his wide-ranging personal diplomacy, his persuasive arguments for negotiations, his small dinners. It was easy to start his guests talking about the problems of serving five years in the army instead of the two months out of a year required of every man until he was forty-five. Well-to-do men of property, who were expected by long tradition to be officers, were not going to rush in to give up a large chunk of their lives. Even those patriotic enough to become so involved were in for a session of annoying paper work before the changeover could be achieved.

Albert Gallatin, the little Swiss-born financier who was Secretary of the Treasury, began to seek ways to raise the money. He first proposed raising customs duties by half, renewing the discontinued import duty on salt and setting up taxes to pay for a loan, suggesting the figure of forty million dollars at eight per cent. When this idea failed, he made up a more comprehensive list of items that might be taxed: auction sales, carriages, liquor, sugar. Any retailer would have to buy a license to stay in business. Import duties would be doubled.

"There isn't a businessman in the whole country who won't be bruised by this sort of thing," Sérurier commented sardonically when he and Foster were thrown in to each other's company at an evening reception. Foster disliked the fellow so wholeheartedly that he could barely hide his distaste, but on this subject he agreed with him. It annoyed Sérurier that the Englishman refused to speak French with him; they could have had private conferences in the midst of crowds. "That's why I speak English to him," he told Baker.

"I suspect Mr. Gallatin is in for some difficult days," he said coolly to Sérurier. "And since the Yankees have not seen fit to renew the charter of their national bank when its twenty-year time limit was up last year, the money won't be easy to find." He found it inadvisable to mention that he knew of Napoleon's offer of twenty-five ships of the line and other good and valuable considerations if the Americans would throw in their lot with the French. When they refused, Foster saw it as a score for his team.

Both ministers had underestimated Gallatin's persistence. Pushing doggedly ahead, he managed to raise eleven million dollars at six per cent. Since the Federalists were sitting on most of the money, the military loan would have to go through them, to support a government they opposed, a President they didn't trust, for an army they didn't want. Those worthies acted as Foster expected them to. He hoped they stuck with it and sat tight.

His great ball would be an excellent base of operations in every way. With some of the legislators, the warmth of his greeting would be enough. With others, he made inquiry about their health and their families.

"How is young Christopher?" he could ask. "A bad bump on his knee last week when he tumbled from his pony, I hear. And Alicia? A beautiful child."

With men inclined to be hostile, or at least wary, a sober request for information and opinion, and a flattering way of listening to the answer. How many men never learned to listen! It was a priceless art.

To all of them he must reflect the virtues of his country: honesty, dependability, solidity. He would not try to hide the fact that he knew many of the things that were going on politically behind the scenes, in spite of their clumsy attempts at secrecy. He understood the whole gloomy picture too well.

He made a careful list of the ladies he should dance with, in strict order of protocol. Memorizing it meant that he could burn the paper.

The President stopped by his office briefly that morning, bringing his wife's regrets, another small disappointment. Foster called on her the week after the ball to tell her so in person. "I love parties, Mr. Foster, as you know," she told him with her disarming smile. "But you realize—politics! I watched much of your preparation and the arrival of your guests from my windows."

"Politics, Mrs. Madison! That's the wrong reason, dear lady! Entirely the wrong reason."

As he moved among his guests he reflected that Washington had never before seen such a colorful assemblage. The Americans, impressed as he knew they would be by the elaborate plans he had made, were wearing their finest. The men who were militia officers came in full-dress uniform; their women were in satins, brocades and laces, with glittering jewels and the latest in the hairdressers' art. The room swirled with delicate pastel colors, backdropped by the men's bright jackets and black evening clothes, many being worn for the first time. Regretfully, Foster had decided against his uniform with its gold braid, epaulettes and dress sword as being too militaristic at a time of so much tension. Formal evening wear it would be.

The real brilliance of the soiree came from the several foreign ministers who were under no such restraint. These people always attended his parties, not just for the charm of his company, he knew, or the delights of his cuisine and the comforts of his embassy, but because he could speak their language.

The Italians, he had found, were more apt to be handicapped in the New World than most other nationals. Now and then one showed up who spoke no English at all, or handled it so badly that he was not understood except in dumb show. At Foster's first words in easy, natural Italian, the bewildered fellow was apt to fall on him with a great emotional outburst that turned him beet-red. He had learned to stay at a safe distance.

Some of the top American diplomats spoke an indifferent French, but even there, Foster's use and understanding of the language outclassed them. His years of schooling in Germany had given him a familiarity with that tongue as well. From his archaeological exploration in the Near East with his cousin Sir John Leslie Foster, he had picked up some Arabic, some Turkish and a smattering of Greek. The one-tongued Americans never ceased to be dazzled by his skill.

To honor their friendship and respect for the Britisher as a person, as well as in consideration of possible political overtones, envoys from the various countries represented in Washington came to the ball in formal native dress. The women were dressed in subtly draped garments of purple, cerise, orange and emerald toned with threads of silver and gold, and wearing great drooping earrings, huge carved combs in their hair, dozens of jangling bracelets; the men wore splendiferous uniforms with engraved or bejeweled scabbards for their swords.

Madame Bonaparte was escorted by her aunt and uncle. She was in filmy pink with a very low décolletage and wore soft kid gloves reaching almost to her bare shoulders. She came up to Foster in a mist of the scent that never failed to set him spinning.

"Your Excellency!" She returned his greeting with a mock curtsy.

"Madame! I am so happy you could come. Senator Smith! Mrs. Smith! You do me honor."

They were pushed on by the crush of other arrivals: statesmen, political leaders of both parties, the great and near great and their ladies. Servants took their wraps and guided them to less crowded areas. The orchestra drew many to the improvised ballroom Foster had created in the wide hallway on the second floor.

Many were watching as he found opportunity for a few turns with Betsy. She slipped easily into his arms, and her tiny feet followed his lead effortlessly.

"I understood that my good friend Lydia Eliza was to be here tonight. Mama has mentioned it in all her letters," she said once.

"I'm sorry, I didn't hear you." He bent his head closer. "This music is a trifle loud."

"Never mind. I was only making conversation. But you do need a hostess, don't you? By the way, putting those large plants in front of areas where you don't want people to go is a stroke of genius!"

"Mrs. Cochran taught me that." He handed her over to Mr. Baker, who had indicated by a lifted eyebrow that Foster was needed elsewhere. "I must find time to show you some of my Italian art treasures. Later?"

She was already giving Baker her undivided attention. Well, he could easily find her again and he knew that he could make first claim on her at any time.

If it had not been for the quality of the fabrics and the carefully modulated behavior of the company, he reflected, the kaleidoscope of color, the noise, the atmosphere of gaiety and excitement could have been that of a carnival. The string orchestra was the best he could hire; the sumptuous midnight buffet had both eye appeal and taste appeal. One servant had been instructed to stay near the caviar and to ask the hesitant visitor if he would like a bite of caviar, thus spelling out the name of the dish and suggesting the size of the serving. There were choice seafoods, English pastries, Caribbean fruits, cold roast fowl, an impressive array of liqueurs, coffee, citrus juices —all chosen with a thought for the food and drink prejudices of many nationalities. He had not forgotten corn liquor for the backwoodsmen, but he warned Baker to keep a watchful eye on those who imbibed it.

In the toilette rooms he supplied rouge and hair powder, as well as the white and blue powders that were favored by Southern belles, who preferred them on their faces to soap and water. Powder made their skins so smooth.

Several incidents indicative of much of the American character, he felt, took place at his ball, although, in general, it was considered one of the most spectacularly successful social affairs of the decade. Children and grandchildren were to hear of it for generations. The party was referred to as "the Great Ball," which indeed it was.

"There was a Person who came uninvited," Foster later jotted in his notes, ". . . whom nobody knew. I went up to him and asked if he knew the Master of the House. He answered No. When I inquired if he had been invited to the Ball, No, he said again, but it was not usual, I said, to come to a Ball without invitation, then the fellow found he had done wrong, but said to excuse it on the score of Curiosity. Having seen the House lighted up and so many people going in, he thought he might also go in to see what there was going on. He was a small Storekeeper of Georgetown and I took compassion on his Simplicity and told him to walk through the rooms if he liked, but to go away immediately after for that he had certainly done wrong in coming and that the Master of the House would be very angry if he knew it. He thanked me very gratefully for my good Advice and walked off so that I saw no more of him."

Some of his buttonholing had unexpected results. Little Christopher's father was so touched by his solicitude that he subsequently reversed his vote on several issues and was almost asked to switch parties. Two of the gentlemen whom he had asked for opinions began giving opinions to one and all on everything.

Baker got a three-day black eye for his vigilance over the corn liquor. When Foster inquired about it, Baker glared out of the other eye and said in a wounded voice, "The oaf was hunting *you,* sir. You will recall my advice against serving that particular beverage."

Late in the evening something happened that he dared not talk about, although the newspapers had no such hesitation. Even getting it into writing for himself was an exercise in semantics. He crossed out and parenthesized some of the phrases to record it accurately but not too graphically for his diary.

He recorded that his guests included ". . . even among the lowest in Station of the Members of Congress several droll, original but unoffending Characters, such as the Tavernkeeper who ~~*Gulliver-like extinguished my fire*~~ committed an Act of great impropriety in my House . . . when the drawing rooms being left empty on the Company going in to Supper, he thought poor fellow that he was alone and unobserved, but two stray Federal members who were rambling about espied his attitude and the Joke was too good to be lost so they had it in all the Papers and all over the States in Prose and Verse (Ringing the Changes on the Extinction of the British Fire). My poor Guest wrote me an humble Letter saying he would rather burst another time and I most graciously answered and hoped to have gained his Vote for Peace by my soothing but the graceless dog voted all the same for War and proved how hard it is by any good Word to sever a Party man from the mass of his political Friends."

The "poor fellow" who had gotten caught in such a compromising situation was the Honorable William Anderson of Chester, Pennsylvania, who had served in the American Revolution with great distinction and had been in Congress since 1808. He might have preferred to remain anonymous, or to have gone down in history in a more statesmanlike way.

The flowers did not freeze, largely because they had been wrapped and rewrapped to protect them, and the stage driver had been paid handsomely to see that they arrived intact and were delivered to the door of 15 South Street as soon as he reached Baltimore. Lydia pinned them to her pillow, overcome with Foster's thoughtfulness in the midst of what must have been enormous responsibility.

Realizing that the nosegay would not long survive without water, she had it taken apart and some of the flowers sent to Thomas's bedside, the others put in a vase beside her own. The fragile blossoms would have to substitute for the Ambassador's company as long as Congress was in session.

"I dare not leave these Members alone two days together," he complained to his mother.

It seemed as if most of Baltimore was ill, some quite seriously. One social function after another had to be canceled. School sessions were curtailed. Even Aunt Debby was finally obliged to take to her bed, although she didn't see how the household could manage without her constant presence.

When Lydia's cousin State Senator Levi Hollingsworth

went up the bay to New Castle, Delaware, to bring Miss Ann Dorsey home as his bride, he stopped in Elkton to deliver two letters, one from Debby, one from Lydia. Mr. Cochran had escaped going to church that Sunday morning of February 9 because he was busy with his books, but the children had been taken to the services, so the house was quiet. Debby bundled herself in a wool robe and curled up close to the fire with her writing materials. Her letter to her sister Ruth would have many personal details, and would end with her signature embellished with curlicues and little swirls that ended in hearts.

"I often wish their was a bridge over the Susquehanna," she complained, as did every thwarted traveler, "then their would be no barrier to our seeing you often." Not bothering to correct her spelling, she went on, "When last I wrote I think I mentioned having a pain in my side. I had flattered myself that it would be slight. The Doctor recommended a pitch-plaster which I wore 10 days. This relieved it a little but shifted to another place. I was at length obliged to give up. The Physician bled me twice the first day. Blistered me the second, then medicine which confined me one week to my room, after all this I was nearly restored, but still have the plaster on my side. I have great reason to be thankful I was so soon restored. The day before I got down my Young Woman who had become vaccinated became exceedingly indisposed. The Doctor pronounced it the Smallpox taken previous to the other. She had been extremely ill going on three weeks, setting up a fortnight. Fortunately I got Hetty the third day after she was taken, who is exceedingly attentive and in her situation which the Physician says was one of the worst cases he ever saw, he had considered her dangerously ill untill a few days ago. She now sets up a little. At several times we thought her departing."

Deborah didn't bother to tell her sister that she had sent over to Ann's to try to "borrow" Fronya for a few nights. The situation there was so serious that they had had to refuse.

Late that afternoon, Mr. Cochran put aside his work and

took little William for a visit to Sam's family on Charles Street, across from the Union Bank, where William loved to go. They reported to Debby that most of Sam's folks were well except for his son-in-law, Dr. Gibson. While Mr. Cochran was gone, Thomas Hollingsworth, Senior, stopped in, so Debby could tell her sister that Thomas, Junior, "mends slow" and that his mother was not very well either. All of their servants had been down with the illness.

In spite of all the bad news, Debby's propensity for matchmaking never failed her. Since Levi was going north and would return shortly with his bride, she suggested that Henry's daughter, Betsy, twenty-seven years old and still single, accompany the newlyweds to Baltimore. "If you see her, tell her I say she must come down and set her cap for Mr. C [Comegys] as he is very cleaver and I have been saying everything for her to him—you see I am for getting everyone married where they can do better. Assure you Levi has furnished his House handsomely. He called for me on Friday to go threw his House. It appears he has thought of everything. I hope it may prove an agreeable Match to all parties."

In any case, Levi's house was ready. Deborah Cochran had made sure.

Lydia, finally recovered, told the relatives up the bay that the bridegroom "has calculated on dining at his own House on Sunday next. Aunt Debby has assisted him in some of his furniture, and says he has everything very comfortable. I told him yesterday at dinner I should take a peep, and he begged we would go and see it all—quite delighted he is with his anticipated happiness. I think the Lady may consider herself very fortunate in her choice, although matrimony is deemed a Lottery!"

The best news she could impart was that her brother had been able to share in the dinner that her parents gave Levi before his departure. "Thomas came down yesterday and remained all day in the dining room; the first time in six weeks. He is reduced a great deal: no calf's to his legs and more hollow in the cheeks than usual. He seems very desirous to be once more on horseback. He rubbed with mercury but could not be salivated and thinks he will not persevere. His throat was sore a few days. The servants are also better. Robert creeping about the yard, and Hannah still in the kitchen corner but they now answer getting better. Both Papa and Mama have colds but they are so very prevalent that we do not consider them an important indisposition. Papa is hoarse, tho his cure is Hoarhound Barley. Aunt Debby is much better."

Lydia knew a little more of Dr. Gibson's situation. He "has been confined with an Inflammatory Fever and cold," she wrote. "He went out yesterday to a patient, of necessity rather than choice, a Gentleman who was stabbed in seven places about a fortnight since by a Frenchman, in the height of passion. He had suffered a great deal since, and the artery was taken up on Sunday week and very near the armpit; it has since broke and bleeds very much, and they think him too weak to bear an amputation of his arm and that he must die by inches. I think this case has agitated Gibson, who thought it very critical when he first saw him. This day his Physicians told him medical aid could not longer be useful."

Yes, William Gibson was "agitated." First, because he had not been called at once, when his surgical skills might have saved the man, and second, because there was no known way of closing up such a severely slashed and broken artery anyway. The incident sent him to his medical books, to all of his notes from the lectures he had attended in Edinburgh, London and Philadelphia, to his memories of witnessing and assisting surgery in both Great Britain and America, but he found no answer. Before the year was over, Gibson would work out his own answer and would become known as the first surgeon to tie, successfully, the common iliac artery. Always before him was the picture of that poor devil bleeding to death on a cold winter Sunday while he, ill himself, stood helplessly and watched the man's life spurt away.

☆

Thomas's weeks of pain and inactivity had drawn him and Lydia closer than they had ever been when he was well and occupied with riding or sailing or fox hunting, all sports she could not share. When they were growing up, the four years' difference in their ages made them feel as if they were of different generations, but the gap between them began to narrow as Thomas grew taller than his sisters and took on more adult ways.

Lydia carried up the tray for his midday meal and brought one for herself so that he would not have to eat alone. Her mother was taking turns with Fronya in watching over him at night, and Ann Maria shared his evening meal. His father stopped in for a few moments when he got home from work each day, but he was the one person who did not spend much time in the sickroom. How could he tell his son that seeing him in such agony was more painful to him than if he had been ill himself? His anxiety always increased as the day wore on and the inevitable hour came for him to trudge home, twenty years older in the past few weeks, and pull himself up the stairs to stick his head in the door and ask with a false smile, "How did it go today, son? You look much better." Young Thomas would reply, just as falsely, "I'm fine, Papa. It won't be long until I am up and out of here."

Torn apart by the boy's courage, Thomas, Senior, noticed the visible wasting of his cheeks, the lifelessness of his hair, which had once been so vigorously curly and dark, the useless look of his twisted hands, the stiff points that his toes made under the bedclothes. He was not better. Not, not, *not!* His fever had decreased after his physicians bled him, and there were no new swellings, but wasn't he still in bed? Had the rubbing helped? Had anything helped? What more could be done?

When the day came that young Thomas could sit up on the edge of his bed with a weakly triumphant smile, he managed an awkward salute to his father, who plunged to his own room and locked the door so that he could pound both hands furiously against the bedclothes to keep from crying out in his anguish and gratitude.

He fell on his knees then and let the tears come. At least the boy would live.

Her brother was the first, and for a long time the only, person to know of the depth of Lydia's devotion to the Englishman. Others suspected it, of course, but she had been careful about committing herself in words. She feared that the gossamer threads that were weaving themselves around her heart might disappear, leaving her only the old emptiness. She was more than a little superstitious; talking about her precious secret could make her vulnerable to some malevolent work of the Devil. Silence was not only golden; it was a form of protection.

After they finished eating, Lydia usually rang for the dishes to be taken away, then fluffed up the pillows to make Thomas more comfortable and sat back in her chair to see if he felt like talking. Sometimes a few moments of idle nothings would relax him enough so that he could drop off to sleep. When his eyelids drooped and his speech thickened, she would make sure he was covered and then tiptoe out.

One day when he was more animated, he started asking her questions, the ones she had been expecting from almost everyone.

"You've made up your mind, haven't you, Sister?" His voice had some of the old banter, but there was an undertone of seriousness.

"About what, Thomas?"

"About the only thing that most women think is important," he said impudently. "A man, of course."

"I guess that is important," she agreed. "But do you think I'm like 'most women,' Thomas? I like to think I'm different. Unique. Special."

"Don't change the subject! I asked you a straight, simple question, didn't I? And I'll bet I know the answer!"

"Mama says it isn't right to bet." Lydia got up to straighten one of the ship pictures and put more fuel on the fire.

"It's all right for me. I'm like Papa. I only bet on a sure thing. That's why I always win. It's Mr. Foster, isn't it? At least I hope it is. He's head and shoulders over any other fellow who ever came around."

She nodded, her face turned away.

"Forever, Sister?"

Again she nodded, not looking up.

"And does he feel the same way about you? If he doesn't, I'll—"

"I don't know, Thomas, not in so many words. Please don't—"

"Have you heard from him lately? Since he sent the flowers?"

"Yes. Two notes. He's very busy and there are so many—"

"Sure. But does he ever make you cross? He can't be all perfect."

Lydia looked out the door to be sure she couldn't be overheard. "Not just cross. *Furious.* When he's here, he's so sweet and thoughtful and—and exciting . . . then he . . . Oh, I don't know how to say it. I could *scream.* . . ."

"I think I know," Thomas said. "He backs off. Isn't that it? What's he scared of, Sister? You're quite a catch, you know. Any man on earth ought to—"

"Don't tease, Thomas."

"Tease? I'm not! I'm speaking God's truth. And did you ever let him know how you get bothered about the way he makes a big fuss over you and then he—"

"Thomas! *Never!* And he's busy. And people shove him around! He's trying to keep us out of a *war.* I don't see how anyone could do anything more important than that—I wish I could help. He does like my letters. He said so."

"Why don't you push him a little? Let him know how you feel?"

"You are out of your mind!" Choking with embarrassment, she picked up their trays and flounced out of the room, her cheeks pink.

As he continued to recover, Lydia helped him down the steps so that he could eat with the family, then back to his room later. Neither of them mentioned their conversation again, but Thomas had planted a seed of doubt in her mind. What was Foster afraid of, if that was really it? He did back off, just as Thomas said. She looked up from her place at the table and saw across the hall beyond her brother's head the old family crest. She hadn't thought about it for years. *Disce Ferenda Pati.* She gave Thomas a knowing smile while he stared blankly back at her.

When he was safely in bed he told her, "You're a pretty good nurse! You can handle an old stiff-legged crab like me who hurts all over when anyone else touches him. You do it exactly right."

"Thank you for saying so."

"You're even better than Polodore." Thomas grinned. "The only thing is he's big and strong. I guess he could toss me over his shoulder if he had to."

"I hope that never happens," Lydia said quietly.

"It won't," Thomas said confidently. "I'm getting stronger all the time. After all, the doctors did say it would take a while." He pulled a quilt around his shoulders. "Say, are girls ever doctors?"

"Girls? Oh, my goodness, no! That would be unthinkable!"

"Why?"

"Why, because. Because, well, doctors have to cut people and do—do horrible things that no—no lady could—oh, no, it would never do. And some doctors have to go out and take care of people at night and get into all kinds of situations. Oh, no, people would never hear of it."

Thomas looked at her quizzically. "You wouldn't have made such a long speech about it if it hadn't been something you'd thought about, Sister. Admit it. And doctors help people, don't they?"

"Yes, of course."

"And don't you like to help people? Aren't you always doing a thousand errands for Cousin Ruth? And going all over town gathering up things for the orphans out at the Benevolent Society? And didn't Aunt Debby think you were the best person in the world when little Elizabeth was sick?"

"I loved Elizabeth."

They were quiet for a while, remembering the lost little one. Finally Thomas began again, although she could see that it tired him. "You know, Mama almost has to be a doctor, to take care of the servants and the people out on the farms and all. No one would call someone like Dr. Donaldson just for a servant, but they get sick too. And how many babies has she helped into the world? How many? Count!"

"Thomas!" Lydia's face was scarlet.

"That's the way everyone gets born, isn't it? And no one ever has a man doctor for that, do they? It's always Mama or some midwife—"

"Thomas!"

"Sorry, Sister." He slid weakly down on his side, wincing with pain as an arm twisted under him. "But a fellow lies here and counts the stripes in the wallpaper and the panes in the windows and the branches on the tree outside—the only one I can see from here—and ends up by doing a lot of thinking. About kind of important stuff too. Like, what will our futures be? Yours, and mine, and Ann Maria's."

"She'll make a good wife and mother some day," Lydia said loyally. "She's very domestically inclined. Mama says she's easier to train than I am. I suppose I should get more interested in learning about running a household but—"

"From what little *I* know about it," Thomas said thoughtfully, "running an embassy is a hundred times harder than just running an ordinary household—"

"An embassy! Thomas!"

When she was out on her rounds of shopping or of gathering up supplies for the Benevolent Society, Lydia began to consider the full extent of her mother's duties. She was purchasing agent, midwife, hostess, confessor, arbitrator, active church worker and keeper of the family conscience, loving wife and tender mother. The anguish of her headaches had valid explanations; when they came on, she still had to keep going, because so much and so many depended on her. Ann Hollingsworth was managing not only one home and one family in Baltimore, but she also had many demands on her from the tenants on their farm properties and had to see to the butchering and to the preserving of fruits and vegetables.

How does she do it? Lydia wondered, considering it for the first time in her previously serene and sheltered life. How does she do it?

An *embassy?* Lydia had thought only in terms of the man himself. But this man had built-in requirements in a wife completely aside from any of the assets she hoped she had as a person. It would not be sufficient just to adore him forever, to feel that everything he did was exactly right, to be willing to take the enormous risk of trying to bear his children . . . but bearing a child for the man you loved. . . . She was beginning to dare to use the word "love" when she thought of him. She had never even come close to such a feeling for any other man.

The social activity that consumed much of her free time could fit her for that phase of life on a public scale, but only partially. She did know how to preside at a tea table, to present and entertain guests, to carry on light dinner conversation, but all that was only a fraction of what she would really need.

She resolved to pick up her French again, remembering Betsy's long-ago advice that "French opens doors." It had certainly opened doors for Betsy, some that might better have stayed locked. Lydia still had her old French textbooks somewhere, with Madame la Comb's artistocratic writing on many of the margins. In hunting for them she stumbled on another about English history and became so absorbed in it that she had to be called for tea.

The next afternoon her brother felt strong enough to stay downstairs until evening. Lydia brought a comforter to wrap around him as he sat by the fire in the back parlor, his feet up on a stool, overjoyed to be a part of the family. She found small cushions to tuck around him and brought him the day's newspaper to read.

"Thank you, Dr. Lydia." He grinned. "And has it occurred to you exactly why you were invited to the big doings in the Federal City, even though you didn't get to go?" He picked up the thread of their earlier conversation while the others were across the room.

"Well, I guess it was—I hope it was because he wanted me to be there. He likes to dance with me. He said so."

"Right. And he wanted you to dip your finger into that whirlpool all the big politicos live in so you could see what it was like. And he wanted to see how you would look in an embassy, my dear sister. Face the facts! That kind of man has to make the right plans all the way round, you know. That may explain why he's so standoffish sometimes."

"Thomas! How can you be so hardhearted? He isn't like that. So calculating. He just isn't."

"Now, don't sulk," he chided her.

"I'm not. I'm just saying—"

"Leave me alone, Doctor. A man must have time to read the news, you know." Painfully he maneuvered the paper so that he could spread it out on his lap, turning it open to the inside page that featured the news dispatches. He would not permit her to help him, bravely determined to do everything for himself that he could manage. He read for a few minutes in silence while the women chatted among themselves and his father went outside for a walk and a smoke.

"Sister! Come here! Look at this!"

"What is it?" Lydia hurried to him, alarmed by the tone of his voice.

"Your man is in the soup! The United States government has paid fifty thousand dollars for a set of letters to the Governor-General of Canada, Sir James Craig, from a number of important New England Federalists. Fifty thousand dollars! How much money *is* that?"

"Never mind! What's the rest of it?"

"The President says that he will publish all the letters, which will show that the Federalists have been conniving with the British. Incriminated in the affair is not only Sir James but also Lord Liverpool, who is an uncle by marriage of the British Minister to the United States, the Honorable Augustus John Foster. Lord Liverpool was formerly Lord Hawkesbury. The letters have come into American hands through an impeccable source, the Count de Crillon, who is said to have gotten them through a Mr. John Henry, a secret agent of the Canadians. It is understood that the names of the American letter writers will be withheld, but they are known. That's what it says!"

"It can't be—"

"Here it is, Sister, in black and white." Thomas's face was as stricken as her own, as he handed her the newspaper and pointed to the paragraphs. "You can read it for yourself. I wonder if Papa knows about this."

Lydia tried to focus her eyes on the damning story, and finally gave it back numbly.

"It . . . can't . . . *be*. . . ."

Chapter Fifteen

Make Ready Thine Arrows

Here is the church
And here is the steeple;
Open the doors
And here are the people!

The familiar finger game shows roughly the shape of Baltimore's inner harbor, the Bason, astride the wide branches of the Patapsco River as it flows toward the Chesapeake Bay. The central longest fingers represent the extension of land between those branches, called Whetstone Point, an ideal location for a fort. Such a fort could act as a sexton at the church door, able to see in all directions. Back him up with men and arms, and the people would have formidable protection, from the sea at least. In the Middle Ages, a robber baron would have had unlimited power just by using Whetstone Point for collecting tribute.

Any enemy penetrating that close to the city would have already breached the defenses out at North Point, at the confluence of river and bay, and other smaller installations at spits of land along the wide river, so the fort must be doubly strong.

Until the time of the American Revolution, the need for

arming Whetstone Point had scarcely occurred to the three or four thousand merchants, bankers, seamen, shipbuilders and traders living there. Vessels of all sizes and registries came and went from the ports of Europe, China, the West Indies, Canada, South America, New England and now and then from Africa. The latter were usually slavers, whose stench betrayed their presence for a distance of fifty miles. Once used as a slaver, a ship could never be successfully converted to another use, because of the smell as well as the horror of its history.

The raucous port, third largest in the Western world, offered many delights for the sailors. Violence in the wharf and warehouse areas was perpetual: brawling, wenching, knifing, clubbing, murdering. Certain professional men made a good living by catering to the visitors' needs. Such advertisements as this one were common:

NO QUACKERY

The Venereal Diseases cured speedily and effectually (without the least injury to the constitution,) by a Physician of experience, at no. 91, Bond Street, Fell's Point, Baltimore. His mode of treatment is the result of twenty years extensive practice in Europe & America. Also, the most inveterate Ulcers, Scurvy, Eruptions of the Skin, Bilious Diseases and Obstructions, Rheumatism, Piles, Worms and Dysentery.

N.B. The Itch cured by one application—

☞ Medicine Chests fitted up, upon an improved Plan.

Carousing on the waterfront was as much a way of life as Sunday services were in the many houses of worship up in the surrounding hills. St. Paul's Church, which was the center of the religious life of the now devoutly Episcopalian Thomas and Samuel Hollingsworth families, was there before the town was a town. The first Roman Catholic diocese was established in Baltimore in 1790, with Father John Carroll as its first bishop; he became archbishop in 1808.

There were Unitarians, Methodists, Presbyterians, Lutherans and members of other branches of Protestantism represented in Baltimore. In spite of this active piety, the city was often called a sink of corruption (or worse) by residents of other cities, who knew only of the life along the docks.

Great wagonloads of produce kept the incoming roads busy, squeaking and groaning into town from plantations, mills, lumber camps, farms and trap lines with goods to be exchanged for sugar, rum, molasses, tropical fruits, iron products, silks, cashmeres and manufactured goods from England, and sometimes for a terrified batch of half-dead blacks brought in on one of the stinking transports.

When the Revolution got under way, the need for a fort became apparent, and by March of 1776 the fort was ready to mount eight guns. By 1781, when the nation was struggling to handle its new independence, the fort had a barracks for its men, a military hospital, a battery and a magazine. With the coming of peace and the need for agricultural, political and economic development at every level, Whetstone Point grew up in weeds. Then in the late 1790's, when America got into an undeclared naval war with France, the Baltimore merchants became alarmed. William Patterson, James McHenry, three of the Hollingsworth brothers and a number of others were so aroused that they began to push for reactivation of the fort. McHenry was then Secretary of War, which gave added weight and urgency to their plans.

Funds ran out long before the work was finished, and so volunteers were requested. The young fellows who responded made a lark of the adventure as they dug ditches, hauled rocks, made mock war on each other and an invisible enemy fleet. Somehow the work progressed anyway.

Little Thomas Hollingsworth, Junior, had tagged along with his bigger cousins and some of the Patterson and McKim boys from across the street. What bothered him most was that he could not find a place high enough to be able to look down and see the shape of the fort, which everyone said was going to be like a star. The talk was that guns could be fired in any direction. There was to be a great high flagpole, so that the flag would be seen clear across the ocean, some said.

"I might make myself a pair of wings," Thomas, Junior, confided to Lydia. "I could climb up on our roof or on that mast of Papa's new schooner; then I could fly from there and look around at everything and come back and tell you all about it. So if the fort *isn't* shaped like a star I could set everyone straight."

"I'm sure you would," Lydia replied. "You'd better not let Mama see how dirty your hands and face are."

"You jus' be a angel, chile," Delia told him as she cleaned him up. "Then you fly whuffo' you please. You see all the sta's."

James McHenry, who had been instrumental in getting the fort back into commission, lived west of town on the Turnpike Road. Because he had been born in Ireland—County Antrim—he could have been one of those persons the British claimed were still British citizens. Taking over *in toto* from the Germans the idea that a man's birthplace determined his nationality, they were using that principle to justify their raids on American shipping.

McHenry was not greatly alarmed for his own sake. He had been through the Revolution as a surgeon; then he was Washington's secretary and later in Washington's and Adams's cabinets. When he was sent to the Constitutional Convention in 1787 he protested vigorously when it was proposed that Congress pass navigation acts and regulate commerce. He could see too clearly that Maryland's export trade, the backbone of its economic life, would then be under the restriction of the four large northern industrial states.

Although he finally signed the Constitution that replaced the old Articles of Confederation, McHenry disagreed with much of its content, but he was man enough to say that his judgments were not completely infallible, and he agreed with old Dr. Franklin that the document was probably the best that could be managed.

When the refurbished and strengthened fort was ready for use, it was named for the surgeon-soldier-statesman who had contributed so much to his town, his state and his country. It was called Fort McHenry.

Early in 1812, when the supposed betrayal of America by the New England Federalists struck the nation like a blow to the solar plexus, activities at Fort McHenry took on greater urgency. Munitions were stockpiled, guns were repaired, new ones were ordered, staples were stored in large quantities to be ready in case of a prolonged siege. Military drills were more frequent and less perfunctory. The watchful sexton was on guard, alert and wary.

On March 9 President Madison sent his message to Congress, accompanied by those incriminating letters that had cost such a staggering sum—fifty thousand dollars. The Chief Executive accused the British of plotting, through the connivance of Sir James Craig, Governor-General of Canada, with certain Federalists—whose names would not be mentioned because their signatures had been clipped from the documents—to destroy the Union and to strengthen their own hand in North America by annexing the eastern part of the United States to the British Isles. John Henry was named as the go-between.

Perhaps Aaron Burr, who had dreamed of becoming Emperor Aaron the First through just such a handy bit of cooperation, had not been too far off the mark.

By the time it became known that the Count de Crillon, who had furnished the letters, was a fraud and an international swindler, he had done so much damage that there was another crisis of imminent war. The letters that he had been so helpful in getting to the President were worth less than the paper they were written on. He had pocketed fifty thousand dollars. A masterly, and profitable, piece of hoodwinking.

"I said from the first," Foster told his secretary, "that something about the whole transaction had a bad smell. I knew for a certainty that Sérurier was right smack in the middle of it.

That fake 'Count' dined at the French embassy almost every day."

"And the money he spent!" Baker whistled. "Trying to impress people."

"One time at Madame Bonaparte's," Foster recalled, "he bragged that he was charged three times the usual amount for lodging because the innkeeper knew of his wealth. He was boasting about his ancestral estates and tin mines in Chile, so I got out a map, a good big one, and asked him to point out their locations. He waved his hand around over the map as if it were a drunken butterfly. He didn't know anything about Chile! He's a rotten cheat. And that bastard Frenchman put him up to it. Probably with American money, if the simple Yankee fools would figure it out!"

When the British Minister made a public statement denying any knowledge of the chicanery, most Americans believed him, some even complimenting him on his straightforward and honorable behavior. Others abused him privately and publicly, called his secretary a spy, and made offers to buy his horses and his wines, as a broad hint that he would soon be leaving.

A Baltimore girl could finally emerge from shocked and miserable isolation, her eyes red and swollen, her heart aching, and take her usual place in her family, convinced that Foster was telling the truth. Her brother, trying to walk again, called on her frequently in his efforts—his own way of letting her know that he loved her and needed her, and that the world had not ended.

When Mayor Johnson came back from a business trip to Washington, he sent his man to Lydia's door with a letter from the British embassy, which he said His Excellency had preferred sending this way rather than by the public post. It was faster. Lydia could smile: it was also more private. She had to resist clutching at the note and ripping it open as she hurried to her room.

"My dear Cousin, You must read and destroy this Note, not showing it to anyone," she read the missive, written in his scrawliest handwriting, as if he had scribbled it off in great agitation. "You cannot, you must not, believe one word about me that is appearing in the public press. I hope you know me well enough to realize that my Honour is important to me and to my Country, especially my dear Cousin when it concerns Relations with *your* Country. I pray, and ask your Prayers for me, that the Matter will soon be cleared up and the real Truth known. A. J. Foster."

At the end he had added a postscript: "When there is time, and when my Company will not compromise you or your Family in any way, I have hopes of coming to visit you, even though it may be briefly. If you care to write me, I shall promise to reply. A.J.F."

Through her tears, Lydia read and reread the message, memorizing it as she did many of his communications. Dutifully, she then dropped it into the fire.

On March 22, Foster went to the home of William Eustis, Secretary of War, for a small evening reception. There was a joke currently going the rounds that Eustis had written Lord Perceval, Britain's Prime Minister, asking for a grant of money to buy blankets. If tongues got too loose at the party, there might be a scene. Poletica, the Russian Ambassador, was among the guests. Foster wrote in his diary: "M^de^ Jerome there—talk of the manners at Baltimore where it is not unusual for a Lady & a Gentleman to walk out into the Country tête-à-tête for 5 or 6 miles."

"M^de^ Jerome" bridled at the slurs on her home town. Poletica's thick accent was a rumbling counterpoint to the tittering of the others. "It eez only vot I hear." He shrugged. "I do not gozzip about your countree. I only qvote!"

"A great many things go on in Baltimore," Betsy said tartly. "Above and below stairs, outdoors, indoors, summer and winter. Walks in the country are nothing!" She snapped her fingers as if to signal a change of subject.

The Russian then tried several ways of finding out what she knew of the political climate in the port city, especially after the recent scandalous fraud. How was feeling running these days? For the French or toward the British? Was some of her father's vast wealth going to be tapped to bolster up the shaky finances of his government?

Betsy got more and more annoyed. The Russian was one man who had no appeal for her; when he and she were in the same room they irritated each other until they both acted like spoiled brats, and she knew it, whether he did or not. Finally she turned her back on him and moved off to join several Italians who had been left behind in the fast-moving party chatter.

At about ten-thirty a message came that her son, Bo, who had been ill, was more feverish and the nurse wished that his mother would come home. Much as she enjoyed most social affairs, Betsy seemed glad to escape. The Russian had so completely dominated the evening that she had been uncomfortable the whole time.

Foster offered to drive her home, giving himself a way out too. His desk was piled high with work. Social functions were a necessity in his job, but he enjoyed them less and less as other demands poured in on him and the political winds blew so erratically and so violently that he had to be constantly on his guard.

"Won't you come in with me, Augustus?" she asked when they reached her house. "I'm so worried about little Bo, and I need a strong right arm to keep me brave." She begged so prettily that he dismissed his coachman, saying that he would walk home. It wasn't far, and he needed the exercise.

The nurse met them at the door, finger on her lips. "He's asleep. Just now. Sh-h!"

"I'll go look in at him. Won't you have a chair?" she asked Foster. "I'll be right back."

The Ambassador had no intention of staying, but he couldn't walk out while she was upstairs, so he went into the parlor and, without removing his overcoat, sat on the edge of a new Empire-style sofa, upholstered in amber satin. The room was furnished in a combination of the conservative middle-aged tastes of her aunt and uncle, whose home it was, and her own more luxurious and sensuous style of elegance. A small portrait of Jerome as he had looked at the time of their wedding stood on a lacquered French console table. A larger one of Bo hung on the wall. The floor was covered with a rich Aubusson carpet in blues, browns and creams. Near the fire a cherry needlepoint stool tempted him to rest his feet. He pushed it firmly away and sat awaiting her return in rigid dignity.

When she came in, she was carrying a small tray with a decanter and two wine glasses. He stood up, murmuring, "But you shouldn't! I really must get home. I have so much work waiting for me."

"It's only a little wine, Augustus!" She set down the tray and handed him an embroidered linen napkin. "I mustn't send you out into this cold night with nothing to warm you! Let me take your coat."

"I can put it right here," he said quickly, not wanting to have her wait on him. "And I had something to warm me at the Eustises'. Too much, frankly. Much too much."

She made a graceful ceremony of pouring the wine into the exquisitely etched glasses. After she handed him one, she raised hers in an unspoken toast, her eyes flattering him.

He sat gingerly on the sofa and lifted his glass in response. "How is the boy?"

"Sound asleep. I told the nurse to get some rest. She was up with him all last night. Since I'm home, I can hear him if he calls. I don't want my aunt and uncle to be wakened. My, there's a cold breeze around these windows!" She drew the draperies shut and went to poke the fire.

Foster wondered if good manners required him to tend

the fire for her, which would imply a certain familiarity, or let her do it, which looked rude. He could not decide, but his face reddened as he considered his dilemma.

"You're blushing, Augustus! A person would think you had never been here before!"

"I—I—" He took another sip of the wine; it was an excellent vintage. "I simply must not stay."

She brought the decanter to refill his glass, then sat down beside him. "I understand how it is, my dear, tired, overworked Augustus. Your nasty old government expects too much of you." She leaned back comfortably, holding up her glass to let the light from the candles shine through the wine. "Isn't this a lovely color?"

"Very." He held his glass the same way, imitating her like a child learning to draw.

"I truly don't see how you manage that big embassy all by yourself, Augustus. Of course you have an excellent staff. Well-trained—*beautifully* trained, actually. And Mr. Baker can help with the business details, of course, but he—"

"I know," he said, beginning to feel sorry for himself. "It's very hard."

She was quiet for several minutes, waiting for him to slide farther back on the sofa. With a quick, unobtrusive gesture, she kicked the footstool to a spot where it fitted exactly under his feet.

The stars were out when he left, and the streets were echoing with silence. The sounds of his heels on the gravel were so loud that he wanted to walk on tiptoe, but that made him feel ridiculous, so he tried to find the grassy edge of the walk. He should get home. At once. Weren't there mountains of paper work piled up waiting for him, with more pouring in every day? Wasn't that why he had left the Eustises' party early?

He began to walk faster. It *was* late! What was it she said that had sent him out of the house so fast? So fast that he had forgotten his overcoat and had to go back for it?

That little minx had a temper! Her display of pyrotechnics had simply dazed him, after he got over his first shock. What was it she had sputtered at him? Had he blurted out something about the true focus of his heart? He must have.

"*Well!* If it's *her* you want," she had thrown the words in his face, "why don't you go after her? If you ask me, *Mister* Foster, you are a kind of *sap!*"

It was April before he got to Baltimore, sending word ahead that he would be in town for approximately two days. The Sterrets were giving a dinner party on one of the evenings, and Lydia was to be invited as his partner. He would like to call on her quite early in the morning of his first day there, on his way to a courtesy visit with city officials. His appointment was at ten. Would Miss Hollingworth consider it rude if he begged to be allowed to come to Number 15 South Street first, perhaps at nine-thirty?

Miss Hollingsworth was up at six. By the time the Ambassador arrived, on the dot, she was nearly consumed with excitement. To her surprise, he was on foot, striding along like a boy released from lessons. Ann Maria and her mother disappeared. Polodore let him in and showed him to the parlor, where Lydia was waiting, attired in a rich gold wool, her hair dressed simply, and with pearl-and-diamond earrings as her only jewelry.

"Miss Hollingsworth!" He stood in the doorway—his round cheeks as pink with excitement as her own—bowing formally, and bringing with him a touch of the cold air outside. "Miss Hollingsworth—"

"Do come in, Mr. Foster. I am so glad to see you. . . ." She was half choking as he approached her and took both her hands.

"I know it is not proper to come so early in the morning,"

he apologized when they were seated. "But would you—would you be embarrassed if I explained quite honestly that I simply could not wait until evening to see you? I knew it would be late when I arrived in this city last night, but to wait another—another whole day. It has been too long, dear cousin."

"Yes." Lydia nodded, unable to take her eyes off him.

"I can stay only a few moments, as I told you, but I needed some—perhaps the word is 'courage,' for the day ahead of me. You know that your Congress has passed a new embargo. They thought at first it would be for sixty days and that they could keep it secret. Then it was for ninety days, and your President was told to call up one hundred thousand men—"

"Oh, Mr. Foster! Papa was talking about it, but I had no idea it was that bad—"

"And there is a presidential election coming up," he said ruefully. "You will understand, or at least guess at, some of the important conferences I must have today while I am in this busy hub of commerce."

"We must not have war, Mr. Foster! *We must not!*"

"So say we all." He drew a long breath. "But your city has already subscribed over a million dollars, more than all of the New England states put together!" He caught her hand and held it tightly between his own. "Now, do you mind if I do not speak of it any more while I am with you? You may have heard the phrase about the world being too much with us. . . . May I just sit, or talk about unimportant things, or just listen? Tell me about your family. And you. And Thomas. Your letters have not given me half the news of all of you."

"We're doing very well. Your flowers were so beautiful—"

"Without you and them, my ball was ordinary, Miss Hollingsworth."

"I hoped so much to come. You know that I did. My friend Betsy gave me a detailed report. The party must indeed have been a splendid one. My brother will want to see you, by the way, if you can manage."

"And I him. Later. Now I just want to spend these few moments with you. Do you mind?"

"I do not mind." The magic that always surrounded him filled the room, the house, the world.

Her mother and sister contrived to move past the door on various household errands, but Lydia ignored them. She thanked him again for the little prayer book he had given her, which had truly become one of her treasures, now that she could bear to open it and use it.

" 'Mercifully grant unto us such a measure of Thy grace,' " she began. Startled, he joined her in a whisper: ". . . that we, running the way of Thy commandments, may obtain Thy gracious promises, and be made partakers of Thy heavenly treasure; through Jesus Christ our Lord. Amen." He raised her fingers to his lips.

Polodore cleared his throat and tapped lightly on the doorframe. "The gentleman's carriage is out front, Ma'am."

"I must go." Foster stood up. "One does not keep people waiting, no matter what the distractions. I shall be a stronger man today, my cousin. Some of your countrymen have been a mite hard on me lately."

"I know. I'm so sorry—"

"Don't worry. I must watch that I don't begin believing what they say about me. What a consummate scoundrel they would make of me! Tonight at the Sterrets'?"

Quickly he bent to kiss both her hands. Lydia could hardly restrain herself from leaning down to kiss the top of his head.

In an instant he was gone. She went to the window, hoping for another glimpse of him, but his carriage was already wheeling around the corner. She stood in the center of the room, taking some time to pull herself together before she went up to talk to Thomas.

"Everything's all right again, isn't it, Sister?"

"Everything." She no longer tried to keep secrets from him.

"And you know he wasn't tangled up in that scandal with that No-Count Count What's-His-Name? At least I knew he wasn't. I hope you did."

"It must have been awful for him," she said in a low voice. "By the way, he asked about you."

"I know. And I heard you talking about Betsy too. I think she has her cap set for him."

"How could you hear us?" She stared at him. "You got out of bed and went to the top of the stairs! You eavesdropped!"

"I tried to. It didn't seem to me that he said much. And I couldn't hear the last part at all."

"You weren't supposed to," she retorted. "And I shall bring you only gruel and dry biscuits for your dinner. That's what you get for snooping."

"He sounded sad, Sister." Thomas ignored her threats.

"Sad? Perhaps he did."

"Of course, I didn't see him. I was only listening. His voice sounded as if the sky had fallen in on him. I think he's been bullied about as much as he can stand. And you know he's trained to be able to stand a whole lot. I don't think I'd like being called a spy and a crook and a traitor and a liar and all kinds of things."

Lydia's face was clouded. "Is that what happens to every ambassador, Thomas? I wonder if they treat our men in England and France like that?"

"We don't even have a man in England any more," he told her. "You know that. You can guess what went on, if Congress was too angry even to send another man after Mr. Pinckney was called home."

"And France?" Expertly she got him into bed, tightening the bottom sheet and smoothing the covers.

"Joel Barlow, that's our man there. His wife likes Paris so well that she wants to stay. That pleases the French, but then the Americans—and, of course, the English—say that she is betraying her country. You're not *supposed* to like any place too well. Any place but home, and if you're a diplomat, you don't stay home."

"I don't see how any man stands it," she said with a frown.

"The married ones manage better," Thomas suggested. "They have someone to listen to their troubles. Someone who doesn't believe all the insults. Someone to pat them on the back and tell them they're marvelous."

"But think, Thomas—think how hard all that must be on a wife too!"

"From what little I know of the great, big, beautiful world," Thomas said with mock gravity, "love makes it go round and round and round."

Lydia would not be teased. She picked up his newspaper, which had fallen to the floor, and folded it with deliberate slowness. "I was thinking the other day about Betsy," she said finally. "The way the French treat her! They call her Mademoiselle Patterson, as if she had never married Jerome! That's the most terrible thing I ever heard of!"

"She thought she would be at least a princess," Thomas said with a short laugh.

"And they want to get her little boy away from her! Can you imagine, those unspeakable creatures want her to give up her son! It would be like asking Mama and Papa to give you up—" She caught her breath. Just such a risk had been too much in the thoughts of all of them in the past weeks. "Well, at least she's getting some money out of them. And Betsy does love money."

"It took Napoleon long enough to get around to giving it to her," Thomas said. "Remember the wedding? You wrote pages and pages to Ruth Tobin. You and Ann Maria were simply green with jealousy because she was marrying a nobleman, from the First Family of France." He turned on some of his old mimicry. "A prince! And now he's a king. And Betsy's just Betsy, not a queen, not a princess, not even completely divorced."

"Well, just because those bad things happened to her,"

Lydia protested, "doesn't mean that everyone who marries a person high up in government would be—"

"You're thinking, thinking, thinking, aren't you, Sister?"

"But Thomas—!"

"I don't blame you," he said simply. "But please forgive me if I don't like the idea of letting you go off to the ends of the earth. You'd have to, you know." His fingers were stiff and fevered as he caught her hand in an unaccustomed gesture of affection. "Even Washington is too far from Baltimore. I heard you tell Ann Maria that. How much farther is it to Athens? Or Madrid? Or Lisbon? Remember when Jacob went? We thought it was forever before we got any word from him . . . but I'd like to go someday myself. . . ." He was yawning wearily. Lydia kissed his forehead and left.

At the dinner and dancing party at the Sterrets', Lydia wore the gown she had had especially made for the January party that she had missed. It was of peacock taffeta with a matching velvet cloak; she wore a sapphire pendant on a slender gold chain. Foster was aware that the color was a subtle, perhaps an unconscious, compliment to his own coloring and that they made a stunning pair. In the whirl of music and laughter he could forget the whole exasperating day he had spent in the city that was about equally divided in its feelings for and against the national leadership.

"As always, it depends on where a fellow sits," one businessman had told him realistically. They were courteous enough to him, and all had expressed deep concern about the steady deterioration of relations between America and Europe, a situation whipped up by the War Hawks. A few had let him know that there should be war to clear the air. The blowup was long overdue. Others indicated that they would go to almost any lengths to find an acceptable workable approach, and all said, as they had been saying for a decade, that it was basically a matter of impressment. The paper blockades and the infringements on their territorial limits were disagreements that they were sure could be negotiated when and if the British stopped hauling away their seamen.

"Now those letters . . ." When he heard that phrase, he had to put himself on guard to have an answer ready. Everyone knew of the letters. Too many had not heard of their falsity. If he explained too earnestly, he saw a look of doubt in their eyes. If he passed it off, they might think he didn't take the whole thing seriously enough. He frequently felt like a tightrope walker. And if he fell, there was no net to catch him.

Forewarned by Thomas, Lydia expected that the Ambassador would want to pour out to her some of the woes of his day, but he was gay and charming and most attentive, welcoming the chance to live in a different world for a while. The Sterrets, always gracious hosts, had planned a sumptuous dinner and had made a careful choice of their guests so that the conversation would be stimulating. A small orchestra came later in the evening, and the floor was cleared for dancing.

As Foster caught her hand to lead her out for a polka, she looked at his face—smiling, confident, eager—and knew that the ends of the earth would not be too far to follow him.

In his turn, Foster discarded forever the notion that an American wife would not be suitable for a British diplomat, war or no war. On his next visit to Baltimore he would make his feelings known and discuss with her his plans.

Chapter Sixteen

Thy Vows Are Upon Me

On a Sunday afternoon late in May, two people sat talking in a small garden, nibbling on fresh strawberries from a pink lusterware bowl placed on an iron table in front of them. They had pulled their chairs close to the table so that the shade of two large lilac trees would protect them from some of the sun's heat. Climbing roses—the fragile new Lady Banks in sunny yellow—trailed over a fence and up to the roof of the stables, which were partly hidden by it. Tulips—red, yellow, pink and white—nodded in front of the trimmed boxwood hedges.

There were sounds of carriages passing in the street, horses snorting in their stalls, a few turkeys making their presence known, children playing jacks, a distant neighbor trying out the keys of a new piano, which was a great novelty and luxury. Sunday afternoon on South Street was usually quiet, because its residents were quiet people—devout people, for the most part, who believed that the Sabbath was a day of rest. It was a day for studying the Bible, for memorizing prayers, and, to several of the older Hollingsworths, for taking naps.

There could have been a raging storm or a violent fist fight going on directly in front of them, but the two enjoying the strawberries would not have noticed. They had been making idle conversation for some moments when the man said, in a tone that showed he had given the matter some thought, "Do you realize, Miss Hollingsworth, what day this is?"

"Sunday," she answered. "I was at St. Paul's this morning, and so were you, so it must be Sunday." She smoothed out an invisible wrinkle from her lace-trimmed India muslin dress. "I'm sure of it."

"You're right. Absolutely right, of course. But what else?"

"Your birthday?"

"No, of course not! You know I was almost a Christmas gift. And you were almost a valentine, weren't you? But think of something else. Never mind, I'll tell you. It is an anniversary."

"Really? Of what?"

"Last week I was going through some of my old notebooks, hoping to find some means of—well, anyway, I was going through my papers and I saw the date. It was six years ago today, almost to the hour, that I first saw you!"

"First saw me?"

"You must remember, my dear cousin! I was sent here on His Majesty's business, and your father was ill and couldn't get out, so he and your uncle invited me here. You must remember! And you came into the room. I saw you first in the looking glass—I believe the fashionable word for it now is 'mirror' . . ."

"Is it six years?" she asked, flushing, knowing exactly how long it was, almost to the minute.

"Much has happened, has it not?" He moved his chair to avoid a bothersome shaft of sunshine and to face her more directly.

"Much! Perhaps I should give you some kind of memento, Mr. Foster, to mark such a great occasion? Shall I pick you a rose?" She started to rise, but he caught her hands and kept her from it.

"An excellent idea. But would you allow me to suggest what I'd rather have for such a special gift?"

Lydia looked up expectantly. "Of course, if it is something I can find."

"What I want more than anything else," he began, his face flaming in spite of his effort to avoid it, "well, it's really quite simple, and it doesn't take any shopping, and only you can give it to me." He hurried on, "I'm saying it badly, my dear cousin—I have had no practice. But the only thing I really want is three short, small, simple words, from you to me."

"I don't believe I understand," she said breathlessly, understanding quite clearly.

"I believe you do." His hands were nearly crushing hers. "But just to make sure they are the right words and in the right order, I shall give them to you first, then you can return them to me. Shall we try that?"

Lydia nodded.

"I—love—you," he said, mouthing the syllables with exaggerated care, then repeating them more rapidly. "I love you! I do, you know."

"Oh, Mr. Foster. . . !"

"You knew, of course! And must I wait forever? Can you not say them back to me? Won't you even *try?*"

She looked into his eyes then, all her long devotion to him no longer hidden. "I truly love you. But that's four words, Mr. Foster."

"Try it again," he suggested.

"I love you." The last word was lost as he jumped from his chair, pulled her to her feet and into his arms, and kissed her as if he would never let her go. When he had released her, she reached up to kiss him again, to his utter joy. He could have touched down on the moon with less exultation.

After a while he asked the question that was at the heart of his deepest concern for her. "Had you thought what it will mean to leave your home and your family and your comfortable life and go—who knows where?"

She did not reply, only looking at him the way he had

dreamed that the right girl would look, as if she would follow him straight to Hell if he asked.

"But if you love me—well, this *shows* that I am not accustomed to such matters! You must know that I want you to marry me! But of course, my beloved cousin! Of course you must know that is what I want!"

"No . . "

"But of course I do! Whenever it can be managed! Knowing that you will have me will give me something to brace me in everything I do. But perhaps I should clear up one other matter as well. Do you think of me as an enemy?"

"Oh, Mr. *Foster!*"

"My name is Augustus," he said, with some of his former starchiness. "A young lady who has just admitted, under great pressure, that she loves me and that she will accept my humble proposal of marriage—you *will,* won't you?"

"Yes, Mr. Foster."

"—should call me by my first name."

"I should have to get used to it, Mr. Fos—Augustus."

"That's better, Miss Lydia, my love. I believe that I should kiss you once more, just to make up for six years of dawdling. Do you mind?"

"I do not mind."

In the early evening, four people sat in the same garden with a large hurricane lantern glowing in the center of the iron table. Each man was waiting for the other to begin the discussion, for such it would be, and each of the women watched them tensely. The Englishman had asked for the meeting, not discounting the immense difficulties that lay ahead, and not hesitating to face them head on in the short time he would have in Baltimore. He must be back in Washington almost at once. The danger of explosion there was frightening, and as far as he knew, the only articulate person who could spell out his own point of view was John Randolph. It was not fair to expect an American congressman to carry the torch for a British minister, and he knew it. Congress wasn't listening to Randolph anyway, any more than they were listening to Foster.

Ann Hollingsworth had suggested the cool garden, and had had Delia prepare a large pitcher of raspberry shrub and plates of fruit and cookies. Foster had called it a conference, although it was not to be much like those that filled his every waking hour and sometimes disturbed his sleep. Bringing a small gift to Mrs. Hollingsworth might help him win, he realized. He had brought her a tin of English biscuits that his mother had sent him from London, possibly hoping to make him homesick At any rate, the gift was warmly received, and the lady was very pleasant to him.

He could not accurately assess how much his attachment to a Maryland beauty might affect the fraying threads of relations between their two countries. He was taking enormous chances, hoping that he was not in any way endangering her, but he had enormous hopes, and he had his own life to live too, he reminded himself when nagging doubts kept him awake. As to his family's shortsighted opposition to an American wife, he would face that when the time came, and Lydia could be her own best witness.

How would they have accepted the American Madame Bonaparte? She was divorced, or partly so. The Church of England frowned on divorce. Her son was Catholic, although she was not. One thing he was sure of: a marriage between himself and Betsy would have pushed everything else out of public and private conversations for some time to come. Even the threats of war might have been forgotten for a while. There were three governments that might be stirred up, one way or the other. He knew he had chosen correctly, and in a left-handed way he was glad for that revealing scene at Betsy's home. The girl was a vixen. And he had been a fool.

As he sat beside Lydia, facing her parents, he saw no harm in openly holding her hand, a tacit symbol of their new relationship. It was all he could do to keep from crushing her in his arms, even if the whole world were watching.

"One of the things they teach us at the Foreign Office, Mr. Hollingsworth," he took the initiative, "actually drill into us, is not to show our true feelings, no matter how provocative the occasion."

"I've wondered about that," Lydia's father answered. "It probably is necessary, but I'm sure it isn't easy. Don't believe I could manage it, sir. When I get riled up over something, I can't fool anyone, not even myself."

"And when you're happy, Mr. Hollingsworth?"

"Guess I want everyone to know it," he conceded. "And if you don't mind my saying so, sir, it would appear to me that you are a mighty happy man this evening yourself."

"I am making no effort to conceal it." Foster smiled. "No effort at all. Your lovely daughter is doing me a great honor."

"And you us, sir. My son is especially pleased." Thomas tried to avoid the anxious frown that overcame him at any thought of his boy. He must keep his mind on the matter confronting him. "I suspect, Mr. Foster, considering the fact that to the public you *are* England—actually, to the government, you are practically the King himself, or the Prince Regent—and consequently the enemy"—he stumbled over the word but went on, determined to pull the issue into the light —"or, at least, one of our enemies, there may be, well, obstacles to your choosing an American girl."

His wife had sat quietly watching as the conversational ball was being tossed across the table. She spoke up quickly, "And you'd be taking her away from us, maybe forever. So far away!"

"I know," Foster answered gravely, squeezing Lydia's fingers. "How well I know! Which is one reason I have been so long in speaking my mind. Of course, if all goes well, I may be in Washington for a long time, although I suppose that is cold comfort."

"I read the papers," Thomas said sadly. "I cannot remember when there has been less hope and less sense in what is going on."

"I know that you realize that I am doing my best," the Ambassador said very seriously. "Twenty hours a day is not uncommon. It is a most difficult and complicated situation."

"But if it does come to war," Thomas said apprehensively, "God forbid—but if it does, you would be in some personal danger, would you not?"

Lydia gasped. She had been sitting close to Foster, saying nothing while the other three discussed the possible direction of her life almost as if she were absent, except for the warm steady pressure on her fingers.

"Perhaps. But I would hope that—"

"There are always people who are violent and vicious, sir!" Thomas interrupted. "And not all of them come from the riffraff element! They can be from the highest and most respectable classes!"

"I am well aware of it. Did I ever tell you that when we had that matter of the *Chesapeake*—I guess we have never been closer to war than at that time, but we did manage to avoid it—" Foster said carefully.

"The United States was not armed and ready then, Mr. Foster!"

The Englishman's face blanched in the flickering light, as he realized that his host knew what he also knew. "At any rate," he went on, regaining control of himself, "I was coming through New York from Boston. Something told me that I should travel incognito. I do not do that very often, I can tell you; a man feels dishonest in not being himself." Lydia noticed the small dimple as it appeared and disappeared quickly. "I had sent my curricle with my groom by another route. A good thing! If it had not been for some cool heads in the mob that attacked him on a ferryboat, the groom, the rig, even the horses, would have been thrown into the North River! And of course myself as well, if I had been in the curricle. They were really after *me*. It—well, it made me think!" He patted Lydia's hand reassuringly. "But that is only one small incident in my years of public service. Usually my life is quite dull and uneventful."

"That hardly seems likely," her mother said gently. "To us your life sounds most active and important and exciting. And of course, now and then, dangerous. You don't mind our saying the truth to you?"

"I should mind anything else," he answered sincerely. "And I'd like to ask you one thing that I have already required your daughter to answer. Do you think of *me* as the Enemy?"

Their startled laughter was his reward. "Never!" both parents said at once.

"Well, I should be honest too," her father added thoughtfully. "As a person, an individual, you are not our enemy, by any manner of means. We consider you an extremely fine and honorable man."

"I thank you."

"But," Thomas spoke slowly in order to use the right words, "I must say, though, that the one point on which I agree with our President and our Secretary of State is that Great Britain is forcing us into war to protect our lives and property. It's especially touchy for me and my brothers because we're English and Irish, just as you are."

"I know." He smiled at Lydia.

"The only agreement that has ever been concluded between us, sir, in these recent years, has been your settlement of the *Chesapeake* affair, if you don't mind my saying so. I know that you must do as you are bid, but in spite of the terrible thing it is to say to you—whom I hope someday to call my son, and proudly so—it is, well, it is your *work* that is our enemy! Not your person."

"I'm sorry. And I know it is true. A man must do what he must do."

"Yes." Thomas nodded soberly.

"May I ask your prayers?"

Surprised, all three of the Americans nodded.

They sat quietly for a few moments, each wrapped in silent worry. "I have not tried to say much of the more distant future," Foster spoke diffidently. "It is impossible to know what I should say, frankly. I may be sent anywhere, at almost any time. I hope that there will be sufficient time before we—before we marry, that you can become accustomed to the idea, or at least to accept it. Neither of us wishes to rush things right now, although if my life were my own to order as I please, we should advise the rector to make preparations immediately."

He glanced down at Lydia. "The days ahead of me are quite uncertain. I almost said precarious, but I do not want to be pessimistic. And I must live and nourish myself on hope and little else. My embassy will be empty of beauty and filled only with dissension, I fear. Alas, my dear cousin, you have never even seen it! I should prepare another great ball, and make sure that you are there!"

"I did help with choosing some of the furniture, didn't I?" she reminded him. "Aunt Debby took me along when she was advising you. I didn't even think I might be selecting things for myself! Oh, Mr. Foster!"

"I had that in mind all along." He chuckled. He snapped his fingers as he thought of something that he had intended mentioning earlier. "I almost forgot, Mr. Hollingsworth! I believe the tradition is that I should prove to my chosen lady's father that I can support her. If you are worried about the matter, I can spell out my situation in a private conference with you or the other directors of your bank. I am not overburdened with riches," he smiled mischievously, "but I can promise you that I am not close to bankruptcy, nor likely to be."

Thomas sat back in his chair, thumbs hooked in his pockets. "That is the least of my worries, sir. The greatest and really the only concern of both my wife and myself is our daughter's happiness. Her happiness and her safety, I believe I should say. She is very precious to us."

Never having made such a sentimental speech in his life, he tried to help himself to another serving of the raspberry shrub, managing to overturn his glass, the pitcher and the plate of cookies. The clatter of broken china against the iron table was the loudest noise in the garden all day.

By the time everything was cleaned up, discolored clothes sponged off and apologies exchanged all around, young Thomas was calling for his mother, and Thomas, Senior, was glad to escape. Both parents bade their visitor a friendly good night and excused themselves to go into the house, leaving the lovers alone by the lilac trees.

A few days after the Ambassador—torn between elation and anxiety, both in a greater degree than he had ever felt—got back to Washington, President Madison sent a war message to Congress, requesting that it be kept secret.

The Americans had also tried to keep their latest embargo secret, setting it first for sixty days, then for ninety, in order to allow them to stop some ships, loaded with flour, that were heading out of the bay. When the news got out, almost at once, Foster had confronted Monroe coldly with the blunt question, "Is this *war,* Mr. Secretary?" Monroe had assured him that the embargo was merely a means of keeping their affairs in their own hands. Senator Smith of Maryland, Betsy Bonaparte's uncle, begged him to soften any report he might send home, feeling that it would put the United States in a bad light in their efforts at conciliation. The President commented to Foster that it was discouraging to hope for any change, because the Prime Minister, Lord Perceval, was as "fixed in his place as his purposes." The stubbornness of John Bull was nothing new.

On May 11, that situation had been dramatically changed, but it was weeks before the information reached America. The Duchess of Devonshire (Elizabeth Foster) wrote to her son that day, "I am sorry to have to add to my parcel the horrid news that Perceval was just now shot dead in the lobby of the House of Commons. I never felt more horror at anything. A murder of that kind has not happened in England since Queen Anne's time and in the midst of the horror of concerns for the particular Event one can't help dreading its opening of a new Epoch in the English Character. Think of his poor wife and children."

Lord Perceval was succeeded in the office of Prime Minister by Elizabeth's brother-in-law Lord Liverpool, Foster's uncle.

Perhaps if Madison had known of Perceval's death and the resultant change of leadership in London, he might have been able to hold off the avalanche of demands for war, in the hope that a more flexible British policy would ensue. Unfortunately, there had been too many months of "perhapses" and "if-onlys," and the War Hawks were sick of it. They were able to put more pressure on Madison by renominating him for the presidency at the Republican caucus in May. He was to run against DeWitt Clinton, then lieutenant governor of New York, who was even supported by some of the more pacific Republicans. Clinton, noted as an innovator, and not completely trusted politically by some factions of his own Federalist party, was a nephew of the late Vice-President, the Honorable George Clinton, who had died in office in April.

(Foster, not informed of the Vice-President's death until the last moment—it was thought inadvisable to upset the diplomatic corps with the news—scored a personal *coup* by sending his carriage with four horses to the funeral cortege. As he had hoped, the Americans were deeply touched by his gesture of sympathy when tempers were so edgy. He could record that his move had been "perfectly right.")

Madison's secret war message declared that Great Britain,

through its three main thrusts at American sovereignty, was practically forcing a declaration of war. First, they were continuing to impress American seamen, despite years of complaint at the outrageous arrests. One senator, Thomas Worthington of Ohio, could testify to the horrors of that experience firsthand. (In spite of that blot, he and Foster were good friends. One of the Englishman's great regrets was that he was never able to accept the Senator's invitation to visit Ohio and sample some apples, fresh from the trees.) In addition, the British were interfering with American trade at every possible juncture by blockades, seizures and searches. No amount of protest had altered the piracy. Then, to top off their depredations on the sea, they were, according to Madison, subverting the Indians up and down the northern and western fringes of the nation, inciting them to ambush and murder white men. The hoped-for westward expansion, which had been dear to Jefferson's heart and which he considered the real destiny of America, was badly threatened.

John Randolph pounced on this point, his thin voice stinging through the uproar, sneering that the War Hawks were not at all interested in the maritime rights of the nation but only in imperialist expansion and the absorption of the whole continent. Roaring off to do battle in the west would leave the east defenseless; it could only be madness.

The battle in the west would be merely a matter of taking advantage of the savages and stealing their vast wildernesses, pinning them up "in nooks" and driving them to retaliation. Behind Randolph's brilliant and biting tirade was basically a demand for common sense tempered with justice. His eloquence fell on deaf ears.

After Madison's secret war message was delivered, John C. Calhoun brought in a favorable report on the declaration of war. Heated debate went on in the House of Representatives until the final vote of 79 to 49, in favor, was taken on June 5. Randolph had called the shots accurately. Forty-eight of the yea votes were from the West and South, the areas most concerned with development of new territory and least occupied with the complexities of shipping and foreign trade.

The declaration of war, supported so enthusiastically by the House, was then sent to the Senate, where almost everyone assumed it would be defeated. The War Hawks did not have a firm hold there; many senators were financially secure Federalists, strongly against war or anything that would upset the functioning *status quo*. The hotheads were in the House.

Britain's harried Minister was not optimistic. He cut down on his hours of sleep, working indefatigably. He sent warnings to British ship captains to stay out of range lest some provocative incident ignite the tinderbox.

Lydia would have real cause to worry about Foster's personal safety then. The British Minister—as well as his government—was extremely vulnerable. He went on about his affairs with his face a mask of confidence and faith.

He noticed, not without a certain acid humor, that the taunts about buying his wines and his horses had virtually ceased. Such jokes were no longer funny.

Then a ship came into port with electrifying news. Samuel Chew, master of the *Thames,* an American brig, reported that out in the middle of the Atlantic Ocean, truly international waters, he had been stopped by a French squadron whose commodore told him they had orders from Napoleon to destroy any and all enemy ships that were going to or from any enemy port—in other words, every ship on the seas that wasn't French! They had just burned two American vessels, the *Asia* and the *Gershorn*. The *Thames* escaped the same fate only by the grace of God. Soon other ships began limping in with similar stories. There could be no doubt as to their authenticity.

So, their friend and ally the Emperor had been lying! He was as much a double-dealer and a skunk and a rascal as the British Ambassador had been trying so patiently and so persuasively to point out. And no one had listened!

Secretary of State Monroe stormed over to the office of Monsieur Sérurier, shouting that the United States was almost at war with Great Britain at that very moment because of its co-operation with the French, and now it had been betrayed! Baldly, insolently *betrayed!*

A. J. Foster found small pleasure in the revelations, even though they vindicated everything he had been telling the Yankees. He feared it was too late. But how totally, viscerally satisfying to watch the guilty squirming of the trapped Frenchman!

"I shall report your complaints to the Tuileries," Sérurier kept promising icily as Monroe scathed him with accusations, waving the proof of his lying under the tip of his nose. "I'll report it at once, of course, Mr. Secretary." It was no answer.

For the second time in recent weeks the French Minister had been caught red-handed. If everyone was accusing Foster of being the puppet and tool of his own government, which, after all, was his job, Sérurier could be called the same and worse, because *his* government was promoting treachery and lies. Foster had some righteous satisfaction in having a clear conscience, whether or not he always agreed with the decisions made in Whitehall. He hoped that his personal standing would rise correspondingly, in contrast.

The only other comfort he had in those critical and dangerous days was Lydia, who wrote him regularly, trying out a French phrase now and then and making him feel loved and appreciated.

When his problems became too pressing, he dropped in for a few moments with Betsy, braced by her caustic comments about the French and by the way she could erase their quarrel as if it had never taken place. He admitted sheepishly that her outburst had brought him to his senses. Possibly he should go so far as to thank her—no, the time for that was not ripe, and might never be. He was privately grateful, nevertheless.

Lydia's first halting venture in speaking French to him that night in the garden had surprised and charmed him. She told him that she knew his knowledge of languages was invaluable to him, and she would learn what she could, if he would but help her.

Help her! He would do everything to see that she had a good vocabulary, a natural accent. His mother might be softened up too if she knew that the American girl, presumed ignorant and one-tongued simply because she was from the Colonies, could speak French! Correctly too! And with diction approaching his own, providing they could spend enough time together to work on it. Maybe later they'd tackle Italian, or German, or both! He wished they could go right at it.

Stupid wars, which kept people from the important things of life!

The scandalous perfidy of the French set off new arguments in Congress. Why not go to war against *both* nations? Many of the Federalists had been urging this approach all along. They were overjoyed when the whole country knew the facts, since these so thoroughly proved their point. The French were *not* their friends and never had been, the shining memory of Lafayette notwithstanding. The wily little Emperor had been playing them for blind fools! And winning! Wasn't it about time to get some sense in their heads and start turning the tables on him?

Sérurier, getting wind of this new trend of thought, suggested cynically that he and the Honorable Minister from Great Britain join forces in order to build up their defenses against such a terrifying enemy with no army, no navy and no money.

This tiny lap dog squeaking out defiance three thousand miles away wasn't going to frighten two huge mastiffs battling to the death off in Europe, but perhaps the mastiffs should kick a little dust in the puppy's eyes, just to let him know they heard him.

Foster did not enjoy the jests.

One of the early proposals in the Senate was to change the declaration of out-and-out war to an act allowing American ships to carry letters of marque, a defensive measure that would permit reprisals at sea. This suggestion lost by only two votes, 15 to 17. There was more argument—some of it explosive, all of it acrimonious. Another vote stood 16 to 16. (Technically there should have been a total of 36 votes, but there were several who abstained on all the voting, so there was never a total of more than 32 ballots cast.)

William Anderson, the indiscreet ball guest and "graceless dog," had voted for war, possibly because he owned property in France. Thomas Worthington, once the victim of impressment himself, nevertheless voted nay. On June 18, after nearly two weeks of agonizing indecision, the bill was passed, 19 to 13, the minimum majority required by law. Attorney General William Pinkney of Maryland, whose former position as U.S. minister to Britain had never been filled in spite of Foster's urging, was asked to complete the final document. It was actually the nineteenth before the President, heartsick and haggard, signed it and released it to the press.

There would be war. It was determined that the enemy was Great Britain; the ally, France. A bone-tired Minister began to know the personal torture of defeat and failure, which not even Lydia's love letters could assuage. In Baltimore, that heartbroken lady sped to the home of Debby Cochran, desperately seeking reassurance and not daring to let anyone see her cry.

Chapter Seventeen

In the Place of Dragons

DECLARATION OF WAR

Declaring War between the United Kingdom of Great Britain and Ireland and the Dependencies thereof and the United States of America and their Territories. Be it enacted by the Senate and the House of Representatives of the United States of America in Congress assembled, that WAR be, and the same is hereby declared to exist between the United Kingdom of Great Britain and Ireland and the Dependencies thereof, and the United States of America and their Territories; And the President of the United States be, and he is hereby authorized to use the whole land and Naval force of the United States to carry the same into effect, and to issue to private armed vessels of the United States commissions or letters of marque and general reprisal, in such force as he shall think proper, and under the Seal of the United States against the vessels, goods and effects of the same United Kingdom of Great Britain and Ireland and of the subjects thereof.
June 18, 1812

Approved, JAMES MADISON

The ominous words appeared in all the newspapers: the *National Intelligencer,* which supported Madison, the *American Commercial and Daily Advertiser,* the *Federal Gazette* and dozens of others.

Spelled out in unmistakable terms was the news that the fateful decision had been made. In drawing up the document, Attorney General Pinkney had neglected to include Ireland with the United Kingdom of Great Britain, which had annexed it in 1801, so the paper had to be rewritten. The declaration was finally signed and sealed on a truly black Friday.

Maryland's two senators split their votes. Betsy's uncle voted for war, and would be centrally involved in it. The other, Phillip Reed, voted against it.

That evening, Foster paid a courtesy call at Mrs. Madison's drawing room in the presidential palace. He noted that the President was "white as a sheet"; the Congressmen were busily shaking hands and congratulating each other. The Englishman knew entirely too well what had transpired, but he had been given no official notification, so he acted as if the day were not any different from others. Dolley Madison was as charming as ever, and went to some trouble to see that he had refreshments and that all was to his liking. He enjoyed his visits there, finding the decorum and graciousness quite different from what it had been during his first years in Washington. Those years seemed centuries away.

Sometime that day he had decided—not without some misgivings that he might be thought doing it for the wrong reason—to make no further secret of his love for an American girl. The die for war was already cast; surely no one could accuse him of using his personal situation to soften the attitude of the Americans toward him. Such an action would have been less than honorable treatment of Lydia anyway.

Offhandedly, as if he hadn't spent hours phrasing it, he dropped a few words about his new happiness to the warm-hearted Mrs. Madison, who had been one of his most pleasant friends during his tenure. He moved on then, as cool and detached as ever on the surface, greeting this one and that, and taking his leave with dignity. Dolley would handle it. And very well. She'd get the facts straight too.

"The President and I wish you well," she whispered as she saw him out the door.

He elected to walk home, taking the long way round so that he could stride along the river, perhaps glance up at the window of his old room. It would be his last time there, just as the visit to the presidential palace would be his last. He felt an infinite sadness. When he first came he had hated everything about America: the people, the food, the architecture, the climate, the manners—nothing had escaped his disapproval.

He could still grumble because the Federal City had no public park, no place of trees and broad lawns and cool refreshment where a person's spirits could be uplifted and his faith renewed. Such neglect was unforgivable in an area where there was such a great potential for beauty. There were vast open spaces that could be developed, with countless native trees and shrubs right at hand. He listed in his notes "The poppinae, gum wood, Bride of China, from ten to twelve varieties of Oak, the liquidambar, Sassafras, Laurus and numerous kinds of Magnolia, and tulip trees with lofty stems, fluted in appearance like Pillars. . . ."

He passed some of Tartar's favorite trees and missed his pet almost unbearably. Tartar would have understood his heartbreak.

"I truly love you. But that's four words, Mr. Foster."

"Try it again."

The tears were stinging his eyes so badly that he turned away from the river and headed toward his embassy. *Packing.* And throwing away, and burning, and forgetting. And remembering.

He dared not slip off to Baltimore for the weekend, strong as the temptation was. He had not been given official notice of the break in relations; he had a hopeless hope that there might be some kind of secret sessions going on even at that late date, which by some magic—young Thomas would have called it Big Medicine—would cancel out the fearful step that had been taken.

"It's madness!" he had exploded to Baker. "Going to war, against the wrong enemy, with only a token, untrained army that *can't* be more than ten thousand men—it may be nearer only four thousand—a leaky navy, no funds to support it, the citizenry either downright opposed to the whole mess or only halfheartedly in favor!"

"War is an incurable form of insanity," Baker reminded him. "I believe, sir, that I picked up that phrase from you."

On Monday he was asked to call on the Secretary of State, which he did with such a heavy heart that he could barely walk up the steps and present himself at the door. Monroe was equally distressed. The two men spent a few painful moments facing each other wordlessly. Finally the Secretary placed the fateful sheet of paper in Foster's hands with a sincere expression of personal regret, and indicated that the interview was over. The Ambassador could not thank the man—there was nothing to be grateful for—so he said a polite good morning and withdrew.

Since Monroe had told him that the President would appreciate a call from him, he went immediately. Madison, looking old and tired and miserable and shrunken even smaller, got up and came around the table to meet him, an unusual and touching gesture. He assured the Britisher that he would do everything in his power to "prevent any serious collision" and that he hoped the war would be only "nominal." Arrangements would be made to permit the Secretary of the British Legation, Mr. Baker, to have custody of the records of the embassy and to be on hand to act as agent for the moneys expected as settlement for the *Chesapeake,* "trusting to the Honour of a People having British blood in their Veins for the safety of the Deposit." An Englishman always paid his debts, war or no war.

They spoke in a friendly fashion for a few more moments.

Then, as he was taking his leave, Madison grasped his hand with unexpected warmth and managed a fleeting smile. "I understand from Mrs. Madison, sir, that you are leaving your heart in America."

Nearly overcome, Foster could only bow.

"Sad, indeed sad for you. Nevertheless, may I give you and Miss Hollingsworth my best wishes? And Mrs. Madison's? Under these terrible circumstances, I presume it will be impossible to take the young lady with you . . ."

Again the Englishman bowed, not trusting his voice.

"I am truly sorry, Your Excellency. Good day to you, sir. May we meet again in happier times."

"Thank you, Mr. President. And please give my regards to your gracious lady."

"And mine to yours."

Foster backed out of the door, afraid that he might begin running. He stopped to post a brief note to Lydia, saying that he would come sometime during the next week.

Lydia had followed the news from Washington with anguished interest, dying a small death every time she knew of another setback for her loved one, and being just as elated when the word was favorable. Writing him every day filled some of the hours, especially since some of her letters had to be redone in order not to pass on to him any of her consuming worry.

She spent a great deal of time with her brother, devising ways of diverting him with such amusements as he could manage. They walked in the garden as he pulled himself along, trying to relearn to use his legs. Nearly eleven months had passed since the onset of his illness. His health had fluctuated from being critical to what Dr. Gibson called "encouraging," although for the past six months he had never been free from pain. The joints of his fingers and of one knee and the opposite ankle appeared to be permanently stiff, so that he walked like a puppet. Holding anything small was impossible. He could grasp a cane and had appropriated a stout oak one that had belonged to his great-grandfather. The thick knob at its top was carved like the head of a lion; the cane was worn to a satiny smoothness by generations of use. The family legend was that it had been a gift from a member of the Penn family in honor of the ship called the *Lion,* on which the first Hollingsworth, Valentine, had come to the New World. The cane itself had a colorful history, for it had been passed to whatever semi-invalid was in need of it. No one knew exactly who owned it. In such a large circle of relatives, it was nearly always in use, and the current user was considered the owner. So, the cane was Thomas's.

It had become more than a tool to him. It was a friend and companion. He was so thin and fragile that he himself wondered whether he or the cane was the heavier. His skin had the ivory waxiness of a man of eighty. He had turned twenty-two on the third of May.

"I wonder how soon I'll be able to ride again," he said wistfully on one of their walks.

"Perhaps you and I can go out in the carriage tomorrow," Lydia suggested, trying not to picture how sober such travel would seem after the years of fun he had had going everywhere on horseback.

"I should start getting used to holding the reins again," he said judiciously, easing himself into a chair. "I wish the Englisher would come."

"So do I."

"I'm happy for you, Sister. But I just don't want him to take you away. I wish we could figure out a way he could get a job right here in Baltimore. Then you could both stay. Forever."

"That would be a kind of Heaven." Lydia smiled. "Shall we go in? There may be a message from him." She helped her brother to his feet and waited patiently until he got his legs aligned so that he could start to move forward like a wind-up toy. She had to turn her back to avoid watching his tormented concentration.

Once when he was in unusual pain he had asked her, "Could you try to find out something for me? I've been wondering for a long time, especially lately. Do you know whether God speaks Dutch? Maybe English is all wrong."

"Thomas! Hush!"

Only her immediate family and the Cochrans knew of her changed relationship to the Ambassador. Ruth Tobin suspected it, but Lydia had deliberately avoided committing herself, showing more interest in Ruth's possible love affairs than in her own. The rejected clergyman had been followed by another of his brothers-in-the-faith, so Lydia could write to tease her cousin: "Pray does our mutual acquaintance, with pastoral staff, find his way to see you? Does he make a long step and lift the latch?"

Lydia felt that Foster should be the one to make their love affair known. There were cynics who would accuse him of basely using an affair of the heart to influence an affair of the government, she knew, so he must choose the time and place. "Discretion is the soul of diplomacy," he had told her half-jokingly. Their romance was not something to hide, but it was certainly not public business, not when the public was in a furor about a possible war, and the least bit of gossip could be blown to sensational proportions.

There was again talk around fashionable tea tables in Baltimore that His Excellency the British Minister had been seen calling on the former Miss Patterson at her Washington residence. One ugly rumor had him staggering home at an ungodly hour, muttering and making wild gestures, but those who knew the gentleman insisted that such behavior was entirely out of character for him. Surprisingly enough, the opinions of these cooler heads were accepted, and the damning story died a-borning.

When the little lady visited her family in Baltimore she managed to drop a few hints that she and the diplomat were "good friends, but that's all." For Lydia it was too much, although she was ashamed of her childish jealousy. Many men were attracted to Madame B., and she was leading all of them a merry chase. Lydia's cousin William was among them, as was young Dr. Mitchell of Elkton, son of Aunt Ruth's trusted physician. Lydia wished fervently that he would turn his attention to Ruth Tobin, from his home town and several times as worthy.

Foster had told her in some detail of his visits to Betsy. He could gain valuable political insights and establish important friendships through the casual conversations in her drawing room. His visits were never private, he assured her, and his reports usually sounded as if she were the center of a voluble and stimulating salon, one of the best listening posts in the Columbia District.

When the vote on the declaration of war was counted, Lydia was as stunned as many others were to see Betsy's uncle voting yea. Apparently Mr. Foster's persuasions had not swayed him.

On Saturday, June 20, while Thomas napped and the rest of the family were over at Sam's trying to assess the extent of their danger if war came to Chesapeake Bay, Lydia was attempting to choke down some of her grief by writing to Ruth Tobin.

"My dear Cousin," she began, as she had since they were children, "I thank you for your kind letter of this day." She spread out Ruth's note so that she could respond to the reports of illnesses and gardens—both flower and vegetable—and to say that she was glad Ruth liked the hat she had chosen for her. "My bonnet is a little larger than yours and trimmed with pink. I will with pleasure get your dress when I am out." She had had a slight cold because "a little party of six walked around Howard Street by the Cathedral, down Charles Street to the City Spring, here we sat in the enclosure which is cold and damp, half an hour, and then came home about nine o'clock. The next day I felt it, with running nose, great hoarseness and cough." She had virtually recovered. Ruth must not be alarmed.

"Sally and the two Nancys and Jacob went last Wednesday to Oaklands to visit Betsy. She had been very urgent for them to go while her strawberries were in perfection. She has an abundance, Jacob says." It was the first visit of either Nancy (Ann Maria and Anne Gooding Hollingsworth, Jacob's bride) to Oaklands, home of Sam's daughter Betsy and her husband, Charles Sterret Ridgely, in Elkridge. They were delighted with the place, which would be filled to capacity during the siege of their city.

Lydia must remember to send along their aunt Ruth's ticket for the Washington Monument lottery. ". . . and yet I know no end it can answer. My other chance met the same luckless fate! And yet I bought half a one in the Medical now on foot, the last venture for a long time I think."

Finally she had exhausted all the chitchat she could gather up, and could no longer restrain herself from bursting out with a hint of her secret. Ruth could surely read between the lines. Lydia chose to get into it through the cast-off Princess from across the street: "The grand prize in our neighborhood has many charms and adventures in the most ignoble sense. I do believe some are who have put in for it. I heard several anecdotes of the swains who went from here and saw her no longer than one would see a shadow, she acted very becoming and dignified I think. I heard William and Mitchell were candidates for her favour."

She pressed a kerchief to her forehead to absorb some of the moisture. The day was so warm and humid. How could she best phrase the thought? "Are they in any way alarmed by their most noble competitor? The elegant, sensible, agreeable, handsome—I am afraid to trust myself with his name

. . . the magical numbers would chill my blood and the thought of his marrying anyone outside this city should overcome me—you must guess this most interesting—I verily believe it will not be a puzzle! He is [so happy] about it and tells anybody and everybody."

If Mr. A. J. Foster could have read what she had written, he might have corrected her gently. "No, my lady, I told only one person, and let her tell anybody and everybody. But I *am* happy! Let it stand."

Knowing that news traveled slowly up the bay, she added, "What think you of war? It is finally declared by our Administration. They are fitting out privateers at the Point."

Yes, they were working round the clock out there. Many merchant ships were to be armed and given letters of marque and were to be legal raiders, with the full weight of the government behind them. Revenge was beginning to give the victims a touch of its sweetness. Thomas and Sam were in a stew of preparation for the installation of guns and gun crews on their ships.

The broad Patapsco River would be an excellent hiding place for the privateers, one of the first observations made about it by Augustus John Foster when he first traversed it. Larger ships could not maneuver themselves into it, but the raiders could dart out like crocodiles and snatch their prey. When they wandered farther from home, the privateers carried double crews in order to have men on hand to sail prize ships back to port. There was no unemployment on the Baltimore docks.

Lydia went to take her brother a cool drink and to sponge off his fevered face and hands. She added a postscript to her letter, for she knew that Ruth would be anxious about him. "Thomas has not been quite well a few days past, and is changing from one room to the other and one chair to the other, with a fan, a book, a newspaper, exclaiming against the heat, he is not sick enough to be patient. Papa will thank

Uncle to send all the wood by Biddle's next trip. A very sudden death has taken place in our city today and one which I am sure will be much regretted, Mr. Benjamin Williams. He had but sipped the pleasure promised by his recent marriage."

Mr. Willams was eighty-one years old and had recently become a bridegroom for the first time. Marriage was indeed a lottery.

There were prayer services all over the city that Sunday, not all of them asking for victory, but for courage and faith and wisdom. Lydia went frequently to St. Paul's, seeking whatever solace and strength she might find. Hundreds of others were doing the same: Protestant, Catholic and Jew, white and black. Whatever war fever any citizens had been able to work up—and it was never much—had disappeared when the sobering reality of war confronted them.

Sometimes Lydia's father sat in the pew with her, holding her hand as if to protect her from the harm that was menacing her. She was greatly moved. It brought back a long-ago moment when he had held her on his lap and asked her, "Will you be my friend again?" Now he was reaching out to comfort her another time in the only way he knew.

On June 23 the *National Intelligencer* printed the dramatic news of the death on May 11 of Lord Perceval from an assassin's bullet, the same day that Foster received his mother's letter about it. Immediately he and Baker hurried to the President. Surely there would now be changes in London! Perceval was the one who had been so adamant; now he was gone. There was every hope for more amicable relations!

Madison was a tragically helpless figure. Congress had disbanded. Many of its members had left. He could not act without their consent. He could do nothing at all.

Foster and Baker tried to seek out such legislators as were still in town, finding them in their offices, their homes, the taverns, the shops, on the streets. The two men begged, cajoled and reasoned.

Human nature being what it is, Foster saw that the probable weakening of the British government in this crisis, which could work to the benefit of the Americans if they could only hold back this war fever, had the effect of turning them into bullies. No one showed any disposition to take him seriously. Doors were literally slammed in his face. He and Baker might as well have been talking in a vacuum.

A few Americans who had listened to him in passing had felt that there was a possibility of some kind of accommodation even yet, if the Orders in Council were withdrawn—but none of these had any power of decision or influence. He could smile sardonically. It was another if-only, and none of these quasi optimists had aided him in any way in his struggle. He asked himself again: was there *any* possible approach he had not tried, any person of even the slightest consequence that he had not consulted? He went down his lists of senators, representatives, cabinet members, even ministers from other nations who might be expected to have the ear of an American. Every name had some kind of check mark against it. Those with a plus sign were few, many being marked with a zero sign to show that they had gone home without any commitment.

Having exhausted every conceivable hope, as well as himself, he set out from Washington on the twenty-fifth.

Because of the lack of quick communication there was no way for Foster, or for the rest of America, to know that the despised Orders in Council had been withdrawn two days before Congress had cast its ballot for war by such a narrow margin. The reason for the war had disappeared before the declaration was written.

His uncle Lord Liverpool (formerly Lord Hawkesbury), the new prime minister, was one of the few people in high places who had taken seriously the complaints from America and the bitter demands of his own people. One of his first acts in office was to abolish those hated Orders that had been blockading trade for so many years and starving Britain's own citizens in the process.

The first word of that long-awaited change of policy would not reach America until late July. By that time Foster would have been gone for a month and a number of lives would have already been sacrificed.

There had been rioting in Baltimore. A mob had sacked the house of a former Secretary of State who was the editor of a newspaper called *The Federalist,* opposed to the government. Mobs, like grass fires, had a way of spreading out of control; for this reason, several people advised the departing Minister that he should go north by back roads.

The Englishman's spine stiffened. Sneak around through the woods like some oaf caught poaching? He had come to the New World with honor, he hoped, and he was not going to leave it like a thief in the night. The main road led through Baltimore, and the central focus of his life was in Baltimore.

Early on that June Thursday, Augustus John Foster turned his back on the Federal City and set his course for the beautiful port city in a cup of hills on the Patapsco River.

After a few moments of greeting, regrets and profound sympathy, her family left them alone in the parlor. The door was partly opened, but no one went past it as a tacit chaperone and none came in with trays of something. All of them knew that this was an ending. At best, it would be a long and tragic separation with unknown dangers. At worst—who could know? Death was padding around openly, in league with horror.

Lydia was shaken to see how tired and hurt he looked. In spite of his effort to appear imperturbable, his eyes betrayed him. Their bright inquisitive blueness and look of superb intelligence had given way to a lackluster gray of humiliation. His posture was erect, his manner courteous, his grooming neat and his clothing fresh, but somehow the fire that had made him what he was had smoldered to ashes.

As soon as the others had withdrawn, he caught her in his arms and buried his face in the curls at her neck. "Lydia! My lovely!"

"My dear cousin!" she whispered, and he bent to kiss her. She had never called him that, and he found it heart-rending. "You mustn't give up! You mustn't!" she soothed, aware of raveling edges of his self-regard. "Come, sit down."

He could talk then, spilling out all his frustrations and his angers, the hopeless futility of his frantic efforts to stem the tide of disaster. "I never thought I would admit this to anyone," he said slowly, "but I found one senator who was known to be perennially in his cups, and consequently unfit to vote. As God is my witness, I shall never think it was wrong that I sent my man to keep him sufficiently under the influence that he could not be summoned. I cannot think it was wrong! But perhaps it was, because it didn't work. Someone got to him and propped him in his seat in time to swing the final outcome by the necessary one vote. Just one! If he had not been there—"

"But he was," Lydia said gently. "And you have done your best. Never forget that."

She could see that he was quieting down and was more like himself. Suddenly he pulled out the heavy gold watch. "I have but an hour," he said sadly. "Less than an hour now, to plan a lifetime, to find some way of strengthening the cords between us in the dark months ahead. . . . I pray it is only months. I have hopes, always hopes, that Mr. Madison's solemn promise of only 'nominal war,' whatever that is, will bear fruit. And when I get to England—" He stopped short. Getting to England would take a minimum of four or five weeks. The world could go up in flames in that time. "Word just came two days ago," he told her, "that Lord Perceval had been murdered and that my uncle is the new prime minister."

"It was in our paper," Lydia said. "You are very close to people in high places."

"I hope so, but that doesn't always help. When I get there, I can go at once and see what the true situation is with the Orders in Council. Because I have heard it so many times from so many directions, I am convinced that the dogs of war could be called off if only my govern— But then, that's later. Too much later, I fear. Please, my lovely, let us talk about us. Only us."

She sat in the circle of his arms, watching the tiny muscles twitching around his mouth, noticing the deep lines from his eyes, the paleness of his usually ruddy skin. She had loved him for so long.

He was like a man crawling out from a collapsing building, still breathless, still wondering what had happened and how he had escaped with his life. "I guess you wouldn't believe it," he said, frowning because he couldn't get away from the shock of what he had been through, "that there could be so many men who put profits above everything else, even above risks to their lives and property and employees. They've been like yellow jackets buzzing around me, wanting me to give them safe passage so they can get through your country's blockades to sell flour to my country for its Peninsular War. Letting them deal with the enemy—your enemy and their enemy!—through my good offices could have made me a very rich man in a matter of hours."

"But you didn't—you—"

"Of course not! I don't need their dirty money! I couldn't make them see that they would be sailing into almost certain death, or at least into the gravest danger. You should have heard some of their inducements—no, I mustn't talk about it." His arms tightened around her.

"Augustus—Augustus . . ." She clung to him like a heartbroken child. "Don't go . . . please don't go. . . ."

He lifted her hand to kiss her ring finger. There was so much to say and yet there was nothing that could be said. They sat for moments, her head in the curve of his neck and shoulder, her fingers curled in his.

"Papa claims there can't be much of a war, without taxes to pay for it." Lydia tried to offer something hopeful. "And Congress didn't muster the army or do anything about a real navy. And the old national bank wasn't reactivated. Maybe there won't be—"

"Won't be any war, my little goose?" he said wearily. "I wish you could have followed me around these last weeks. I don't think you would be so confident. It would have shaken your soul, as it has mine. There are forces of violence that seem to be riding the whirlwind—" He shook his head as if to drive the thought from his mind. "I do have a small memento for you. It will have to stand in my stead for a while." He took a flat parcel from his pocket and put it in her hands.

Lydia pulled off the wrappings hesitantly, looking from the gift to the giver, blinking away her tears. "Augustus—"

"It was said to be a very good likeness," he told her, with the first smile he had been able to give her. "I was about five, I guess. The artist was Richard Cosway, if that matters to you. His initials and that little phrase in Latin on the back will prove it to you. My father knew him."

Lydia stared at the delicate miniature painted on ivory. The child's face was round and serious, the eyes deep blue and looking out from under pale lashes and brows, his head a cap of red-blond hair. She kept turning the gold-framed portrait over in her hands, finding herself quivering at the reality of looking at the little boy, just such a child as she had dreamed of for the years she had known the man that the boy had become.

"I was more devilish than I look there, I can tell you." He

grinned. "I was no sissy angel. They had me tied to a chair while the fellow worked furiously to catch some kind of likeness. Fifteen minutes was the outside limit. Once they tried to bribe me with a toy, and I threw it straight through a window. Believe me, I heard about that! For a long time!"

"You were quite a fellow, weren't you?" she said tenderly.

"I still am," he assured her with some bravado. "We must not let it be too many moons, my precious cousin, until I can take you to the spot where this was made, perhaps even present you to the man who did it. I have always dreamed that someday he could paint my own sons. . . ." His fingers stroked her hair. "Does anyone ever live on anything but hope? Do we dare make any real plans? Like, how will it be when I come to get you? What will you look like at our wedding? I can picture you in—"

"Don't—please don't!" she begged.

"Do you think that our minds—really our hearts—could somehow reach across the sea?" he asked impulsively. "That we could in some way—that we could find a means of communication? I don't quite know what I am trying to say, but I'm convinced that there must be something in this communion-of-saints thing in religion, some way that living, *loving* people—ordinary people, not saints—can reach each other. I want desperately to believe it. Do you think it can be done?"

"Yes, I do!" she answered eagerly. "I have tried many times to reach you in these terrible weeks."

"I knew it! It was true! I knew it! And now I have only moments of the magic of your company. You must keep this forever in your heart: for me, you are magic." He embraced her again. "Will you try to reach me? Maybe every day? And I will try to get through to you. Will you?"

"Yes . . . yes. . . ."

"At, say, five o'clock? Could that be it? Because that was the hour, twice, six years apart . . . Even the one that comes around in the morning too? You know it's five o'clock twice a day!"

"That will be harder." She let her arms twine tightly around his neck, her face touching his cheek. "But will it be five o'clock where you are? Isn't the time different? It must be."

"Yes, but I can always figure it out. I have a theory that between here and London, for instance, there's five hours' difference. Don't worry about that part. Just to try to reach me. I shall try too. Every day, and forever. Do you love me? It seems that I must hear you say it."

"I love you, Augustus," she told him shyly. "And if I should use four words, I shall say I truly love you, Mr. Foster."

He looked deeply into her eyes. "I live on your promises, my beloved cousin. And now, if I am to preserve this life of mine in order to give it to you for safekeeping, I must start on my long journey. I can only hope I am not being pursued—I have learned a great deal lately about the evil that lies just under the surface—"

"Don't . . . go . . . don't . . . go. . . ."

With a last crushing kiss, his eyes wet with tears, he hurried down the steps, not trusting himself with a backward glance.

He had forgotten to leave a book he had brought for Thomas. It came by messenger two hours later, when he was already out of the city, heading dejectedly for New York, where the Governor of Nova Scotia had sent a British brig of war to take him safely to Halifax.

The book was a thorough, well-illustrated study of astronomy and navigation, leather-bound, with marbled end papers. Many dog-eared pages showed that he had studied it extensively. At some points there were question marks in the margin, as if he wished to dispute with the author.

His name was on the flyleaf with the date of his purchase. Under it, Lydia's brother painfully scratched his own and the date he received it: "Thos. J. Hollingsworth, Jr., June 25, 1812." Then, for the second and final time in his long illness, he burst into tears.

Hearing him, Lydia crept from her room; they could weep together.

Out of two hundred sea battles the English had racked up two hundred victories. They had no reason to fear, or hardly notice, the halfhearted belligerence of their onetime colony. A skiff was not much of a threat to an armada.

The War Hawks were on the warpath, armed or not. De-Witt Clinton was soundly defeated by Madison, by an electoral vote of 128 to 89. As a price for his renomination and reelection, the President was committed to the ones who had supported him and the program they were pushing.

"On to Canada!" whippoorwilled John Randolph. "And leave the broad reaches of the Chesapeake unprotected!"

"The broad reaches of the Chesapeake are centered in the docks and shipyards and homes of Baltimore," Sam said angrily to his brother. "Norfolk and Baltimore. Those are the real targets. And we're in Baltimore, sitting ducks. So, as far as I'm concerned, we're the *only* target in the whole damned mess."

"And my house is a block closer to the water than yours," Thomas, Senior, said wearily. "How is your company of militia getting along? I'm too old to fight, I guess, at least for the government, but, by damn, if they come to my door, they're going to find out they're up against something. I'm still a straight shot. And no one ever said I wasn't stubborn."

"But still, isn't the Ambassador—?"

Thomas's face darkened. "It's a hard thing to say, Sam, but we love that man. I don't care what he is or who he is. And for Lydia's sake—well, it's pretty hard on all of us. I don't know when the whole caboodle of us has been so—I'm sorry, I just can't talk about it. I hope you understand. My daughter—"

"There are lots of other men," Sam began, trying to be genial. "Good, substantial *American* men—"

"Not for Lydia, I'm afraid. For her, there's only one, forever."

Chapter Eighteen

They Who Watch for the Morning

The departing Ambassador went to Halifax in the brig *Colibri*. "We sailed with the *Amanda*," he wrote, "which had been taken from the Americans and now was loaded with Flour. We were her Convoy and she sailed nearly as well as we did. Our Poop was decked with flowers of the Hydrangia—the Drums were beating, the Ladies looking out of the windows waving their Handkerchiefs at the Officers & General Cheering."

In Nova Scotia he waited restlessly, hoping for some break in the tension. After some days he received word that Admiral Sir John Warren was en route with an offer of cessation of hostilities. He pondered whether he should wait for the Admiral, and perhaps accompany him to Washington to plead their case. In his heart he knew it was useless; he had already trod every inch of that rocky, dead-end road. The members of Congress had scattered; Madison could not act without them; reaching even a quorum would take weeks or months. Even then—he knew too well the tenor of their thinking. There was no reason for hope or for further pursuit of a lost cause.

On July 23, nearly a month after he had torn himself from the arms of his American sweetheart—almost rudely, so that he would not break down in front of her—he decided to board the *Atalanta*, a sloop of war bound for England.

After the sloop was well under way, in a heavy fog, word came that they might be meeting up with an American frigate, the forty-four gun *President,* under the command of Commodore John Rodgers, the Harford County Marylander who had done in the *Little Belt.* The twenty-eight-gun *Atalanta* had been built in Bermuda of cedar, a wood that Foster's well-stocked mind knew to be inclined to splinter. Foster held the *President* and the Commodore in proper awe. The frigate was fitted out as a privateer and was lighter, faster and more maneuverable than the sloop of war, but the British captain trimmed his ship for action.

His sailors were advised to leave their hammocks on deck, the bulkheads were all taken down, and boxes and baggage were stowed out of the way. The men were warned that there were important passengers on board: a general, an ambassador, a consul and the Governor of Bermuda. Woe be if anything happened to that illustrious cargo! On the other hand, meritorious behavior might be significantly rewarded.

When the fog lifted, the ominous frigate turned out to be British. The apprehensive Ambassador had been wondering whether the Americans might possibly have spared the ship if they had been told who was on it. He was enormously relieved that he had not had to find out.

That near miss seemed symbolic for him, as if it meant that his life had been spared for a purpose. He must now turn his face steadfastly homeward and have no more idle dreams of peace on earth and a quick reunion with the one who had promised to adore him forever. Achieving that hope might best be brought about by doing well at whatever came to his hand in the British Isles. His efforts, which were usually considerable in whatever he tackled, might combine with those of President Madison to keep the war "nominal." He must remember that word "nominal." It said so much without saying anything at all.

Late in the afternoon he stood again at a ship rail, a lonely figure as he looked and looked and looked into the west. The horizon was only water, centered by the blazing orb of the setting sun. Beyond him he noticed the gulls floating thirty or forty feet above the sea, taking advantage of the air currents. The slightest movements of their wings could improve the angle of their bodies to the winds. He observed how their legs, some black, some orange, fitted sleekly into their gray-white underbellies to lessen their resistance to the air. When the birds wanted to alight, the feet appeared from their hiding places, acting both as brakes and as a means of support while they snatched at bits of food on deck.

As the ship gained distance and all evidences of land disappeared, the birds gradually began to go back, one after another, wheeling around as if they were detaching the golden lines that had been keeping the ship tied up. Just so had they come to meet him and pull him to shore. Scarcely more than a year had passed!

Now they were releasing him, gracefully, silently, completely. Was it to be forever?

He watched until the last one had disappeared into the coral-tipped spray and mist. As he turned from the rail, the General, who, unknown to him, had been standing near and watching the same phenomenon, observed, "Those with the sooty heads and the long white streaks at the front edges of the wings are known as Bonaparte's gulls, sir. Did you know that?"

"No, I didn't," Foster said slowly. "I didn't know."

At least two sets of marauders were in action within days of the war vote. Commodore Rodgers had swept out into the Atlantic to rid it of British raiders and to protect the American ships, which had previously had no protection at all. Commodore Isaac Hull raced out of the bay and up toward Boston, there to engage the British ship *Guerrière* and give it a sound trouncing. The *Constitution,* with its heavily timbered sides, was quickly given the nickname of "Old Ironsides."

Hull's first set-to with the British brought about a rare escape. Becalmed off the coast of Massachusetts and surrounded by the enemy, also becalmed, he ordered his men to attach the *Constitution*'s rowboats to its bow, then to get in them and row the ship to safety. The idea worked. They slipped into Boston harbor like Cleopatra's barge, an unforgettable picture.

Privateers began streaking out of the Patapsco and making swift, deadly assaults on any British shipping within range. These, combined with Hull's and Rodgers's successes, shot national morale, and consequently the fever for war, sky high.

The War Hawks had been insisting that Canada could be taken in six weeks, so that invasion was to be the first order of business. As a matter of fact, Henry Clay had been boasting that the Kentucky militiamen could take Quebec by themselves.

The attacks would be launched from three key points: at Lake Champlain, south and east of Montreal; at the Niagara River and the narrow neck of land that separates Lake Ontario from Lake Erie; and at Detroit, where a powerful fort controlled traffic between Lake Erie and Lake Huron. Detroit was considered the most vital objective.

Before the war was two months old, aging General William Hull, governor of Michigan Territory and commander of the American forces there, marched into Canada and marched right back again, with British and Indians hot on his heels. Fort Detroit surrendered. Across the Peninsula on Lake Michigan, Fort Dearborn (Chicago) was captured by Indians.

These swift and disastrous defeats galvanized the residents of the Great Lakes region into a frantic mobilization. In the village of Kinsman, Ohio, close to the Pennsylvania state line, every man in town, young and old, went off to war.

They gathered up muskets, rifles, blunderbusses, axes, kitchen knives, pistols, clubs, even pitchforks. They grabbed blankets, boots, whiskey, corn meal, whiskey, sacks of apples, fatback, tobacco, ammunition, whiskey, coffee, sugar and a few skillets. They kissed wives, children, parents and sweethearts in tear-choked farewells and roared away, some in wagons, some on horseback, a few younger ones on foot.

The first night the hastily organized company camped under some trees at North Williamsfield, the next village, and found themselves enjoying military life far beyond their wildest dreams. There was a large campfire, they had plenty of food and drink, and the late-summer sky was cloudless and benign.

There were no women to nag them and make them wash their feet, no children quarreling and stirring up trouble, no animals to be fed, milked and bedded down. The horses, enjoying the change too, were grazing peacefully on the pasture of a farmer, who surely had not expected such a horde of company but took it stoically. The only sounds, except for the singing and storytelling, were of owls, crickets, frogs and the joyous yapping of the expedition's dogs.

By the second night the rolls of the company were greatly depleted. Word had come—several words, to be exact—that the women and children left at home were not able to cope. They could not possibly run the farms, milk the cows, harvest the grain, tend the chickens, ducks, pigs, geese and turkeys, manage the two or three stores in town, cultivate the vegetable gardens, pick and preserve all the fruit, chop the firewood, operate the blacksmith shop and mend the fences. There were also passels of children to be fed, clothed and educated. The woods were full of Indians.

Particularly hurtful to the volunteer soldiers was the remark from younger men that no army needed men past sixty. Or even fifty. That cut-off point took nearly half the warriors, who certainly could not be blamed for grasping at a heaven-sent chance for a vacation, their first one ever. They dragged themselves home to more familiar fields of combat.

By the third night the hard-core survivors had found another decimated band of gladiators at the town of Jefferson. A military unit with muscle could then begin to shape up and get down to business.

There was little social life in Baltimore. The women's morning calls were cut down, as they were in summer's broiling heat anyway. Now it was too depressing to try to make small talk, when spirits were so low. Lydia stopped all her visiting except to her Aunt Deborah's, where she found affectionate but unmeddlesome sympathy. Mr. Cochran might put extra warmth into his handclasp and Debby pat her on the arm every time she came near, but they said nothing. From being a radiantly happy fiancée whose entrance to a room was almost incandescent, Lydia was becoming a frightened recluse, measuring her days by the arrival of the post, and then to the hour of five, when she tried faithfully to evoke some image of Augustus and to feel him reaching out to her.

One short note came, mailed from New York on the eve of his departure and couched in careful phrases. "Four are better than three, but five is best. Every day. To me you are magic. Pray it will not be long." Because he had signed it with only a cryptic "A," she knew he feared that his mail was being opened. The folded page gave no evidence of tampering. After two days of reading it, she put it between the pages of the prayer book, along with the pressed flowers from the corsage he had sent her from Washington in the winter.

One afternoon she was sitting where they had sat on the sofa in the front parlor to say good-bye. Her head was down, her eyes closed, with every other thought shoved from her mind as she concentrated on him. There was a pleasant scent in the room, the faint odor of shaving soap that always surrounded him. She opened her eyes blankly and looked around, but she was completely alone. "Augustus . . . ? Mr. Fos—Augustus . . . ?" She closed her eyes again, waiting.

It was as if she saw a sunset, a magnificent orange orb sinking toward the water, which must be the ocean. There were birds skimming and soaring gracefully through the air, their feet neatly tucked under them. They were wheeling and turning away. Soon there was only the sea, the broad empty sea. She had a feeling that fragile lines were being broken and were trailing behind the departing birds. As clearly as if she had been present, she watching the lines drifting and blending into the crimson-tipped surface of the waves. She sat for some moments, hoping for more, almost fearing to breathe. A hoarse whisper sounded like the word "Bonaparte's," then faded away.

As suddenly as it had come, the moment was gone, and as truly as if he had slipped into the room and caressed her, she had felt the touch of his heart on hers. She sat there quietly crying for perhaps five minutes. They *could* reach each other.

On a humid night in late summer she woke with a scream and sat up in bed, looking dazedly around in the growing morning light. She thought she had been trying to shriek a warning to someone. "Watch out! Watch out! There is danger! *Watch out!*"

She rubbed her cheeks briskly to be sure she was awake, shivering in spite of the stifling heat. Fronya, who had been spending every night in the hall on a pallet because Thomas had been worse again, slipped into the room, her small lumpy shape making a grotesque shadow on the floor.

"Yes'm?"

"Oh—oh, it's you, Fronya."

"Yes'm."

"Never mind. I'm all right. I must have been dreaming." Lydia began thumping her pillow to make it more comfortable. "What time is it?"

Fronya brought her the small clock from her dresser so that

she could squint at it. "Is it only five o'clock, Fronya?" She held it to her ear to make sure it was running. "Five?"

"Yes'm."

"You can go back. I'm all right. I hope I didn't waken anyone."

"No'm."

By the eighteenth of August the sloop of war *Atalanta* had passed the Scilly Islands off the coast of England at Land's End. A messenger got off the ship at Falmouth in order to get the returning Ambassador's messages to the Foreign Office with all possible speed. Before he finally set foot on English soil himself, Foster had another brush with disaster, this one real. He began to feel as if something were after him.

I should never have left her, he thought for the thousandth time. I should either have found a way to stay or to bring her with me. What price must we pay, both of us?

In the heavy fog off the Channel coast the navigator somehow mistook St. Alban's Head, a rocky, dangerous promontory, for the Isle of Wight, some miles farther east. Foster could hear distinctly the smashing of breakers on the rocks, getting louder and more menacing every minute, while the sloop plowed blindly along.

There were shouts of alarm from several of the passengers as well as the crewmen. The captain leaped to the tiller himself, wrenching it furiously to starboard to avoid a crash, as the ship's timbers groaned and screeched from the strain.

The shaken Minister went below to comfort himself with a stiff drink. His heavy watch, which he had left lying in his cabin, showed that the hour was just past ten in the morning. If his navigational observations were correct, he had gained about five hours in the course of his eastward passage, and it would be just daylight in Baltimore.

The news that he found when he got to London, of several American victories, even though they were small ones, told him all he needed to know. The Yankees were savoring the taste of blood. His judgment, bitter and difficult as it had been to arrive at, was correct. He was disturbed to learn that Lord Castlereagh, the Foreign Secretary, was greatly annoyed with him for not waiting at Halifax for Admiral Warren.

By the time he was received at Carlton House by the Prince Regent, who was ruling in place of his permanently insane father, George III, that gentleman had been advised in detail of his reasoning and of his profound regrets. To Foster's immense relief, the Prince Regent told him that he agreed with him. In addition, he had been so generous as to say so to Lord Liverpool, so Foster felt vindicated.

He practiced assiduously the effort to reach Lydia. It had been his own suggestion, and he was so hopeful that it would work. He had not one small memento of her except for some of her letters, which he could not part with because they had reached him in moments of his sorest distress.

I should have asked her for her scarf so that I could wear it into battle, he thought, as he tried to remember her voice at his ear, the feel of her lips as she had returned his final, passionate kisses, the softness and warmth of her fingers as they lay curled in his. He could best picture her eyes as they looked at him with such fire and depth as he had never seen except when he caught a glimpse of the way the fluttery and engaging Mrs. Cochran looked at her husband.

The Lady Annabella Milbanke was still available and unmarried, although admitting her interest in Lord Byron. Her mother and Foster's mother expressed pleasure at seeing Annabella and Augustus together again on an afternoon at Devonshire House. He had bowed as politely as he could. He could not recall why he had been so disturbed at having to leave Annabella. Of course, she was vivacious and witty, if a trifle moody. She alternately flattered him and scorned him, in a kind of game that he found wearying. In her stead, he could picture the quiet, devoted, beloved Lydia in the great rooms of the mansion, emptier now, since the Duke had died soon after Foster left for America. His mother had been so devastated at the death of her husband that Foster feared for a while he might have to return to help her pull herself together. Lydia . . . Lydia!

Young Thomas was better for a while; then several things conspired against him. His face developed a series of unpleasant swellings and eruptions, something like the attack of sumac poisoning he had had when he and Starfire went off on a camping trip one spring and he had built a fire of fresh twigs. This new misery was as painful as that had been, and, if anything, was uglier, but it was not the same, and he had not been camping.

He had been hoping to go to the country, to spend some time out at the Benevolent Society, where there was plenty of room. It was cooler there and its high location airy and pleasant, but, as Lydia wrote to Ruth, "the Servants' illness kept him from going away, until a long spell of wet weather came on and he was so severely affected with rheumatism as to use a crutch, and not be able to dress himself." Ruth would know how he hated both inconveniences. Moving from cane to crutches was an admission of his need for greater support. Not being able to dress himself was the most unmanly thing that could happen to him. He despised his weakness.

"His shoulders, elbows, wrists and ankles were all affected," Lydia wrote sadly. "He is better but his legs continue swelled and very painful. Yesterday he drove himself out. He had not walked out, and the weather is now against him, wet and heavy."

In October, Jacob Hollingsworth, Sam's oldest son, had both personal and political news to send up the bay. "I shall feel much gratified at hearing of your having sold your Wheat," he wrote his Uncle Stephen, "which now is rather declining at 17 cents and will be still lower. Flour is sold faster than we can make it at 10½ Dollars, Sixty days. Many of the Millers have large quantities engaged and not yet delivered. Many flying reports of an accommodation to take place immediately between G.B. and U.S. but I place no faith in them and consider them more electioneering stories which are made by the Madisonian Party which is much the strongest here, notwithstanding the Whig is so decidedly opposed to Madison and his friends."

Jacob also reported that his cousin Thomas, with whom he had shared so many adventures when they were growing up and who had been best man at his wedding, was improved. "I am glad to tell you of Thomas being on the recovery and he is up an hour in the day. You may suppose how very weak he is but as the fever has left him I hope sincerely he will have no return of it."

On the twenty-fifth of that month, off the coast of West Africa near the Canary Islands, Stephen Decatur, already an American military hero from the war with Tripoli in 1803, won a decisive victory over the British *Macedonian* with his frigate *United States.* When the news reached home there were no further "flying reports of an accommodation." Wars were fine when you could win so handily.

In London, Augustus John Foster decided, with the active encouragement of his uncle the Prime Minister, that he would stand for Parliament as the member for Cockermouth. The town had been in existence since Roman times, but he knew it especially as the birthplace of William Wordsworth, whom he considered the greatest English poet since Milton. Representing Cockermouth would be an honor, he felt, and apparently the people agreed, because he was elected. He would stay in England.

Lord Liverpool wanted his nephew to present the government's arguments in the issues that had brought about the recent Anglo-American split. Once on his feet for the moment that every rising diplomat looked forward to, his first speech in Parliament, he was confronted by questions from Alexander Baring, who had an American wife and who was known to oppose the Orders in Council. Foster would have liked to ask *him* some questions, about how it had all worked out and what advice he could give in handling the delicate negotiations of bringing home an American girl.

He felt that he had his material well thought-out and well prepared, but before he could get halfway through, his throat became so dry that he could not continue. In overwhelming embarrassment, his face the color of a poppy, he was forced to sit down. Why hadn't he had the wit to bring an orange with him, so he could suck on it and moisten his throat? He would never have the chance to find out whether he could then have continued; the moment had passed, irrevocably. Perhaps his humiliation had come about because he found it too difficult to present the government view; he knew the other side too well. At any rate, the experience was humbling. He never tried it again.

Actually, he had planned to sputter off a little—there in that assemblage where he knew his hearers would be responsive—about the Americans' unbelievable greed for land, which was the most obvious trait he had observed in his two sojourns in the New World. Not content with cherishing and improving the acreage that fate or inheritance or hard work or a fortuitous marriage had given him, an American always had a wild dream of pushing west, always west, even into the limitless, useless desert that lay beyond the Mississippi—or the Metché Sépé, as his Indian friends spelled it. He found the attitude incomprehensible and not altogether admirable. Acquisitiveness had never seemed to him to be a virtue.

Even the question of slavery, which lurked just below the surface of economic, political and social life in the United States, did not disturb him to the same extent. He had seen how John Randolph's several hundred slaves had a better life with their master than they could possibly have made for themselves, although the Virginia aristocrat used to awaken them in the morning with a hunting horn, a peculiar practice.

The importation of slaves was supposed to have stopped, but there was still traffic in human lives. There were dark rumors of black breeding farms, one an island in the Caribbean—he found even the thought of such a business revolting. His reports to his government indicated that he felt, as had all his predecessors, that sooner or later the United States was going to split wide open on the slavery issue and that the northeastern states would become a separate nation, with its base in industry instead of agriculture. Josiah Quincy of New England was greatly agitated when Louisiana came into the Union as a slave state, shouting that this was the final straw and that a breakup was imminent, because the slave bloc could outvote the free states. Foster reasoned that New Orleans would be strategically, and perhaps sentimentally, the logical site of a new capital if the split came.

He wrote to Lydia once a week, sometimes pouring out his heart to her then tearing the letter up. He would then rewrite the message in more circumspect tones, asking about her family, the weather, and sending greetings to each one and especially to Thomas. He felt that she knew him well enough to use an inner eye, to know that what he was not writing down was actually the important part of his message. A laconic "three or four" at the end of his letter was a plea to hear again that she loved him.

He was still in touch with Baker and could manage to send his letters by diplomatic pouch, asking that they be sent on to her. He was annoyed with himself that he had not thought of it before he left so that he could plan the exchange with her.

It was a note from Baker, which came to him while he was cooling his heels at Halifax, that had given him the idea. Baker had met Madame Bonaparte on the street in Baltimore, where he spent more time with the embassy's archival records than in Washington. He and Madame had agreed that even though Baltimore was moribund in the summer, Washington was deader than dead. She had inquired about Foster and had asked Baker to send him her best wishes. She hoped he would soon be back in the States.

But if Baker could send him these personal messages, of course he could send the same kind in return and Baker could deliver them! How blind and unthinking and just plain stupid could a man be? He wrote back at once to suggest the plan, and when he reached London, the message from Baker was that he would be glad to co-operate.

Baker was quite young and was known to have an eye for a pretty girl, but Foster was not worried about him as a competitor. Baker never liked the quiet ones.

When the first batch of four letters for Lydia arrived, Baker thought to accept Madame B's casual invitation to call on her when he was again in town, so he went there first. When he got back to Washington, the letters were still in his pocket. Should he send them by post? He thought not. If they were waylaid or wrongly delivered, he'd be in the soup for his carelessness. Best to wait until his next trip there.

The weeks stretched into months. Neither Lydia nor the Englishman had the slightest communication from each other. There were rare moments when both of them felt that the other had responded to their five o'clock reaching-out, but because no mail came, there could never be any confirmation.

Lydia knew that the Ambassador would want news of Thomas as well as of herself. In late October she wrote nearly identical letters to him and to Ruth. "Thomas is certainly better, no fever, but the pain has continued and does still severely affect his limbs," she told her cousin. "Somedays he sits up half an hour, never yet longer; but the weakness caused by sitting up the Doctor says injures, and as it increases his pain, he recruits faster in bed. His spirits are very good and I hope he will recover his health, though indeed Cousin, I do not calculate on a quick recovery. He is rubbed twice a day with Steers Chemical Opeduldoc by Mama, which he thinks has relieved him considerably. I hope sincerely that after he recovers from this spell his constitution may be renovated. His appetite is pretty good, still inclining to Gingerbread."

One cheering thing for Ruth would be that Lydia could think about shopping for her again. "I went yesterday to Aunt Rachel's and got a square of Pelice cloth, Cousin. It was 10$, and divided it between you. Aunt will line hers and put in wadding. I priced the fur. It is from 62½ [cents] to 2 dollars the yard and will take near 5½ yds. to go all around, the ribbon will be very little I imagine. I avail myself of your indulgence and do not yet shop for anything . . . the streets appear crowded with goods, tho' I have been but three times out, then to see the sick. Thomas does not like to see us leave him at any time. . . . I see not one China aster. The Turkeys have gobbled them up and left not a leaf in my border. I will try for the larkspur seed."

One evening, when there was a large family gathering, she sat in a quiet corner near Dr. Gibson. Something was said about the limits of pain, beyond which the awareness of pain could be no greater. He and some other physicians had been discussing it, and although he was normally reticent, he began talking with intensity and feeling. Was there a point at which pain got no worse, no matter how much a disease progressed? Did accepting pain help the patient recover faster than fighting against it and refusing to let it become one's master? How much did the patient's basic character and temperament have to do with it?

Lydia wanted to ask him why it was that if a positive, steady inner strength was good medication—Big Medicine—in Thomas's case he was always worse? His courage in the face of his obvious deterioration was amazing, and it made her ashamed of her own less tangible pain.

Gibson rarely if ever discussed medical matters outside his office, but Lydia was such an absorbed listener that he expounded for several minutes before his wife's slight frown hinted that perhaps the conversation should be more general. Lydia got no real answers from him, because, in truth, he had none, only questions. Her cousin-in-law was a physician who cared deeply, and because of his caring he might someday find some answers. This glimpse of his great concern for his work gave her a new resolution to try to strengthen herself; perhaps in that way she might also be a stronger ally of her brother.

After five months of silence had passed, she took the precious miniature from the table near her bed and slipped it into the drawer with the prayer book and the pressed flowers. In its place she put her French grammar, to remind herself to study.

At almost exactly the hour of her marriage nine years previously, Betsy Patterson Bonaparte brought her seven-and-a-half-year-old son across the street for a Christmas Eve visit to the Hollingsworths. Little Bo was an attractive youngster, handsomely dressed and rather formal in his manners. He was being brought up in the Catholic faith and had the best of tutors, in preparation for what his mother hoped would be some kind of royal connection and position in Europe.

She had no interest in any possible future in America for the child. After all, he had royal blood in his veins. Wasn't he the son of a king? The Emperor had recognized him and had made several efforts to get his hands on the boy for his own purposes. Betsy was always vigilant that any move involving him be the right one and that she keep control over him; with careful planning and manipulation she could still succeed in most of her ambitions.

Lydia couldn't remember when Betsy had last been in their house. Certainly not since her marriage. She was genuinely glad to see her, and welcomed the two with much warmth.

Young Bo regarded her with solemn interest and acknowledged his mother's introduction of Lydia like a grownup. Lydia reflected that the boy needed some rough-and-tumble outdoor life of the kind that Thomas had always enjoyed—and that Betsy herself had shared, come to think of it! He was too sheltered, too protected for his own good.

"We can't stay," Betsy said simply, "but we did want to come over to wish you the joys of the season and to say a word or two to Thomas. Bo has always wanted to know him. I've told him so much about Thomas." She handed her furs to Polodore. "I've hardly seen him since we've grown out of our childhood."

"Can we see his horse?" the youngster asked soberly.

Betsy laughed. "He has heard so much about the way Thomas always rode Starfire and what fun he had with that horse. I'm negotiating for an Arabian stallion for Bo. Maybe we should ask Thomas if we could name it Starfire, son. I'm so sorry he's been ill, Lydia. May we see him?"

"Of course. He's right upstairs. He'll be so pleased."

When Madame Bonaparte came back down after the briefest visit with her old friend her face was ashen. "I didn't know," she kept saying. "Can that be *Thomas?*" She sat down abruptly. "I had no idea. . . . Oh, my dears . . ."

Getting control of herself, she asked Bo to report on his school and to inquire about Lydia's parents, who had gone to call on the Cochrans. He and his mother rose to leave. While Polodore was getting their coats, Betsy said suddenly, as if she were coming back from a great distance, "I almost forgot one of my real reasons for coming over." She reached into her reticule and brought out a small packet of letters. "Mr. Baker asked me to deliver these. I've been so busy—I hope it is nothing urgent. . . ."

Ann Maria had come down from Thomas's room to say good night to the pair. She slipped to Lydia's side and, with her arm firmly around her sister's waist, assured their neighbor that they had been simply delighted to see her and that they all hoped she would come again very soon and that she and her family would have a pleasant holiday.

"I'll bring my horse over for Thomas to ride," Bo promised.

Chapter Nineteen

Thine Arrows Are Sharp in the Heart of the King's Enemies

Christmas and the Holy Festivals were as quiet at 15 South Street as the same season the year before, except that the holiday balls were greatly curtailed because of the threat of war. Six months had passed since the break in relations with the mother country, which had sent A. J. Foster away. The belated packet of his letters had helped to put the sun back into the sky for Lydia. Even knowing that he had arrived safely back in England was some comfort.

The day after Christmas, Great Britain announced a blockade of both the Delaware and Chesapeake bays, the second more serious. Delaware Bay was too shallow for good harbors and successful shipping.

By the first week of February, a British fleet under Rear Admiral George Cockburn, who would become one of the most hated men of the war, was stationed across the nine-mile mouth of the Chesapeake, and the deadly game of trying to outwit him was under way. American ships took advantage of the unpredictable winter weather and frequent fogs to slip through and out to open sea. Thomas Hollingsworth, Senior, aged ten years in those spring months.

Not content with guard duty, the British commenced attacking everything within range and probing into the myriad coves, inlets and rivers farther and farther up the bay. There were only scattered shore batteries for protection; the fearsome Congreve rockets could fire as far as two miles and were so hard to aim that they might hit almost anything. The countryside was nearly paralyzed with fear.

By April, the fleet was threatening Baltimore itself, using the island of Tangier as a base.

Betsy's uncle, General (and Senator) Samuel Smith was in charge of the militia and the defense of the city. He set up a battery of forty-two-pounders, pressed insistently for the strengthening of Fort McHenry and Fort Covington southwest of it, and demanded that every weapon in the city be made ready and supplied with ample ammunition. The army engineers towed several old scows to the mouth of the channel and into the inner harbor and sank them. Gunboats were stationed near the Lazaretto, on the northwest branch of the Patapsco, opposite Fort McHenry. A city-wide campaign quickly gathered up a half-million dollars. There was little sleep for anyone.

After the first feint the British withdrew, possibly taken aback by the extent of the city's preparations. They skimmed down the bay and into the Severn River to terrorize the capital at Annapolis. A week later they were back, lined up just outside the mouth of the Patapsco. No ship went in; no ship went out. The Governor sent a frantic request to Washington for the men and arms that Congress had promised to any threatened state.

While they were throttling Baltimore with economic strictures, as well as with the ancient weapon of terror, the British darted out to plunder islands and bayside towns. Anything that might have challenged them or taken revenge against them was either bottled up in the harbor or kept at sea by the base at Tangier. Shore batteries couldn't reach them.

"Don't try to keep the news from me," young Thomas begged his father. "I've got to know what's going on, even if I can't get out there to fight those pirates myself. I can't believe that those snakes can be from the same nation as Mr. Foster. Have they gone clear up as far as Elkton? Lydia's worried about Ruth Tobin, and so am I."

"They got to Frenchtown," his father growled. "The men drove them back twice, even with their old-fashioned, worn-out blunderbusses, but they came a third time and burned everything. Five vessels, all the wharf installations where the packets tie up to make connections with the overland stage to Philadelphia. Some British were killed, thank God, but I don't think they got any of ours. I haven't got all the details yet."

"But Elk Landing? Are they safe at the Landing?"

"So far, I guess. They put up two forts there, a small redoubt with some cannon called Fort Hollingsworth, and a bigger one on the north side of the Elk River, farther down, called Fort Defiance. They've got chains suspended across the river, hooked up to windlasses so they can draw them up—*smack!*—and finish off any boat that gets that far."

"I'd like to be there," Thomas said sadly. "I could wind up their old chains, I bet, even if I couldn't aim a gun. I'd find a way."

His father turned away to hide his face. "I guess they could use both of us, son. One of their problems is that the militia was called up and brought to Baltimore. They said the redcoats stopped at Hyland's Fishery on the Elk River and took a hundred barrels of shad and herring. They're living off the land. Damned well too. Fresh vegetables, poultry, hams, fish."

"They're like a pack of dragons, Papa."

The dragons lashed back and forth across the upper reaches of the bay, burning Havre de Grace and finally heading up the Sassafras River where it widened to make a natural boat basin. The residents of the towns on either side of the river, Georgetown and Fredericktown, knew of the attack long enough ahead of time to ambush them but were outnumbered and the scarlet-tunicked invaders swarmed ashore for bloody hand-to-hand combat. The British won the day, sending more tremors of fear throughout the land.

Dr. Edward Scott, an eyewitness to the subsequent wanton destruction of the two riverside villages, wrote to the Federalist Congressman Charles Goldsborough on May 6, in order to keep the record straight and to convey to the government some of his sense of outrage at the invasion.

Dear Sir: As some allusion may possibly be made in Congress as to the conduct of the enemy at Geo:Town and FredericTown on Thursday the 6th Inst. I consider it a respect due to you as the Representative of the District that you should be furnished with a correct statement of the insult offered and the injury done there. Those villages you know are situated on the Sassafras where the River is about a quarter of a mile wide, opposite each other and about fifteen miles from the Chesapeake Bay, the former in Kent County, the other in Cecil. Geo:Town contains a meetinghouse, tavern, one or two merchants' shops, as many old storehouses and granaries with thirty dwelling houses, all the buildings but the meetinghouse and eleven dwellings with some of their outhouses are reduced to ashes. FredericTown contained a small tavern, a storehouse, two large granaries and seventeen dwelling houses. Only the tavern and seven dwelling houses escaped the conflagration.

It was the order of the Admiral as acknowledged by his officers to destroy every house but some were spared at the entreaty of the women and aged and the fire was extinguished in some others after the enemy had abandoned them. A large sea schooner and three small ones were burnt in the stream. Mr. Joseph Ward's and Mr. John Ward's farmhouses about a mile from FredericTown were also consigned to destruction. At some little distance here as a spectator of the scene exhibited I saw the smoke and flames rise in quick succession from the burning villages and as soon as the enemy departed, visited their ruins. Without one or two exceptions the houses saved are most materially injured. Their doors, windows, mantelpieces and staircases being burned and hacked with hatchets. Some of the inhabitants had removed their furniture; others had not been so provident and suffered more severely. No property however trifing, valuable or sacred, escaped the rapacious hands of the foe. Women and children and even Blacks were plundered nearly of their All. Beds were cut open and the feathers scattered abroad. Desks, Looking glasses, cupboards, tables, chairs, clocks, etc., were shivered to fragments, even Bibles were taken off for the avowed purpose of making cartridges. With the honourable exception of Capt. Myers and one or two others, Admiral Cockburn's officers behaved in the same inhuman indecent style, saluting respectable citizens and even delicate females with the most vulgar blackguardism. While this scene was acting in Geo:Town and FredericTown a party from two of their tenders stationed eight miles below went on shore and plundered the house of Mr. Ag. Meeks. As the Admiral returned in the evening, he stopped with his squadron at Tuoney Creek and it was there declared by this ferocious Banditti that if they caught Mr. Madison they would hang him to the first tree and that every person taken with a rifle in his hands should have a similar fate.

Considering the extent and viciousness of the attack, it was remarkable that no one was killed. Several were wounded, and large quantities of staples, such as flour and sugar, along with four boats and many cords of lumber, were destroyed in the basin. It was said that one house in a prominent position overlooking the water was spared because of a young charmer named Kitty Knight, whose pleas were so beguiling that the Admiral told his men to overlook it as well as the one next door.

In both Elkton and Baltimore the Hollingsworth relatives were frantic with worry about one another and had to depend on the whims of Lady Luck to get any messages through. Lydia, heartsick at the exposure of the despicable side of the enemy—and Mr. Foster must be counted as one of them, whether or no—wrote to soothe Ruth Tobin. "My dear Cousin," she began. "Since I received your affectionate letter we have experienced more fully the agitation which you had been thrown into by rumors and alarms. Those with regard to the enemy's landing were altogether without foundation, but you can perhaps conceive the state of mind which predominated. All who could remove their effects either hurried them off or put them in trunks to be sent away as speedily as possible. It really produced a melancholy sight, the men running with great alacrity, which did them honour, the women in extreme agitation for those exposed at North Point and fearing a powerful foe to destroy them. Happily it did not long continue, and we felt assured it was false! But the impression made by it was not to be obliterated, Cousin; and the dry goods merchants hired Teams and sent their property into inland Towns; some stores are naturally empty; and household and other furniture was continually going day and night to a place of security. There seemed at first a panic through the city, then a decided resolution to save what conveniently could be done, from a future attack. Our waters are now free; and the fear has partially subsided. Why they are concentrating their forces we are ignorant. Some conjecture to attack and destroy more effectually the seaboard; others, the news of a French fleet having left Toulon had reached them, and driven them away. I hope the French will keep their own fleet, and let us fight our own Battle for I think an alliance with Napoleon produces only subjugation in the end to his views and we are in evil enough without their alliance."

Word had just come to Baltimore of the destruction of the Canadian city of York by the Americans and of the loss of an important officer. "The death of Gen. Pike is truly lamentable," Lydia said, "a brave, good officer, so unexpectedly destroyed, on the road to success and conquest is very distressing to the Army there, and to the States in general. The country looks enchanting at present," she continued. "I have not seen the Forest Trees since they put on their spring dress (until ten days since) and that greatly alters the face of Nature. We only wait a few warm days to move bed and board into the country. The Physicians are anxious that it should have a trial for Thomas, whose recovery is scarcely perceptible; and he is anxious himself. They think one week there would more restore him than two months here. Papa has taken the first floor of the Benevolent Society which will accommodate us all. You have been to the School, I think, and perhaps recollect the situation. It is airy and high, we have two rooms larger than three at home, one smaller and a Hall. Already Mama has sent some bedsteads and beds, china, trunks of cloathes, groceries, etc., to be ready in case we went off in a hurry. It keeps us in a state of confusion, so divided are our cloathes and the cart moving away slowly."

She stopped her writing in order to supervise Fronya's packing of what Thomas would be needing, with one set of trousers, shirt and everyday jacket that he could wear if he got well enough to sit on the porch out there in the country. He should have at least two different dressing gowns, so that he could always have a clean one if he could be out of bed at all. He had an extensive wardrobe of nightwear, since he had not worn anything else for so long. While she was busy choosing a shirt, her cousin Jacob stopped in on his way to Elkton, so she rushed to complete her letter to send with him.

"Jacob is here now . . . he will say more of us than any paper will permit me. I had another cousin married last week, Mary H . . . the first party, Cousin, since November. . . . I have not worn the India muslin dress since last June. . . ." She hoped Jacob could not see the sudden tears in her eyes. She added a postscript: "Thomas is still on milk and rice, or bread. There is a Pitcher under my nose now, with Tar-water prepared for him to drink. His cough continues, but freer, I think and less frequent, he is yet very weak, Cousin, but his stomach a little stronger I think."

The day before they were to move to the country, Thomas was brought downstairs early for tea, at his insistence. It was as if he wanted to go through as many parts of the house as possible, touching once more the things that were precious to him, looking eagerly out the windows for a different view from the one he had had for the many months he had spent in bed.

With Lydia at his elbow and the lion cane supporting his other side, he pushed relentlessly from room to room, through the front hall, both parlors and the dining room, pausing often to rest but smiling at Lydia with such joy that she could hardly look at him.

"It's different in here! The room's larger or something," he said.

"Mama sent the china closet and many of the dishes to the country. She and Ann Maria are out there now, getting settled."

"Oh, of course." He sat down abruptly in the nearest chair, puffing for breath. "Is that gingerbread? Is Delia really making me *gingerbread?*"

"I think so. She wanted to surprise you."

"I've just got to go watch her, maybe give her an extra thank-you. I haven't been in the kitchen for—I've just got to!"

He pulled himself to his feet, caught up the cane, and with the other hand using the wall to support him, he began trying to race toward the kitchen, stumbling forward as if he were being pushed, not waiting for his sister to help him.

"Thomas! Wait! Let me hold your arm! Watch out for those steps!"

He was thumping eagerly along the back hallway. "Yum! Gingerbread!"

The *ssssss-sst!* of Fronya's testing of her irons told Lydia that she was there and at work, getting their clothes ready for the move out to the Benevolent Society. Beyond her, Delia hummed as she baked.

"Thomas!" Lydia was screaming, to no avail. Her brother's

momentum carried him headlong beyond the top one of the three steps that led down to the kitchen. Since there was no part of his stiffened, crippled body that could bend, for a split second it appeared that every bone would be broken.

It was then that Fronya, for possibly the only time in her short life, moved with lightning speed. In one leap she placed her misshapen little body so that Thomas would fall across her. He went down like a pole, knocking over the ironing board with the little ruffling iron. The base of the iron, with which Fronya had been doing up the girls' frilly blouses and petticoats, was filled with hot coals. Somehow Fronya fell directly on the iron and at the same time the side of the broad ironing board hit her across the back of her neck. Thomas skidded on his cheek and one elbow into a kitchen chair. He lay there panting and helpless.

It was never really known whether Fronya died from the blow on the base of her skull or from the burns of the iron, which left two sets of neatly corrugated ridges across her middle, one deeper than the other. The kitchen, once so fragrant with the smell of fresh gingerbread and clean laundry, reeked of scorched human flesh. The quiet domestic sound of busy people at their work turned to screams of nightmare.

Polodore was there in an instant, scooping up Thomas and getting him back to his bed, taking the steps as lightly and swiftly as a cat. With the skilled fingers of an intelligent man who had trained himself to do many things, he went over Thomas's suffering body and determined that there were no broken bones, only bruises and the bleeding, torn skin on his arm and face. Without waiting for confirmation from anyone, he found the laudanum and prepared a dose for the lad, hardly taking his eyes off him until Lydia burst in the door.

"She saved me! She saved me . . ." Thomas was moaning hysterically.

"Never mind now, Thomas. Are you all right? Polodore, get me some salve. And some clean cloth."

"Shall I send for your papa?" he asked her.

"Yes. And get Robert in to help in the kitchen. Where's Hannah? Oh she went with Mama. Find Louis. Get Shagram in from the stables. Make every one of them stop screeching. Oh, why doesn't Mama get home?" She knew she would have to get herself calmed down somehow, because there was no one else to take responsibility. She stumbled to the door to call after Polodore. "Send somebody for the doctor too. And hurry! And I need some water and a cloth to wash him. And fresh towels . . ."

"I'm all right. . . . I'm all right. . . ." Thomas had changed the burden of his frantic chanting as the painkiller began reaching him.

Not waiting for someone to carry out her orders, Lydia got water herself and sponged her brother's face and arms of the blood, pulled a sheet gently over him and slipped out to the hall, where she could lean against a door and let herself cry. It took only a moment; then she was strong enough to head toward the kitchen to see what could be done.

The London night was clear and cool as Augustus John Foster, M.P. for Cockermouth, strode along Whitehall past the Admiralty, where so much of his life had been regulated, trying to get himself sufficiently tired that he could sleep. He was again too well acquainted with loneliness, as he had been for much of his life. His innate shyness kept him from making friends easily, and his bachelor status threw him automatically into male company for much of his time.

Occasionally he was asked to a dancing party or a formal dinner or other state function, but most of them bored him beyond words. There were women around, but he had resolved a year ago that he could not be content with second best. He knew what his heart wanted.

In the eleven months since he had left America, he had not received one word from her. He no longer had the privilege of sending mail by the diplomatic pouch; Betsy had been so upset by her glimpse of Thomas that she had completely forgotten to explain to Lydia that Mr. Baker could get letters through for her, so Lydia had not tried that way of communicating. She kept dispatching mail by the regular post until her father came home one afternoon with a handful of it and told her sorrowfully, "It's so hard to speak of this, daughter. They keep bringing me these letters and saying there is no possible way to get them to England. I don't know why they don't just return them to you instead of to my office—but there is no way, my dear. The mail does not get through."

"I guess I knew, Papa. I must have."

For answer, her father put his arm around her and kissed her twice on the cheek, something he had not done since she went off to school for her entrance into Miss Becky Love's first grade. He was not a demonstrative man, and she was much moved by his gesture. "It's a kind of empty world," he muttered as he turned away from her.

The war, instead of being nominal, was going to be full-blown, and both sides knew it. The burning of York had incensed everyone in England, and there was little sorrow that the Yankees had lost one of their finest men, General Pike, in the engagement; it served them right. Foster knew that his countrymen would be shouting for swift retaliation at the loss of the city. Revenge! All war is revenge, he thought with some surprise. Revenge in return for revenge! And it multiplies into holocaust.

He had not thought of it that way when he was in the Royal Horse Guards Blue when he was nineteen. War was a glorious way of paying tribute to one's country, of showing manliness and courage in defense of its honor. War was man's destiny, both a duty and a privilege.

He began to walk faster, turning into St. James Park by the duck pond; then he stopped short, thinking he had heard his name. "Augustus—Mr. Foster! Augustus!" It could not be. There was no one near except for some intertwined sets of lovers, ignoring him. Ahead of him he saw a pair of luminous dark eyes, beseeching him.

"Lydia . . . ? Is it . . . is it Lydia?" The warm eyes were filled with love for him. "You need me . . . ? Lydia . . . ?" He started to run, with no sense of direction. "Lydia . . . ?"

The eyes were soon gone, and he was alone in the night. Through the quieter sounds of the ancient city on the Thames he could hear the monotonous voice of the watch "Ten o' the clock and all's well. . . . Ten o' the clock and . . . all's . . . we-e-e-e-e-lllllllll. . . ."

She needed me. She needed me. . . .

Lydia was to reach through to him successfully only once more. In no case did he understand what she was trying to tell him, except that she loved him.

Word of Elkton's spunky resistance to the enemy when they approached Fort Hollingsworth reached Baltimore in record time. Stephen Hollingsworth, sixty-three years old and considering himself unfit for any kind of military duty, made a unique contribution to the war effort in his own quiet way. Along with several other men and a uniformed guard of militia, he took his heaviest wagon with two teams of horses and pulled up in front of the Elkton Bank.

With exaggerated secrecy, a number of large boxes were loaded into the wagon. They were then driven, still under heavy guard, to the inland city of Lancaster, Pennsylvania. Obviously the bank was taking every precaution that its specie be kept out of the hands of the marauders, a wise and provident move.

The boxes were empty. The bank's capital was under the bed of Levi Tyson, one of its directors, who owned a grist mill on the Big Elk. The Negroes who had helped carry and hide it there were told that it was ammunition to be used against the British, just in case. The conspirators could laugh about their ruse for the rest of their lives.

George Adams, Lydia's uncle, wrote to congratulate Stephen on his exploit. "I am very happy the Enemy have left you, as well as us. I hope they have left us with an Intention never to return. And I hope you have not been indisposed from the hardship of fatigue you endured whilst under arms."

Stephen and Ruth Tobin chuckled quietly at that phrase. Possibly George was one of those who had been fooled. Hardship? It was a lark. And he got a nice trip out of it too. "You citizens of Elkton," George told him proudly, "deserve the greatest credit for it was through your energy and spirit you saved it."

George had news about Thomas from Baltimore, but he did not know of Fronya's tragic and heroic death. "They removed Thomas on Tuesday last to the Charity School," he wrote. "He rode in the carriage. Dr. Donaldson rode with him. The Dr. says he bore the ride remarkably well. He still continues much as usual but he thinks he will now mend himself. The physicians think if he can mend anywhere it is there for the situation is delightful. The house is remarkably large, in a very good neighbourhood within two miles of town. . . . There is nothing new. Everything is very dull with us. It is impossible to say how long things will continue in their present state. Several of the Dry Goods merchants and likewise grocery merchants have removed their Goods to Frederick Hooks toward York and opened stores there. The reason is they say they cannot sell as much in town as will pay rent."

Lydia had to turn her head while Polodore and Robert carried her brother up the steps and to his waiting bed. Thomas was humiliated; being carried was for infants and puppies. A man should get around on his own two feet. Polodore had had to tote him twice within a week. He hated it.

☆

In the pitifully small store of Fronya's worldly goods they found nearly six hundred dollars in cash and a small loaded pistol. What, or whom, had she feared? And what had she planned to do with her fortune?

Thomas, Senior, appropriated the pistol and decided to teach his daughters to use it, a melancholy task. There was no telling what even more critical need for defense they might have, after the recent scares.

His wife, after a long consultation with the new rector, Dr. Kemp, decided that the money should be used to buy books, slates and pencils for a school being set up by a young free Negro who was bent on bringing some education to his people. For want of any other name, the money would be designated the Fronya Fund. When the full import of what was happening to him finally got through to the surprised young educator, he fainted in his tracks. He had never heard of Fronya. Or the Hollingsworths.

In mid-July they moved Thomas back into the city, in spite of the heat and the noise and the smothering humidity there. He had told them many times how much he enjoyed the fresh country air and the serenity at the Benevolent Society, but there came a day when he was very weak, unable to feed himself and barely able to speak.

"I think, Mama," he whispered, "that I should be home. Would it be too much? I don't like to bother anyone." He tried to grin, to let the old Thomas shine through. "I guess I'm homesick, Mama. I'll be all right as soon as I get into my old room. You'll see."

He lived until the end of the month, slipping away as gallantly and unaffectedly as he had done everything else. Lydia was sitting by his bed, as she had for days, supporting him tenderly with her arms when it was hard for him to breathe. His eyes, always so merry and vivid, appeared to get larger and more luminescent as his face wasted away beneath them.

On this hot, still evening they suddenly flew wide open, as if in surprise, then slowly shut like those of a child dropping off to sleep, the straight long lashes making dark fringes on the sunken cheeks. His heart, which had fought so long and so valiantly to keep his failing body functioning, stopped its weary ticking, like a clock that has run down and leaves a deafening silence in the room.

One piercing, unearthly scream from his mother was the only sound as Lydia slid her arms away from him, kissed him on the forehead and eased him down on his bed. Deborah Cochran, who had been with them through the night and the long day, caught Lydia as she moved back. Ann Maria, Thomas and Ann fell into each other's arms as if by clinging together they would not collapse. The servants clustered by the door and in the hall, solemn and frightened. There was no need to send for a doctor. Both Donaldson and Gibson had been there within the hour, knowing there was nothing to be done.

"Now he see all the sta's." Delia sobbed into her apron. "He always want to see all the sta's."

Two lines in the newspaper marked the passing of his bright spirit: "Thos. J. Hollingsworth, Jr., aged 23, died at his home, 15 South street last night." The months of agony were over.

"We have indeed experienced a sore affliction in the irreparable loss of our beloved Thomas," Ann Maria wrote Ruth because Lydia could not. "He was more than brother, a sincere friend, and everything that was dear to us. You well know his amiable and cheerful disposition, but it is almost impossible to imagine the fortitude and patience with which he bore his long protracted illness. For more than 10 months he was confined and during that time frequently suffered the most severe pain and anguish, yet he never murmured nor discovered the least impatience at his hard fate. How inscrutable are the ways of Providence! We could not but hope that he would have been restored to us, but we must all submit to our All-Wise Creator, who afflicts for our good. Indeed, we have all borne up surprisingly well. My dear Mother, whose heart was wrapped up in her son, makes great exertions, never was more devoted attention paid than by her. Papa too has received a severe blow. Indeed, Papa looks many years older, the last winter was a solitary one for him and he felt it most keenly. The great composure and resignation with which my dear brother left this world of trouble gives us great consolation. I think he must be happy. Amiable, dutiful, unostentatious, and added to these virtues the highest sense of honour and integrity. We could not have wished for more."

It was fortunate for Lydia that her sister had taken on some of the necessary tasks that flooded in on them. Memorial gifts in Thomas's name had to be bought and sent to all the closer relatives. Lydia was probably better acquainted with the stock of all the city's shops, dwindling because of the blockades, than any of the others, but she found that duty the most harrowing she had ever undertaken.

Their mother was quite ill after the long strain. She had had a bed moved into her son's room so that she could spend nights as well as days watching over him, after Fronya's death. Even when he slept, she could not allow herself complete relaxation, fearing that he would waken and she might not hear him. She refused help from anyone, although there were numerous offers from friends and relatives. She was a woman of great determination and character, traits inherited by her son. She felt that if she were but strong enough and stubborn enough, she could save her boy.

When she could not, it was as if every phase of her life had counted for nothing; she went into a severe withdrawal and depression. Her husband—if anything, more bereft than she—could not reach her by word or touch or thought.

Once the necessary shopping was done, Lydia was confronted with one more woeful duty, preparing the letters to go with the gifts. "My Dear Cousin," she wrote to Ruth, "Your letter of June lies before me unanswered and until now I felt as if I could not write you. My last was penned under feelings so totally different, alternate hopes and fears then possessed me for a dearly loved Brother, whose life was doubtful, but superior wisdom has removed him from us all and I firmly believe, my dear Cousin, to happiness. His last hours could not else have been so perfectly calm, the last words he addressed to me were expression of a wish not to remain long here. His Fortitude, and truly it seemed Christian, never forsook him, in pain or in parting moments. Aunt Debby can tell you more fully of the change, she was with us. I had never been with one in that fatal flattering complaint before, and felt unfeigned satisfaction in being able to have administered a little to his comfort. The dawning of this year was the most painful anxiety for him; and the middle of it finds him not among us; what the remainder has in store, we know not! Favour, in the sight of our Maker and Redeemer, outweighs all the brightest joys of Earth, and I do not murmur, though I feel, at times deeply feel. This adversity of feeling is doubtless for our good, and we must seek the proper channel for it; and not repine, Cousin, that our schemes of present happiness are diverted. . . . Mama presents her affectionate love to you with a silk dress, and gloves; and to Aunt Ruth, gloves and a Love handkerchief, which you will do her the favour to accept on this occasion."

Wrapping up the parcels and enclosing the black-bordered memorial cards made her accept that their loss was real, and that it was permanent. Thomas was dead. His wasted young body lay forever in St. Paul's Cemetery, waiting for a Judgment Day that all must someday meet.

Ruth Tobin, receiving the word of his passing, collapsed in grief and spent four days in a darkened room, inconsolable. She would not let Stephen write to Baltimore, other than a short note she dictated for him, telling Thomas's family how deeply sorry they were, and that they had all loved Thomas and hoped he was now in a better world, where there was no pain and no sorrow. Stephen signed it for all three of them: himself, Ruth Hollingsworth and Ruth Tobin.

Chapter Twenty

Mine Enemies Are Lively

A sudden summer storm brought A. J. Foster galloping through the great iron gates at Chiswick House, drenched, his horse lathered and his morning's shooting ruined. The rain had come in such torrents that he had barely been able to see his way, trusting largely to the horse's instinct to get him to the right road.

He sent the animal to the stables with a groom, tossed his gun to another servant to be cleaned and put away, and squished disconsolately inside. Once out of the weather, he sat down to take off his boots and ring for hot water and fresh clothing to be made ready in his room.

He didn't particularly mind the soaking, but he was disappointed in having to come in so soon. Shooting had always been his favorite sport, but he had too little time to spend at it. There were still superb mounts in the Duke's stables, although his mother had disposed of some of them before she went off to Italy to dig in the ruins around Rome. She would never live in London again; he supposed he should be happy that she was spending some of the Duke's vast fortune in that way and that she was finding a new life for herself. The new Duke had made him feel welcome at Chiswick and Devonshire houses but the old gaiety was gone. London had a great emptiness for him. The city was steadily encroaching on its lawns and parks, but at Chiswick he could still ride through green forests and meadows, past the tranquil little lake and along winding country lanes toward the Thames.

There in the country he could escape some of the bitterness and bickering that characterized public life and avoid the news dispatches of victories or defeats on the battlefronts. War, war, *war!* It had its built-in horrors, not the least of which was the separation of people who loved each other, regardless of the decrees of their governments.

Perhaps he enjoyed shooting because he was killing off some of the ogres that were keeping him from her. *Smash!* If some small creature perished in a burst of feathers he felt no guilt, only the satisfaction of having power over something that stood in his way. He'd reload at once, ready for the next ogre.

In dry clothes, and aware that he would be housebound for several hours if the storm kept up its pounding, he went to the big library, looked along the shelves at the lines of books and chose several to read.

As he was about to seat himself in an alcove where the light was good, he heard a thump against the window and looked up to see a few feathers sticking to the wet glass, still fluttering. Obviously a bird had been slammed into it by the force of the storm, or had mistaken it for an unobstructed opening. He went closer to look out through the sheets of rain. The bird lay broken and helpless under the window, still alive. He could see its quick fast breathing under the soft grayness of its feathers, and the peculiar in-and-outness of its sharp eye. It was a sea bird that had apparently been driven inland from the coast.

He opened the curtains wider, then decided to light a candle to relieve the gloom. The somber power of the storm made him feel uncomfortably solemn. Although it was midsummer, he was so chilled that he would have welcomed a fire and thought briefly of ringing for one. Instead, he buttoned his jacket around him and settled into his chair to read. He must try to lose himself in something outside himself, drive away the stifling loneliness that was creeping through the room like a fog, penetrating every nook and every window bay.

The bird would not let him rest. He went to look out again and saw that it was quite still and lifeless. Poor thing, he thought. Not the quick death and the merciful one that he and other good Christians prayed for. Neither quick nor merciful, this one, but final. Why should it have such a tug at his heart?

He felt a pang of unspeakable sadness, as if some appalling loss had come upon him. Giving in to it, he put aside his book and tried to concentrate on solving the riddle. Perhaps something new had happened in the war, either on the Continent . . . or at sea . . . or . . . in America? When he thought of America, he knew instinctively what had occurred. He sat for some moments with his head down and his fingers rubbing his temples.

Because of course it was Thomas. Thomas, the gay, intelligent, curious, eager young one, the boy who was the model of the son he dared to dream he might have for himself someday. Thomas was dead. Young Thomas, who had so much ahead of him, who had never made any secret of his admiration for Foster and his joy at the plans for having him in the same family—the boy was gone. He knew it as truly as if it had been painted in mile-high black letters against the menacing sky. Thomas was gone.

Lydia would need him more than ever, as he had known she needed him earlier, although he had not known why. Now she needed him with what amounted to despair. She needed the shelter of his love for her, the hope of their future life together, the solid faith that he was still there.

Lydia—Lydia Eliza—my lovely cousin . . . How could he let her know that he knew?

God, why can't I go to her?

Not bothering to hunt for oilskins, he plunged out into the storm, his head bare, his throat choked with sobs. He went stumbling along until he could smash through the shrubbery to the spot where the bird had fallen. Finding it, he took it into his hands, rubbing it with a frantic urgency, trying to force some life back into its graceful, silent body, holding it against himself for warmth.

Then, in a gesture he would never understand, he lifted the bird high above his head and opened his hands, as if expecting the lifeless wings to lift and carry the frail body into the heavens. The rush of feathers past his face as the bird fell again to the ground made him kneel, pick it up and place it tenderly against an ancient gnarled root close to the wall. There was nothing he could do.

It took nearly two weeks for news of young Oliver Hazard Perry's victory at Lake Erie to filter south. On September 10, 1813, with a total of fifty-five guns and fewer than a dozen ships, he had flushed out an enemy fleet with at least ten more guns, at Put-in-Bay at South Bass Island. The battle raged for three violent hours; then Perry's flagship, the *Lawrence,* was disabled. He scrambled into a small boat and boarded the *Niagara,* ordering her into close combat even though she was surrounded and being shelled from both sides. By sheer guts and skill he goaded his battered men to victory, the first of any consequence in the fifteen months of the war.

Laconically, the twenty-eight-year-old Captain sent a message to his commanding officer, old "Tippecanoe" Harrison. "We have met the enemy, and they are ours." The nine words would electrify the country.

When Baltimore found out about it, thirteen days later, the celebrating started out with a city-wide illumination. There were bands, parades, dances. Strangers stopped on the street to exchange word of the good news.

The Hollingsworths, to take their minds off their grief, and to give Ruth Tobin a rest from the confining care of her aunt, invited her down for one of her rare visits. Polodore and Robert were sent to the packet to meet her, bringing her and her suitcases to the door, where the family was waiting. There were tears as the wound of their loss was opened up again, but at last Ruth and Lydia went upstairs to get Ruth settled for her stay with them.

Lydia Eliza watched her cousin as she moved around, taking out dresses, lining up her shoes in a careful row, putting her comb and mirror on the washstand in the guest room. Ruth was not herself. Something more was affecting her, weighing her down, making her so quiet—something besides the oppressive and demanding care of a sick old lady. The two spoke of the weather as it influenced her trip down the bay, exchanged greetings from various relatives, noted the beginning of autumn color in the forests. The superficiality of their conversation was covering up the need for deeper communication, which would come, Lydia knew.

When her clothing was hung up and everything was in order, Ruth went to the window to look out at the garden. As she turned to answer a question, Lydia was startled to see the expression on her face. Her large eyes, her most distinctive feature, had a look of withdrawal and deep hurt. Her thin shoulders were stooped.

"Ruth!" Lydia blurted out. "You don't look well! Was the trip so very tiring? Shall I ring for some tea?"

"No, I'm all right. Thank you anyway."

"But you aren't yourself. There's something really wrong, I know. Won't you tell me what it is? Maybe you're lovesick?" She made an effort at banter. "One of Uncle Stephen's preacher fellows? You've never mentioned the new one in your letters—I found out about him from—" She stopped, noticing Ruth's stricken face. "Cousin! *What is it?*" She rushed to her and pulled her, weeping, on to the chaise longue. "What is it? You can tell me. We have no secrets, do we, Cousin? We promised each other, long ago. Is it a secret?"

Ruth nodded, dumbly. "It was. It doesn't matter now."

"Ruth!" Lydia cried as the girl collapsed in her arms. "It was Thomas, wasn't it? *You were in love with Thomas!* Oh, my darling—"

"I thought—" Ruth began, trying to get control of herself. "I thought I couldn't come here, to this house, to everything that he—but then I knew—I knew I had to—somehow. . . ."

Lydia sat with the weeping girl's head cradled on her lap, finding her own heart torn to shreds all over again, feeling a hundred years old. After a long time she asked, "Did Thomas know?"

"I don't think so."

"I wish he had," Lydia said in a pinched voice.

"It wouldn't have saved him." Ruth got up and went to the window again. "I would have given my life—don't tell the others—*my life*. Please don't tell them. They have enough suffering. And so do you. I want everyone to think I am having a wonderful time while I am here—and I will be really—but—"

"I think I know a little bit—" Lydia began, but Ruth interrupted her in a soft whisper, "You still have hope."

When the two of them came down for tea, Ruth had changed her clothes and their faces were masks of smiles, their conversation light and noncommittal.

A list of invitations for Ruth had already been made up: to the Cochrans' for an oyster feast, Sam's for dinner, the George Adamses' for tea and a drive in the country, at Oaklands for a family evening. Ruth entered into all the plans with pleasure, especially the city-wide rejoicing for Perry's victory. Maybe now, they all told each other, the horrid war would take a turning and soon be over. There had been so few crumbs of encouragement to build on.

On the twenty-third, Ruth sat down at Lydia Eliza's writing desk to report home on her visit and to assure her aunt

Ruth that all was well. "The Cannon is now firing at the Fort [McHenry] in honnor of the late Victory obtained upon the Lakes. The Town is to be illuminated tonight. It will be a new Scene to me."

She added a prophetic postscript: "I have been looking out the window in the upper Story where we have a fine view of the Fort. Could see the Companys and the flash of Cannon. There were a great number fired in quick succession. The flags flying from the Vessels there [make a great deal] of bustle in Town." And well they should, because they were the banners from captured ships. Baltimore was swiftly becoming known as "a nest of pirates." Privateers and raiders were adding daily to the brilliant display of colors out at the Lazaretto. Those smaller, less dramatic victories might be put with Captain Perry's to make an impressive record.

When it was time for Ruth's visit to end, Aunt Debby came in her carriage to take her to the packet, to save Thomas's family the public appearance that they could not yet face.

The next packet brought Ruth a letter from Deborah, recounting her fears. She related that ". . . just after we parted from you we met the Captain, whom I perfectly remembered." Stephen smiled when Ruth read that line. Probably the Captain remembered her just as perfectly. Deborah Cochran's ways with ship captains were well known to the brotherhood. "I asked him how the wind was, he observed as fair as can be, and said he expected to run up in six hours. I thought this would be to swift, beged him not to carry too much sail, and take great care of you and Mrs. Cooch as you where both timid, he promised he would. Mr. C. laughed at my timidity, at the same time observed he was fearful that you would have more than was agreeable. I stoped at Brother Thomas's to say how you were fixed, as to your company, etc. There the wind whiseled so loud that we all expressed our fears and regretted your departure. . . . I never left there untill one o'clock. I then bid them a good morning . . . on going home I asked

Sally if I had ordered dinner, she laughed and said I had not, but that her Master had. This was the first omission of the kind ever I kept house. So you will see how much you was thought of."

Debby had had many worried hours until she was sure that Ruth had arrived safely. "I wished anxiously on Saturday that we could hear from you, this was impossible. I yesterday morning sent to South Street to know if there was a letter. none. then to Mr. Levi Hollingsworth the same, I then told Henry to go to the Warf and inquire if the Packet had returned. to my very great relief he brought word that it was. The Captain told him you had left here at tenn o'clock and arrived safe at four, all well. After Church I sent down to let them know which they were much gratified at hearing."

Since Lydia was having trouble with an infection in her eyes, Ann Maria wrote to report Debby's anxiety and their own relief at Ruth's safe arrival after the dangerous fifty-mile journey: "The wind was so very high and the weather so cool the day you left, as that we could not help fearing you would suffer great inconvenience. . . . Aunt Debby returned from the boat and continued to 1 o'clock, she would every now and then exclaim dear me! the wind is prodigiously high!" Ruth could laugh at this description. Aunt Debby was an accomplished worrier.

Not being permitted to use her eyes spared Lydia the knowledge of some of the British outrages, because she could not read the papers. The enemy was still infesting the bay but without doing significant damage, but nuisance raids were still menacing passenger lines and other necessary civilian shipping. She heard enough of their depredations anyway, through listening in on conversations. She was also spared the daily practice with Fronya's pistol that her father demanded of all three of his womenfolk. Lydia Eliza hated trying to use the weapon. It forced her by every motion she made with it to try to think of Augustus John Foster as the Enemy; she wanted to toss the gun into a junk heap, it filled her with such revulsion.

It was weeks before she could safely try any close work. It was a relief to take up her pen again after her long idleness.

"My dear Cousin," she began on November 5, "I thank you for your very affectionate Favour of last week, wherein you express great solicitude for my poor Eye. . . . I was yesterday for the first time since your return home, at church, it was Thanksgiving Day; and did not walk out for four weeks. The idleness I was compelled to practice was a great labour for though my work avail but little it amuses me and makes me contented."

The Thanksgiving service had been almost more painful for her family than young Thomas's death. There were more women than men in attendance, since it was a Thursday and not many businesses were closed. Because Thomas's family had gone into deep mourning and almost total retirement from any public contacts, many had not seen them since the funeral. Their inquiries and sympathy came from genuine concern, but each sad look, each touch of a hand was like a new wound opening up the scar that was just beginning to heal.

Dr. Kemp's sermon reminded his parishioners that there was much to be thankful for, and Lydia supposed he was right. So far, the city had been spared, the fury of the summer's rampages from the British had lessened and it was said that the enemy fleet was going off to the Caribbean for the colder months, so there was hope of some relief. Not peace, he reminded them regretfully, but a respite from the sword. Their faith had been sorely tested and probably would be again; the days of terror were not ended. The number and types of uniforms scattered throughout the congregation were mute testimony to their condition.

After church Lydia went alone to visit her brother's grave, hoping to find some strength and consolation in silent communion with him. She was thinking not only of herself but of Ruth. Might he have known? On her return home, she begged to be excused from dinner, asking for some tea and a small lunch to be sent up to her room. Her mother brought the tray herself, knowing instinctively that her daughter was coming to a new crossroads in her life.

"The world does not end in a season," she said gently. "We must bear what we must bear. It is the only thing in life that I know for sure."

"Yes, Mama. But—"

"It is not only Thomas. . . ." Her mother's voice caught on his name. "For you, it's not just your brother. Papa and I know. It's Mr. Foster. We had learned to love him too, you know." She brought a creamy Merino shawl and slipped it protectively around her daughter's shoulders. "You probably feel that you have lost the two most precious men in your life."

"I still have Papa," Lydia whispered, knowing that her mother had exactly defined the dimension of her grief.

"Yes. And he needs us, all of us. We mustn't forget that." She poured some tea from the Lowestoft pot. "Papa and I, and your sister, think the time must surely be close when your Mr. Foster can come back to us."

"Don't say that, Mama! I don't dare hope that it can be true."

"We have faith. And just because no mail comes—it's always hard to get messages through when there is war—we remember the last one. And now there are thousands of miles of ocean. . . ." She dropped a kiss on her daughter's cheek and slipped from the room. "We must . . ." The interview was so painful for her that she left without finishing the sentence.

Resolutely, Lydia went to the drawer where she kept the few mementos she had of the man she loved. There was a total of nine letters. She had read and reread them so many times that the folds of the paper were getting ragged and some of the wax seals had dropped away. With them were the dried, pressed flowers, the well-read prayer book and the gold-framed miniature. That was all. All she had on which to build a hope, a dream, a life. There were her own letters, the ones she had written to him that had never left town. Without opening them, she tore them to bits and sprinkled them over the fire. Some fragile remnant of trust kept her from doing the same with his. She found a small box, put into it her little hoard of treasures and went to the third floor. In the back room far under the eaves there was a little niche where she and her brother and sister had hidden things from each other when they were children. So long ago!

The room was cold. They had not used that space since the flood of relatives had come for Thomas's funeral and the house had been filled to capacity. After the last sorrowful visitor had departed, the servants took off all the bedding, cleaned the rooms, drew the blinds and went back to helping the household assimilate its loss. As far as Lydia knew, no one had been up there since, except for those fifteen minutes during Ruth Tobin's visit. The servants all lived in rooms at the back of the house or over the stables.

There was an air of spookiness, of clammy chill that made her shudder. The place smelled of carnations.

She looked down at the box in her hand and at the shadowed hiding place under the eaves. Hugging the box to her as she stifled a cry, she flew back down the steps like something being pursued, slamming the door behind her and falling into a chair, out of breath.

Her tea was nearly cold, but she drank it gratefully, nibbling at the slice of pound cake and the orange that lay near it, glad that there was no gingerbread. Finally she sat at her dressing table, staring at her reflection in the cloissoné looking glass with as much honesty as she could muster.

She was twenty-seven, going on twenty-eight. Well-born, well-educated, reasonably attractive, she admitted, with a quiet flair for choosing clothes that looked well on her. She was never first to take up the new or last to forsake the old. She had found the man she loved. Wasn't this the end and aim of every woman's life? The long months had brought her to the realization that he might be gone forever, but she would always love him. That could not change.

The thought of even absent-mindedly considering another sweetheart or another husband could find no lodging in her mind or in her heart. Even the specter of spinsterhood was less ominous than it used to be.

Could she ever face the prospect of a marriage of convenience? With what kind of man? And for what reason? She did not need wealth; there was enough of the world's goods at her disposal to cover any need or want she might have. She and Ann Maria would divide between them her father's—she could not yet face the awful thought that some day he, like her brother, would be gone. In any case, there was no reason to marry for the sake of money.

She did need companionship and love, the only real reasons for marrying, she had always felt. She had had glimpses of the richness that could bring. Only glimpses, all too brief, but they had illuminated her life like a series of Roman candles. Just remembering the sound of his step in the hall, or the way he sometimes hummed when he danced to a tune he liked, or his response to a flowering shrub, could bring back an instant of rapture.

She did not need social prestige or an entree into select company. She already had both, for whatever they were worth. The only kind of more select company for which she might yearn was the one whose circles would be opened through her marriage to a diplomat. "Three short, small, simple words, from you to me . . ." He had known what *he* wanted, and had offered himself in return.

So what do I need? What do I want? How shall I get it?

What she needed and what she wanted were identical. A

husband whose name was A. J. Foster, a home to be shared with him and children to be had with him. It sounded simple. The present impossibility of achieving it was what had brought her to her room for a confrontation with herself. She could not survive any longer in this frozen cave as she sought to deny her brother's death and her sweetheart's silence.

If I were a man, I could go out and shoot up the town, she thought realistically. Being a woman, I'm not even supposed to scream. Or throw things. Or curse. Or drink myself into blessed oblivion.

Tears were the time-honored feminine weapon and escape valve, but she was beyond tears. Centuries beyond tears.

She sat with the soft shawl enfolding her as Foster's arms had sheltered her on their last day together. She was not alone. She knew it. Someplace far away he was reaching out to her as well. His problems might be even greater than hers. She could not know.

A great sense of peace came over her. It was as if young Thomas had said to her in his old teasing way, "Face up to it, my dear sister! You can't spend your time living in a yesterday that's gone or a tomorrow that may never come. Today! That's the day to live!" She broke into an involuntary smile, as if returning her brother's affectionate grin.

When she came downstairs her face was drawn but tearless, her manner reserved as always, her attitude that of a person who has come to a decision and would follow it through without whimpering. Her mother looked up, her eyes questioning and hopeful.

"I must live each day for itself, Mama," she said with finality.

Her mother kissed her cheek. "In the end, Lydia Eliza, there is only faith."

In January, Baltimore's sagging spirits were greatly raised by the news that Oliver Hazard Perry himself was coming to town. Merchants, caterers, city fathers, hairdressers, tailors, dressmakers and all the military organizations were galvanized into new life. Tickets were sold for a gala dinner honoring the hero, who would be escorted to his place by the President of the United States.

All three of the Baltimore Hollingsworth brothers were there to pay him honor, along with several of their sons. Thomas Hollingsworth had much to tell his womenfolk about the evening, especially about the appearance of the young Captain. He had wide-set, intelligent eyes, curls of brown hair above the ears, a pleasant open face; above all, he was a man. A real man. Married, yes.

Lydia passed the information on to Ruth: "The public spirit of Baltimore seems to have awakened to the beams of his Glory, and shone forth yesterday in a Dinner to him. a Large Company and an elegant repast, with splendid decorations for the occasion. Tonight he gratifies the Ladies by being present at a Cotillion party. . . . It appears that he is as modest as he is brave—a married man, that the Ladies may wear their happiest faces and air, and yet not be accused of overstepping their proper bounds. he has met with a namesake in this City—a Brother Sailor, who had once been in the same vessel with Perry, had a son soon after the Victory on the Lakes; and called him Oliver Perry. the child was presented to him by Mr. Johnson on his supping at his House and the Commodore was pleased with the compliment."

Perry was also pleased to be dubbed Commodore. It was a rank that he did not achieve during the few years of distinguished service to his country that were left to him.

"I wish you had been at the Ball," Lydia told her cousin, "for I think his presence was more flattering than Miss H's or any other Belle's who attended. I regret I did not see Perry, as two opportunities presented themselves and I missed them both. In one instance I did not know he was on the bridge with me; and in the other my excessive anxiety to see him heightened my colour so much that I was actually ashamed to present myself before the window, and I only caught a view of his figure."

Blushing! Would she never outgrow it?

"Perhaps a short account of the decorations of the Ball-room may amuse you. Nancy [Ann Maria] and I went with Col. Howard and Mr. J. Carroll the next morning to the House, as they were not then removed and had no interruption to our gaze. Over each window in the dancing room was gracefully hung an American flag, formed in a rose at each corner, and at the head of the room hung a very large elegant Painting of the Battle. It represented the moment when Perry in the *Niagara* had broke the British line of Battle Ships and was receiving the fire of the enemy on both sides. an awful splendid sight, and the Commodore says, faithfully depicted. on the top of this vessel in distinct characters were 'Don't give up the Ship,' which you know were the last words of our poor Lawrence, and I doubt not cheered the crew. there were many other vessels in the piece, and I must tell you, by an invisible hand the British colours were struck, in compliment to Perry who in reality had raised his country's above them.

"In attempting to hoist the American flag over on shore I mean, the machinery was a little wrong, and they could not succeed, the Gentlemen mentioned their mortification to Perry at this defeat but he with great presence of mind and politeness replied the upper rope (he used a technical word) was only shot away. the dancing ceased, and Washington's March announced him. The supper room was also decorated. a table in the form of a quarter deck was covered with delicacies for him, and some other distinguished gentlemen. He sat on an elevated chair, covered by the flag of his country, and on a pillar opposite, were the names of our naval conquerors, then a ship; then those who fell in Glory, a ship, and so on, as they gained laurels; with his own name at the top, then a crown, and above 'we have met the Enemy, and they are ours.' These were his own modest words. The Ladies were all, with his appearance so much charmed that they were induced to beg an introduction, and have a passing word with him."

A most satisfactory hero. Americans could stand taller and straighter because of him. Even though he had been born in Rhode Island, one of the states pulling vigorously against the Union and against the war, he was still an American and represented in every way all that any young American could want to be.

Without firing a shot, Oliver Hazard Perry had conquered Baltimore.

In addition, the victory on the Lakes made possible an invasion through Detroit to Canada, the invasion that had been impossible by land.

Supplies and men could now be transported by water instead of slogging through the swamps of the Maumee Valley. "Tippecanoe" Harrison took over from the defeated General Hull, recaptured Detroit and, within three weeks of Perry's spectacular success, had sped up the Thames River to a victory that effectively stopped further British aggression there. Perry himself had led the decisive push.

That battle took the life of the great Indian chief Tecumseh. The man who could put a new star in the sky or turn off the sun was as mortal as anyone else.

Sadly, Lydia wondered if the gay spirit that had been her brother might find the fearless one of the redoubtable old warrior, on some bright forest trail in the Happy Hunting Ground.

Chapter Twenty-one

The Proud Have Forged a Lie Against Me

The tempo of war picked up in the spring of 1814, when the Tennessee frontiersman Andrew Jackson effectively ended the co-operation of the British with the Creek Indians on March 27, in a frightful massacre known as the Battle of Horseshoe Bend. He then rampaged into Florida and captured the Gulf city of Pensacola, which was owned by the Spanish, who had also been supplying the Creek Indians.

America was rapidly forging ahead on land, which was the kind of conflict the War Hawks had been calling for from the beginning. Maybe now even the New England Federalists would see the light, would stop driving great herds of cattle across the Canadian frontier to feed the British and stop shipping thousands of barrels of flour to the same enemy in Portugal. Maybe they'd open some of their fat purses, swollen with the profits of this traitorous traffic. Maybe.

On April 11, the fabulous empire of Napoleon Bonaparte collapsed at Fontainebleau south of Paris. Abdicating his throne, he fled for safety to the isle of Elba, ninety-four square miles of real estate off the coast of Italy, the only remnant of his vast fiefdom he could still control.

Foster's brother Frederick was in Paris during the rioting and subsequent setting up of a provisional government. On

May 1 he wrote to Augustus: "The noise drove me away from the Hôtel de Bruxelles and I am now at the Hôtel des Ministres de l'Université, still more noisy but in a different way. Mme. de Staël is arrived. I called on her yesterday and found her to be in high spirits, surrounded by a crowd of admirers, and all talking of course of Napoleon. They say he took opium, but the dose having failed he considers himself as preserved by destiny for great things yet. Says he was formed to rule the world."

In a few days Augustus himself was in Paris, sending back to his mother a running report of what was going on, in several dispatches: "Napoleon is off; he embarked at Fréjus; and he has Elba in Soveraineté; he was obliged to put on a white cockade near Avignon, to ride and pass as Lord Burghersh or Col. Cambell, and even to cry 'Louis 18.'" And on May 7: "Yesterday we went to St. Cloud. The concierge says there is no servant with Bonaparte but Alie Mamelouk . . . whom Napoleon is too happy now to have. He can shave himself fortunately. I suppose the account of his journey will be in all the papers. He cried a good deal, I hear; but how flattering to us his confidence in us. . . . It is impossible to stand higher than the English do here; people of all sorts are striving which shall best express the feeling to us. The French too open themselves to us without scruple upon their affairs . . . the Prussians behave well in the great towns but commit a great deal of injustice in the villages. One told us they had Champagne enough to bathe in in Champagne."

The deposed Bourbons, who had seemed like such tyrants before Napoleon showed them something worse, were back on the throne. Early in May, King Louis XVIII re-entered the city of Paris like a conquering hero.

France, all of Europe, and especially England, went mad with joy. There were massive fireworks displays, parades, concerts, speeches, victory balls and general hullabaloo. Flags flew from every pole and every house. Hats in France flaunted the white cockade, the symbol of the royalists. The victims of the Emperor's vaulting ambition felt that they had been delivered from bondage, as indeed they had. Churches were open night and day for prayers and thanksgiving.

America, France's reluctant ally, joined the festivities. The *Federal Gazette* gloated that "The cruel are always cowards," and gave considerable space to publicizing plans for Baltimore's city-wide illumination, the first since Perry's victory. In New York City Gouverneur Morris rejoiced that the long agony was over and reminded the American Francophiles that "Those who would know the idol of their devotion [should] seek him in the Island of Elba."

With all the exultation it seemed not to occur to any but a few of the wiser heads that the dissolution of the Empire would free thousands of British soldiers and sailors for combat in North America. Great Britain's fleet, said to contain a thousand ships, could be released from blockade duty. It could be augmented by vast armies no longer needed on the Continent.

The British set about planning their new strategy. There would be invasion and subsequent victory at three points: Lake Champlain in the north, where they would vindicate the defeat of "Gentleman Johnny" Burgoyne in the Revolution; the Chesapeake Bay on the central east coast; and the mouth of the mighty Mississippi at New Orleans.

On June 11, a squadron of eleven British ships, the forerunner of the great fleet to come, slipped out of the French river Garonne into the Gironde, heading west for a final thrust of the harassment out in North America.

Deos fortioribus adesse, they confidently quoted Tacitus. The gods assist the stronger.

When Foster got home from his firsthand look at the change-over in France, one of his friends at the Admiralty told him with pleasure that the British had captured an armed

American merchant ship that had been delivering flour, leather, gunstocks, tobacco and black powder to France. Both sides had lost several men in the engagement, but the ship was saved and towed in as a prize. The master and several of his crew were in prison right there in London.

"It was quite a catch." The officer grinned. "The ship is a big one, only three years old, belonged to that Patterson chap. I'm sure you've heard of him. His daughter married one of the Boneys. Had a whole fleet at one time, I hear. This is the third one we've picked off. And we can use that cargo too, Mr. Foster. This has been a very good day!"

"A Patterson ship, eh? That would be a prize," Foster said thoughtfully.

Before the week was out he had located the prison where the ship's master was being held. In the faint hope that he might get some word from Baltimore, he went to see the man.

The prison shocked him. Located near the Thames, it was damp, moldy and filthy, not much like the model facilities he had been shown in Philadelphia, which had greatly impressed him. (He had not seen the others.) The men there were treated humanely, taught some skills if need be; the cells were kept clean and whitewashed frequently; the plank beds had thin mattresses; the slop pots had covers and were dumped regularly. It was not without reason that some of his colleagues in Parliament sneered behind his back that he was not to be trusted because he was pro-American. When it came to jails, he certainly was.

The stench came out to meet him, and he nearly turned back. The jailer, not knowing him but recognizing from his bearing and his clothing that he was a man of importance, mumbled some apologies about its being early in the day and all their clean-up work not finished yet. Now if he had just come a little later . . . Foster stared him down.

"Ye'll have to excuse it, Guv'ner." He rapped his heavy keys across the bars of a cell. A prisoner got up from the pile of straw that was his bed. "Company fer ya, Finch!"

The man—gaunt, unshaven and hostile—at first refused to speak to him. Foster couldn't blame him much. The chances of his getting out of there alive were poor. He began persuasively to tell the fellow of the reason for his visit. "I was in America for several years, Mr. Finch," he explained. "Before this war, of course."

For the first time, Augustus John wished that he had learned to turn on an American accent. He had tried it in jest several times, and it never failed to convulse his British friends, but now, when a less clipped and precise enunciation might have softened the prisoner's attitude toward him, he didn't dare try it for fear it would come out as dangerous comedy. He was aware that his words were like a series of razor cuts to the poor devil's sensitive hide.

"I have some friends in Baltimore that I thought I might inquire about, Mr. Finch. Do you, perhaps, have any acquaintances there?"

"I live there," was the sullen reply. "Or I did. Thirty-six years I've been livin' in Bal'mur."

Foster jumped. That was the way the residents pronounced it, with no "t." He hadn't heard the name said that way in nearly two years. He would try it too.

"I'm especially interested in any news you may have of the Hollingsworth family in Bal'mur," he said.

"Which one? Lots of 'em there."

"Thomas. They live across from the Pattersons."

"Known 'em all my life," Finch answered. "Worked for him eight, maybe nine years." If the place had not been so murky and dark, the visitor would have been instantly on his guard, because the American had realized who the man was. He knew a great deal about this Mr. Foster; he knew Lydia, had always known her or known of her, and he knew of the love affair, as did most of the town. On his last shore leave he had seen some of the family and had guessed at the loss and loneliness that the girl was feeling.

Mr. Finch could not sympathize, because Mr. Finch hated

everything English. His grandfather had been killed in the Revolution three months before Finch's birth. His father had been blinded and lost an arm in the same war, at the age of twenty. His childhood had been strangled by poverty, and now his life and his work had been blown to Hell, all because of the English. He hated them in his bones and in his viscera. His days in this stinking prison had only increased his loathing. He had lost his ship, his cargo, his men, his freedom and perhaps his life. He doubted that he would ever see his wife and four children again.

Inspired, and knowing that all was fair in war, if not in love, he fabricated an out-and-out lie, telling it as simply as if it were true, and adding embellishments as he saw that his thrust struck home.

"Fine folks, the Hollingsworths," he said, more genially. "Lost their boy last summer. Very sad."

Foster caught his breath. So he had been right. It *was* young Thomas.

"Things going better there now, though," Finch went on. "Remember that second daughter, one of the Bal'mur belles, as they call 'em? The brown-eyed one?"

"Yes—yes?"

"Getting married. Right away, I guess. Big society weddin' up at St. Paul's Church, flock of bridesmaids, relatives pourin' in from all over."

The Captain saw by Foster's horrified silence that he had scored, so he drove the blade in deeper. "Some Frenchman, they say. Can't remember whether he was the top man the Frenchies sent over to Washington or one of his men."

"Sérurier?" the name whistled past Foster's teeth.

"Doesn't sound quite like it, but it was one of those Frenchies from the Federal City. Mr. Patterson's daughter Betsy . . . you may know her? The feisty one? Madame Bonaparte? She got them together."

Craftily, the American finished the job. "Understand the

Frenchies are pretty happy about it. Beautiful American girl, lots of money, important family. We're allies with the French, you know."

"Yes, I know. Well, thank you very much, Mr. Finch."

"Come again, Mr. Foster. Any time."

The news that the lying Captain gave him so glibly, and that he had no immediate means of proving or disproving, struck him with the force of a lethal blow. He groped his way back into the daylight, dismissed his coachman and pounded blindly toward the river. The cobblestones were slippery from a recent rain; more than once he nearly fell. At the water's edge in that dingy area where he had never been before, he looked out at ships' masts of many registries, some of them newly captured prizes, their flags struck in humiliation, others British war vessels of every description home for repairs. A few swarmed with men making them ready to shove off and sail back into the fray.

The sight of the sleek Patterson frigate stabbed him. How long it had been since he had seen an American ship! Her whole starboard side was smashed in, but she was still afloat. His first impulse was to try to board her to question her sailors; then he scoffed at his own stupidity. There wouldn't be any Americans on her; they were all either dead or in prison or impressed for duty on British warships. Even if she carried a full complement of men, those sailors would not have been of Lydia's social class and would never have heard of her. They might even laugh at him. How big a fool could a man make of himself?

He headed back toward Westminster on foot, walking faster and faster to keep from leaping into the black waters of the Thames and ending his life. A ridiculous and ignominious exit. And he didn't have *proof*. He had only the word of a viciously embittered prisoner of war. Finding his way to a street, he hailed a hack and went despondently to his rooms.

Who would know, or could find out, the truth? Only someone in the States. Or, as a remote possibility, in France; but he could not look there for help. Who in America then? John Randolph—he should be willing to investigate, if there was a way to reach him. Madame Bonaparte? She would know, if anyone did. Baker? But where to get hold of him? The Foreign Office people said he was in New York, in Baltimore, in Washington—they never knew where he was, and it took weeks for a response to come through diplomatic channels. But why try Baker anyway? Using him as a go-between had been a failure. Perhaps the young man had done as Foster feared he might: begun courting Lydia himself. That still seemed unlikely. And Finch insisted that Lydia's new love was a Frenchman. Well, he'd write to Baker anyway. He thought fleetingly of approaching Dolley Madison but backed away. There were certain friendships and certain relationships, even the warmest ones, that one could not impose on, especially in wartime. Mrs. Cochran? Yes! Of course!

He wrote letters like a madman, far into the night, begging, imploring, pleading for any scrap of information that anyone might have. Even as he went to post the stack of them the next morning he knew that none would ever reach its destination. And if any of them did, Lydia's wedding in the old sanctuary at St. Paul's Church would by then be a thing of the past, and irrevocable. And she would have been so beautiful. . . .

At least the feverish hours of writing had served him as a kind of healing ritual in his extremity.

Among other countries freed by the crash of Bonaparte's empire was Denmark, whose capital had been badly damaged by the British in 1807 when they forced the Danes to give up their fleet so that it could not be used against them. In anger over this highhanded tactic, Denmark had joined Napoleon, to its sorrow. When the Honorable Augustus John Foster was suggested as Britain's first minister to the newly-liberated country, he leaped at the chance. There would be new scenes, new challenges, new problems. Denmark was almost on its knees financially, and he felt that his going there might be of benefit to it. He knew it would to him. He would get away from England and much farther away from America.

Finch, in his degradation and hatred, had been striking at a whole nation, but only one man's world had splintered to bits because of it. Foster realized anew that he had been living and planning and *holding on* just for Lydia. He had not been an outstanding success in Parliament; even though he was a proud man, he could admit that. But when the war was over—ah, then he could go claim his bride and hunt for a situation where his talents could be put to better use. The long silence between them, frustrating as it had been, he accepted as another of the brutal side effects of war, a war which some shortsighted persons were blaming on him.

But Lydia—was she already some other man's bride? A *Frenchman's* bride? Part of his sorrow at her betrayal of him focused on that point. Perhaps she had already had the man in mind before Foster had even left the United States! Hadn't she been eagerly practicing her French, having him help her with her vocabulary and her accent, correct her grammar, teach her new phrases?

How could she have forgotten him so soon? Her eyes, so full of love for him, always haunted him, adoring him, speaking to him. . . .

For several days he was perilously close to suicide. He was not afraid of death; it would come sometime anyway. Whether soon or late was a matter of indifference to him. Homer's "raging impotence of woe" was nearly consuming him. As with Lydia in her desolation, there was no one in whom he could confide.

It was only when some inner voice asked him bluntly if he were more afraid of life than of death that he got hold of himself. Providentially, the appointment to Denmark was waiting. He plunged into the assignment with the greatest vigor of anything he had ever undertaken.

On August 10, he reported to his mother from Copenhagen: "Never was Minister's arrival so grateful to a People as mine here. The Queen said such things to me as proved how delighted they are. Fortunately I had to use my own discretion in a great Measure and had to use all the Grace of conferring on a Country the greatest Obligation it can receive. I was first in recognizing the state of Peace here and the Queen said today my coming was the first moment of Happiness they've had in a long time."

Lydia, totally unaware of what had happened to the man she loved, and would always love, had decided to live her life as if the war were going to continue forever, which it surely seemed to be doing. There were skirmishes reported in the papers, on both land and sea. Her father's several business interests fluctuated enormously, dependent on the chances of ships getting through. He and his brothers were supplying huge quantities of goods for the military needs of their country. Since the loss of his son, which had nearly ended his own life in the depth of his heartbreak, Thomas had grown closer to his daughters, especially to Lydia, who had more interest in business and finance, and less in household affairs, than her sister. They never discussed Foster, although he was often in their minds. There was nothing more to be said. Thomas noticed on rare occasions that her eyes were puffed and red, but he kept silent. He wished that he might cry too.

Lydia had gone back to her shopping, in spite of the war-induced shortages and high costs of everything. She knew that Ruth would enjoy the gayest of the new headgear. "My dear Cousin," she wrote. "This is the season for straw bonnets and I wish they may reach you in safety and peace also. I have not supplied myself, but yesterday directed that one should be enlarged in front, to protect more than the fashionable ones do.

They are very generally coarse and not white, of various shapes. Ann M. got these for you, a little different, as she imagined you would not wish them exactly alike. High crowns are altogether worn and the trimmings high (on chip hats, flowers are put around the very top).

"My dear Cousin, we procured a small box, and have not placed the ribbons on them with the hope of their going in nicer order. In each bonnet near the top you will see a pin, then fix the bow; and the strings across the crown and simply pin at each side. The Hats were each $5 and the bonnet 4.50. Ten yards of ribbon at fifty cents are 5, the box 25 cents which leave in your favour a quarter of a dollar from the twenty which I now enclose to you. I hope the Ladies will admire them. It appears a great price for straw. I shall deposit my letter with them in the box, and send your dress also. It is a Wellington cotton. Nancy had a pattern washed, which stood very well. 5½ yards at 75 cents. The few plaids we saw were not handsome, too large."

Dr. Gibson's famous teacher and mentor had favored Baltimore with one of his rare visits. "I must tell you that the celebrated Dr. [Phillip Syng] Physick has been here, a part of two days, though he did not operate on Mrs. Campbell as they expected him to do. My curiosity was gratified by seeing him and hearing him speak. Perhaps you have heard me express my wish to see so eminent a man. I think him the boast of the United States and was more desirous to see him than almost any other person."

The halcyon interval of shopping and going to lectures was soon over. On the sixteenth of July, George Adams wrote some alarming news to Stephen Hollingsworth in Elkton. "I am sorry to have to give you the following unpleasant information. There was a letter received in town yesterday from a respectable merchant in Norfolk stating that four seventy-fours and five frigates had arrived in the Bay. Another letter mentioned that a flag of truce which was sent down to the

Draggon 74 with story for Mr. Schwertchkoff, the Russian Minister who is on board that ship, returned last evening. The officer who went in the Flag stated that Captain Bavois of the *Draggon* said he expected that Sir Thomas Picton would soon arrive in the Chesapeake with 12,000 men. Cousins Nancy [Ann Maria] and Lydia and Madame Bonaparte are going on Monday to spend a week at Owing's Springs (about seventeen miles from Town)."

Two days later his older brother Levi also sent Stephen some news, from Philadelphia.

Dear Friends: It is with heartfelt distress that we hear the enemy are again at Frenchtown and fear they will also advance to Elkton. It is said they are in great force. Should this be the case, you will not be able to oppose them. The women had better fly as fast as possible. Let Sisters Ruth and Jane with the young ladies come to this city. They will be in safety here, and as you are too infirm to do much as a soldier and can possibly leave your property, after driving off your stock to some place of security, you may follow them.

Cursed war! For what was it made? If you have warfare, write to us how you are and how you have fared under its horrid calamity. We can accommodate two or three families. Send the women off as soon as possible. It is no time to trouble you with markets. Flour is dull, 6½ to 6¾ $. God bless you and take you under His Holy keeping. Your Brother,

LEVI HOLLINGSWORTH

Since writing this I have a letter from W. H. Jr. Am glad to hear things are not as bad as reports in the morning represented them.

Stephen frowned at his brother's letter, with little appreciation for its thoughtfulness. His household, except for slaves, consisted of himself, aged sixty-four, his widowed sister-in-law, barely able to walk without help and increasingly confused in her mind, and his niece Ruth Tobin, so thin she looked like one of his bamboo fishpoles. The enemy surely would not consider any of them "dangerous" and might even pity them. He snorted when he came to the word "infirm."

"Who's he think he is?" he asked of the two Ruths. "He's ten years older than I am! Infirm! Hmph!" And where was there a "place of security" for his animals? And his servants? Levi had lived in the city too many years. What should a man do, just turn cattle, sheep, horses, pigs, turkeys, guineas, chickens, dogs and cats in to some other farmer's fields and go skedaddling off to save his own skin? And what if other cowards were to turn their livestock into *his* fields?

Stephen and his womenfolk and their goods and chattels would stay put.

Baltimore, the bull's-eye of the target, was getting ready for siege. Lydia saw steady streams of wagons, carts and drays pulling out of the city night and day as the residents sought to salvage what they could of their worldly goods. Silver was buried in yards and under rosebushes. Small treasures were suspended in deep wells. Family records were carried to the churches for safekeeping, with some thought that holy ground would be immune from danger. Larger pieces of special value were sent to whatever haven of security could be found, the owners trying to outguess potential pillagers.

Country kin far from town and on unfrequented back roads had their attics, cellars, barns and spare rooms stuffed with Baltimore's household furnishings. The Baltimore residents who remained in their stripped homes got along with worn-out things that had been marked for discard or charity. Rates for haulers and draymen went out of sight. The men were never idle and were charging at least double rates, explaining that they never had a return load and must come back empty. Their teams knew no rest; it was not uncommon for one or both of a pair to fall in their traces.

Thomas Hollingsworth's household, like Stephen's, would not leave. He and his women were armed, with one small pistol, one Revolutionary War musket and an inheritance of Saxon courage.

Fort McHenry was bristling with firepower and ready for a scrap. Men sent their families away to safety so they could be at the Fort full time. The activity there and at Fort Covington went on night and day: drilling, training of recruits, issuing of weapons, digging of trenches, stocking supplies of food and medicine, strengthening of barricades, laying in of military stores.

Above Fort McHenry flew the bold red, white and blue flag made by the young Widow Pickersgill to the orders of Brigadier General John Stricker (whose daughter had been young Thomas's sweetheart), Will McDonald, commanding officer of the Sixth Regiment of the Baltimore Militia, and Joshua Barney, the millionaire buccaneer and one-man navy. The flag was large: thirty by forty-two feet, with fifteen stripes and fifteen stars that were twenty-six inches across at their broadest points. It had taken four hundred yards of fabric—stout British wool, to be exact—and its ninety-foot pole carried it so high that many insisted that King George himself ought to be able to see it if he had sufficient wit to try.

While Baltimore was putting all its energies into preparing for the worst, the capital city was left unprotected as it drowsed by the Potomac, a sleepy village with little commercial life when Congress was not in session. Secretary of War John Armstrong had some peculiarly shortsighted ideas of national defense. What did the Federal City have that would be of interest to an invader? Only the seat of government—no shipping, no manufacturing, no markets. The enemy, Armstrong contended, would head straight for Baltimore; fortunately, that busy center was aware of its danger and was ready to defend itself. Washington would not be worth the enemy's time.

With constant reports of raids along the shore from advance forces of British invaders, and the obvious evidence that they were working their way methodically and inexorably north and could whip out at Washington en route, the village slept, undefended, an ostrich burying its head.

The President, stuck with a war he had not wanted, nevertheless showed moments of rare courage and common sense, and had the spunk to stand up to Secretary Armstrong. He sent a delegation to Europe, hoping they would come up with some agreement with Great Britain through the good offices of the Russians, who had offered to mediate. Madison knew better than to put all his reliance on those men—skilled, capable and hard-working as they were. Those long-range negotiations were important, actually essential, but short-range emergencies were right under his nose. That British fleet snarling up the Chesapeake was very real. There was not another moment to spare.

His dander finally up, James Madison called a meeting of his cabinet, got an order to create a militia guard of approximately fifteen thousand men for the capital and had the area set up as a separate military district, with a nephew of Maryland's Governor Winder in charge. Three thousand of the militiamen would be stationed between Washington and Baltimore; the remainder would be in a state of ready alert.

Armstrong jeered at the President's alarm and his demand for all that protection. It would not be needed! Washington was not a target.

By mid-August the European fleet had arrived. General Ross and Admiral Cochrane joined forces with another rear admiral who was too well-known on the Chesapeake Bay already, the despised Cockburn, and his large force of men and ships. Their plans were carefully laid out.

Washington, an easy mark and farthest south, would be first. Then, the rich and strategic city of Baltimore. The entire bay would be under British control and the sea-borne forces could connect with the land troops coming down from the north and east.

For his headquarters, Cockburn took over the elegant residence of a sixty-five-year-old Scottish-born physician, Dr. Edward Beanes, in Upper Marlboro, moving in his aides, bag and baggage, and announcing that they would pay for whatever they used. Beanes's only duty was to stay out of the way and keep his mouth shut.

Beanes saw that they meant business. Within hours the British had routed the unprepared American forces in a fierce, one-sided battle at nearby Bladensburg and were pushing on into the undefended Federal City.

Confident and cocky, the British sat themselves in the Capitol building, and in a mockery of the American Congress took a solemn vote: should they burn the city? There was a brief flurry of debate. Then someone reminded them that the Yankees had burned York, up in Canada, for no sane reason. Now was the chance for a memorable reprisal.

By the night of August 25 there were few walls left standing. The ruins of the capital were still smoldering. Dolley Madison had had the wit to cut the portrait of George Washington from its frame before she fled for her life, leaving a hot dinner waiting. The original Declaration of Independence was in a farm wagon, headed south. Dolley was refused asylum by at least one frightened householder. The fugitive First Lady was a far cry from the gracious hostess Ambassador Foster had admired so much. It was hours before she and the President found each other.

Seeing the smoke from his windows, Dr. Beanes took revenge. With the help of two friends he began seizing straggling soldiers making their way back leisurely to the ships waiting for them at Benedict and slapping them into jail at Queen Anne, nine miles away.

Enraged, the British burst into his house at 1:00 A.M. and took the doctor and two of his house guests as hostages. The latter, not involved in the arrests, were released, as were the British prisoners, but Beanes remained a captive. General Ross declared that Beanes was a traitor because he had given haven to his own countrymen, then had betrayed them. Hadn't he been born in Scotland? If so, he was subject to the

Crown, and must expect the usual punishment, death by hanging. The frail old man was taken aboard a ship, in chains.

In the scramble of friends trying to rescue him was a brilliant, thirty-five-year-old, socially prominent Georgetown lawyer, Frank Key. When he agreed to try to get Beanes released he did two things. He went to the President to ask for a pass through enemy lines. Then, because he knew that the wounded Britishers were receiving the finest care, he went the rounds of the makeshift hospital wards and let drop a few words about his forthcoming truce visit. He just might be persuaded, he hinted, to carry messages from the prisoners for their families back in England.

In no time Key's pockets were crammed with letters. On his way to Baltimore, where he was to board a sloop to hunt for the physician with John Skinner, another lawyer acting as liaison officer, he glanced at some of the hasty scribbles. The men were lavish in their praise of the humane treatment they were getting from the Americans, who had been pictured to them as such barbarians. One of the notes had some paragraphs that might open the ears of the brutally cold and militaristic General Ross. That letter home, from a certain Sergeant Hutchinson, might help to save an old man's life.

After two days of scouring the bay, the attorneys found their quarry. Dr. Beanes, still in irons and not allowed any comforts, was on the Admiral's flagship *Tonnant,* which was riding at anchor near the mouth of the Potomac River with the rest of the fleet, poised for its forthcoming attack on Baltimore.

Key presented his case to the General and the two admirals. Cochrane glared, shocked at his audacity. Cockburn denounced him. Ross turned him down flat. Key's heart froze at the General's contemptuous indifference, but his courtroom experience saved him. Simply and without dramatics, he showed the General the letter from Sergeant Hutchinson.

The officer's stony face began to soften. Not much, but enough. He swung around in his chair and looked out at the great fleet of waiting ships. Some of those men, drilling, polishing guns, repairing sails and rigging, stacking ammunition, were going to be hurt. Some of them would surely be killed and others—how many?—taken prisoner. No battle was ever won without such cost.

Did Ross's own jailers and medical men treat prisoners with such humanity as the Sergeant had just described? He had serious doubts. If the word got back that he had refused amnesty to a sixty-five-year-old noncombatant whose eyesight was so dim that he could hardly tell the Admiral from an ordinary seaman . . . if he refused, when his men were getting such superlative care . . . if the news got around, and he was sure it would because too many people knew . . . President Madison knew. Beanes's worried, influential friends knew. The wounded prisoners knew. In the tense silence, the throbbing at the General's temples was almost audible as he weighed his decision.

At last, his voice dripping icicles in the stifling cabin, he turned to deliver his verdict. The prisoner would be released, but *only* because the Americans had given the British such humane treatment, and not because the old man was not guilty. He *was* guilty. Everyone, Beanes included, knew it.

None of the three Americans would be allowed to land, however. They were taken from the flagship, without even a chance to thank the General, and put aboard a small cartel, named the *Surprise*. It was not a combat craft, so it was a safe place to keep the three, who knew entirely too much.

The fleet pulled up anchor and headed north. Francis Scott Key, who had already been separated from his beloved Polly for too long, had time to reflect that their separation might well be permanent. He remembered her best as she had come through the elaborately carved doors into the parlor at her parents' home in Annapolis to promise to share his life. That life might very well end in the next few days by an accidental shot from his own countrymen; Mary Lloyd Key would then have the enormous burden of raising their six young ones alone.

It was nearly five days before the fleet reached Baltimore and the spires of the distant city, like eyelashes over the wide eye of the river, came into view. To keep his sanity through the almost unbearable tension and to ward off some of Beanes's anxious questions and speculations, Key began humming to himself a rollicking tune he often sang at the tavern in Georgetown on vaporous occasions when the ladies were not present. Polly didn't know the song; there was no memory of her that was connected with it. He certainly would not have taught it to his children either, so it was a good one to think about in his despair. Hadn't the tune had its start in something about a Greek poet who was almost always drunk and who composed poetry—or was it music?—only when he was in his cups? Anacreon, that was the old boy's name. Now how did that second line go?

Another day and half a night passed, with increasing bombardment; the sky was afire, the air ringing from the constant concussion. Toward the second morning, exhausted by the days of anxiety and astonished to find himself and the two other Americans still alive and unscathed, Key made his way to the deck of the *Surprise,* anchored out of range in the Patapsco River. The doctor was at his elbow, shading his eyes and trying to focus into the smoking dimness. Key scanned the horizon with his glasses.

"What can you see out there?" the old man's voice kept repeating, in a fretful singsong. "My eyes aren't too good any more. What can you see? Is there any sign of the flag at the Fort? Are we close enough to see the Fort?"

"Smoke. Flames. Explosions, probably rockets," Key reported, trying not to show his irritation.

The anxious voice kept pounding at him. "Didn't they say it was the biggest flag in the whole world, Mr. Key? Didn't they?"

Chapter Twenty-two

The Snare Is Broken

"The uniforms in church were so pretty, Papa," Lydia said thoughtfully as the two of them walked down the hill after a noonday prayer service at St. Paul's. "I tried to think only of how cheery and bright the sanctuary was with all those colors and shiny buttons and gold braid. And their swords looked so manly and brave—until I remembered what swords are for."

"That stack of rifles out in the vestibule wasn't pretty," her father said bleakly. "Guns in a church—"

"When do you think they'll attack us?"

"Any time! There are reports every few hours of their progress, if you want to call it that, up the bay from what's left of the Federal City after they put the torch to it."

"The last time they only scared us, Papa; then they went away."

"This time it will be the real thing, daughter. We may not survive it."

"Papa!"

"Well, if they break the defenses out at the Lazaretto, and at the forts, and they come along North Point by land, we're goners. There is no hiding place."

"We could go to Elkton, couldn't we?"

"How? The routes by both land and water will be blocked by redcoats. And Elkton is in just as bad a way as we are."

"I wish it would be over, Papa."

"I feel the same way," Thomas said, sighing, "but let's not mention it to your mother. She tries to convince herself that all this horrible war talk is a bad dream."

"It's a nightmare," Lydia said as they crossed the street to walk in the shade. "There is something I must say, Papa, before we get home. Promise not to laugh at me, or to tell Mama or Sister."

"Of course." He took her hand and realized that she was quivering.

"If by some fate I do not live through this," she said carefully, "I—I shall not mind. Don't grieve for me. Will you remember that?"

"Lydia Eliza!"

"I never talk about it, Papa. I simply can't. But life without Augustus is not living."

"He'll come back, daughter. Of course he will! It's this awful war—"

"He may be dead." Lydia began to walk more slowly, so that their conversation would not be cut off by their arrival home. "I have had no word from him since those letters Mr. Baker brought me. And who would let me know, or could let me know, if he had died? No one. So, if my life ends, I shall not mind. Perhaps I can find him over there."

"Lydia!" Her father's voice was full of pain.

"I used to get angry," she went on, "thinking he should write me, that he should answer my letters. He might as well have died. And I know this war will go on forever."

"Perhaps he's in the military, daughter."

"Don't even think that! He'd be an officer, and he'd have to order his men to kill Americans, perhaps even us! And he did get to love America, at least a little bit—oh, please, I hope that has not happened to him!"

Thomas had no answers. As they neared their street, Lydia asked, "Is it a sin, Papa, to say I shan't mind dying? I can't believe it is. I think it is simply facing facts, and having faith in Providence, and trusting that I will find Augustus somewhere . . . someday. . . ."

"I guess it is not a sin," he said as they went up the steps, "but it breaks your father's heart. You and Ann Maria are all I have left."

On Sunday, Colonel Sam—in close touch with the situation because he was on duty with the militia round the clock—put his foot down. The women and children were to leave. There was no more time; he would not put up with any nonsense. His daughter Betsy Ridgely had sent word several times that there was room for all out at Oaklands, in Elkridge. If they were to be safe anywhere, that was the place. With some exceptions, the families obeyed Sam's orders. Debby Cochran kissed her little son a tearful good-bye and sent him and his two half sisters with Lydia. Mr. Cochran, stubborn beyond any imagining, would not budge, although he was too frail to offer even token resistance to any violence. If Mr. C. was to stay, Mrs. C. would stay with him. Sam knew better than to argue.

There was no sense in arguing with his older brother either. Thomas Hollingsworth made sure that Fronya's pistol was loaded and in the keeping of his women as he sent them away with Sam; then he braced himself in his home with his ancient musket, fully prepared to die rather than surrender. Even his servants had left.

When the actual shooting began, Deborah Cochran used her vast nervous energy to keep a running account of the battle, not knowing whether she or any of her loved ones would live through it, or whether even the words she was writing would ever be read. At least she would make the effort. Being busy might also keep her from twittering over Mr. Cochran.

"To Miss Ruth Tobin, Elkton. *To Mail*" she wrote nervously.

Baltimore, 15th Septr 1814. My dear Ruth: Nearly half past four in the morning—our alarm guns were fired twenty minutes past twelve, since then the bells rang, drums beating, the houses generally lighted; we have all been up since that second. We know not the hour when we may be attacked. Last night passed here one Brigade of Militia to encamp at Silver Garden on the west side of Town where it is thought the British will make the worst attack. The city looks deserted, some moments I feel very resolute, the next quite the reverse. God only knows what the event will be. I put my trust in Him and I fervently trust He will protect us all. Mr. Cochran and Joseph [a servant] are with me in the dining room, our domestics all with us. You no doubt heard the firing on Tuesday which commenced early in the morning and continued until Wednesday morning.

Throughout the day I have often been agitated, near three o'clock when Mr. Cochran and Joseph returned from the encampment, the British was then within one and a half miles from the city, they saw the fires very plainly. Mr. Cochran was extreamly solicitous my leaving town. Although I felt dreadfully, I reluctantly assented to his sending for a carriage. The Boy returned without being able to get one, sent again. Mr. C. proposed taking me out seven miles then to return, the idea of his being here without me I could hardly reconcile, the firing fast approached and we supposed the enemy. I consented to go to Mr. Barnabus (the Spanish Consols) who very kindly offered us protection under his Flag. We set out, distance one mile. There we met with the most cordial reception from them both and their family.

The bombarding still increased, half past ten we retired, I cannot say to sleep. Entering my chamber, Mrs. B. and I discovered a considerable light which we supposed the Fort. We called Mr. B. who said it was not quite in that direction. We have not yet been able to say what it was but Oh my dear Ruth, such another night I never experienced! From one to three incessant firing, we all thought it impossible that the Fort could hold out. The flash from the bombs distinctly shone in the different parts of my chamber, it was like continued flashes of lightening.

As to my feelings, it is impossible to describe them. I thought we must all inevitably go. There was part of one Bomb picked up near the Powder House; two, Mr. C. thinks must have lodged, on the Point. Mr. C. at home, our dear Son and children at Mr. Ridgely's [Oaklands].

I looked anxiously for day. I thought the hours would never roll round and then thought if it was light, I would wish to be forty miles off. After day broke, we with great pleasure, observed our Flags at each Fort still flying.

After breakfast, Mr. Barnabus mentioned his intention of going in. I told him I would accompany him, this they all wished me to decline, I could not feel satisfied. Whilst Mr. B. was getting ready, I drew on a pair of boots, being very wet, and went up to see Mrs. Z[ebulon] Hollingsworth, with whom I found her daughter, Nancy, Miss Bonds, several others in her Family. Horatio slightly wounded in the leg, Levi Hollingsworth in the hand, Mr. Cheston in the leg, a brother of Dr. Gibson, thigh broken, Mr. James H. McCulough's thigh broken, and many more. One Hundred killed and wounded.

The Enemy, it is said, has lost three hundred in the engagement on Tuesday. Is not this dreadful? I never saw Sister Sally [Sarah] so much distressed. I was with her when Samuel returned. I cannot tell how greatly rejoiced I was to see him. I endeavoured as much as possible to console Sister, I assure you it was a task. Samuel attended me home after a little while. I heard of each of their households having returned safe except Mr. C. of whom I have mentioned. How greatly our friends as yet have been favoured.

Poor George [Adams] suped and lodged at our house. He looked almost worn out, their duty is extreamly hard. He yesterday dined with us in fine spirits, looks much better.

When I began this letter I continued on until breakfast came on, with the candles. My mind was as I before observed. I began on the half sheet without thinking of looking for more. It is now past eleven o'clock. No British yet. I hope we may not experience such a night as the last.

Mr. Sterret Ridgely stopped in for a few minutes this morning. On asking him 'What news?' he told me Commodore Rodgers was of the opinion they were embarking, he differs in opinion, such is the state of uncertainty we are in.

Sister Sally, Cousin Sally with Mr. William Creek and Brother

Thomas came down yesterday. They mearly dined and left about five in the evening. Brother Thomas called up during the night between one and two, during which time I answered a letter which I had received from our dear little Son, whom I have not seen since Sunday. Therefore you can suppose how anxious we are. The dear little fellow, with the rest, are quite happy. Although Sally told me yesterday morning at seven when he awoke, he asked where the British was, how near to Baltimore and how were Father and Mother. I can never forget Betsy's attention. William Scott and Mr. L. L. slept in Cousin Betsy's room.

Mr. Barnabus has this instant called soliciting our going out there this evening, finding the dreadful situation we experienced last night. However, as it has passed, we have great reason to be thankful we are still in being. I fear I shall tire your patience.

With Mr. Cochran's, Levi's with mine to you and Sister. Wishing to hear particularly how you all are, Compliments to Mr. Hollingsworth, Mr. Partridge and other friends, Your Affectionate Aunt, D. C.

Betsy Ridgely somehow supervised the large company of Cochrans and Hollingsworths in spite of her anxiety about her husband, who was a general in the cavalry, and her two brothers-in-law, as well as her father. Dr. Gibson was on surgical duty night and day, and James Cheston, Molly's husband, was in the thick of the fighting.

All of them were in greater danger than they dared to contemplate. They were spared largely because General Ross was killed early in the fighting as he sought to carry out the land-based attack through North Point. The death of the coldly efficient leader completely demoralized his men; no one came forward to take his place. Uninstructed, disorganized and vacillating, they scattered and gave up all they had won. Soon it was too late, and Ross's forces lost their initial advantage, never to regain it. South of the Fort, six vessels tried to slip through the bombardment but were quickly repulsed. Could the invincible and mighty men of Great Britain have possibly misjudged the temper of their adversaries?

In spite of, or possibly because of, their fright, the refugees found that being besieged was almost a lark, as many owners of large homes away from the heart of the city or the bay area opened their doors to them. Madame Bonaparte, caught in Baltimore, took her young son to Belvidere, home of her friends the John Eager Howards, where she was out of range but not out of sight and sound of the fury of the battle.

The gaiety of the house parties, which many recalled later with a sense of unreality and guilt, might have been that of people doomed. They could not know what the outcome of the fighting would be or what their individual fates might bring, so they ate and danced and sang and laughed.

When affairs had calmed down a little, Lydia also wrote to Ruth.

Sept. 30th, 1814 . . . I determined to write you a long letter. I came to Town one day and asked for a sheet of paper from Aunt Debby for that purpose when she told me the day previous she wrote you on the subject of our attack and most gallant defence, and I thought it not necessary on my part as she gave you an account of our families both retreating to Oaklands.

We have been most signally protected and all the officers and men I have heard express their sentiments, agree that a kind Providence saved us and the early death of Gen. Ross. Tho' we had a very considerable force for the defence of our entrenchments, if the enemy that night had followed up retreating regiments (as some of their own Generals warmly desired but all would not consent to after their General was killed) we had not been as we are now.

Though I had not been so frequently on the Philadelphia Road where the enemy were a whole day, yet I could scarcely believe our armies were so very near, until I rode around after my return home with Aunt. Our sentinals heard the British sentinals at night distinctly. A party of them went to Col. Joe Sterrets and took possession of his house, dined and were all day there. They forced his closets, etc., and took off all his old wine in baskets, left their names in a note to the Colonel, inquired particularly for his wife, who one of the officers had dined with at her Father's table many years ago, and regretted to the servants that she had not remained at home.

From the lane which leads to his house, they had a full view of our best and strongest works and it made quite a formidable appearance. Of our Forts we may be very proud, they are constantly at work making the magazines bombproof. I am told by everybody it was an awful time from the cannonading till the fleet stood under sail down the Bay. I cannot think it is ended, but feel persuaded we shall again be attacked.

Cousin Levi had a bullet wound through the left arm, Cousin Zeb's second son [Horatio] a wound in the ankle, and Cheston one from a spent bullet but they are all doing well. Our citizens have been more mercifully preserved in both engagements. I suppose your own villagers will give you a full account of the battle, our defence, their own privations, of which too many have cause to complain, and all the interesting topics.

Mama and I were a week at Betsy's. She had all our family. Aunt Sally, her nurse and child, Nancy, ditto, Mr. Cochran's three children, Mr. and Mrs. Cook, in all twenty-one whites in family. Papa was there one day and night, and I assure you there were so many we were not a depressed set by any means. We heard constantly from Town. Papa could not stay away from home and we came in Wednesday, after the engagement on Friday, and suffered less in our feelings than if we had been more distant. . . . Mr. Ridgely dismissed, to his gratification. There has been little use for the cavalry yet; tho' they have encountered great fatigue. Every man is a soldier, a part of each obliged to be in arms.

True to long habit, Lydia had investigated the shopping as soon as it was safe to venture out. "It is difficult to get a pair of shoes," she commented, "or any job from any trade. Some stores are open and if you wish any article they have and will write me, I will endeavour to suit you. I have near $15 of yours, goods are higher. I forgot to tell you when I wrote you, in August, that no Smyrna silk but brick-dust colour or straw were to be met with & they are not pretty. Very pretty Canton crepes at $1.75 per yard, variety of colours. I see in the papers another Victory on the Lakes. I wish most sincerely we could have peace to cheer us all and that state of happiness we once enjoyed. . . . your attached Cousin, L E H."

The *Commercial Daily Advertiser* gave specific details of the siege and their providential deliverance in its Friday edition.

On Tuesday morning at 6 o'clock, the first division of the enemy's fleet consisting of six bomb ketches, some rocket ships and barges with a number of frigates were formed beyond the reach of the guns at Fort McHenry when they commenced the bombardment of that fortress. The firing continued near 2 hours without any intermission, during which time 1000 bombs were sent at us. On Wednesday morning from 12 till half past 2 the frigates, sloops-of-war and barges within gunshot kept up a tremendous and incessant roar which was answered and repelled with the greatest spirit and firmness by Maj. Armistead and his garrison in Ft. McHenry and the officers and men of the Battery at the Lazaretto, North side of the Bason, the Sixth gun Battery and Fort Covington on Patapsco South Branch.

During more than an hour the incessant blaze of fire was emitted from the naval semi-circle of several miles Northeast and South of the Fort. The fire from the Forts was equally animated and constant. At one time a rocket ship and five barges passed through the shower South of Fort McHenry and cheered, thinking themselves sure of reaching the Cove at the Sothwest end of the City whence they could, unannoyed, have burnt the town, but as they passed from the 42s of the great Fortress the narrow channel brought them under the 18s and 24s of the upper Batteries. Here, crippled and discouraged, barges began to tow out the disappointed squadron. The Fort, being warmly besieged at every angle continued the cannonade until the Fleet drew out of their line of safety two and a half miles. The bombardment continued until daylight when the Fleet was called off. There were four men killed and about twenty wounded in Fort McHenry during the gallant defense.

In a few days, word reached Baltimore that even before its own fantastic reprieve and victory, there had been another spectacular rout of the British on September 11 at the Battle of Plattsburg, on Lake Champlain. That area was the second of the three focal points where the British were planning to bring America to its knees.

The fleets lined up against each other were fairly well matched, but the British army was three times that of the American and was well trained, well disciplined and well supplied. Just as had Baltimore, Plattsburg looked easy. Nevertheless the doughty Americans overcame the invaders, who turned tail and retreated to Canada—permanently. Their scarlet coats made superlative targets there in the forests.

That left only the third focus of attack, the strategic Mississippi Delta. Britain strengthened its fleet and lined up its ships in a fan outside the harbor of New Orleans. It imported scores of tough, hardened veterans of the successful Peninsular War and laid in enormous supplies of food and ammunition. The British were taking no chances on failure.

Facing them would be even tougher Andrew Jackson, with as raggle-taggle an army as was ever gathered up, including Negroes, Indians and frontiersmen like himself. Jackson's nondescript army was equipped with every available kind of weapon, but most significantly with squirrel rifles.

Men of the wilderness had long been dependent on the plentiful common gray squirrel for survival. When his children's stomachs are empty, a man had better learn to draw a bead on one of the fastest and most elusive of animals, and fell him with one shot.

There were those who claimed that the whole War of 1812 was won by the gray squirrels. They had given American marksmen a long and effective discipline, helping to develop a breed of sharpshooters that was the best in the world. For a man who could say modestly that he felled all his squirrels by a shot through the left eye, and only the left eye, a red jacket moving however cautiously through the woods was almost too easy a mark.

The squirrel rifle was an answer that the deskbound, city-bred strategists in the Admiralty found absurd. Augustus John Foster would have understood it and believed it, but he was far off in Copenhagen, stubbornly trying to forget that he had ever been in America. When the exiled Aaron Burr approached him, in an effort to renew their acquaintance, Foster rebuffed him, thinking the relationship unwise and unprofitable.

There were bitter moments when he wondered where Lydia's Frenchman had taken her for safekeeping, or if he had been gentleman enough to do anything to try to save her. Had she lived through the horrible battle in her city? Did the Frenchman love her and cherish her the way she should be loved and cherished, care for her the way Foster would have cared for her? What he could not yet consider was the picture of Lydia in the Frenchman's arms, in anyone's arms but his own.

He was still refusing to join the majority of his countrymen in believing that all Americans were traitors. There *must* have been some situation he didn't know about that could have changed her so abruptly.

Lydia, miraculously alive, but with no Frenchman in tow, dared to think that all the recent victories might mean that the war would soon be over. When would he come? Or would he send for her instead? What kinds of preparation should she make for her new life? Where in all the wide earth would her future take her?

At least she could go back to her neglected study of French. Perhaps Betsy B. would help. She was in town, bored with the emptiness of wartime social life, although the officers' uniforms did add some welcome color.

Lydia was busily filling up a second large dower chest with needlepoint and other embroidered linens. Thomas's months of illness had given her many extra hours for her needlework as she sat by him, relieving her mother of his care and keeping herself busy so that he would not feel guilty for requiring so much attention. They could talk of Foster too, and she could remember with a pang in her heart how the Englishman had looked as he sat in the same room visiting with her brother. Her love for Augustus John Foster had been woven tightly into every stitch.

A few days after the stinging defeat of the British, while the humiliated fleet was slinking down the bay, the taverns, coffeehouses and theaters of Baltimore were ringing with an inspiring new song which began with Dr. Beanes's worried question, "Oh say, can you see?" Mr. Key had first put the words with the phrase "through the dawn's early light" but that did not quite suit him, so he changed the preposition to "by." From there it was easy to race along through four stanzas.

As soon as he and his companions were safely on shore, he took his poem to a printer. The fly sheets of "The Star-Spangled Banner" were quickly on the streets. Key's first version of his immortal verses was:

O say can you see by the dawn's early light
What so proudly we hail'd at the twilight's last gleaming,
Whose broad stripes & bright stars through the perilous fight
O'er the ramparts we watch'd, were so gallantly streaming?
And the rocket's red glare, the bomb bursting in air,
Gave proof through the night that our flag was still there.
O say does that star-spangled banner yet wave
O'er the land of the free & the home of the brave?

On the shore dimly seen through the mists of the deep,
Where the foe's haughty host in dread silence reposes,
What is that which the breeze, o'er the towering steep,
As it fitfully blows, half conceals, half discloses?
Now it catches the gleam of the morning's first beam,
In full glory reflected now shines in the stream,
'Tis the star-spangled banner—O long may it wave
O'er the land of the free & the home of the brave!

And where is that band who so vauntingly swore,
That the havoc of war & the battle's confusion
A home & a Country should leave us no more?
Their blood has wash'd out their foul footstep's pollution.
No refuge could save the hireling & slave
From the terror of flight or the gloom of the grave,
And the star-spangled banner in triumph doth wave
O'er the land of the free & the home of the brave.

O thus be it ever when freemen shall stand
Between their lov'd home & the war's desolation!
Blest with vict'ry & peace may the heav'n rescued land
Praise the power that hath made & preserv'd us a nation!
Then conquer we must when our cause it is just,
And this be our motto—"In God is our trust,"
And the star-spangled banner in triumph shall wave
O'er the land of the free & the home of the brave.—

"Didn't they say it was the biggest flag in the whole world, Mr. Key?"

In July at Lundy's Lane, on the narrow strip of land between Lakes Ontario and Erie, young Major General Winfield Scott was gravely wounded; a bullet was imbedded so deeply in his shoulder that he was not expected to survive. After having two horses shot from under him, the six-foot-five-inch 237-pound soldier, who had gone into military service from law school after witnessing the shocking revelations of Aaron Burr's trial, had to be carried off the field. The job took four men: first, because of his great bulk; second, because he didn't want to go.

The depth of his wound, soon badly infected, meant that his life could not be saved because "invasion" of the body by a surgical knife was considered immoral and against the will of God. Surgery was confined largely to amputations, common on the battlefield, and to removal of external tumors.

Not wanting to waste his great talents in the short time supposed to be left to him, the army dispatched Scott to Baltimore to take charge of its defenses. The whole bay area was still quaking from its narrow escape, walking on eggs for fear the enemy would return to finish the work they had botched. Lydia saw Scott on the street early in November.

"The Commanding Officer has been changed since then," she wrote. "The Major General is a young, brave unmarried man who had distinguished himself on the frontier, and the gentleman seems well-pleased with the appointment. He has a house in Water Street and has three aids-de-camp residing with him. We are a garrison and the defences (lest the British should return) which is highly possible and another Fort has been chalked out by Gen. Scott. He is an invalid from his wound, one arm in a sling, very tall, thin and pale. I am told his manners are engaging and polite. I hope we are safe for this winter in our city. We have brought no things home but flannel and a chamber carpet, and live very plain yet awhile, old carpets, very little plate and no apology as is the case most everywhere . . . the times are bad for new establishment, every article higher and higher. The dry goods stores are pretty [empty] . . . if you want any purchases I will be glad to serve you, as there seems no hope of Peace and imported goods will be dearer."

Both imports and exports were short. Since 1811, a poor year itself, the export trade of America had dropped to one-seventh of that year's figures. To keep crews busy, as well as to harass the British, many ships became privateers, spreading out across the Atlantic and even into the English Channel. British insurance rates doubled. In 1813, one raider, Captain David Porter, accompanied by his young adopted son, David Glasgow Farragut, cruised in the *Essex* off the coast of South America with such devastating success that he decided to branch out to the Pacific. There he and the boy terrorized everything afloat, took many valuable prizes and claimed the Marquesas Islands for the United States, who did not follow up the claim. Porter's luck ran out in 1814 off the coast of Chile, but the British and Spanish paid dearly for him.

By the end of 1814 American raiders and privateers had accounted for approximately fifteen hundred ships and millions of dollars in money and goods, an extraordinary score for a nation without a navy.

At long last, on Christmas Eve, in Ghent, Belgium, the two countries concluded a treaty of peace, in the making since August. One delay had been caused by the British desire to set up a buffer state for the Indians, between themselves and the Americans. That idea was indignantly rejected.

There was a great deal of bickering among the American delegates. Albert Gallatin had to act as peacemaker between the former minister to Russia, John Quincy Adams, who had deserted the Federalist camp to support Thomas Jefferson's embargo, and Henry Clay, the War Hawk who was sick of war.

The negotiations dragged on for four and a half months, as autumn turned to winter and men went on dying. When the paper was at last in its final form, there was no mention of the issue of impressment, which had brought on the whole war. The matter was never again discussed or argued, although impressment did stop, simply because the British no longer needed extra sailors.

Territories gained were to be returned to whatever country had owned them before hostilities began, and the fighting was to end as soon as both parties had ratified the agreement. Each side was almost exactly where it had been two and a half years before, except for the destruction, the waste, the losses, the senseless killing and the heartbreak.

While the men at Ghent were haggling, the New England Federalists, who had been whispering of secession for a decade or more, held a large general meeting in Connecticut, the Hartford Convention. A young New Hampshire congressman, Daniel Webster, who had done everything in his power to discredit and undermine the administration's conduct of the war, was one of its most vocal leaders. Feeling that Madison's government was in such dire straits that a Federalist threat of withdrawing from the Union would bring them begging on their knees, they laid out a set of demands—really ultimatums—including seven amendments to the Constitution, all designed to protect the industrial North and East from the developing power of the South and West.

Soon after they dispersed, confident and optimistic, news came of the treaty and of the smashing victory of Andrew Jackson's squirrel-shooting frontiersmen at New Orleans. The Federalists never recovered from the blow, or from the humiliation of being known as would-be traitors. As a party, they were done for.

Possibly the only lasting value of the senseless war was that it made a nation out of a scattered collection of sectional states, all pulling in separate directions. It had been "hang together or hang separately." A secondary benefit was that the government would settle down once and for all in Washington. There was no more loose talk about moving back to Philadelphia or any place else. Most tragic was the fact that if cool heads had prevailed and the war fever kept in check until the inevitable fall of Napoleon, there would have been no need for a war at all.

Lydia's spirits were rising that Christmas and as the New Year began, with its annual promise of better things to come. Early in February she got word of Jackson's victory a month earlier and sat down to share her excitement with Ruth. "Well, my dear Cousin," she wrote, "what do you think of the resistance made by our brave citizens at New Orleans? It has diffused much sunshine on our citizens here! And I do hope, although the British Army be reinforced, which I calculate largely on being done, that our troops may continue brave, united and successful, The battle seems to have been bold and bloody and dreadfully fatal to the British. *Our loss* astonishingly small and it would have been incredible if we did not know that in the battles nearer home the number was much less than had been generally calculated on. Gen. Jackson appears able to lead them and quite a guiding star . . . from various letters he is said to be a stranger to fear and a lover of war. Even the poor Sisterhood have changed themselves once more with the world and are patriotically employed in making clothes for the soldiers and in nursing the wounded. The nuns who have not been long immured within the walls of the convent I think must welcome the busy hum of social life with delight. Those Sisters whose habits of monastic life are deeply rooted know no other and are well satisfied. The Abbé du Bourg was an instructor of ours and we remember him well. His eyes spoke very decidedly."

His eyes were still speaking decidedly. First president of Georgetown College, founded by Archbishop Carroll, then president of another of Carroll's projects, St. Mary's College, he was sent to New Orleans as administrator apostolic of that diocese. Inspired by Andrew Jackson's preparations for siege, the Abbé gave aid wherever he was needed and made the Ursuline convent a haven and a hospital. When New Orleans was celebrating its victory, the Abbé stood on the steps of the cathedral to welcome General Jackson and put a crown of laurel on his head.

"I think the people of the Southern States are in a wretched situation," Lydia went on. "Those of Georgia who are now contending with British, blacks and Indians are worse off than any other class of citizens and they appear to fear the latter foe the most. I fear the time is distant that will find us all in the enjoyment of peace. Though it may seem strange to you that Baltimore should be so gay, yet it is true almost to dissipation! Dinners on dinners, parties on partys! The military, Belles and strangers unite in producing it. Ever since Christmas there has been a round of Frolic kept up. Very many private dancing parties and I am sure some of the Belles more French in their dress and more . . . than before. I can say nothing of myself for I have not seen one, and from all I hear feel not the smallest desire to behold so profuse an exhibition of charms."

She took so long with her letter that she missed a chance to send it up the bay with relatives—usually the safest route, since the British were still sniping and were especially eager to get their hands on the new steamship, the *Chesapeake,* which was running from Baltimore to Frenchtown. She could add a hysterically happy postscript on February 14, the day after her twenty-ninth birthday.

"The news of the last days is so prominently delightful I rejoice to give it to you. I feared when I wrote the pages of this letter that War was to molest us for a long time but I acknowledge I prophesied falsely. Our Commissioners have made us a peace which the bearer Mr. Carroll has said our President and Senate may confirm with honour to the Nation. I hope in a very few hours we will hear they have ratified it and that the British agent who has also come out in the *Favourite* may speedily return with the tidings to Great Britain, and all hostilities cease. These are to continue until our government approve the Act, and he, the Secretary Mr. Baker is to inform the Armies and fleets of His Majesty in this quarter of the globe of the ratification. I give you, Aunt, Uncle and all of you joy. It is a feast for the Nation that we have an honourable peace and I am convinced you rejoice in the cessation of arms and sparing of human blood. We are all elated and are to illuminate and proclaim aloud our grateful thanks. This is the subject for Nancy's next letter, who has been reproached by her conscience for a long silence."

The news of the peace treaty completed on Christmas Eve had taken seven weeks to reach South Street. When the treaty was finally ratified and signed and all the tag ends tied up, the second war for American independence would be over. Jackson's slaughter of some seven hundred redcoats at New Orleans had not actually taken place after the conclusion of peace, because the treaty had specified that the war would continue until both sides had signed. There was still skirmishing as late as March 23, when the American *Hornet* captured His Majesty's sloop the *Penguin*.

Small wonder that the last armed conflict between English-speaking nations became known also as the War of Faulty Communications. It might also have been called the War of If-Onlys.

The downfall of the Bonapartes and the easing of tensions in Europe had one special result on South Street. Madame Elizabeth Patterson Bonaparte had gotten the Maryland legislature to pass a special act releasing her *a vinculo matrimonii* with the one-time King of Westphalia. She was now free by the laws of both church and state, ten years after the "wedding of the century," and could live her life the way she wanted to, escaping once and for all from the suffocating dullness of Baltimore.

On March 27, Lydia told Ruth of Betsy's prospects. "Our fair neighbour Bonaparte is on the eve of her departure for Europe at last. She goes with our Ambassador to Holland, afterwards to France. It has been the predominate desire of her life for years. She is unattended to Europe by her family or child. He is at school at Emmetstown. I sincerely wish her well. The scheme requires a decided character to go through with it. May it eventually prove to her good. If I write more it will meet more eyes there than in the little room here so I conclude with Mama's, Papa's and Nancy's best affection, Believe me, as ever L E H."

It was all she could do to keep from asking for a serious personal talk with Betsy, to suggest that she might be able to send home some news of Mr. Foster. The restrictions of wartime had helped her and Betsy renew their early friendship. Not to have heard from her beloved for more than two years had left her drained of emotion; to try to live on hope made for an extremely restricted diet. She dreaded letting herself get back into the hated groove of watching for mail. The five o'clock effort at spiritual communication was not satisfying, because there was never any tangible confirmation, although she kept it up religiously. There had been one or two occasions when she had felt the warm flood of his love pouring into her heart, and those rare moments had had to sustain her.

Perhaps I don't have enough faith, she thought as she studied herself. But I do, I do! She was sitting by a window, looking out at the dried-up winter garden, where she would soon be helping her mother plant annuals and decide on the borders. A strange thing happened, actually for the second time. The first had been late in the spring or early summer. The experiences were nearly identical.

On this afternoon she was concentrating with unusual zeal. The war was over. Mail was getting through. People were getting through. Travel for nonmilitary persons was no longer restricted. Regular sailing schedules to and from Europe were advertised in the papers and at the docks. Privateers were being refitted as commercial vessels and the river and bay were blossoming with sails. The long dark night of separation should be coming to an end.

"Augustus . . . ?" It was one of the few times she had spoken his name aloud. "Augustus . . . ?"

There was an audible *snap!*, as if something precious were breaking. Had her loved one died? It was the only answer she could find. If so, there would eventually be news in the press of his passing, since he was of more than ordinary interest to Americans. She would have to wait. Sadly, she said a wordless prayer for him and went to join her family for tea. Ann Maria glanced at her with affectionate understanding and a question in her eyes, but Lydia did not respond.

Within a few days Madame Bonaparte set out to conquer Europe, unaware of Lydia's feverish yearning.

Chapter Twenty-three

As the Flower of the Field

Sam Hollingsworth lost no time in trying to persuade his new commanding officer, the ailing General Scott, that there was a man in Baltimore who might be able to save his life, young Dr. William Gibson, Sam's son-in-law. Scott, noted for his edgy temper, which had not improved during his increasing disability, sent for the physician for a consultation. The next morning, Gibson, by a courageous combination of skill, speed and great faith, went against all accepted medical practice and extracted the bullet that was sapping Scott's life. Within a week, the officer was recovering rapidly and telling everyone of the miracle that had happened to him.

Knowing of Lydia's interest in his work, Gibson told her briefly of the operation at the next family get-together, leaving out the details and stressing Scott's legendary fortitude and his own profound belief in the unlimited potential of medical discoveries. "We're on the brink of a great new world," he told her enthusiastically. "We must study and explore and learn and never stop trying!"

"And not be afraid of anything?" she asked, smiling.

"Not anything, except ignorance. We must get the best possible men interested in medicine. We must recognize it as both a great art and a great science. We must demand more training, more experience, more study!"

"What about women as doctors?" Lydia always found that she could speak more freely with him than with anyone else.

"We aren't that desperate!" he answered, his face flaming.

"Dr. Physick said in his lecture here"—Lydia tried to cover up her embarrassing mistake—"that he and Dr. Rush are interested in cutting down the length of time an apprentice must serve and the amount of training he must have."

"No, no, no! They are wrong. I've argued with them time and again—" He stopped short. Conversation about his work was rude. He must change the subject. "Tell me, Miss Lydia, what do you hear of the fine young man . . . ?" Noticing that her face was gray and her eyes devastated, he asked courteously, "Would your mother care if I asked you to show me her garden? Sally has been after me to help plan ours at the new house, and I'd suppose I'd better put my mind to it."

Gratefully, Lydia rose and led him outside. There he showed a desultory interest in the pansy plants and the low-growing ageratum and babies'-breath. Finally, he asked her bluntly, "What has happened, Miss Lydia? Remember that I am a friend, a relative and a physician. It doesn't take a wizard to know that you are greatly disturbed. Perhaps I can help."

Overcome, Lydia poured out the whole story as coherently as she could. He sat on one of the garden chairs, leaning forward, listening intently, asking a soft question or two as he nodded his understanding.

"Let me suggest something," he said when she had finished. "I truly don't mean to interfere, but perhaps, under the circumstances, you will not consider it intrusion. You probably know that Bonaparte, who was supposed to be gone forever, has descended again on France?"

"No!"

"Yes. About the middle of March. At any rate, I know there will be battles. France and Europe—and the world, for that matter—have no place for that—that man. So, I am going over there. A surgeon can learn on the battlefield faster than anywhere else, and I have so much I want to explore, so much I want to try. And maybe my simple skills can save a life or two while I'm at it."

"You wouldn't—?"

"Yes, if you want me to. I can see what I can find out. I feel that he is alive; I think there is no question of that. If he weren't there would have been a notice about it long ago in our papers. I shall not embarrass you in any way by my questions over there, I can assure you, and I should be able to locate some fairly knowledgeable people who can give me some information."

"Oh, Dr. Gibson!"

"I'd suggest a good out-and-out crying session, Miss Lydia. It is long overdue, and your health demands it. Thank you for showing me the garden. I shall report to Sally that we should have lots of pansies. They're such friendly little people."

The physician's letter was harder for him than any surgery he had ever performed. He would so much rather have talked with Lydia than to send an impersonal piece of paper, but he did not know when, if ever, he might get home again, and he knew that her anxiety was severe. This surgery was also going to require skill, speed and faith. He approached it with dismay.

Finding news of Mr. Foster had been easy. There were many extra editions of the newspapers because of Napoleon's ill-starred return to France, and short items were useful in filling in a few lines of space at the ends of columns. Almost every paper reported that the Lady Albinia Jane Hobart, daughter of the Honorable George Vere Hobart, had been married early in March to the Honorable Augustus John Foster, British Minister to Denmark, well known in France, et cetera. The ceremony had taken place in London, and the happy couple would live in Copenhagen. Mr. Foster, formerly a Member of Parliament, was the first emissary sent to Denmark after the resumption of diplomatic relations with that country. Previous to the recent war, he had been ambassador to the United States, in North America.

Gibson read the news in both English and French in five or six papers before he could accept it as fact.

Knowing only what was before him in black and white, and no longer able to tell himself that the information must be a mistake, the American spat out two furious words: *"That bastard!"*

He waited another twenty-four hours before he felt steady enough to take up his pen and try to compose a message to be sent off to the New World on the next sailing. In less than a month, it was in Lydia's hands, and she knew the worst.

Unable to touch or scarcely to look at the furniture that had once known the magic of Foster's presence, or to walk the streets where he had stridden so briskly on the long walks he enjoyed or had driven his team with his jaunty curricle, Lydia threw some clothes into a portmanteau and caught the next packet for Elkton. Her mother and sister watched helplessly. Her father couldn't bear to talk with her. He tried to stay out of her way after one silent hug and kiss when the letter came.

Lydia had dreamed so many times of taking her sweetheart to Elkton, not only to meet the relatives but also to show him the lovely countryside. She knew he would enjoy it. He was a man who hated the confinement of the city and whose soul, like hers, could find its greatest refreshment in the outdoors. He had never gotten there. Now he never would. The hot sun blazing down on the water took on a brassy unreality. Perhaps death in the brutal siege of her city would have been preferable. Surely it would have been more merciful. And final.

Since she had come without warning, there was no one to meet her. She left her luggage at the wharf and hurried up to the house at Elk Landing. Her cousin William was the owner now; both Zeb and Polly, his parents, had died. It seemed curious to knock formally at the door of the house where her father had been born, but one didn't walk in unannounced, even on relatives.

A servant, recognizing her, ushered her past the banistered staircase into the dining room and sent a boy to hunt for William, who was somewhere out in the fields. Still a bachelor at that time and frequently absent on political or business affairs, William was in and out at the Landing. Lydia was lucky to find him home; the boy located him at one of the stone barns and soon brought him in.

While she waited she looked nostalgically around the big, comfortable room. It seemed a lifetime since the Celebration had brought such a large crowd of them together to welcome the new century. The Hollingsworth crest hung, as it had for decades, over the fireplace. Blue for the sky—and for his eyes, she thought tearfully; silver for the rivers and for innocence—she had been the innocent one, believing so deeply in him; and green for the holly in the Land of Hol, but green also for love. The ribboned motto underneath told her forever to bear patiently. The Saxon stag topping the crest told her of courage.

What was courage anyway? Mostly it was a matter of *accepting:* accepting what an inscrutable fate threw in one's lap; accepting the savage limitations built into a crisis, and going on from there; accepting the cruel knowledge that life could end just when it should be beginning.

Do I have courage? No.

She kept her self-control until William took her to Stephen's after tea. Ruth Tobin nearly fainted on seeing her, and went into a prolonged coughing spell, her face nearly purple, that frightened them both.

"Ruth! You mustn't! Let me get you some water!"

"I'll be all right in a minute. But Lydia! Cousin! Why have you come? This is *wonderful!* I never dreamed . . ." Ruth choked out words and phrases between coughs. "Is it bad news?"

"In a way."

"Let's go up to my room so we can talk."

Her paroxysm over, Ruth shut the door behind them and put her hands on her cousin's quivering shoulders. "It's Mr. Foster, isn't it?"

Giving in at last to her grief, Lydia threw herself across the bed in an anguished torrent of sobs. Ruth sat beside her, patting her, weeping too, trying to make some sense from Lydia's tangled words.

"Is he dead?" she asked. Lydia shook her head.

"Hurt in the war? Did some terrible thing happen?"

"Terrible for me," Lydia blurted out. "He's married, to some woman with a title."

"Are you sure? How did you find out? Where is he? Didn't you ever get any word from him after those letters? Are you absolutely sure? It isn't some cruel joke?"

Lydia fumbled through her reticule and handed her Dr. Gibson's letter with two newspaper clippings, one in English, one in French.

Ruth read them, then reached out to put her thin arms around Lydia and rock her back and forth as a mother would soothe her child. Finally, exhausted, Lydia stood up and tried to wipe her face and smooth out her clothes.

"There is nothing we can do, cousin. We or anyone else," she said tremulously. "But please—I—I hope you will let me stay here until I have learned some way to live again. I know now what you meant when you said—"

"I am trying to live without Thomas," Ruth said tenderly. "And without hope. Perhaps we can find a way to sustain each other."

Some weeks later, word came from Ann Maria that their father was not well and that perhaps Lydia should come home. "He fatigues himself by walking about," Ann Maria told her, saying that he complained a great deal. This was so unlike him that Lydia began packing to go to Baltimore the next morning. Deborah Cochran was coming through Elkton from a visit with her Christiana relatives, so the two could be company for each other.

"Pray for good weather," Lydia told Ruth in mock seriousness. "You know what kind of sailor Aunt Debby is. And how hard it is on the captain if he goes too fast or too slow or too close to the shore or too far out. I wish we were going by steam, but she's afraid of that too."

As they usually did on their last evening together each summer, the two cousins wandered around the big lawns, looking at their aunt Ruth's once lovely flower gardens, which, tended almost entirely by servants in recent years, were now weedy and unimaginative. On an impulse Ruth and Lydia crossed the road to the old family cemetery near the Manshon House, where the first Henry and several of his children and grandchildren were buried. That small plot of hallowed ground was precious to Lydia. She bent to read the old-fashioned lettering on the green slate tombstone of her grandfather Zebulon, who had rested there near his father since 1763.

Happy ye man whose tender care Relieves ye poor distrest
When he is by troubles compassed 'round
Ye Lord shall give him rest.

"Perhaps that has something special to say to me," Lydia said in a low voice. "I'm glad we came here. Strength—maybe it can give me strength. . . ."

To Lydia's surprise and pleasure, her father was at the dock waiting to meet her and Debby. He was in excellent spirits, overjoyed to have them safely home, asking questions about all the relatives but thoughtfully ignoring the reason Lydia had skipped off so suddenly.

Mr. Cochran and little William had come with their carriage to take Debby to Calvert Street, and soon whisked her off. She blew an affectionate kiss to Lydia and Thomas, her sunny, attractive face smiling and giving no hint that the sight of her brother-in-law had told her more than she wanted to know of his condition.

Deborah was not surprised when Polodore came early the next morning, bringing an urgent note from her sister Ann. As soon as she saw the proud black man, she knew why he had come. In moments she was on her way. Not even some of her special custard would be of help now. She and Thomas's womenfolk fell wordlessly into each other's arms, as the faces of the doctors told them that time was running out.

"My dear Ruth," Debby began a shaky letter about noon, to keep herself from pacing all over the house, "I am writing you from Brother Thomas's where I have been since nine o'clock, Brother being taken with a very severe chill about two o'clock this morning, succeeding with a very high fever, perspiration exceedingly great, and what is more alarming, a considerable stupor . . . he has only answered Yes or No. . . . God only knows what this event may be. . . . Sister and the Girls very distraught."

Thomas J. Hollingsworth, Senior, died that evening, September 5, 1815, aged sixty-eight years, and was taken to lie near his beloved son at St. Paul's Cemetery.

The mystical rule of three had come full cycle for Lydia. With the loss of her brother, her sweetheart and her father, a portion of her life came to an end, closed off forever.

It was more than two months before she could emerge from the blackness. "My dear Cousin," she wrote in November, "I have wished for several weeks to answer your letter but could not conquer my reluctance or rather my feelings. They were woefully changed in a few hours after we parted. I was quite unconscious even of the feeble state of health that others saw increasingly and the eventful blow was altogether unexpected to us all. I cannot tell you how grateful I felt and do feel under the stroke that we met in love and passed one evening all on earth again. When we visited the tombs of our friends that day before I returned I dreamed not that my dearest one was so soon to be united with his parents in such a soil.

"From our friends we have all those attentions that mitigate grief. Aunt Debby devoted herself some days to us, and you judge right of our good friend the Bishop [Kemp] whose friendship has been extended to us all. Through the autumn we have wished you had it in your power to visit us, more particularly Cousin, with a view of benefit to your health. We have sent several messages. I thought I could not write.

"The shawl Aunt requests Mama will send with this. She gave 3.50 and if it answers Aunt can keep it. I took the liberty of deviating in her directions for an Angora as the spun silk were handsome and I thought would accord with her own ideas of beauty and propriety. They are now much worn in mourning."

Aunt Debby found it hard to leave the three forlorn women at Thomas's house when her beloved Mr. Cochran became so ill that they had to go off for expert help. Lydia said that "they reached Philadelphia without any inconvenience to Mr. Cochran and William. She was sick on the way thither but thought it would be beneficial to her. My dear Cousin, they have not decided on a sea voyage. It is spoken of in banter and may finally be resorted to but will not, I think, unless absolutely necessary. Aunt anticipated no pleasure from it herself as her fear of the water is very great, but if one of the family goes she will not remain and it may be recommended to Mr. C. whose health is very delicate. He looked very badly when they left here. Sally Gibson has another son."

Dr. Gibson was more than happy at the birth of that child because he was safely home from Europe, after having been wounded at the Battle of Waterloo. The baby later became nearly as famous as his father. He was Charles Bell Gibson, named for the London doctor who had been Gibson's teacher; his medical career would be centered at the medical college of Richmond, Virginia, where he became a distinguished professor of medicine.

Dr. William Gibson's famous patient, Winfield Scott, survived his dangerous operation for another fifty-one years. He was defeated for the presidency by Franklin Pierce in 1852. The phrase "Great Scott!," referring to his gigantic size, came into the American language from that campaign. Scott was credited with adding more than eleven million acres to United States territory in its westward expansion, which would have delighted Thomas Jefferson's heart. Scott laid out some of the strategy for the long-prophesied Civil War, but he was enraged at being refused a battlefield command. He was then eighty years old.

Lydia and her dear cousin Ruth were to share only two more summers at Elkton. Their aunt Ruth died quietly on April 13, 1817. Shortly after the new year of 1818, the dreaded consumption claimed yet another victim. The county clerk filed this paper:

Manumissions dated the 6th day of January, 1818

Ruth Tobin, of Cecil County in the State of Maryland To Sundry Negroes

Manumits the Negroes hereinafter mentioned at the following periods:

Lewis six years old the second day of November 1817, to be free on the second day of November 1836

Charles four years of age the twenty-second day of December 1817, to be free on the twenty-second day of December 1838

Sophia one year old the tenth day of December 1817, to be free on the tenth day of December 1841.

Recorded on the 7th day of January 1818

Ruth's spinster sister Rachel took over the duties of taking care of Stephen and keeping in touch with the Baltimore relatives. Lydia wrote to her as she had written to Ruth. "To Miss Rachel Tobin, Elkton. My dear Cousin: . . . . The friendship of my dear Cousin Ruth was long cherished and mutually sincere and warm. . . . You have indeed lost a dearly beloved and valued Sister, whose life seemed prolonged suffering, after the decease of our good Aunt—and so little prospect was there of ease or comfort in health, in her complaint, that had her life been spared, she could not have anticipated happiness, for I think when the Lungs once decay, all medical skill is in vain. It is sure, tho' often very lingering death. Her Piety, my dear Cousin, now consoles and reconciles you more to the bereavement than the warmest encomium of friendship can do. I have heard much of her great patience under sufferings very acute, and resignation to the Divine will. She was quite aware of her situation, for a long time. . . . believe me, with affection, your Cousin, Lydia E. Hollingsworth."

The Honorable Augustus John Foster had met the Lady Albinia shortly after he was sent to Copenhagen. He was soon to be thirty-five years old, and if he didn't take steps to remedy the situation he would indeed become one of the "Diplomatic old Bachelors" who were sprinkled through so many branches of the Foreign Office. That solitary life had never appealed to him. It was with great joy and hope that he married her in March of 1815. Early in 1816 she presented him with the first of their three sons.

"Albinia has made me a Papa!" he wrote exultantly to his "Dearest Mother" on January 6. "He has got blue eyes and light hair, his mouth said to be like mine and his limbs well-shaped and we hope he will be a perfect Person."

The British diplomat occasionally saw the gay little American exile Betsy Bonaparte in the fashionable and political centers of Europe, but he rarely had time to exchange more than a few words with her until a snowy winter day about eight years after his marriage. He had taken his family for a holiday in Switzerland. Madame B. was living in Geneva so that her son could go to school there and have every opportunity for contact with children of crowned heads.

The onset of a heavy fog sent all the merrymakers inside, grumbling about the weather and welcoming the blazing fire in the big lobby of the lodge.

Foster was carrying one of his sons, bundled warmly in heavy leggings and several sweaters. Near the fireplace he noticed that Betsy was holding court for a small circle of admirers. She saw him almost at once, and left her friends to come to him with a warm greeting and a coy request to be introduced to the child. While he took off the boy's wet outer garments and rubbed his little hands to get them rid of their chill, he thought to ask her some questions. She had not been in the States for a long time, but he supposed that she probably kept in touch with her relatives and would know a little of what was going on.

She and her father were half-estranged. She claimed that he should have been more manly than to permit a willful eighteen-year-old girl to lead him around by the nose that way. A man was not much of a father who could be so easily swayed; he was a fool to have let her marry that Jerome, both of them children.

"Tell me, please"—Foster tried to keep his voice low and nonchalant as he tugged to get the heavy jacket off the child—"do you ever hear of the lady who was formerly Miss Lydia Hollingsworth, a neighbor of yours? After she married that Frenchman—I understand it was a big wedding at St. Paul's—I never had any further word of her, and I have always wondered—"

"A *Frenchman?* Big church wedding?" Betsy's tinkling laugh swirled over his head. "There was no Frenchman that I ever heard of! Oh, my, what ever gave you that idea?"

Foster stood up to look incredulously into her face. A touch of her old archness returned as she told him, "Everyone I knew always felt that there was only one man in her life, Your Excellency, and that man was *you*. She still lives across the street from my father, with her sister and her brother-in-law, John B. Morris. A *Frenchman?* Oh, *no!*"

In 1824 Foster was transferred from Copenhagen to Turin, where he remained for the rest of his professional life. Several honors came to him in middle age. He was knighted in 1826 by George IV, who as prince regent had sent him to America in 1811. He was elected to the Privy Council, and in 1831 he became a baronet of Glyde Court, County Louth, in eastern Ireland. In the 1830's he began collecting and organizing his papers, diaries and notebooks for a book about his experiences in the New World, to be called *Jeffersonian America.* More than a hundred years after its first printing it was re-edited and republished because of its continuing interest, both as a record of an era and of a man.

As he was scribbling out some random thoughts that came to him during this study, he put down these prophetic words: "I was induced to moralize upon Death, which I do not seek but am not afraid of—I mean in a moral sense—on the contrary I look to it as perhaps many a girl does to marriage, with a Curiosity very great to know where it leads and to clear up a mystery."

He enjoyed excellent health and vigorous activity for most of his life but was observant enough to be constantly at odds with accepted medical practice, especially that of bleeding by opening the veins or putting on leeches or a heated cup. He wrote pityingly of watching a woman die while a bevy of doctors stood near, wringing their hands because there was nothing more they could do after they had drawn off her blood. A teaspoon of water had been put near the poor creature's mouth and her parched tongue had reached out to try to lick it up and give her dehydrated body some kind of nourishment.

Perhaps he remembered the incident when, for one of the few times in his full and honorable life, he became quite ill in the summer of 1848, at the age of sixty-seven. He was at Branksea Castle in Dorsetshire, in the south of England. The illness increased in spite of his stubborn efforts to throw it off by sheer force of will. He became steadily more despondent: the threat of being helpless filled him with horror.

On the dark and thunderous morning of August 1 he picked up a freshly sharpened razor and sliced his throat.

"I truly love you. But that's four words, Mr. Foster."

"Try it again. . . ."

"*A* Frenchman? *Oh . . . no-o-o . . .*"

". . . to clear up . . . a . . . mystery . . ."

Epilogue

Setting her face firmly toward the future and away from the past, Lydia Eliza got back into the busy social life of the belles, spending some of her talents and energies in guiding and grooming younger belles. Those bright pretty creatures had heard legends of Miss Hollingsworth's tragic romance, but they tossed the stories off lightly. How could a woman over thirty know what love was?

When Lafayette revisited the New World in 1824—the fabled Frenchman must have been the busiest social lion in all recorded history—he sought out the slender spinster who was considered the best dancer in Baltimore, the one her nephews, John Morris's boys, called Miss Silverheels. The aging Marquis was so charmed with Lydia that he gave her a gold-and-crystal pendant shaped like a teardrop and containing a lock of hair from the Father of his Country, the sainted General Washington.

Lydia was not aware of the irony, but if it had not been for the nineteen-year-old Lafayette's help to the struggling colonies in the 1780's, the American President in 1812 might not have felt so obligated to repay the debt to France by joining forces with them instead of with the English. The idealistic young nobleman had cast a long shadow.

Shortly after Thomas, Senior's death, Mr. Cochran died too. Although he was only forty, his lungs were destroyed; without the central orb of her life, Debby did not long survive him. His daughters were both married. The orphaned little William spent the remainder of his twenty-four years in a weary search for health, wandering over America and the British Isles and staying with Irish relatives for a year.

The Cochrans' idyllic love affair ended too soon. Lydia's devotion to the British aristocrat never reached fulfillment. The Bonaparte-Patterson romance was an international fiasco, but the fiery little Betsy would outlive all the six people involved in the three amours.

Jerome, the most flamboyant and extravagant man in Europe, if not in the world, who would postpone a battle if his uniform fitted badly (although he was actually quite effective at the business of war), died in the arms of his last mistress when he was seventy-five. His military entourage was of the stuff of legends. He needed a half-dozen wagons to carry his wardrobe of uniforms, several hundred shirts, a variety of headgear, countless silk kerchiefs and sixty pairs of handmade boots.

Other wagons carried a complete dinner service, almost any type of furniture he might require, all kinds of toilet needs, a mobile, superbly equipped kitchen, stacks of bedding with deerskin draperies for his bed, silver-lined saucepans, and, most important, a silver chamberpot, which could be easily warmed in inclement weather. The people accompanying him could have constituted a small village: a doctor, a crew of secretaries, menservants, barbers, a chef who cooked only for Jerome while a lesser one took care of the ordinary folk, and at least one mistress. On long and strenuous campaigns he might carry a spare.

And then there was always Le Camus, Count "Furchetintin."

Once, in 1823, Foster's mother had written her son from

Hamburg: "We had a shocking event here two nights ago. The nurse at . . . was found murdered by her husband from Jealousy and himself a corpse at her side. The wretched man left a paper saying that his wife had sold herself to Jerome Bonaparte and thus should all husbands avenge themselves. He was handsome and only nineteen."

Betsy became a sharp-tongued, parsimonious near-recluse, living in cheap boardinghouses, finally dying in an uncarpeted room at the corner of Richmond and Cathedral streets in Baltimore on April 4, 1879. She was ninety-four.

Her acid remarks about marriage, about the ugly duties of childbearing and child rearing that fell on those so unfortunate as to be born women and about any and all phases of romantic love contributed to the spicy legends that grew up around her. Never remarrying, she became a familiar figure in the port city, stumping around town with her red umbrella.

She had made arrangements for her body to be placed at her death in an ice casket for five days before interment because she had such a fear of being buried alive. She lies in a large plot all by herself at the highest spot in Greenmount Cemetery in a white marble tomb inscribed at the end: "After life's fitful fever, she sleeps well." Around the edges of the lot, setting her apart from ordinary souls, are long, low border stones, also of white marble. She never did escape from Baltimore.

Betsy left her two grandsons—who were twenty-one-years apart in age—an estate of one and a half million dollars, kept together by her penury and her shrewd business investments. One of these was the Baltimore and Ohio Railroad, founded by her father in co-operation with several others, including the last surviving Signer, Charles Carroll, and Lydia's brother-in-law, the banker John B. Morris.

Her son, Bo, had greatly disappointed her by marrying, for love, a charming Baltimore girl, Susan May Williams, and taking a house at the corner of Charles and Pleasant streets. Betsy had trained him so assiduously for a royal match, suited to his imperial heritage. She never quite forgave him.

She and Jerome never saw each other after the day in 1805 when he left her in the harbor at Lisbon so that he might plead for her with his brother the Emperor. In the 1820's he and his Prussian princess caught a glimpse of her in Florence, Italy, but they did not speak. After having spent one and a half tempestuous years with him, she lived seventy-four years without him. In her letters from abroad she frequently inquired about her childhood friends, the Hollingsworth sisters.

"Florence, 7 Sept. 1829 . . . Mrs. Morris and Lydia Hollingsworth have been friends & favorites of mine thro' life—our habits & tastes & countries are different, but I ever recollect them with pleasure & interest."

During their last years, she and Lydia, fading relics of a long-gone era, met now and then on the street in Baltimore or in the shops, pausing for a word about the weather or the Morrises' children and grandchildren, to whom Lydia was devoting her life and heart, even more so after Ann Maria's death in 1847. One of the Morris daughters, named for her aunt Lydia, married a grandson of Francis Scott Key, and the two old ladies sometimes reminisced about his poem concerning the flag they too had seen on a far-distant September morning, the defiant flag that had spelled both deliverance and freedom.

They never spoke of princes.

The Morrises had taken over the family home at 15 South Street and Ann had moved to Number 17, to be out of the way of Ann Maria's five children but yet close by. Thomas's old room was turned into a nursery, with the family crest hung over the fireplace.

In addition to helping with the youngsters, Lydia found a

natural interest in the business of the Mechanics Bank at Number 19, of which Mr. Morris was the president. She wrote many of the bank's letters, especially those concerned with investments by members of the family.

In June, 1834, she wrote, addressing Rachel as she had Ruth: "I am not surprised, my dear Cousin, that you are anxious, nay even distrustful, Cousin Rachel, of Banks. One of ours has been so wantonly managed and other moneyed institutions so pillaged. The Union Bank has had its share of dement, and has fallen greatly. We are pretty large stockholders in it, and I really wish the move now making for a change in its Directors may operate to the advantage of the stock. I presume it will give a dividend at the usual period in July. It is really distressing to know so many Ladies, reduced by the losses in those Savings Banks delusively called; and industrious mechanics, who had invested their money in them, to find all squandered after the bubble burst, and secrecy was no longer practicable. I know a single Lady advanced in Life, who has lost four thousand dollars in one Bank and fourteen hundred in the Savings. There is a Savings, conducted upon pure principles, which receives deposits, and lends on real estate which is good, that is highly approved, there are but two pay officers in it."

In June of the next year she reported on the family illnesses, a lifelong topic in her letters: "The day after we came to the Country my nephew Thomas was attacked by a bilious fever, severe but quickly conquered, by the Doctor who bled him freely and commenced with quinine as soon as the pulse would admit it. He is unused to sickness and felt feeble for several days, but is again at College. Mr. Morris was a sufferer too from St. Anthony's Fire, which was in his leg and ankle, and had 36 leeches applied, and was on the bed some days and from Town longer. My dear Cousin I have consulted with Mr. Morris about the price of Stock and he requests me to say the quoted price is three hundred fifty-six to fifty-eight for the Baltimore Bank stock per share, and from seventy-two to seventy-three dollars a share for the Union Bank of Baltimore, and that it will give him pleasure to serve you in any manner you desire. If you wish to dispose of it, Mr. M. says the dividend declared on the Union Bank is but one and a half percent, for six months, and he thinks the Stock will not bring the quoted price."

It was nearly six months before she wrote to Rachel again. Her world was badly shaken up. The mismanagement of several banks had created the utmost public indignation. Mr. Morris, whose bank was not involved, volunteered as a public-spirited citizen to act on a committee to look into the squabble. His action was misinterpreted, in spite of a statement he published in the paper, and his bank became a target for the mob's fury, along with the guilty ones.

In the ensuing rioting, the home where Lydia Eliza had been born, had given up her three men and her mother, and had spent her life, was so badly damaged that it was a total loss and had to be destroyed. No one was killed, by some miracle. The precious mementos of the one great love of her life were totally lost. The family portraits—of her parents, painted in 1810 by John Wesley Jarvis, and of herself and the Morrises done in 1823 by Thomas Sully—were buried for safekeeping under some straw in the barn by the servants, two of them Polodore's grandchildren.

Her anger had still not completely cooled when she wrote to Rachel in December 1835: "I presume you are acquainted with the outrages of the Baltimore Mob in August last. But one opinion exists here, with regard to the ruin of our house, that it was wanton, unprovoked, and unlooked for by all but the abettors. My Sister and I were ignorant of threats, and did not know until Sunday it was necessary for us to leave home which we did with the children and found refuge at Mr. Ridgelys. Mr. Morris the same hour left us for Bel Air, where the Bank Books had been sent under guard at daybreak the same morning. That night they profaned in the utter destruction of every article within our long cherished paternal home. Oh Cousin what a horrid State has been brought upon individuals; upon the morals of the young and old who united in the revelry, by the wickedness of these men, who are acquitted by a Court Temporal. The testimony produced of their guilt and dishonesty was too well established not to impress those who attended the trial, although the jury acquitted them.

"Our House in South Street was sacked, the very doors, shutters, mantles, stove carried off in the open during this misrule, and all the valuables there, even to private papers, letters and cherished memorials, which had been our parents', grandmothers' and relatives'! A young servant man with a neighbor's buried some plate, which thus escaped for we had not moved anything. The contents of one drawer containing shawls and some little things of value of mine were saved by a friend before the attack, and a servant girl of my Sister's of her own accord saved her wardrobe, or rather a part of it, and took to a friend's house. All our Beds, bedding, table linen, in fact everything was lost.

"A silver vase has been returned, one family Bible, a doz. spoons and some scraps of curtains. We are residing in [22] Mulberry Street near the Cathedral, a fine large House, owned by the widow of Mr. Eaton R. Partridge, which we had rented in September of her. An agreeable situation, but there is no feeling of home, no furniture the eye has rested on all our lives, but our lives were preserved and I was, and am, grateful to Providence for His mercies. My Sister unites her most affectionate love with mine for you. Mr. Morris presents his respects to you—believe me ever your attached Cousin, L E H."

All of her aunts and uncles had passed away, Sam and Sarah being the last; they died within four days of each other in 1830. The loss of her home seemed like the end of still another life. Venturing back several days after the mob's destruction,

Lydia Eliza got down on her knees to look for some cherished treasures. It was a most undignified position for a decorous and genteel spinster nearing fifty, but she was frantic and angry. In the trash she found fragments of the beloved miniature, the remainder ground to powder by a boot heel. The frame was bent beyond recognition or repair. The prayer book was in charred shreds. Thomas's lion-headed cane, which had never been passed on, sat undisturbed in what was left of a mahogany wardrobe. Ann Maria's younger son salvaged the old crossed-hands fire mark from the front of the house, but the framed replica of the family crest was stolen. Nothing else of value was ever found. Looters had finished carrying off what the mob had left.

On June 1, 1865, Lydia Eliza Hollingsworth—who had lived through another war much more horrible than the one a half-century earlier, the civil war foretold for so long by all the British ministers—set out for her last journey to visit her dear cousins. She had had a secondhand motherhood through the generations of orphaned boys at the Benevolent Society, who probably never completely realized the extent of her devotion to them or of her contributions to their essential needs. More personal was her joy in her nieces and nephews, and grandnieces and grandnephews, as she took them for walks along the river and bought them little pretties to bring a sparkle to their eyes. They forgave her if she stopped short when some mention was made of a visiting ambassador and seemed for a moment to drift off into another world. Such behavior was common to fragile old ladies who clung to the past.

She never learned of Sir Augustus's tragic death. She was seventy-nine when she went to find him. The ormolu clock she had purchased to replace the French one destroyed by the mob was chiming out the hour of five when she closed her eyes forever. A niece, awe-struck, whispered to the doctor, "She looks as if she's saying 'Hello' to someone she loves!"

Lady Albinia Foster lived two more years, having been

tenderly cared for by the remaining two of her three sons, Vere and Cavendish, Sir Frederick, the oldest, having died in 1857. Only one, Cavendish, a minister of the Church of England, married. All three were noted for their enormous contributions to the public good, especially Vere, for his interest in education.

Cavendish's granddaughter Dorothy lives in the rambling estate at Glyde Court, County Louth, Ireland, where Sir Augustus was made a baronet after being knighted. The many family treasures that surround her and her husband, Arthur C. W. May, are watched over by a full-length portrait, halfway up the beautiful old staircase, of her distinguished ancestor. Another of him, done in America, probably by Gilbert Stuart, hangs in the breakfast room.

The surrounding gardens are colorful with blossoms, and the rural countryside abounds in songbirds and small wild things.

"Mercifully grant unto us such a measure of Thy grace that we, running the way of Thy commandments, may obtain Thy gracious promises, and be made partakers of Thy heavenly treasure; through Jesus Christ our Lord. Amen."

Acknowledgments

A century after the death of Lydia Eliza Hollingsworth, one of the celebrated Baltimore belles, and half again as long after the passing of her "Dear Cousin" Ruth Tobin, I first learned of a collection of letters between them and other members of their families. There are 115 altogether, 59 of them written by Lydia; they span the years from 1802 to 1837 and were preserved by descendants of the Tobin family. One letter, from Lydia's father to one of his brothers belongs to Mrs. R. H. Blanchard (Margaret Jamar), of Columbus, North Carolina, a descendant of Lydia's cousin William Hollingsworth, but all the others are the property of Mrs. Elizabeth Hurtt Westcott, of Kennedyville, Maryland. She is a descendant of Ruth Tobin's sister Sarah Tobin Moody, and has generously allowed me full use of the letters. She has also given me help in a number of ways.

At first, I worked with typed transcripts of the originals, copied some years ago, and did not see the actual letters until nearly a year after I had begun the extensive study that was necessary. The reality of the various kinds of handwriting—Ann Maria's neat script, Lydia's legible but not quite so perfect writing, Aunt Debby's gay flourishes, the men's businesslike, broad black strokes—gave new life to the characters I was hoping to re-create.

Following up several veiled hints and clues in Lydia's letters, I was led to Sir Augustus John Foster as the unrequited love in her life. Sixty-five of his notebooks and diaries and a large number of letters are in the Library of Congress Manuscript Collection, and the first draft of his book *Jeffersonian America* is in the Huntington Library, San Marino, California (as are some later Hollingsworth letters not important to this story).

The historical facts are as nearly accurate as possible, traced with the discerning help of Mr. and Mrs. Calvin Criner and especially of Miss Iola Parker, long-time teacher of American history on WUNC-TV for the North Carolina public schools. Some incidents have been given several versions and interpretations by various chroniclers; I have arbitrarily chosen the one that seemed the most reasonable or best fitted the story line. On occasion, the situation, or the people involved in it, was described by A. J. Foster as he observed it firsthand, and in these instances I have used his viewpoint.

Real people and places appear throughout, except for a few minor ones who *might* have been real. Polodore and Robert did in fact exist. The houses at Elk Landing, Hollingsworth Tavern (where Ruth Tobin lived) and Partridge Hill (where Colonel Henry Hollingsworth lived), are still in use in Elkton, Maryland. A portion of the 1712 Manshon House is still standing. When the Elkton Cemetery was opened in the 1880's, the Hollingsworth bodies were moved there from the family burying ground beside the Manshon House.

Part of the fun of undertaking such an enormous project as this one is the interest it generates in other people, as well as the opportunity it provides for making new friends on both sides of the Atlantic. So many persons have given help and suggestions that to name them all would take a dozen pages. Since I am neither a Hollingsworth nor an Adams descendant, I tried to approach the research objectively, but I found myself constantly caught up in the great sweep of their contributions to the making of this country.

Topping the list of thank-yous must be my good husband, who gets his own breakfast and never complains about the books and papers strewn all over the house, or about the ghostly visitors from a hundred and fifty years ago, or about the necessary absences of a writing wife as she goes on trips to track down facts and people.

Hollingsworth and Adams descendants who have been espe-

Writers and the Writers' Workshops at North Carolina State University, under the direction of Sam Ragan, have all helped me to find Lydia and to re-create her on paper. Mr. Ragan's interest brought me to the attention of Hiram Haydn, one of America's great editors; the several writing clubs have, among them, listened to almost every word of *My Dear Cousin* as it took shape.

PEGGY HOFFMANN

Raleigh, North Carolina